Be My Baby Tonight

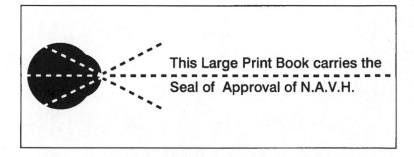

This Large Print Book carries the
Seal of Approval of N.A.V.H.

Be My Baby Tonight

Kasey Michaels

Thorndike Press • Waterville, Maine

Published in 2003 by arrangement with Kensington Books, an imprint of Kensington Publishing Corp.

Thorndike Press Large Print Romance Series.

The tree indicium is a trademark of Thorndike Press.

The text of this Large Print edition is unabridged. Other aspects of the book may vary from the original edition.

Set in 16 pt. Plantin by Myrna S. Raven.

Printed in the United States on permanent paper.

Library of Congress Cataloging-in-Publication Data

Michaels, Kasey.
    Be my baby tonight / Kasey Michaels.
      p. cm.
    ISBN 0-7862-4984-6 (lg. print : hc : alk. paper)
    1. Baseball players' spouses — Fiction.   2. Pregnant women — Fiction.   3. Large type books.   I. Title.
PS3563.I2725 B4 2003
    813'.54—dc21   2002075021

*To my father, Eddie Charles, — the only man
I know who can keep tabs on games on two
television sets, monitor a third on the radio,
and do a crossword puzzle, all at the
same time — who gifted me with
his passion for all sports.
I love you, Dad.*

One time I got pulled over at four a.m. I was fined seventy-five dollars for being intoxicated and four hundred for being with the Phillies.
> — Bob Uecker
> (former Phillies ballplayer)

There comes a time in every man's life, and I've had plenty of them.
> — Casey Stengel
> (former Yankees manager)

One

I think everybody gets caught up in super-stitions. But I don't put much stock in them — knock on wood.
       — Minnesota Twins pitcher,
       Jim Deshaies

The sun shone brightly, with a better than average breeze blowing out to right, making it a good day at the plate for a left-handed hitter.

The stands were full for the Sunday afternoon home game, because it was July, and because the Phillies were actually still in the race after the All-Star break. Usually, they were pretty well out of it by late June. Hell, there had been years when they had been crossed off by the sports columnists before spring training was over.

If they won today, they would only be two games out of first.

Phillies catcher Tim "the Tiger" Trehan stood in the on-deck circle, swinging his weighted bat, watching the reliever's windup, as the guy was newly traded from the American League, and this was the first time the Phillies had seen him pitch other than a single inning during spring training.

Good move to first, Tim decided as the pitcher stepped off and sidearmed the ball to the first baseman, making Dusty Johnson dive back to the bag. What the hell was Dusty thinking? With one out, a long fly ball would score a run. Nobody could make the hotshot, base-stealing rookie realize that making the second out at second was never a good deal for anyone.

Tim smiled as Dusty got up, not bothering to dust himself off, because what would be the point? Dusty attracted dirt like a magnet collected iron filings, and had been given the nickname Dusty only because Charles Shultz had already named one of his *Peanuts* characters Pigpen.

Tim's grin widened as his manager, Sam Kizer, his face beefsteak red, hung on the dugout railing and yelled to the first-base coach to by damn keep Dusty's ass glued on first or he'd — Sam shut up before he said the words Tim was pretty sure he'd heard before, because the manager had recently begun an anger management course, at the request of the team owners.

Tim's head went up as Rich Craig

popped to shallow left, making the second out, and leaving Jeff Kolecki stuck at third, Dusty still hanging on first. The first-base coach had probably grabbed Dusty by the uniform belt, to keep him from trying to tag up and take second. The kid was fast, but nobody was that fast.

Two out, runners at the corners, and Tim was up. Bottom of the eighth, down six to five, and the Braves were sure to bring in their ace closer in the ninth, planning to shut the door on the Phillies' comeback that had begun in the sixth, when they had scored those five runs after Tim's lead-off double.

It was time. It was his time. It was what he'd been born to do, all he'd ever wanted to do.

Tapping his bat on the ground to knock the doughnut weight free, Tim then stepped to the plate, oblivious to the yells from the stands, the blowing horns, the waving white towels, the word *Charge!* flashing on the screen next to the scoreboard.

"A real bitch having to strap on your gear in a hurry after making the last out," Tony Rodriguez, the Atlanta Braves catcher, said, lifting his mask to grin at Tim.

"Nah, Tone," Tim said, smiling back at him, because the two men were friends. "The bitch is standing at the plate with your jock strap flapping, watching three runs come across after I land one in the right field bleachers."

"In your dreams, Trehan," Rodriguez said with a laugh, pulling down the mask once more as he folded himself into his crouch behind the plate.

Tim went into his usual ritual, born in Little League, and never varied. He put out the barrel of the bat, ready to draw an imaginary line across the center of the plate.

Except he wasn't holding a bat.

He was holding a crutch. And his left leg was in a metal brace from ankle to thigh.

"Time!" he called out, stepping out of the batter's box as he wiped at his eyes. He looked at his bat. It was a bat again. No brace on his leg.

But his right arm was in a cast, just the way it had been last September.

What the hell?

He went back over to the on-deck circle, grabbed the pine tar rag, made a business out of rubbing down his bat before returning to the batter's box.

Okay, the bat was still a bat. And the cast was gone.

This was good. This was very good.

Tim took two quick half swings before cocking the bat over his left shoulder, another ritual, then looked to the pitcher's mound.

And there stood Jim Harris, leaning forward, his gaze locked on the catcher's, shaking off a pitch.

Thing was, Jim was wearing a wedding gown.

White one. With a big skirt and a veil and everything. His mitt was gone, and he was holding a bouquet of white roses.

"Time!" Tim called again, holding up his arm as he stepped out once more.

"Hey," Rodriguez said, standing up. "You thinking Jimbo's going to get too old to pitch, waiting on you?"

"Funny, Tony," Tim said, blinking. "I've got something in my eye." He looked out at the mound, and there was Harris, in his uniform again. "I'm okay now."

"Play ball," the umpire said, pushing up at his chest protector as he hunched behind Rodriguez.

Tim took two more quick half swings, cocked the bat, then trained his gaze on Harris. He figured a curve ball, high and tight, for the first pitch. And he was ready for it.

What he wasn't ready for was the baby — *a grinning, giggling, arm-waving baby* — that came winging through the air, released by Harris, and heading straight for the plate.

"No!" Tim yelled, jackknifing to a sitting position in his bed, his eyes still closed, his arms stuck out in front of him to catch the baby. "No!"

"Tim? Tim! Hey, Timmy-boy, wake up. Come on, wake up now."

Tim opened his eyes as Dusty Johnson shook him by the shoulder. He blinked in the light Dusty had turned on between the two beds, looked at the rookie standing there in his BVD's and Superman shirt, his bright red hair standing on end like a rooster's.

Dropping his head into his hands, trying to control his breathing, Tim said succinctly, "Shit."

"The dream again?" Dusty asked, heading for the hotel room's small refrigerator and pulling out a bottle of grape juice. "Man, and you're supposed to be some sorta calmin' influence on me? That's the third time this week."

Tim stacked his pillows behind him and sat back. "Put a sock in it, Dusty," he said, glancing at the clock. It was five in the morning, and he was sharing a hotel room in Pittsburgh with a guy who wore Superman T-shirts. And drank grape juice, for crying out loud.

Damn Sam and his psychology classes, which had ended with the veterans rooming with the rookies on the road. Rich Craig wouldn't even mention a bad dream. Hell, he'd have slept right through it, and had done so for most of last season.

Or had he?

"Dusty, toss me a can of Coke, okay?" he said, quickly popping the top when he caught it. "Rich ever talk to you about . . . you know? My dreams?"

Dusty shook his head as he returned to his own bed, sat down cross-legged, and chugged half his Yoohoo. "Naw. Just said you get antsy once in a while, that's all. He figured I could handle it."

"And can you? Handle it, that is?"

"Sure," Dusty said, finishing off his drink. "I'm used to gettin' up early. Do the milkin', you know? You okay now?"

Tim rubbed a hand across his forehead, realized that his breathing had returned to normal. "Yeah, I am. Thanks."

"No problem. Which one was it? The crutch again? The weddin' gown? I like that one. Pay down real cash money, I would, to see Jimmy Harris in a weddin' dress. Don't think I'd like to see a baby come wingin' at me, though. Does the baby say anythin'? You know? What does the baby say? Da-Da? Or maybe — *duck!*"

Tim put down his Coke, pressed both hands against his temples. "It was all three of them. First time that ever happened. It's getting worse, a lot worse. I thought it would get better, but it just keeps getting *worse*."

"Oh, man, that sucks, don't it? All of them? You know, maybe you oughta talk to the skipper. He's doin' all that psychology stuff now. Maybe he'd know why you keep havin' these dreams."

Tim snorted. "Sam? You want me to talk to Sam? Cripes, Dusty, the man thinks anger control means throwing only one bat out onto the field and not his usual half dozen. Besides, nobody's getting me on a couch."

Dusty nodded. "Because you know why you're havin' the dreams, right?"

"Right," Tim said, wide awake, knowing he wouldn't sleep for the rest of the night. And, since it must be close to milking time somewhere in Dusty's internal clock, if the kid wanted to talk, they would talk.

"It's like a superstition, ain't it? Like

wearin' the same socks, like you do when we're winnin'? You got yourself one big superstition."

Tim shrugged. "I guess. Something like that. We've all got superstitions; it's part of the game. But this is worse. This is like I've got this sword hanging over me, and the thread holding it is getting thinner and thinner, and there's nothing I can do to stop it . . ."

"I still don't get it, you know. So what if your brother got himself injured and outta the game? Got himself a baby, a wife. You're not him, right?"

"I'm his twin, Dusty," Tim explained as he had several times before, reaching for the deck of cards he always kept on the table beside any bed he slept in, ever. "We've always done whatever the other one's done."

"Like playin' baseball, right?"

"Right," Tim said, dealing out the cards for solitaire. "Like breaking the same bones, like coming home with the same grades, like getting crushes on the same girl, like smashing up cars the same week. Jack's older — seven minutes — and he does stuff first, and I always follow."

He looked at the cards, saw he was already out of moves, and gathered them up in one hand. "Almost every damn time, I end up doing something the same as Jack has already done. Call it superstition, but I've been looking over my shoulder ever since Jack retired from the game."

"That long? Your brother had to quit baseball after that rotator cuff thing, right? That was over a year ago. You're still here, right?"

"Right. Except I missed the last month of the season last year after that finger surgery."

"Yeah. What was that, anyway? The guys were laughin' about it one time."

Tim dealt out the cards again, put a red queen on a black king. "I tore a tendon in the middle finger of my throwing hand."

"Wow, how'ya do that? In a game? I don't think you ever said."

Red ten on the black jack. "After the game," he said, not looking at his roommate. "In the club house, taking off my sock. I — I stuck my finger down into the sock, tried to pull it off my foot, and the damn tendon snapped."

"Naw. Get out," Dusty said. "Takin' off your sock? Man, that's somethin'."

"Sports writers seemed to think so. The jokes? Damn. But then they started making noises about the Trehan curse."

"Wow, a curse. Superstition's bad enough, but a curse? You mean, because your brother ripped his rotator cuff takin' off a sock?"

Tim laughed. Okay, so maybe rooming with a rookie wasn't so bad. The kid had made him laugh. "No, Dusty, because the writers had noticed, long ago, that almost everything Jack did, I did. We were signed the same month, him with the Yanks, me with the Phillies. We moved to Triple-A within weeks of each other, came up to the majors exactly two months apart. Jack first, me second. Always. If Jack does something, I do it. Not all the time, granted. It's not always follow the leader, you know. But at least two out of every five. I don't like the odds."

Dusty nodded. "So, okay, so Jack gets hurt, and everybody thinks you're next? Am I gettin' this?"

"Yeah, you're getting this. And I was, too, after never missing a game since I got beaned my senior year in high school." He lost another game of solitaire, picked up the cards, replaced them on the nightstand. "I got away with it last year, with the tendon thing, but the clock's ticking. Any day now, Dusty, it could all be over."

17

Dusty was silent for some moments, then grinned. "But you said only two out of five, right? From what you're tellin' me about these dreams, you've got three this time. Would that make it one out of three, do ya think? Do one, and the other two go away."

Tim shrugged. "I don't know. Yeah, okay. One out of three. Big damn deal. Out of the game? A baby left on my doorstep, like Jack? *Married?* Cripes, Dusty, it's not like there's anything real good in those choices."

"There's nothin' too good about wakin' up almost every night, screamin' because you're havin' that dream again. You struck out three times today, Tim. Not that it's my place to be sayin' nothin', you understand. You're still the best."

Pressing finger and thumb against the bridge of his nose, Tim let Dusty's words echo inside his head. O-for-three today. One-for-five yesterday. And that passed ball. Damn, that one hurt. Should have been ruled a wild pitch, not a passed ball. Still, he was off his game, and he knew it.

"So," Dusty said, slipping his skinny, hairy legs under the covers once more, "which of the three is the worst? Leavin' the game, I'd say. Wouldn't you?"

Tim nodded. Leaving the game would be the worst. The very worst. He wasn't yet thirty, had plenty of good years ahead of him, even if Sam had started making noises about moving him to first base when Romero retired next year, to save his knees. As long as he could swing the bat, he had a home in Philly, and he knew it.

Dusty kicked off the covers, stood up. "Gotta go brush my teeth," he said, heading for the bathroom. "My ma'd skin me if she knew I didn't brush after that grape juice."

Tim absently waved the kid into the bathroom, thinking about what Dusty had said. Yes, definitely. Leaving the game, being forced out of the game, was the worst of the three.

Sticking his head, and his foaming mouth sporting the handle end of a toothbrush, out of the bathroom, Dusty said, "No babies around, right? Rich said you're gettin' a new nickname — Tim 'the Monk' Trehan."

"Remind me to shoot some shaving cream into Rich's cleats," Tim said, pushing the pillows lower as he lay down, trying to believe he'd actually be able to fall back to sleep. They had one more game in Pittsburgh tonight, before having a day off and starting another home stand.

"Yeah, sure," Dusty said, smelling like mint as he crawled back into bed, then reaching toward the toggle on the bedside lamp. "Hey, I got it. One out of three, right?"

"I don't know. I never had the dream with all three in it before. Probably. But they're all lousy."

"One out of three, two out of five. That's what you said. So get married. Can't be worse than the other two, right? At least then if it's two out of three and the baby comes along, you'll have somebody to raise it, right?"

Dusty turned off the light, leaving the room dark and silent. Tim stared up toward the ceiling, Dusty's last words going round and round inside his head.

Married? Get married? Sure, that would work. He could do that. Right after he jumped off a bridge. . . .

Suzanna Trent stood outside the new Pittsburgh Pirates' stadium, not ten feet from the players' entrance, wondering when it was she'd lost her mind.

It was bad enough that she'd bought tickets to the entire weekend series, then sat in right field, her binoculars trained on

Tim Trehan as he squatted behind home plate, and each time he came up to bat.

But this was worse, much worse. What in hell had possessed her to bribe the guard with a twenty so that she could get inside the gate, be there when the team members headed for the bus that had to be taking them to the airport and the trip back to Philadelphia?

She didn't even have a pennant for him to sign, or an autograph book.

Not that she'd ask him for his autograph. Why should she do that? She still had every note he'd ever passed to her in Mrs. Butterworth's world history class:

"Suze — you coming to practice? Bring my cleats, okay? They're in my locker."

"Suze — think fast, when was the war of 1812? Hahaha!"

"Suze — you think Mindy Frett will go to the dance with me Friday night? Ask her, Suze, okay?"

Oh, yeah. She still had every note. Had cried over most of them. She didn't need no *steenking* autograph.

So why was she here?

Hey, she was in town, that was why. She was on a job, straightening out the Harrison Manufacturing Company's screwed up computer system, a job she'd just wrapped up Friday morning.

It was Sunday. So why hadn't she gone home to Allentown? Why had she stayed, gone to all three weekend games?

"Because you're certifiable, that's why," Suzanna grumbled to herself, hitching her large bag back up on her shoulder, preparing to leave before Tim came out, saw her, and walked right past her without recognizing his old classmate, pal, and general gofer.

Yes, that was it. She wanted to see if he recognized her. Why not? She looked good. She looked damn good.

Then again, anything would be an improvement over frizzy, carrot-orange hair, the teeth braces that had nearly become a permanent part of her, and the baby fat she'd carried all the way into her early twenties.

God, the crush she'd had on the man. Ever since kindergarten, and straight through their senior year.

From the beginning, they had been together, thrown in close proximity through simple alphabetics. Every classroom, every year, it was Trehan, Trehan, Trent. Jack, then Tim, then Suzanna. Every blessed year.

Jack, Tim, and "good old Suze."

That was what Tim called her: good old Suze.

She didn't call herself that. Inside her notebooks, where nobody could see, she'd scribbled, year after year: Mrs. Timothy Trehan.

Not that he'd ever had a clue. She'd have died if he'd known. If he'd laughed, told his brother, told his friends. She would have just *died*.

But, damn him, he should have known.

After all, it had been Suzanna who could always tell the twins apart, when no one else could. It was Suzanna who had done Tim's homework for him when he'd forgotten, Suzanna who had always made sure she had bubble gum for him because he swore he couldn't play ball for spit without it.

It was Suzanna who had volunteered to be statistician for every team Tim had ever played on, just so she could be near him. It was Suzanna who Tim had thought of as his great pal, his buddy, his friend, his "good old Suze."

The jerk.

Thank God she'd wised up and not followed Jack and Tim to college. Instead, she'd deliberately headed to UCLA, as far away from Tim as she could get without leaving the continental United States.

She'd graduated near the top of her class, built herself a career, a damn good career, acting as a troubleshooter for a major software firm headquartered back in Allentown. She traveled the country now, remained heart-free, and believed she had a pretty good head on her shoulders.

A head with short, tamed, now carefully colored dark mahogany hair with touches of soft blond highlights, atop slim shoulders that belonged to a size-eight body.

Oh, yes. She wasn't good old Suze anymore. She was woman, watch her soar.

So what in *hell* was she doing here?

"Nothing good," she told herself, hitching up her purse once more as she stepped away from the shadows, intent on getting herself out of here and back to sanity. She should have left long ago, when the game had gone into extra innings, instead of sticking around until the bitter end.

Thing was, the door had just opened, and Suzanna found herself trying to fight the tide of yelling autograph seekers, from six-year-old boys to seventy-year-old grandfathers, that converged on the area as if they had been tossed there by a tidal wave.

Fighting that wave was hopeless, so

24

Suzanna turned around, allowed herself to go with the flow.

What the hell. She was here. Why not at least look?

"Dusty! Dusty! Over here, over here! Sign my book, sign my book!"

Suzanna looked down to see a young boy standing in front of her, a pair of crutches propped under his arms and a cast to his midthigh. Poor kid, he'd never make it through the crowd. She looked around, hoping to see a parent, but the kid seemed to be alone.

"Here, let me help you," Suzanna said, proving yet again that, yup, here she was, good old Suze.

Good old Suze used polite "pardon me's" and a couple of well-placed elbows as she helped the boy to the front of the crowd just as Dusty Johnson — his shock of bright red hair easily recognizable — headed out of the door and toward the bus.

"Yo, Dusty," Suzanna called out, waving her hand high in the air. "Over here. There's a kid wants your autograph."

The rookie shortstop smiled, nodded, and headed for the crowd. "Yes, ma'am," he said, then bent down, lifted the boy's Phillies cap, and ruffled his hair. He ignored the other books and programs and hats being aimed at him and instead took the autograph book from the boy as he knelt down in front of him, getting on eye level with the kid. That was nice.

"See that triple I hit tonight, son? Did that just for you. Bet you didn't know that."

"Ah, man," the boy said, shifting on his crutches. "You're so cool. Sign it to Joe, okay? Not Joey. Joe."

"Got ya," Dusty said, scribbling on an empty page. Then he stood up, looked back at the door and the few stragglers still heading for the bus. "Hey, Tim. Hey, roomie. C'mere. Sign this kid's book why don't ya."

"Sure," Tim Trehan said, tossing a light jacket over his shoulder as he headed their way.

Time stopped. Reversed. Older yes, but he was still Tim. Her Tim. Long, lean, a ballplayer to his toes. Thick, unruly dark blond hair, with that lighter streak on the left, just above his temple. That same wide smile, those same whiter-than-white teeth against his constant tan. Those same bright colbalt blue eyes. That same lazy walk that some might call a swagger.

She'd know him in the dark, on the

moon . . . and in her dreams. Always in her dreams.

Suzanna could have done a quick melt into the crowd, except that it wouldn't be easy. Especially since she didn't want to move.

"Oh, man oh man. Tim Trehan. Tim the Tiger." The young boy nearly fell off his crutches as he leaned forward to get a better look at Tim.

"Hi, son, what's the other guy look like?" Tim asked, taking the autograph book and scribbling his name.

"Naw, it was just me. Fell off my bike."

"Bummer. I did that, a couple of times. You wearing your helmet?"

"Yes, sir," Joe said, nodding. "My mom'd kill me if I didn't. You okay, Tim? Sanchez hit you pretty hard, huh?"

Suzanna, holding her breath, trying to pretend she was invisible, listened as Tim told the boy that he was fine, that he'd been slid into plenty of times, blocking the plate.

"Yeah, but you were down for a while. My dad said it's the Trehan curse. Did you see him in the clubhouse? I'm waiting for him out here. He writes sports for our paper, you know? He said all the writers know."

Suzanna watched as Tim stiffened, a slight tic working in his right cheek. "Oh, yeah? Well, you tell your dad to —" He shut his mouth, shook his head. "Never mind. This your mom?" he asked, jerking a thumb in Suzanna's direction.

"No, sir. She's just some lady helped me up here."

Suzanna winced. The story of her life. Just some lady.

Well, the hell with that!

"Hi, Tim, remember me?"

Tim looked at her, glanced in her direction actually, and shook his head. Then he tipped his head to one side, narrowed his eyelids. "No. No way. Suze?"

"Yup," she said, knowing full well that her cheeks were turning bright red. And her neck, and her forehead. She was the most *thorough* blusher she knew. "It's me, Tim. Good old Suze."

The next thing she knew, she was enveloped in a bear hug that all but squeezed the breath from her body.

"Suze, I don't believe it. God, it's been years." Tim took hold of her shoulders, pushed her slightly away from him, ran his gaze from her head to her toes, then back again.

She looked good. She knew she looked

good. Anyone who took three hours bathing, dressing, and putting on her makeup had damn well better look good. She'd even worn a dress, and heels. For the love of God, she was hopeless — she'd worn heels to a ball game. Who did that?

"You've changed," he said, and she didn't know if she should give him points for his observant comment, or punch him in the nose.

"I've lost weight, the braces, and about two feet of hair, yes," she answered, trying to keep it light. *Gotta keep it light with Tim Trehan, always keep it light.* Otherwise, all she'd see of him would be his back, as he ran away. "You look good, especially for a guy who had his bell rung today."

"Yeah, well, it wasn't anything," Tim said quickly. "Just a part of the game."

"I was listening to the post-game wrap-up on my car radio while waiting around for a while," Suzanna said. "They said Sanchez might get brought up in front of the League president. Fined, even suspended."

"Could be," Tim said, shrugging. "I don't get into that stuff."

"I know. It was Jack who threw at a few guys' heads as payback when he was pitching, as I remember it."

"You know Jack. He lived by Don Drysdale's motto. Remember it? 'My own rule was two-for-one. If one of my teammates got knocked down, then —' "

" 'I knocked down two on the other team,' " Suzanna ended, laughing. "I remember."

Tim smiled with her. "God. It's great seeing you, Suze. You live in Pittsburgh now?"

She shook her head. "No, I'm just here on business. I'm still in town, Allentown actually. After Mom and Dad died, I sold that big house in Whitehall, took an apartment. You're still there in Whitehall, right?"

As if she didn't know. One-thirty-seven Hill Avenue and Thirteen-thirteen Mockingbird Lane; two addresses she'd never forget. Tim Trehan and Herman Munster. She really ought to think about having her head examined one of these days.

"Yeah, still there. When I'm home, which isn't often during the season."

"Yo — Trehan! Today, okay?"

Tim turned to wave at Rich Craig, who was standing on the bottom step of the bus. "In a minute." Then he turned back to Suzanna. "Look, I know it's kind of late, but God, Suze, it's been forever since I saw

30

you. Do you want to go for something to eat? I have to go back on the bus, team rules, but you could follow, meet me in the hotel, and we could grab something to eat, catch up on old times? Our plane doesn't leave until tomorrow morning because we went into extra innings."

"Something to — well, sure. Sure. My . . . My car's parked right outside this gate." She half turned, pointed toward the gate, as though she was giving directions. *Smooth, Suze, real smooth. Why not drool, too.* "Where, um, where are you staying? Just in case I lose the bus on the road."

He told her what she already knew — because she was booked at the same large hotel — then turned, walked partway to the bus before turning again, giving her a grin that melted her insides. "Good old Suze. Is this something, or what?"

Suzanna nodded, smiled, then stepped back, half tripped over Joe's crutch, and nearly fell. Good old klutzy Suze, suddenly thirteen again.

Yeah, it was something all right.

But what?

Two

And the ball is out here.
No, it's not. Yes, it is.
No, it's not. What happened?
    — Yankees announcer Phil Rizzuto

Tim snagged two more beers from the bar and walked over to the table in the corner, where Suzanna waited for him. He put down the beers, sat, and grinned across the table at her.

"This has been great, Suze. It's been forever. I'm getting a real kick out of hearing about all the guys. And the girls, of course."

"Of course. You never came back for either of the high school reunions," she said, using her tongue to swipe some foam from her upper lip. "Last one was this past May. Ten-year reunion, if you can believe that. It should have been last year, but you know Bobby Freedman. Late for everything. Why we ever elected him class president is still a mystery."

"He gave everybody gum in exchange for votes, as I remember."

"Yeah, that's right. But you should have been there. This one was fun. And Mindy Frett was fat."

Then she sat back, her eyes wide. "Oh, I shouldn't have said that. That's it, no more beer for me. Three's my limit, obviously."

Tim laughed. "No, no, I want to hear this. Mindy's fat? What happened?"

Suzanna lifted her frosted mug, using its wet bottom to make rings on the tabletop. "She took over her dad's pizza place. Guess maybe it's all the mozzarella?"

"Biggest attraction Mindy had, her dad's pizza place," Tim said, half lost in memories. "She used to sneak me into the back room, and I'd gorge myself on pepperoni. I was crazy about her pepperoni."

"I thought you were crazy about her — her, well never mind. That's the beer talking again."

Tim's grin was evil, and he knew it. "She had quite a set, didn't she?"

Suzanna took another sip of beer. "A lot you know. She stuffed."

Tim collapsed against the back of the chair, goggling at her. Man, he was loving this trip down memory lane. "No. Mindy stuffed?"

"Trust me. I took gym with her sixth period for two years, remember. If I'd had the money, I'd have bought some Kimberly-Clark stock, for all the Kleenex she used." Suzanna put down her beer. "Guess the rumors were wrong then, Tim. You never got to second base with Mindy?"

Tim grabbed his beer, took several deep swallows. "Don't tell anybody, okay? I've got my killer reputation to protect."

Was Tim even more handsome than he'd been at eighteen, or was she looking at him through rose-colored glasses?

Okay, beer-bottle-colored glasses.

". . . and then, just when Jack is about to slit his own throat, the doorbell rings, and there stands this woman, this interior decorator our Aunt Sadie hired because Jack may have bought the house, but he hadn't planned to be living in it so soon."

"Because he didn't know his rotator cuff was going to be shot," Suzanna said, her chin balanced on her hand as she tried to count the golden flecks in Tim's eyes. "Then what?"

"Hey, you know Jack. He's got my cousin Cecily's baby in the kitchen, and a female at the front door. Baby, female. Female, baby. He grabs the female, takes her to the baby. Ah, they match. Perfect."

"They match?"

"Sure," Tim said. "Females, babies, diapers, throw up, midnight feedings. A perfect match."

Suzanna watched him down the last of what had to be his, what, sixth glass of beer? That would mean she was on her fifth, because she'd turned down one, but she hadn't turned down two. Or was it her sixth, his fifth? Oh, well, they were small glasses. What time was it anyway?

"So Jack married this woman because she could change diapers?"

Tim held up his hands, shook his head. "No. No way. Jack's nuts about Keely, and she's crazy about him. Although it was pretty hairy there for a while. But Cecily signed Candy over to them, all nice and legal, and now Keely's pregnant. If my big brother got any more domestic, he'd scare me. Hell, he does scare me."

As Suzanna watched, Tim's smile faded, and he began tearing up a soggy napkin, avoiding her eyes. "What?"

"Nothing. He doesn't really scare me. I just said that."

"Uh-huh," Suzanna said, then reluctantly looked at her watch. Damn, it took a few seconds for her eyes to focus on the watch face. Standing up was going to be a real trick if she didn't watch herself.

It was dark in the bar, but when her mind finally sorted out the big hand from the little hand, she was pretty sure it was nearly one in the morning. Did hotel bars close at two? "Well, Tim, guess it's time to go."

"Go?" Tim took her hand as she began to rise, held it, so that she quickly sat back down. Good thing, because she was feeling pretty shaky.

"It's late, Tim, and you said you have to catch a morning plane? So do I, and I have to return my rental car first."

"But you didn't tell me anything about you. All this time, and all we've talked about is high school, my trip to the All-Star game again this year, and Jack. What about you, Suze? What've you been up to?"

"I told you, Tim. I work for a software company. We sell the software; the company we sell it to thinks they can work it. They can't, they screw it up, and then they call me in to fix it. I travel, a lot, and . . . Well, it suits me."

"Traveling's okay," Tim said, "for a while. Used to be I loved it, but now these long road trips, especially to the coast, can be a real drag." He tipped his head to one side, looked at her. "The coast. That's where you went, right? How come you never wrote?"

"Well . . . I . . . I guess I was too busy?" She didn't remind him that he hadn't written to her, either. Even though she'd written the address of her dorm in a birthday card she'd sent to both he and Jack. There had been a giraffe on the front of the card, she remembered. A two-headed giraffe.

That was what she always did with Tim. Kept it light, kept it funny. Hid everything else. Otherwise, the little she had might become nothing.

"Busy. Tell me about it," he said, leaning forward.

She blinked, startled by his question. Tell him about the giraffe? No, that couldn't be what he'd meant. Man, she'd better get out of here, pop a couple of Tylenol, and hope she made it to the bed before she passed out.

"Come on, Suze. Tell me what it was like to go to college in sunny California. Did you wear flowers in your hair?"

"Wrong decade, Tim," Suzanna said, laughing. But then he asked her again, and he looked so cute when he begged; so she told him about what it had been like in

California . . . right after he got them both another beer.

She never knew she liked beer so much. She hadn't had any since college. She never had more than a glass of wine, ever since she'd turned twenty-one and the thrill of sneaking an illegal sip was gone.

But this was fun. She felt sort of soft, and liquidy, or something. And she wasn't nervous anymore.

That was nice.

"Last call, folks."

Tim checked his watch. "Wow, almost two." He smiled at Suzanna, who was looking sort of sleepy. Sort of fuzzy around the edges. Really cute.

She smiled back at him, her chin cupped in her hand. "Somebody whistle for my pumpkin," she said, turning to the purse sitting on the extra chair, pulling it onto the top of the table so she could rummage in it for her room key.

"Don't you mean your coach, Cinderella?" he asked, taking her wallet from her so that he could find the key card to her room.

"Nope, my pumpkin. It's already after midnight. Ah, thanks, Tim," she said, holding out her hand for the card.

He moved his own hand slightly, and she hesitated before she could follow, her movements slow, a little clumsy.

"How many beers did I feed you?" he asked, holding on to the key card as he helped her to her feet. His own head felt a little scrambled. He reached into his pocket, threw four twenties on the table. "Man, how many beers did we both have? Let's get out of here."

He slipped an arm around Suzanna's slim waist, and she sort of melted against his side as they walked out of the bar, into the large lobby. She felt good, pressed against him. Not too tall, not too short. And she smelled good, too. And he liked her hair. All sort of short and spikey. Like Dusty's, but a much deeper, darker red, and it looked a hell of a lot better on Suze.

"You didn't feed me, you know," she said when they stopped in front of the bank of elevators.

"I didn't? Sorry, Suze. Didn't you eat at the ball park? You love hot dogs at ball parks."

Suzanna held on to his arm as she lifted one foot after the other, stepping out of her high heels. "That was hours ago, Tim, and I only had one. All I've had for hours are the pretzels the bartender gave us, and you ate most of those."

"You're right, sorry," he said, helping her into the elevator. "Here's another question, since there's no number on the key card. What floor, Suze?"

"Fifteen," she said. "Fifteen-twenty-three," she concluded, grinning at him as if she'd just said something brilliant. "See? I'm not drunk, Tim. I'm in fifteen-twenty-three . . . two, fifteen-twenty-two."

She held up two fingers. "Three. Fifteen-twenty-three."

"So much for waving you goodbye from the elevator and going on up to nineteen." The doors opened on fifteen, and he took her hand, led her onto the floor. "Pick one, Suze," he said as he walked down the hallway and she sort of *danced* along beside him, lazily waving her high heels. "Two, or three?"

She stopped, giggled. "Does it matter? Why don't we just try them both?"

"Oh, boy, Suze is snockered," Tim said quietly, pulling the key card out of his pocket and inserting it in fifteen-twenty-three. Always go with first instincts; that was his motto. The light turned green, and he pulled down the handle, opened the door. "Here we go, home again, home again."

"Oh, you're so smart," Suzanna said, sliding past him, trailing her fingertips across his chest as she went.

"Are you going to be all right?" he asked, flipping the light switch just inside the door, then following Suzanna. "Suze?"

She'd stopped, just beside the king-size bed that took up most of the room, dropping her shoes onto the floor. Expense account, he figured instantly, looking around the room. Nice enough hotel, but let's not spring for anything too fancy, spoil the hired help.

Yeah. Like he cared. He was in enough trouble, looking at Suze in that body-hugging dress that ended a good three inches above her knees.

Looking at Suze looking at the bed.

"Isn't that funny? I've been here a week and never noticed. Big, isn't it?" she said, looking down at the bed.

"Yeah, sure," Tim said, rubbing at the back of his neck. It was that. Big.

She turned to him, her smile sort of wobbly. She pressed both hands, palms flat, against his chest, and sort of leaned into him. "I have a confession to make."

"No, you don't," Tim said quickly, deciding that he was the sober one here. Well, the least drunk anyway. "No confessions,

41

Suze. They're bad for the soul."

"No, silly, they're *good* for the soul." Suzanna looked up at him, her huge green eyes sort of dreamy. And deep, like some wild, bottomless ocean. A guy, if he wasn't careful, and sober, could drown in those eyes.

"Tell you what, Suze," he said, ignoring the fact that her lips were fuller than he'd ever remembered. Julia Roberts lips, opening over a set of perfect white teeth that he'd never known could be a turn-on for him. Teeth? Who would have thought it?

"Hmmm?"

"What?" he asked her, swallowing down on the sudden lump in his throat.

"You said you'd tell me what, Tim. So . . . what?"

"Oh, right. Tell you what, Suze," he said, realizing that, somehow, his hands had found their way around her waist, "we'll have breakfast tomorrow morning — this morning — and if you still want to make this confession, you can do it then."

She closed her eyes, shook her head. "No. No, Tim, it's got to be now." She slowly walked her hands up his chest with the tips of her fingers, locked those hands behind his neck. "I've always been crazy about you."

Then she pressed her face against his shoulder.

"You have?" Tim heard himself say. He thought he'd sounded at least a little bit incredulous. *Good save, Trehan. Like you didn't know. Like you haven't always known.* "Gee, Suze, I didn't know."

Her head moved against his shoulder. "I didn't want you to know. I was just good old Suze to you, Tim."

He put two fingers under her chin, lifted her head so that he could look into her eyes. "You were a great friend, Suze. A great friend."

She was silent for some moments, then took a deep breath, let it out slowly. Looked at him. "I could be a better friend," she said at last, lifting her lips for his kiss. "I could, Tim. Really."

He put his fingers against her mouth. Man, what was next for him? Sainthood? "No, Suze. It wouldn't be fair. I'd be taking advantage of you."

And he hadn't been with a woman in months. Months. That damn Trehan curse thing. Oh, yeah. Sainthood, at the very least.

Her eyes lost their glow. "You don't want me."

"Oh, no," Tim said hurriedly, giving a

moment to wonder if Suzanna was numb from the waist down. Otherwise, how could she have missed the fact that he was pressed against her, and he was hard, ready. "I want you, Suze. I do."

"Great!" she said in her cheerful tipsiness. And the next thing Tim knew, she was sort of falling backward with her arms still locked around his neck, and he was falling with her, and she was flat on her back on the bed, and he was on top of her, being kissed by her.

He kissed her back.

He wasn't nuts.

The kisses deepened, especially as Suzanna moved beneath him, working on his belt buckle, pulling down his zipper. For a lady who'd had a little too much to drink, she was damn good with zippers.

So was he. The next thing he knew, Suzanna's dress was on the floor, and he was gulping over the sight of her well-formed, long-waisted, flared-hip body in bikini-cut pink lace panties and pink lace underwire bra.

Front-closing pink lace underwire bra.

He knew how those worked.

"Damn," he breathed quietly as the hook slipped open and Suzanna's breasts, her perfect breasts, were revealed to him.

He had to touch.

He had to kiss.

He had to . . . he had to . . . he —

"No," he managed to say between quick, labored breaths, "nothing with me. Are you okay?"

"Never better," Suzanna said tipsily, hooking her thumbs under the waistband of his briefs, tugging them down over his hips.

"No," Tim said, trying again. In between running his tongue up the side of her throat, rimming it inside her ear. "Are you . . . ?"

She found him, wrapped her fingers around him. He heard her moan, low in her throat as she raised her hips, pressed against him.

"Oh, hell . . ." he said, and that was pretty much the last thing Tim remembered until the grinning, laughing baby came winging in from the pitcher's mound.

"No! No!"

"Tim. Tim! Wake up, wake up! You're having a nightmare."

He opened his eyes, not surprised to find himself sitting up in yet another hotel bed, his arms stretched out in front of him.

But Dusty's voice had gone an octave higher. . . .

He turned on the bed and saw Suzanna sitting there beside him, naked, the sheets tangled around her hips, her dark red hair even more spikey, her breasts . . . damn, her breasts. Those gorgeous breasts.

He remembered now.

"Are you all right?" she asked him, pulling the sheet up to cover herself.

He swallowed, ran his hands through his hair. "Yeah. I'm . . . I'm okay. How are you?"

She averted her head. "I've been less embarrassed," she said quietly, then turned to look at him once more. "I . . . I really don't do this . . . you know, what we did? Really."

Tim was still shaking off the remnants of the dream, the nightmare, but he wasn't so self-involved that he didn't know that Suzanna might be feeling a few regrets.

"No?" he said, pushing her back against the pillows. "That's a shame, Suze, because you do it really well."

Her frown only deepened. "Not because I do it a lot. I mean, I'm twenty-nine years old, Tim. I've . . . well, I've . . . you know. In college there was this one guy. And maybe a couple of times since. I'm only human. But I never meant to . . . you know . . . with you."

"You talk too much," Tim said, capturing her mouth with his own, even as he moved his hand to mold it around her breast.

She didn't want to think; he was pretty sure of that. He didn't want to think. Touching Suzanna, holding her, he knew he didn't have to think.

He couldn't think.

But he could feel . . .

Her hands, tugging at him, pulling him close.

Her nails, digging into his back.

Her softness. The curves, the valleys, the secrets that became his, yielded to him.

The scent of her, the taste of her.

The wild hot heat of her.

Her legs came up around his hips as he plunged between her thighs, burying himself there, being reborn there. Taking, giving, taking more, taking more.

He caught her soft, rather surprised exclamation of pleasure with his mouth, held her as she went toward the edge, then tumbled over with her, the two of them lying there, holding each other.

Falling asleep once more, in each other's arms.

When Tim awoke at the sound of the alarm Suzanna — practical, good old Suze

— had probably set before heading out to the game last night, he realized that he felt rested. Actually rested.

The nightmare hadn't come back.

The Trehan curse? Hell, maybe it was Tim "the Monk" Trehan that had been the problem all along.

Then Suzanna snuggled against him, sliding one long leg over his, and murmured in her sleep.

No, that wasn't it. Close, but it wasn't it.

He'd found a solution; that was what he'd found. *If you can't beat 'em, join 'em. Right?*

He began stroking Suzanna's arm, patiently waiting for her to wake up.

"Hmmm . . ." she said at last, her hand moving on his bare chest, leisurely exploring.

And then, suddenly, her hand stilled; her body stiffened. "Tim?" she said, her voice small.

"Still me, yes," he answered, picking up his head enough that he could plant a kiss on her hair as she lay against his shoulder.

"Oh, God!"

Suzanna pushed hard on his chest, putting space between them, obviously ready to leap out of the bed. But then she hesitated for a second, reaching back to tug on the tangled sheet, which she dragged off the bed with her, wrapping it around herself — and leaving him totally naked and exposed to her.

He could reach the bedspread if he wanted to. Easily. But he didn't want to. It was much more fun watching Suzanna look at him.

She held the sheet with one hand, pressed the other against her forehead as she looked at him. Sort of *goggled* at him.

"I . . . I thought I'd been dreaming." Her eyes were wide, her cheeks pale. "Oh, God, my head. My head is killing me."

"It's called a hangover, Suze," Tim told her, grinning.

"Oh, shut up," she said, flipping the end of the sheet over her shoulder as she turned away from the bed. "And put some clothes on. And go away. Please."

"I'd rather go to Vegas," he heard himself saying.

"Fine," she said, heading toward the bathroom. "Go to Vegas. Just *go*."

He half leaned across the bed, so she could hear him, so he could watch her walking away. "I don't have another game until tomorrow night. Instead of heading back with the team, I'm betting Sam will let me fly to Vegas when I tell him I'm going to get married."

Suzanna had reached the bathroom, and the door slammed on his last few words. But she'd heard him. He was sure she'd heard him.

So he waited. "One . . . two . . . You're back?"

She stomped, actually stomped, toward the bed. "What do you mean . . . *married?*"

He was standing next to the bed now, pulling on the briefs he'd found beneath a chair. "I mean married. You and me, married. You know. Shoes and rice? The little woman? Legal sex? Scratch that — *great* legal sex."

The sheet safely wrapped around her, Suzanna pointed both index fingers at him, then at herself, then at him again. Then she got fancy. One index finger pointed at him, the other at herself. Back and forth, alternating fingers.

He had this wild thought, remembering a quote from the very quotable Yogi Berra: "He hits from both sides of the plate. He's amphibious."

Tim grinned. Who wouldn't have grinned?

"You? Me? You and me?" Those talented index fingers were still flying. "Are you talking about you and me? *Married?*" Then her eyes narrowed. "Am I still drunk?"

"Maybe," he told her, pulling on his slacks. "So, you want to do it?"

Now the index fingers went in circles. "We already did . . . it. Twice, as I remember."

"Yeah," Tim said, smiling as his head poked free of his polo shirt. He smoothed his hair with his hands. "And, this way, we get to do it again and again."

The fingers stopped their dance as Suzanna folded her hands together, pushed them against her stomach. "How . . . romantic."

Tim reached up, scratched at a spot behind his left ear. "I play ball, Suze. I don't make speeches. But we're good together, aren't we? We've known each other forever, so it probably came as much of a shock to you as it did me, but we're really good together. And neither one of us is getting any younger."

"Gee, real smooth, Trehan. Flattery will get you everywhere," Suzanna said, rummaging in the hotel dresser for fresh underwear that she quickly hid beneath a fold of the sheet.

Tim walked around the bed, laid a hand on Suzanna's shoulder. "Come on, Suze, marry me. It makes sense."

"Because we've known each other since we were kids?"

"That's one reason, and a good one. Here's another. We like each other."

"Don't forget number three. Because we aren't getting any younger, remember?"

"Hey, an argument is an argument. I gave it a shot, but I'll take it back if you want."

She slammed the drawer shut. "Yeah, I want. Take it back."

"Taken back. I'm not getting any younger. You, however, are close to jailbait. I'm just lucky nobody carts me off to the pokey, being here with such a lovely young thing."

"Don't overdo it, Trehan, we graduated in the same class," she said, then sighed. "Okay. I'm hearing your reasons. We're friends, we've known each other forever, and you're right, neither one of us is getting any younger. And we had . . . we . . . We made love," she ended in a rush.

"Wrong. We made some damn fantastic love, Suze. I don't know about you, but I think I heard fireworks going off."

"I . . . I wouldn't know. It . . . It's not like I have a whole lot to compare you with . . ."

He leaned close, whispered in her ear, "Trust me, I'm good. I'm very, very good."

"Trust Me Trehan," she said, stepping away from him. "Oh, yes, I remember now. Last time I heard that one I think I ended up letting you borrow my mom's car. You drove it into a ditch, and I was grounded for a month."

"We won't drive; we'll take a jet to Vegas. I'll charter one."

She sat down on the edge of the bed, looked up at him. "You're serious, aren't you? I mean, you're really serious."

Tim had a quick flash of himself lying on his back, all his wind knocked out of him after Sanchez had come barreling into him, full force, in yesterday's game. It was only a matter of time before that one out of three happened, until he fell victim to his own superstition, or to the Trehan curse. Who cared what it was called. He just cared that he believed it, that one of those three things had to happen to him.

"I'm serious, yes. Marry me, Suze. You've been my pal forever. You've always come through for me in a pinch. I . . . I need you."

She looked at him for a long time, long enough for him to feel the guilt begin to seep into his bones, take up residence.

But was what he was doing so bad?

She'd always had a thing for him. He'd

always known that, and she'd admitted it to him last night.

And he liked her. He'd always liked Suze. Good old Suze. Now good old Suze was a grown woman, and man, had she grown up great.

They would be okay. She liked baseball. He loved baseball. She loved him. He liked her.

It could work. It *would* work.

As long as he didn't tell her the truth.

"Suze? Please?" he asked, going down on one knee.

"Oh, get up," she said, heading for the bathroom once more. "And you'd better order us both some breakfast. I hate airplane food."

"You got it," he called after her, high-fiving an imaginary hand as he headed for the telephone. Sam was going to bust a gut, but he'd get over it.

His manager would get over it the minute Tim "the Tiger" Trehan started hitting them into the bleachers again.

Three

Holy cow!

— Phil Rizzuto, former
Yankees announcer

"Would you care for a glass of wine, Ms. Trent?"

Suzanna tore her gaze away from the bluer-than-blue skies and poofy, whiter-than-white clouds outside the small port-hole window and looked at the stewardess, one of the two on this chartered flight.

What was the plural of stewardess? Oh, yeah, that old joke from her dad's favorite comedian, Shelly Berman: "the plural of steward-ess is steward-ii."

Except they weren't steward-ii anymore. They were flight attendants. Probably trained in CPR and antiterrorism tactics, and braver than she'd ever be.

Shame this one, who probably spoke three languages and could efficiently employ the Heimlich maneuver while serving dinner to two other people, couldn't seem to recognize a hangover when she saw one.

"Um, no thanks," Suzanna said, hiding

behind her dark sunglasses.

"No? How about a soft drink?"

"Uh-uh, thanks."

"Beer?"

"God, no," Suzanna said, then did her best to smile. Poor woman. Two attendants, two passengers; one of them sprawled out over two seats, sound asleep. *The woman has got to be bored out of her skull.* "But if you have some water and a couple of Tylenol?"

"Certainly, Ms. Trent," the attendant said happily, and walked off in her sensible two-inch heels and marvelously well-cut navy blue suit.

This plane had to be costing Tim the earth, and maybe even a sizable down payment on the moon. Pilot, copilot, two attendants, and seats enough for at least fifteen people.

How nice for him to not have to worry about things like money. Not that she sat up nights worrying about bills herself. Still, her money, piled next to Tim's money, would look like the proverbial molehill next to his mountain.

Was that going to be a problem for her? No, she didn't think so.

"Oh, thank you," Suzanna said, accepting the glass of ice water and a small packet of Tylenol from the attendant. "You're a lifesaver. Tell me, when do we land?"

The attendant looked at the watch strapped to her wrist. "About ninety minutes more, Ms. Trent. Would you like me to bring you another pillow? A blanket?"

"No, that's okay. I think I'm going to go prod Mr. Trehan with a stick. It'll help pass the time."

The attendant blinked, then grinned. "He's been asleep almost since we took off, hasn't he? Big game yesterday, I guess. I heard the pilot and copilot talking about it. Fourteen innings?"

"At least that," Suzanna said weakly, remembering the "innings" she and Tim had put in *after* the game was over.

Suzanna watched the attendant walk toward the front of the small jet once more, then released her seat belt and headed to the back, where Tim was curled up on a wider seat, a fuzzy blue blanket draped over him.

"Tucked you in, did they?" she asked quietly, sitting down on one of the facing seats.

She looked at him, his head on a small pillow, his hands tucked up near his chin, his long legs bent to fit on the seat now that the center armrest had been pushed out of the way.

The sleep of the innocent. Whoever had written that line surely had never met Tim Trehan.

Married. He said they were going to be married as soon as the plane set down in Las Vegas.

And she'd said yes.

And, much as she wished she could tell herself otherwise, she had been sober when she'd said it.

She was sober now. Her headache had even begun to fade, so that she couldn't say she wasn't thinking clearly.

Clearly, she was *nuts,* running a close second to *pathetic.*

God, look at him. His dark blond hair mussed, and yet sexy as hell. That lighter blond streak making her fingers itch to run through his hair.

Once, a million years ago, he'd fallen asleep on her bedroom floor, after half a night spent cramming for their trig final.

She'd gone downstairs to get them each another soda, and when she'd come back, there he was, curled up much the same as he was now, out cold.

She'd sat on the edge of her bed and watched him sleep, watched him until it was nearly dawn, then finally woke him and slipped him out of the house before her parents could wake up and have a cow.

Have a cow? Where had that come from? She had regressed to high school speak.

Okay, so it went quite well with her resurrected high school crush, didn't it?

Except she was a grown-up now. Tim might still be playing ball, playing at life, but she was a grown-up. She had a responsible job. More than a job, a profession. What did Tim have? His face on a baseball card, that was what Tim had.

They had had fun last night. *Before* they went up to her room. Talking, laughing over old times.

But it had been ten years, almost eleven. Did they have anything in common anymore, other than their memories?

And some really great sex, a small part of her brain, the lascivious part obviously, reminded her.

But, as Tim had said, and had clearly meant, neither of them was getting any younger. He must really be ready to settle down, and he had decided to settle down with her.

It was a dream, all her dreams, come true.

"Oh, God," she said, burying her face in

her hands. "Am I about to make the biggest mistake in my life?"

Tim tilted his head slightly, smiled into Suzanna's face. "Hi, Mrs. Trehan," he said, then gave her a hug as the little old lady in the purple dress and matching hair cried *"Weeee!"* and threw confetti at them.

"Can we get out of here now?" Suzanna asked, and Tim realized that she was shaking and seemed close to tears.

"Sure, Suze. Let's go."

He slipped an arm around her shoulders and led her out of the small chapel with all the white latticework on the walls, festooned with plastic flowers, and through an archway of white balloons, out into the hot Las Vegas sunshine.

"Pretty creepy, huh?" he said apologetically, looking back at the square white clapboard building with the makeshift steeple on top. "Sorry we couldn't wait for the chapel at one of the casinos; but I've got to be back in Philly by tomorrow morning or Sam'll murder me, and then he'd fail his anger management class."

"I understand," she said, quickly slipping into the long, black rented limousine ahead of him as the uniformed driver held open the door for them. "Are we going straight back to the airport from here?"

He slid in beside her, planted a kiss on her nose. "Suze, we landed, we hit the courthouse, then the chapel of the damned, or whatever that place is called. Before we leave I want to get something great to eat, and then maybe we can hit one of the casinos. Sam made me promise I'd put twenty on number twelve for him. That's roulette, Suze."

"I know it's roulette," she told him, sinking lower in the seat. "And I could eat, I suppose."

"Great," Tim said, knowing he wasn't quite playing the role of attentive bride-groom. But it had just hit him. He was married. Cripes. Married.

To good old Suze.

"Steak?"

He frowned at her. "Oh, steak. Yeah, sure. I could eat a steak."

"Good, because suddenly I'm starving." She leaned forward, knocked on the glass separating them from the driver. "Steak and the nearest casino, in that order, or to-gether, if you can manage it?"

The driver grinned at her. "Yes, ma'am. And may I say, ma'am, congratulations. Nice work. Tim Trehan. Man, that's cool."

Suzanna sat back once more, her expression, to Tim's mind anyway, rather mulish.

"What's the matter?"

"What's the matter?" she repeated. "I'll tell you what's the matter. The groom is supposed to be congratulated, and the bride offered best wishes. *You*, Tim, are supposed to be the lucky one because *you've* got *me*."

"Yeah, all right. I wasn't listening. What did he say?"

"He congratulated me; that's what he did. Nice work, he said. Like you're some huge fish I landed with my rusty reel and a couple of wiggly worms. Is that what everyone's going to think?"

"Prickly," Tim said, slipping his arm around her once more. "I forgot that about you, Suze. You could get really prickly. I married you because I wanted to, and that's what I'll tell anyone who asks."

She slightly lifted her chin as she closed her eyes. "People are going to ask, aren't they? Reporters. Fans. Jack."

Tim nearly knocked the top of Suzanna's head off as he jumped forward in the seat. "Oh, cripes. Jack. I didn't tell him. Or Mort."

"Who's Mort?" Suzanna asked, rubbing at the back of her head.

"My agent," Tim said, reaching for his cell phone and hitting number two on the speed dial, Mort's private number. "Mort will handle everything, the publicity, all that junk. And he'll go ballistic if someone calls him to ask about our marriage and he doesn't know about it. I mean, he'll blow a — *Mort!* Hey, hi. It's Tim. Yeah, I know you know my voice. Look, Mort, I've kind of got something to tell you."

The limousine pulled under a canopy of sorts and stopped. Suzanna got out when the back door opened, and Tim followed, still listening to Mort tell him about an endorsement deal he was working on, one that would feature both Tim and Jack and a huge four-by-four pickup truck.

He covered the phone for a moment, told the driver to wait somewhere for them, then trotted after Suzanna, who had already stepped inside the casino. The loud casino. Bells ringing, people yelling, music playing, kids running for a big gift shop right next to the front doors. "Mort? You still there? Suze! Suze, wait for me."

"Suze? What's a Suze?" Mort asked from behind his desk in his office in New York. Tim could see him there: pudgy five-foot, nine-inch frame stuffed in some modern leather chair, his Ferragamos propped on the desk top, either rubbing hair restorer into his scalp or hiding that scalp beneath one of his many toupees, his black bean eyes somewhat squinted as he listened to Tim. That was Mort "More and More" Moore.

"Here's the thing, Mort," Tim said quickly. "I got married a couple of minutes ago."

Then he waited for the explosion.

"You *what?*" Tim imagined Mort's feet swinging down off the desk top as his agent hopped to his feet, tried to force himself through the telephone wires so he could strangle his client. "And you didn't tell *me?* Where are you? I can have press and cameras there in five minutes. No, no press. Not if I'm not there. Just cameras."

Tim had caught up with Suzanna, who was standing in front of a slot machine showing a computer image of dancing frogs. Well, some were dancing. One was puffing up like a blowfish, another was wearing a crown, and there was a chicken in there somewhere, laying an egg.

He slipped his hand into his pocket, pulled out a twenty, handed it to her. "Here, babe. Play the machine while I talk to Mort, okay? But it's too loud in here to think straight, so I'm going to go back outside so I can hear. You stay here, where it's cooler. I'll be right back."

She gave him this sort of funny look. "Yes, master," she said, taking the twenty, then turning her back on him.

"Right back, Suze. I mean it. And then we'll eat."

"Uh-huh," he thought she said, her back stiff.

Tim looked at that stiff back for another moment, ignoring Mort's ranting in his ear, then sighed, headed for the doors once more.

Once outside, he listened as Mort wrapped up his tirade about who was going to tell Aunt Sadie, and who was going to tell Jack, and what in hell was he going to tell the press?

"Mort. Mort, take a breath. And get a pencil and paper," Tim said, walking in a circle as he shoved a hand through his hair. "I'm married. Bride is one Suzanna Trent, whom I've known since kindergarten. Jack can fill you in on the rest of it, where she lives, all the usual stuff. And she works for a computer software company, something like that. We flew to Vegas this morning, we're married, and we'll be back in Philadelphia in time for tomorrow night's game. Honeymoon to follow . . . follow . . . hell,

65

follow the end of the season. That's the best I can do, right?"

"Since kindergarten? So this isn't just some bimbo you picked up somewhere? You've only gone a little nuts, not totally nuts?"

"Smooth, Mort, real smooth," Tim said as a young boy walked up to him, holding out a paper bag with *Treasure Island* stamped on it, and a pen with a pirate's grinning skull attached to the top.

Tim scribbled his name on the bag, rubbed the kid's head, then turned away, walked a few steps, hoping for more privacy.

"Look, Mort, I've gotta go. Suze is inside, playing some frog game, and neither of us has eaten in hours. Unless you want to be handing out a press release on our divorce before you can announce the marriage, I've got to go make nice, okay?"

"You aren't husband material, you know," Mort said. "I've heard Sadie say it at least a million times. Jack had to grow up, with his injury and all, but you're still a kid, playing a kid's game."

"And with that vote of confidence, Mort, I'm hanging up. See ya," Tim said, hitting the END button, then folding up the phone, jamming it into his pocket.

Then he pulled it out again. Jack. He had to call Jack. Before Mort could call Jack.

He hit the first number on his speed dial and anxiously bounced on the balls of his feet as he listened to three rings, then four, before a female voice said, "Hello?"

"Keely," Tim said, relaxing a little. This was good, this was very good. At least Keely wouldn't go ape-shit on him. "Is Jack there?" he asked, hoping his brother was anywhere but "there."

"No, sorry, Tim, he's not. He and Candy are off to Dorney Park for the morning. There's a new ride, or something. We can only hope Jack fits in one of the seats, because we both know he's more crazy about the rides than Candy is. The rides, and the cotton candy. You just caught me, as a matter of fact, because I have my monthly with the obstetrician this morning. Three hours in the waiting room, five minutes with the doctor. Jack took a raincheck this month. Anyway, can I help?"

Tim hesitated, suddenly not so sure he should tell Keely first instead of Jack, then realized that he didn't have much choice. And he already knew it would be easier to tell Keely. "I'm in Vegas, Keel," he said, turning his back on a bermuda-shorts-clad man who was looking at him with that "don't I know you from somewhere" look. "I just got married."

Silence. Complete and utter silence.

He took the phone away from his ear, tapped on it, then put it up again and said, "Keely? Keel, babe? You still there?"

"Sitting down, Tim, sitting down," she answered, her voice a little strange. "Did I hear you correctly? *Married?*"

"Yeah, married. But it's okay. It's Suzanna. Suzanna Trent. I know you don't know her, but Jack can tell you all about her. We're heading back to Philly later today, because I've got a game tomorrow night. Do you think you two could grab a baby-sitter and come down?"

"Meet her, you mean? Tim, are you at all familiar with the term 'wild horses couldn't keep me away'? Of course we'll be there. The Yankees aren't on TV, so Jack is free."

"Okay, good. Great. Thanks, Keel. You're the best."

"Only because I have so many questions I can't get one out of my mouth with any hope of coherence. But be ready, buddy, because tomorrow night, I'm showing up with a list."

Tim laughed, said goodbye, and ended

the call even as he trotted back into the casino.

He found Suzanna right where he'd left her, sitting in front of the slot machine with the frogs. Except there was some sort of bar blinking on the screen now, a red light flashing on top of the machine, and both a loud ringing and the most god-awful tinny song emanating from somewhere inside.

"What happened?"

She didn't look up at him. "I'm not sure. Lots of frogs in a row," she said quietly.

He peered over her shoulder, read the message flashing on the screen: "Hand pay required. $248.65. Please call attendant."

He sat down in the empty seat beside hers. "Damn, Suze. You won. And with nickels."

"Yes, I'd figured out that part. But now what?"

"Now we wait for the attendant. They come over when they see the red light flashing. So, steak's your treat?" he asked, leaning over to kiss her cheek.

"Deal," she said, twisting her hands in her lap. "Then what?"

"I don't know. I have to play that twenty for Sam. You seem to be lucky, Suze. Maybe you'll want to play some more slots."

She twisted on the chair, glared at him. "And that's it? We come to Vegas, we get married by a guy who called me *Susan*, I watch some frogs dance, I gamble, we eat steak, we both gamble, and then we get back on the plane?"

He grimaced. "Not the best time you've ever had, huh? I mean, when you say it that way . . ."

The attendant showed up, blessedly turned off the ringing bell, the tinny music.

"Jack," Suzanna said as they both stood back so that the attendant could open the machine, do something with the insides. "I don't want to sound bitchy or anything, but have you noticed that my finger's turning green?"

He immediately looked down at her left hand, where he had placed the ring he'd bought at the chapel. Twenty-five bucks, but it was better than nothing. Besides, she'd exaggerated. Her finger wasn't green. Not yet. But it probably would be, any minute now.

"Damn."

"It doesn't matter, honestly. I guess I just had this white gown and veil dream, you know? An elopement and the proverbial ring out of a Cracker Jacks box isn't as romantic in practice as it is in theory. I'm just being silly, and I know it."

"The hell you are," Tim said, gathering her into his arms, kissing the top of her head. "Ah, Suze, don't be such a good sport."

"It's what I do," she mumbled into his chest, so that he had to laugh, although he felt like a heel.

"I know, and I took advantage of you."

"Swept me off my feet," she said quietly.

"Plied you with beer."

"I don't remember you forcing a funnel down my throat."

"Seduced you."

She lifted her head from his chest, but he kept her held close inside his arms. "Good," she said, looking straight into his eyes. "That's how I want to remember that moment. At least then I can live with myself."

"Flew you out here and married you," he continued, grinning at her. Good old Suze. What a brick.

" 'Dear Diary,' " she said, a smile growing on her own face. God, he was crazy about that smile of hers, those full lips, those white teeth. She had a smile as big as center field.

"Huh?"

"I said, 'Dear Diary,'" she repeated. "'Today I got married, met a frog, and ate a New York strip steak.' Does that sound romantic to you?"

"Hell no," Tim said as the attendant politely cleared his throat, so that Tim let go of Suzanna and she could hold out her hand as bills were counted into it. She pulled out a five and handed it to the attendant, who probably didn't get too many tips from the nickel players, because he thanked her, three times.

"You're very welcome," she said, and Tim shook his head. That was also good old Suze. An only child, she'd been brought up to be polite. Far from the rough and tumble of his own youth, his and Jack's.

"Hey, just a sec," he said as the attendant turned to walk away. "This place have room service?"

"Yes, sir, twenty-four hours a day."

"Great. Where's the check-in desk?"

The attendant pointed to his left. "Over there, sir. Say, aren't you . . . ?"

"Nope. I'm only his twin brother," Tim said quickly, already steering Suzanna toward the large foyer and registration desk.

"Hey! But if you're his twin brother, then you're — ha! That's a good one, Jack.

Or Tim. Or whoever you are . . ."

Suzanna had a hand pressed to her mouth as they made their way through lazily strolling tourists, covering her giggles. " 'Nope, I'm only his twin brother,' " she said at last. "When did you think up that gem?"

Tim sort of leered at her. "I've got a million of 'em, babe," he said as he walked straight up to the manager's desk and turned on the considerable Trehan Irish charm.

"Hi," he said, sticking out his hand, "I'm Tim Trehan. I was really hoping we could get a room. The bridal suite, if it's free?"

"Nothing in Vegas is free, Mr. Trehan," the manager said, with no hint of a smile.

"Funny line. I'll bet he's got a million of 'em, too," Suzanna whispered as she turned her head into Tim's shoulder, her own shoulders shaking.

"Good one," Tim agreed, letting go of the manager's hand, leaving the two one-hundred-dollar bills behind. The guy looked at them and slipped them into his pocket without so much as a blink.

"Our bridal suites, I'm sorry to say, are all occupied, Mr. Trehan, but I do believe we can have a most lovely suite ready for you . . . and Mrs. Trehan? . . . in about an hour. Will that be satisfactory? Would you care to have one of our bellpersons take your luggage?"

"No luggage," Tim said, and Suzanna squeezed his arm a little too tightly. "That is, it's being sent over later. But not an hour. We'll be back in twenty minutes, and the suite will be ready, right? In the meantime, where's your jewelry shop? You've got one of those?"

"Yes, sir, we pride ourselves on our fine jewelry shop." The manager stood up, pointed to his right. "Just follow that hallway to our galleria."

"Come on, wife," Tim said, feeling pretty in charge, pretty competent. "The jewelry store awaits. You think that jackpot you hit will cover it?"

"You want *me* to buy my own ring?" she asked, almost skipping to keep up with his long strides. He wanted this shopping business out of the way, so he could concentrate on other things. One other thing: Suzanna.

"You think I should pay for it, huh?"

"That depends. How rich a widow would I be if I killed you right now?"

Tim laughed, feeling better, *freer*, than he had in longer than he could remember. Since Jack had gotten hurt, found Candy,

74

gotten married, probably. Over a year. One long, scary year for a guy who used to think he owned the world and all the good luck in it.

A song began on the casino sound system, some oldie but goodie with a strong back beat, and Tim impulsively grabbed Suzanna into his arms and began dancing her down the hallway, sidestepping tourists, turning circles as Suzanna gasped and giggled, not stopping until they were standing inside the jewelry shop.

You knew it was a good shop. There were diamonds glittering in the window display. And rubies. And those blue things.

And no price tags.

"Wedding rings, my good woman," Tim said with a smile, pulling a suddenly reluctant Suzanna over to the counter and the heavily bejeweled woman behind it. "And engagement rings. We'll want to see both, won't we, Suze?"

She shook her head at him. "Oh, I don't know, Tim. I'm glad you want a wedding ring, but do you really want an engagement ring? Some of the guys in the clubhouse might make jokes. Or are you thinking about a diamond in your ear?"

"Me? Oh, funny, Suze, funny." Then he took hold of her elbow, moved her away from the counter. "Suze . . . no joking here, okay? You knew I meant that I want the lady to show us some rings for you."

"Yes, I know that," she answered, looking past him, to where the saleslady was standing, hands folded together on top of the glass case, doing nothing.

"And you know that I can't wear a wedding ring. I mean, not during a game. And if I didn't wear it during the game, then I'd probably leave it on a shelf in a locker somewhere, forget it, lose it. So I probably shouldn't have one. You see that, don't you?"

Was it getting cold in here? How low did casinos turn their air-conditioning anyway? Because, suddenly, there was a definite chill in the air.

"Suze? Suzanna? Say something, okay?"

"Sure, I'll say something. No rings."

"What do you mean, no rings?"

"I mean, no rings. Don't play dumb jock with me, Tim. I sat behind you in school, remember? Straight A's. If I say no rings, then you know I mean — no rings. Not for you, and not for me."

At that, she pulled off the cheap ring and tossed it over her shoulder. It landed in a potted plant strung with little white fairy lights. "See? All gone."

"Damn." Tim jammed his fists on his hips, glared at her. "Send a girl to California, and she comes back one of those women's libbers. You could have warned me."

"Gender equality, Tim, and don't tell me your mom wouldn't have washed out your mouth with soap if you'd said *women's libbers* within earshot. She took me to a Gloria Steinem lecture my junior year in high school, remember? Poor woman, surrounded by men who left the seat up."

Tim rubbed at the back of his neck, almost sensing his mother standing behind him, telling him that good manners and women's rights were two different things, so he'd better still open doors for his dates or she'd know the reason why.

One tough lady, his mom.

"All right, Suze, I get it. And I'll get a ring. Just don't shoot me if I lose it and have to get another. Tell me, are you going to take my name? I'd really like it if you took my name."

"Nut, of course I'm taking your name," she said, standing on tiptoe to kiss him on the mouth. "Come on. I'm thinking matching gold bands. We'll get you two."

"You two ready now?" the saleslady asked, looking bored as they walked back to the counter. "We only sell, you know. We don't buy."

"Man, we must look worse than we think," Suzanna whispered to him as the saleslady went into the back room once Tim had brought out his American Express card and plunked it on the glass. "No limit," he'd said, pushing it toward her. "Here, take it. Go check."

Tim looked down at his wrinkled slacks and the golf shirt he'd slept in on the plane, wondering how he'd gotten light blue fuzzy stuff all over his shirt. Then he turned to Suzanna, who looked just fine, damn it, in kelly green slacks and a soft yellow blouse — her matching jacket left behind in the plane.

"You look great," he told her honestly. "The green matches your eyes."

"And for a while, earlier this morning, my complexion," Suzanna said, and he remembered how difficult it had always been to compliment her. She just didn't believe in herself as much as she should. Never had.

"Mr. Trehan?"

Tim and Suzanna turned at the sound of the man's voice. "James Freethy, Mr. Trehan," he said, holding out a hand sporting a diamond the size of a pigeon's egg. "I'm the manager, sir. How may I help you?"

Tim smiled at Suzanna as if to say, *See? That's more like it.* "Hi, Jim. I'd like to introduce you to my wife, Suzanna Trehan."

"That's James, sir." He nodded to Suzanna, who nodded right back at him. "Madam."

"Yeah," Tim then continued, "Suzanna Trehan. We were just married, sort of a spur-of-the-moment thing."

"We get a lot of that around here, Mr. Trehan," James Freethy said with a small smile.

"I'll bet you do. So . . . rings. Wedding rings for both of us. Gold, the lady said. And a diamond ring, just for her. What've you got?"

"Our selection is quite extensive, sir. Shall we begin with the wedding rings? Then, if I might make a suggestion, I believe an exceptional three-carat emerald ring I'm thinking of, surrounded by the finest diamonds, would be perfect for Mrs. Trehan. Match those lovely green eyes."

"Keep talking, Jim," Tim said, leaning on the glass counter. "I think we're playing in pretty much the same ball park."

"Ball park, sir? Would that be baseball?

I'm afraid I don't know much about sports."

"Neither do I," Tim said, keeping a straight face. "But it sounds good when we say stuff like that, doesn't it?"

"Yes, sir," James Freethy said, looking at Suzanna, who was coughing into her hand to cover a laugh. "Now, I'll leave you alone to look at this tray of wedding rings, and go retrieve the emerald from our safe."

"He doesn't know you," Suzanna said once James Freethy was gone. "I don't think the hotel manager did, either. Are you insulted?"

"Relieved, to tell you the truth. Mort wants to break the story."

"It's a story? Our marriage is a story?"

Tim ran his finger over her furrowed brow. "We've covered that, Suze. You already know it is. But we'll get through it, I promise. And Mort will do the heavy lifting for us. He always does."

"If you say so, Tim," Suzanna said, then sighed. "I feel like I'm on a roller coaster. You know what I mean?"

"Yeah," he said, kissing her forehead. "I know, babe. I know."

Four

It ain't braggin' if you can back it up.
— Dizzy Dean, pitcher

"I don't think James liked you," Suzanna said as Tim shoved the key card in the door of their suite ninety minutes later.

"Who?"

"James, Tim. The guy who sold you this rock I didn't ask for but am very happy to be wearing."

"Oh, you mean Jim. I didn't notice," he said, pushing open the door. "Wow! Would you look at this, Suze. You could bowl in here."

Suzanna stayed where she was, entertaining thoughts of Tim carrying her over the threshold, then gave it up as another girlish dream that had bitten the dust. "Let's see," she said, walking past him, through the massive foyer, and into a huge round room with raised platforms, marble pillars, enough gilt to redo the dome at Notre Dame, and a sea of white couches. "You're right. Wow."

"The manager told me it's usually reserved for high rollers," Tim said, walking around, opening doors, peeking down hallways. "And how about that view?" he commented, pointing to the floor-to-ceiling windows that looked out over the city, all the way to the mountains.

"I'm speechless," Suzanna said, trailing one hand over the back of a snow-white couch. "It's a good thing we decided to have those steaks downstairs. I'd be afraid to eat in the middle of all this white."

"Yeah, I remember. Suze the slob. You used to wear everything you ate. But you were okay downstairs, so I guess you grew out of that one, huh?"

"I still have lapses," she admitted, heading for the windows and the view. There was a bedroom in here somewhere, probably more than one of them, and she was feeling distinctly nervous. Maybe she shouldn't have said no to the wine Tim had wanted to order with their meal. "With chocolate ice cream, mostly. Mom used to beg me to try vanilla."

That's it, keep it light. A little joke, a little laugh, a little seltzer down your pants. Something like that.

Man, this wasn't as easy sober.

She jumped slightly when Tim spoke from directly behind her. "Seen enough yet, Suze?" he asked, tickling her ear with his breath.

She nodded. Nodding was good, when a person was trying, without much success, to pry her stupid tongue off the roof of her mouth.

"Good, because I've found the bedroom."

The next thing she knew, she was being held high in Tim's arms, and he was heading toward one of the hallways. Her head buried against his chest, she tried to mentally explain to her heart that two hundred beats a minute was probably overdoing it, when Tim put her back on her feet, held her loosely locked inside his arms.

"Open your eyes, Suze," he said, kissing her forehead. "You aren't going to believe this."

She already didn't believe this, any of this, but she opened her eyes anyway, then gasped. She pulled free of his arms and began walking around the huge room.

Enormous round bed on a raised platform. Sheer draperies hanging all over the place. More gold-veined mirrors than she'd like to think about.

She stopped as far away from the bed as she could manage. "My god, Tim. This is like something out of the *Arabian Nights*. Or maybe *Aladdin*. Disney goes porno, I don't know. Wow."

She looked at him, and he had already stripped off his knit shirt, was smoothing down his hair as he grinned at her. Oh, lordy, but the man had a body. . . .

"How about a nap?" he asked, walking over to the bed and yanking down the bedspread in one strong pull, sending the pillows scattering.

"You slept on the plane," she reminded him. He was working on his belt buckle now, and she wondered if there was any water in this suite, because her mouth had gone as dry as the desert.

She pressed her fingertips to her temples. What was the matter with her? They were married. Legally, if tackily married. And she was the one who had hinted that there had been a definite lack of romance about their marriage so far.

That was why they were here, in this movie set for Debauchers 'R Us, instead of safely on the casino floor, betting Sam's twenty bucks.

It was her fault. It was all her fault.

Hooboy, she thought, eying the bed once more. *Every once in a while, Suze — for a woman who thinks she's a practical, level-*

headed, feet-on-the-ground sort — you bite off way more than you can chew.

And then Tim was standing in front of her, his talented hands slipping her blouse buttons from their moorings, and he was asking her in that teasing way of his, "So, are you having fun yet?"

And she was answering, her voice low and — yes, definitely — sort of sexy, "I could be having more."

Omigod, did I just say that? she thought, panicked. *I couldn't have just said that, could I? But I did, I said that. Shame on me. Shame, shame on . . .*

Tim's lips skimmed the side of her throat, his tongue doing these talented things to her skin, the lobe of her ear.

Shame, shame on . . .

His hands were kneading at her shoulders now, her bare shoulders, because her blouse was gone.

Her slacks had disappeared, too.

Her body felt cold, then hot, as he moved against her, pressed his hard body against her.

Man, he hadn't been kidding. He was pretty good. She hadn't even noticed when her bra and panties had bit the dust.

He caught her sigh with his mouth, and on contact, her body gave this small, involuntary convulsion of delight.

And sudden hunger.

She wrapped her arms around him, drew him closer, attempted to press her lower body even closer against his. Slipped one bare leg through his, raised it slightly, pressed again. Gloried in his arousal.

Shame, shame on . . . Oh, the hell with it.

They tumbled onto the bed together, his hands everywhere, hers mimicking his as she skimmed his body, learned his body, rejoiced in his body that fit so well with hers.

"You taste so good," he said, then sluiced his tongue between her breasts, sucked lightly on the side of her throat. "And you smell good, too."

She said something that disproved four straight years of A's in vocabulary. "Uh-huh." And then she ran her hands down his back, glorying in the ripple of his muscles as he shifted above her, brought his mouth to her breast again.

All things considered, with her body singing, her heart hammering, her breath catching in her throat, "Uh-huh" was pretty damn articulate.

He moved his hand lower, slid it over the flare of her hip, then concentrated for a moment on her navel, circling it with one finger even as he pressed his palm flat against her lower belly.

The pressure he created deep inside her made her swallow down hard on the low moan that threatened to escape her.

She moved her hips, raised them slightly as she braced her bent legs against the mattress, wordlessly pleading for more, more.

And then he was there, between her legs. His hand, his fingers, touching her, opening her, stroking her, giving all the proof she'd ever need that the man didn't brag. He was more than good. He was very, very good. A master of his craft.

Her hips went on autopilot, moving on their own, pressing up against him each time he seemed to threaten to leave her, stop what he was doing.

Heat, deep inside her. Building, building. She clamped her teeth together hard, all her concentration on his hand, on what he was doing to her. On his mouth, how it suckled on her, how his tongue flicked at her nipple, sending wave after wild wave of tingling awareness from her breasts to her belly, tying her up in a huge knot that just had to be untied so that she could break free. Soar.

And here it was, coming toward her as she stood poised on the edge, waiting.

Closer it came, that exquisite tightness, that glorious pressure that built and built and built. The hunger that consumed her.

A hunger she'd never known existed, until Tim. Never even imagined.

She beat on his back with her fists, unable to speak, unable to breathe, her heels digging into the mattress as she thrust her hips high, then held them there for him. Open to him, spread wide for him, eager for him.

More than eager.

Demanding.

No inhibitions, for he had teased them all away.

No shame, because he wouldn't allow shame.

No second thoughts, because thinking was something to save for another time, another place.

"Yes," she breathed at last, as the tension turned liquid. Turned blue and white behind her eyes. Flashed red, and deep purple. The colors of passion, exploding all around her. She was drowning in color, in sensation, in that tight coiling that at the very last, frightened her.

His thumb on her, he slipped two fingers inside her and drove them up, up.

"Yes!"

And it all came tumbling down, the mountain of need, of want, that he'd built inside her. Tumbling, tumbling down in a wild explosion of pulsing, rippling sensation.

She lowered her hips — her legs could no longer hold her, because she had gone all soft and liquid. But the need was still there, a different completion than he had given her, one that included them both.

The *want* clogged in her throat, the *need* to give.

Dragging her fingers down his back, she urged him with her body, pulled him toward her. Up and over her.

He sank between her legs, filling her even as his mouth claimed hers again, his tongue mimicking the thrusts of his lower body.

She broke free, gasping, biting on his ear. "More, more," she urged him, wanting nothing else in this life than to give him everything he wanted, everything he might not even know he needed. "More, Tim. Faster. Deeper."

"Oh, babe. Babe," he said, and increased his tempo. Deep, hard, fast. And faster. And faster. Driving into her as she opened to him, gave him all she had.

All he probably would ever want. . . .

★ ★ ★

"Nice," Tim said, looking around after dropping her two suitcases on the floor of the small foyer of her Allentown apartment. "When did they build these?"

Suzanna deposited the case containing her laptop on the paisley-print chair just inside the living room. "Last year. That's when I moved back home for good, sold the old homestead," she told him, looking around the room that could have fit inside the bathroom of their Vegas hotel room. With room left over for a horse. A Clydesdale.

"It was really great of you to do this, Tim. Fly into ABE instead of Philly, and all of that. I'll just be a minute," she said nervously, heading for the door once more. "There's soda in the fridge. That way," she ended, pointing toward the kitchen.

Once outside her apartment, Suzanna leaned against the wall, took a few deep, steadying breaths. Other than her trips to the bathroom in the hotel and on the plane, and a brief moment with the frogs in the casino, this was the first time she'd been alone since saying hi to Tim. Ever since she'd gone temporarily insane, to be more precise.

But it was okay. She'd get used to this.

Being married to Tim, the love of her life, a man who called her "babe" when they made love. Did he always do that? Just so he wouldn't goof up, call somebody by the wrong name?

"Don't think like that. Maybe he's got a thing about Babe Ruth, that's all. No, that's just too weird," she told herself, pushing away from the wall and heading across the square hall for 4B.

Mrs. Josephson opened the door as far as the security chain would allow, then smiled at Suzanna. "Oh, it's you. Just a moment, dear."

The door closed, then opened again, the security chain undone, and Suzanna stepped inside the apartment that always smelled like cinnamon sticks. "How are you, Mrs. Josephson?" she asked. "I got your message on my cell phone. I hope Margo wasn't any trouble?"

"No, no, dear, Margo's never any trouble. But when my sister called to tell me her husband fell and broke his hip, well, I knew you wouldn't mind coming home to take Margo back. Stupid Walter. Tell me, what is a seventy-year-old man thinking, to climb up on a roof like that?"

"He fell off the roof?" Suzanna winced, then went to the corner of the room to pick up Margo, who had been sleeping on the floor in a patch of sunlight coming through the window. Margo wasn't much on big welcome home celebrations.

"The lower roof, luckily. Putting up one of those satellite thingies, Mary said. Five thousand channels, Mary said, all of them sports, to hear her tell it. Well, I'll be off," she said, picking up an overnight bag. "I phoned for a cab when I saw you walking across the parking lot. I thought my cab had come early, but then I saw you get out of it."

Suzanna buried her smile against Margo's soft brown fur. That was Mrs. Josephson. The town crier. She waited for what would come next.

And here it came. . . .

"Such a nice-looking young man, Suzanna," Mrs. Josephson said, reaching for her huge handbag. "Anyone I should know about?"

"He's an old friend, Mrs. J. Tim Trehan. The ball player?"

"Ball player? I'm afraid I wouldn't know, dear. Well, the cab will be here any minute now, and then there's that long bus ride to Pittsburgh. I think I'll be able to make the ten o'clock bus. I may be gone for a while, dear, but don't you worry. I know how busy you are, so I've asked Mr. Horvath to water my plants for me and bring in my mail. He'd have taken Margo, too, if you had to go out of town again, except he's allergic. Nosy old coot, I'll grant you, but he's sure to bring in my Social Security check next Monday."

Suzanna held open the door for Mrs. Josephson, then waved her on her way before reentering her own apartment.

"Here she is," she said, rather proudly, depositing a squirming Margo on the carpet. "One Princess Morgana Margret of Leeds, to be precise about the thing. But I call her Margo. I couldn't resist her."

The brown tabby Persian stretched out one back leg, then the other, before walking over to the couch where Tim sat. She sat on the floor in front of him for a few moments, examining him for flaws, then gracefully hopped up onto his lap.

"Pedigree, huh?" Tim said, scratching behind Margo's ear. Suzanna could hear the cat purring from halfway across the room. Margo *never* did that. "You know, I have a cat, too. Lucky. Big black tomcat. He's got muscles like Arnold Schwarzenegger, I swear it."

"No, I didn't know you had a cat," Suzanna said, watching Margo melt under

Tim's touch. She knew the feeling. "Who takes care of him when you're on the road?"

Tim grinned at her. "Guess we're finally getting around to talking, huh? I should have told you."

"That's okay. You didn't know about Margo until I picked up my messages on our way to the airport."

"True enough. Okay, you know I have a house here, right?"

She smiled. "Right."

"It was one of Mort's ideas. Jack bought a house; I bought a house. Tax write-off, that sort of thing. I had been in a condo, but the bigger the house, the higher the taxes, the bigger the write-off. At least that's what Mort and Aunt Sadie said."

Suzanna's smile widened. "Your Aunt Sadie. I remember her. She worked at a bank, didn't she? Trust officer, something like that? Never married."

"That's Aunt Sadie, although she doesn't work at the bank anymore. She, with some input from Mort, manages Jack's and my finances now. Among other things."

"Other things? Oh, you mean because she's retired now? What does she do? Garden?"

"You wish. Last time I checked, she was auditioning for a project at some local theater," Tim said, putting Margo to one side as he stood up, headed for the kitchen. "You want a soda?" he called back over his shoulder. "Then we'd better get moving, okay?"

"Okay," she said, following him. "And I did know you built a new house last fall. Near Jack's, right?"

He straightened after bending to grab two sodas from the bottom shelf, then looked at her overtop the refrigerator door. "Keeping tabs on me, huh?"

She shook her head. "Don't get too puffed up, Tim. You remember Ron Laub? He did the tile work on your place."

"Ronnie? You're kidding." He popped both tops, handed one can to her. "I haven't seen him in years. He was going to join the navy, wasn't he?"

"Until Babs told him she was pregnant, yes. Now he does tile work with his dad, and he and Babs have three kids. I saw them at the reunion you didn't go to, remember? Now, just give me a minute to change my clothes, feed Margo, and we can go."

"She'll be all right here until tomorrow? Because I really want us to stay at my place in Philly tonight."

"She'll be fine. I'll leave her lots of water and dry food."

"Or you could leave her with Lucky?"

Suzanna had taken three steps toward the hallway leading to her bedroom, but then stopped, turned back to look at him. "Yeah, how do you do that? Who takes care of Lucky for you when you're on a road trip?"

He stepped out from behind the bar in the kitchen. "I guess the old Whitehall High rumor mill missed one, huh? But it's simple enough. I have this huge house I'm barely ever in, and this cat, who really needs company."

"And . . . ?" Suzanna prodded.

"And so I asked Mrs. Butterworth to sort of move in, take care of Lucky for me."

Suzanna put out one arm, steadied herself against the wall. "Mrs. Butterworth? *Our* Mrs. Butterworth? Our history teacher Mrs. Butterworth? *That* Mrs. Butterworth? You're kidding."

"Nope. Our Mrs. Butterworth. Her husband died, you know. Last year. They never had any kids, and she was all alone. Aunt Sadie told me about it. It was pretty sad, you know? So I asked her to be my housekeeper, move in, take care of Lucky

96

for me. She lives in a small apartment attached to the garages, the same way Aunt Sadie lives in an apartment attached to Jack's garages. It works out great, really."

Suzanna looked at Tim for long moments. "When did you get Lucky?"

"Honey," Tim drawled, dropping a kiss on her forehead as he walked past her, back into the living room. "I wuz *born* lucky."

She followed after him. "No, seriously, Tim. When did you get Lucky — the *cat* Lucky? Before or after you heard about Mrs. Butterworth's husband dying and her being left all alone in the world?"

He collapsed onto the couch, shrugged his shoulders. "I don't remember. About the same time, I guess. It doesn't matter. It worked out, right?"

"Right," Suzanna said, then turned and headed down the hallway once more.

God. That great big goofy ball of marshmallow. He bought a cat just so he could convince Mrs. Butterworth he needed her to move in, where he could keep an eye on her.

How she loved this man. He tried never to show it, ever, but she knew. She'd always known. The guy had a heart as big as all —

She wheeled around, trotted back into

the living room. "This cat. Lucky. You said something about muscles. Tomcat, right?"

Tim was once more scratching behind Margo's ears, as that fawning feline sat on the arm of the couch. "Yeah," he said, not looking at her.

"And he's fixed?"

"He was never broken."

"Funny," she said, walking around to the front of the couch to glare at him. "And you know what I mean, Tim. He's been — snipped?"

"Snipped?"

"You know. What do they call it? Castrated?"

"Now, there's a word I try never to work into a conversation," Tim said, scratching beneath Margo's chin, so that she stuck out her neck, closed her big golden eyes in ecstasy.

"Tim, Margo's a pedigree animal. I mean, I don't show her or anything like that; but she is pedigree, and I may want to have her mated one day, have kittens. Persian kittens, Tim, with another Persian cat. She's nearly one now, and will be going into heat any day now. So I can't leave Margo with Mrs. Butterworth unless you tell me Lucky's been fixed. Now, did you have him fixed? Look at me, Tim. Is Lucky fixed?"

He looked straight at her. "Sure. The vet took care of all of that. Shots, flea stuff, you name it."

Was he lying to her? Tim could lie with the best of them. She certainly knew that. But would he lie about something like this?

"Okay," she said at last. "As long as he's fixed. I'll be right back, and then we can go drop Margo with Mrs. Butterworth. I'm dying to see her again."

"That's because you were always her pet," Tim called after her.

"No," she yelled back at him. "That's because I wasn't twins and never tried to pretend I was my own brother. Margo's crate is in the hall closet. Load her up for me, okay?"

By the time she had brushed her teeth and changed into a denim skirt and soft pink summer sweater, Margo was safely locked into her carrier, and Tim had loaded dry cat food and two dishes into a clear plastic bag, along with two fuzzy toy mice and a packet of Margo's favorite organic catnip.

"Small kitchen," he said as she headed for her purse. "It was easy to find this stuff."

"I know. I'm ready." She carried, slung over her shoulder, a soft carry-on bag she'd found in her bedroom closet and quickly stuffed a few things into, and now picked up her overnight bag that held her toiletries.

"I hope you didn't mind me opening cabinets, finding this stuff. I think Lucky eats another brand."

"We're married, Tim. Everything I have is yours." She took the plastic bag from him anyway as he followed along, holding Margo's carrier.

"Yeah," he said, giving her a slight pat on the backside with his now free hand. "I like this part pretty well. Thanks."

"Don't mention it," she told him, locking the dead bolt. "Please."

"And I like this part," he continued as if she hadn't spoken, bending to kiss the tip of her nose. "And this part . . ." he went on, lowering his head to kiss the bit of skin revealed by the vee in her sweater. "And this —"

"Okay, okay, I get it," she said, quickly stepping away from him. She was so nervous! "Here, carry my overnight bag. I think you need your hands occupied."

"Yes, ma'am," he said, looking about as innocent as a thirteen-year-old with a copy of his dad's *Playboy* stuck between his mattress and box spring. "But everything I have is also yours, remember. What parts do you like best?"

She raised her eyebrows, lowered her eyelids, tried to look stern.

He grinned at her.

Oh, what the hell.

"Your eyes," she admitted. "I've always been crazy about your eyes."

"Really?" he said, following after her, out into the parking lot. "But they're the same blue eyes Jack's got. Same color, same eyes."

She stopped, turned, handed him the car key she'd fished out of her purse. "No, they're not. They're not even close. How do you think I was always able to tell you apart? Now, come on. We've got to drop off Margo and get to Philly, before Sam Kizer puts out an APB for you."

He trotted after her, to keep up. "We'll talk about my eyes again, later? Because this is interesting, Suze. I mean, Jack and I are identical twins. So what is it about my eyes that's different from Jack's?"

She blew out a quick breath. "Okay, but only because you're going to drive me crazy until I tell you. It's the devil, Tim. He peeks out through your eyes. Jack got the angel, and you got the devil. Happy now?"

He sort of tipped his head from side to side, as if considering what she'd said. "Yeah, okay. I kind of like that. Ready to roll, babe?"

She sighed. Someday, in twenty years or so, maybe she'd tell him she hated when he called her babe.

For now, she'd just go with the flow. . . .

Tim steered Suzanna's late-model four-door sedan down the narrow macadam road, past Jack and Keely's place and several other large homes built on three-acre lots sold to them by Jack, who pretty much owned this entire small mountain. They crossed over the small, one-lane bridge that spanned the narrow Coplay Creek that flowed in front of Tim's property, then pulled into the long drive that led up to his own house.

"There's no time to stop in, see Jack and his wife?"

Tim shook his head as he parked the car on the circular drive outside his mansion — his "pseudo Tudor" mansion his Aunt Sadie had informed him — with lots of brown brick, dark wood, and that stucco stuff. "We've got about ten minutes, tops, to see Mrs. Butterworth, drop off Margo, and get moving again. Come on, we'll go through the house, out the kitchen, so you can see some of the place. But just look, don't stop."

"Bossy," Suzanna said, opening her own car door as Tim reached in the back, removed Margo's carrier.

When he joined her, she was standing very still, looking up at the house. "So? What do you think?"

"It's big," she said. "Very big."

"I know. Aunt Sadie sent me all these books, with pictures in them, floor plans. We were out west, on a long road trip, and I didn't have much else to do anyway, so I looked at the books. This is the one I liked best. I moved in just before Thanksgiving last year."

"Henry the Eighth would have liked it, too," she said, heading up the three brick steps that were fashioned in a huge semicircle around the front doors — two dark brown wooden things with leaded glass inserts. A battering ram couldn't get through those doors.

He fished in his pocket for the key, then opened one of the doors, waved Suzanna in ahead of him, then waited for her reaction.

He liked his house, really liked it. Liked all the dark wood, the dark colors on the walls. Those things Keely had called "accent sconces" that were on the walls. The place might be almost new, but it looked as if it had been here forever.

"Keely decorated the place, top to bottom," he told Suzanna as he pointed toward the rear of the house and the kitchen. "She's really good."

Suzanna nodded, and kept on walking. "It suits you, Tim. Like a great big cozy den for Tim the Tiger." She stopped halfway down the hall. "Oh, wow, is that a real tapestry, or a reproduction?"

Tim looked at the wall hanging that stood at least eight feet high in the two-story foyer and fifteen feet wide. It was one of his favorite things in the whole house, and it pleased him that Suzanna had noticed it. "Keely got it from some place in New York. An auction house."

"Sotheby's?" Suzanna asked, her eyes wide as she looked at him. "You're kidding."

"No, I think that's the place. I saw it in a catalog she had at the house, and told her I wanted it. All those great faces, all those people. The castle in the distance? I don't know. I just liked it."

"This from the man who had posters of Vanna White on his ceiling," Suzanna said, shaking her head. "And the poster of that guy with the green tongue."

"You remember that? That was during my professional wrestling fan phase. What were we? Ten, twelve years old? What was that guy's name again? Oh, yeah. George 'the Animal' Steele. Hairy shoulders, green tongue and all. Remember the time Jack and I took you and Jan Overly to the Allentown Fairgrounds to see the wrestlers?"

Suzanna shuddered. "I remember sitting in the first row, wondering how flat I'd be if that Andre the Giant guy fell out of the ring and landed on me."

Tim laughed, putting an arm around Suzanna's shoulders. "So that's why you and Jan spent most of the night in the ladies' room?"

"You got it. It's also why I practically fell on your dad's neck in thanks when he showed up to drive us all home again," she said, smiling with him. "Hey, we're wasting time. Where's the kitchen?"

"Back through here," he told her, guiding her, "but don't look. Keely really outdoes herself with kitchens, and if you're anything like any other woman who's seen this place — meaning Aunt Sadie and Mrs.

Butterworth — you'll start *ooh*ing and *aah*ing, and Sam will have a breakdown waiting for me."

"Um, Tim?" Suzanna said as they walked through the huge kitchen — complete with fireplace — and out the back door. "Remember what a great cook my mom was?"

"Buttermilk pancakes with blueberries? Chocolate cake that was so moist it was almost black? Sunday afternoon and roast beef, mashed potatoes, and gravy? Oh, yeah, Suze, I remember."

"Well, hold that thought, Tim. Because I can't cook."

Tim stopped on the wide brick patio and stared at her. "Your mom never taught you?"

"Nope," she said, shaking her head. "I have all her recipes, packed away somewhere, but I've never tried any of them. I . . . I eat out. Or microwave stuff."

Tim rubbed a hand over his chin. "Do you *want* to know how to cook? Because Keely's a great cook, and if she had your mom's recipes, she could, you know, *teach* you?"

One thing about Suzanna Trent, now Suzanna Trehan, that Tim remembered well. When she got mad, you knew it.

He knew it now.

It was simple, really. When they had been little, she'd punch him in the gut. When she got older, grew out of that punching business, she'd just tell him to go to hell.

She said it now: "Go to hell, Jack."

"Knew it," he said, tagging after her as she walked toward the large three-car garage, still carrying Margo.

They were doing all right, he and Suze. They would probably do better as time went on.

But he'd have to remember that temper. . . .

Five

Players like rules. If they didn't have any rules, they wouldn't have anything to break.

— Lee Walls, coach

Sam Kizer had the most interesting vein on the side of his rather large, bulbous nose. The redder his nose got, the bluer the vein got. And when he began yelling, it throbbed.

Fascinating, Suzanna thought, watching the vein do its thing.

Intrigued as she was by his nose, there was a lot of Sam Kizer to look at. The Phillies' skipper was short, with a generous belly that overhung the belt on his home uniform that fit him like a second skin. He had a mop of white hair that bore the imprint of the cap he'd hurled across the office a few minutes ago, and if there was ever a set of legs that didn't look good in red stirrups socks, Sam owned them.

"Sam," Tim was saying. "Sam, Sam, Sammy. I'm here, aren't I? I said I'd be here, and I'm here. So what's the problem?"

"What's the problem? What's the —"
Sam put out both hands, as if pushing his
temper away. "No. I'm not going to go
nuts. Lesson seven, Tim. When faced with
idiots, do not say anything. Just walk away.
Lesson seven, Tim. I'm on f-ing lesson
seven, and you aren't going to make me
blow it."

"Oh, I don't know, Sam. I think you
oughta blow," Tim said as Suzanna
stepped in back of him, because if the guy
was going to explode, she wanted to have
already ducked for cover.

"Tim. He said he didn't want to get
angry," she whispered, hoping he'd hear.

"I know, Suze," Tim said back to her as
Sam Kizer walked back behind the desk in
his jumbled office and sat down. "But if he
doesn't blow at me, he's going to blow at
an umpire, and the owners aren't going to
like that. He's been warned. He can be
thrown out three times this year, and that's
it. I wouldn't want him to waste one of
them on me."

Tim raised his voice slightly. "Isn't that
right, Sam? You don't want to get thrown
out of tonight's game because you really
want to yell at me? Come on, Sam, you
know you have to do it. Give it to me, both
barrels. You know you want to."

Sam looked up at Tim. He raised his hands from the desktop, slowly curled his fingers into claws. His eyes grew wide and showed white all around the irises. "I don't want to yell at you, Trehan. That's too f-ing easy. I want you boiled in oil. Tarred and feathered. Hung up on the flagpole. I want," he said, slowly rising from his chair, "I want to —"

"Wait outside," Tim said with a grin, at the same time Suzanna mumbled, "I think I'll go wait outside."

She closed the door just as Sam's almost polite "f-ing," that had probably been cleaned up for her benefit, was discarded for a more definitive term. She walked down the lime green painted cinder block hallway, as far as she could safely go without getting lost and yet still far enough away not to hear every word Sam Kizer said.

Tim hadn't been kidding. The man had a definite temper. And, in Suzanna's considered opinion, a really good reason to go ballistic on Tim.

She and Tim had met at the stadium in Pittsburgh Sunday night. Monday, they had jetted off to Vegas. In the very early hours of Tuesday morning, they had flown back to Pennsylvania. Who would have thought the world would miss Tim Trehan so much if he disappeared for a little over twenty-four hours?

They had driven down to the stadium in Tim's sports car, after he'd stopped in the driveway to transfer her bags into his trunk.

An hour. That was all it took to get from Whitehall to the stadium. There were players who lived in New Jersey, Tim had told her, right over the Walt Whitman or Ben Franklin bridges. There were players who lived in other Philadelphia suburbs. Sometimes it took players who lived closer *longer* to get to the ball park.

But not Tim. Because there was nothing but super highway and generous speed limits between Whitehall and Philadelphia.

So an hour. Hour and ten minutes, tops. That was what Tim had promised her, assuring her that flying into the local airport instead of Philadelphia International and taking care of Margo wouldn't be any problem. They would still get to the ball park on time, in plenty of time.

Unless there was an accident on the turnpike, or a backup on the Schuylkill Expressway.

Today, they had had both.

So here they were, at the stadium, with a

seven-twelve start time, and it was already five-twenty-two.

The manager probably had a legitimate beef — but Tim's late arrival time was only one small part of Sam's anger.

Because, according to Sam, there had been reporters milling around all day, driving him nuts, asking questions about Tim's absence.

Why hadn't he flown back on the team plane? Did that hit from Sanchez do more damage than anyone was telling them? Was it true Trehan was in a Pittsburgh hospital, checked in under another name, and in some sort of coma? Hey, no, someone else said it was a punctured lung, and they had found him unconscious in his hotel room. Or was management thinking trade, because everyone knew Tim became a free agent at the end of the season, and the Phillies had so typically refused to talk contract yet. Was Trehan boycotting the team?

Suzanna had heard it all, both on the all-sports station Tim had turned on in the car, and in the hallways as they walked toward Sam's office. Sam had then told them all of it again . . . as little flecks of foam had gathered at the corners of the manager's mouth.

Two reporters entered the hallway, and Suzanna turned her face toward the wall, hoping neither of them recognized her from the quick sprint she and Tim had made between his car and the players' entrance.

"I say he's pulling a fast one, faking an injury," one reporter said, adjusting the press pass hanging around his skinny neck. Then he pulled out a cigarette, lit it. "Man, I needed this. Let's just stay here a while, okay?"

"Why in hell would he do that?" the second one asked.

"Do what?"

"Pay attention, at least to yourself, for crying out loud. Fake an injury. Why would Trehan fake an injury? And blow that damn smoke somewhere else, okay?"

"I'll tell you why. It's simple. Sit out a few games, show management how much they'd miss him if he goes. When are they going to wise up upstairs? *Sign* the man."

"The way I hear it, Moore wants over a hundred million for six years," the second reporter said.

Suzanna sort of choked, coughed, and put one arm against the wall, bracing herself, pretty sure anyone who looked could now see the white all around the irises of *her* eyes.

"Chicken feed, Alex. Look at the Rangers, throwing down more than twice that for a ten-year deal."

"Yeah, but what happened in Texas is never going to happen again. Damn sure not here in Philly. Hell, they let Shilling get away. You could damn near field a team of All-Stars with ex-Phillies who are still out there, playing. He's gone, I'm telling you. If they don't cough up the bucks, Trehan's gone at the end of the season. Off to greener pastures."

"Unless the curse gets him first," the guy named Alex said, and Suzanna perked up her ears once more. The curse? Hadn't that kid in Pittsburgh — Joey, right? — said something about a curse?

"Right, there's always that. So is Moore playing games? Or is Trehan really hurt? He didn't look hurt, Herb told me, and he saw him walking into the clubhouse with some hot babe on his arm."

"They don't put a sling around a concussion," the other reporter said. "And maybe his ribs are taped. I'm telling you, something happened out there in Pittsburgh. Something's going on. Why else would Moore have called a press conference for after the game?"

Suzanna was beginning to feel very conspicuous, all alone in this hallway with the two reporters. She decided she might feel safer on the other side of the double doors she and Tim had come in through earlier, and headed for them now.

She should have kept still, kept playing at being invisible.

"Hey, miss?"

Suzanna stopped, but kept her back turned.

"Excuse me, but are you the gal who came in here with Trehan?"

Keeping her back turned, she shook her head. "No, I'm only her twin sister."

And then she took off, not quite running, for the door marked Women that she'd passed on her way to Sam's office.

Once safe inside her sanctuary, Suzanna walked over to the sink, washed her hands as she stared at herself in the mirror.

Hot babe?

That was nice. Very nice.

But what was this business about a curse?

"Well, that's one down, babe," Tim said as he took hold of Suzanna's elbow and led her toward an elevator tucked deep inside the stadium. "Sam's fine now."

"Poor man. Is that vein in his nose still

throbbing?" she asked as she stepped inside the elevator and waited for whatever came next.

Good old Suze. She just went with the flow. No muss, no fuss, no hassle.

"Just a little," Tim told her, grinning, as the doors closed and the elevator car started up. "But now I've got two minutes to get you upstairs to my private box, and get back down to the clubhouse, change, and get out on the field. There's a rumor going around that I'm dead, you know. Guess somebody missed the bulletin about us running in here."

"Do you think Jack and his wife will be there yet? In your private box."

He looked at his wristwatch, shook his head. "No, not yet. Keely will want to wait until Candy's gone to sleep before leaving her with Aunt Sadie. I figure they'll be here by the bottom of the second. But Mort will be there."

"Oh."

Tim looked at her quizzically. "What 'oh,' Suze? What's the matter, babe? You're not afraid of the big bad Mort, are you?"

"No, of course not. But he's going to have questions, isn't he?"

The elevator stopped, and Tim bounced on the balls of his feet, waiting for the doors

116

to open. "Only about six dozen. You can handle him. I mean it, he's a big pussycat."

"An example," Suzanna said, stepping out into yet another hallway. "Give me an example."

Tim grinned. "Okay. Mr. Bendix."

"Benny the Bear?"

"You got it. Algebra two, tenth grade. Remember him?"

Suzanna nodded. "Growled like a bear, but he was always fair. If you worked hard, he gave you credit for trying."

"And he was a sucker for compliments, remember? Jack once got the class out of a pop quiz just by complimenting Benny on his new tie."

"Your brother was shameless," Suzanna said as they walked along the hallway, toward Tim's private box. "His tie, his new sports coat. One time, I remember, he told him he liked his crew cut."

"He probably did."

"Are you kidding? The man looked like he'd been attacked by a table saw."

"Just remember," Tim said, opening the door to the box, "Mort loves compliments. He can be in the middle of one of his rants, and a compliment brings back the sunshine. Honest."

Suzanna nodded, then motioned for him

to precede her into the box.

"Mort, hi!" he said as his agent scrambled out of his seat and headed toward them. "You look great. Is that a new jacket?"

"Blow it out your ear, Tim," Mort shot right back at him. "Where the hell have you been?"

"I see what you mean, Tim," Suzanna said from slightly behind him. "Works like a charm."

"Mort," Tim pressed on, knowing he should already be on his way back down to the clubhouse, "keep a lid on it for a moment, okay? I want to introduce you to my wife, Suzanna Trent Trehan." He hesitated a moment, then added, "Be nice, Mort. She's on our side."

"Mrs. Trehan," Mort said, extending his hand, which Suzanna took.

"Please, call me Suzanna."

"Suzanna. I like that. Good solid name. And I'm Mort. You can call me Mort." Then he glowered at Tim. "And you can call *me* — before you so much as take another deep breath. You got that?"

"Yes, sir," Tim said teasingly. "Your wish is my command, sir."

"Smartass," Mort grumbled, still holding Suzanna's hand in his beefy one.

"Come on, Suzanna. We'll get to know each other while this idiot here goes down and gets into his uniform. Maybe we'll bury him in it."

"Tim?" Suzanna said, looking back over her shoulder.

"It'll be fine, Suze, honest. And Jack and Keely will be here soon. If Mort gives you any trouble, just tell him how you've been thinking about doing that shoot for *Penthouse*. What's it called? Oh yeah, Baseball's Babes."

"Tim Trehan, you know I'd do no such thing," Suzanna said accusingly.

"Exactly. See, Mort? She knows there are things you do, and things you don't do. I'm telling you, you two are going to get along like gangbusters."

"Yeah," Suzanna said, shooting him a look that actually had him thinking about wincing. "We're going to form a club, with Sam Kizer. I think we'll call it the Kill Trehan Club. What do you say, Mort? Does that have a nice ring to it?"

"Oh, Tim, I like this girl. Now go away. No, wait. How about you tell Suzanna here that you're going to hit a home run for her tonight."

Tim rolled his eyes. "I don't do that stuff, Mort."

119

"I know, but if you do happen to hit a home run, then I can tell the press it was a wedding present to Suzanna here. If you don't, hey, then I don't mention it. Now go. We'll meet up with you in the press-room after the game. I'm holding a press conference."

"I heard," Tim said, looking at Suzanna one more time. He felt as if he was deserting her. "Are you going to be all right, babe?"

"I'll be fine. Oh, and Tim? Right center, okay? I'd like you to hit that home run to right center. Work on it."

Mort's chuckle followed Tim out the door.

Mort was a sweetheart. He asked a million questions, definitely, but then, when the game was about to start, he went hunting up refreshments for her.

He'd made sure she had soda, fresh roasted peanuts, even a cheese steak. He'd actually begun to explain the game to her, until she'd pulled out the program Tim had snagged for her earlier, opened it to the correct page, grabbed a pen out of her purse, and began writing in the lineups so she could record the stats.

"You know the game?" he asked,

watching as she recorded the first out.

"I used to do the stats for Tim and Jack's teams, yes. I love baseball."

"Amazing. Keely didn't know squat, except that she insisted she was a Mets fan. With Jack a Yankee." He shook his head. "But she's getting better at it, now that Jack's colorman for the Yanks. This is good, really good. So, you've known Tim since kindergarten?"

"Yes. Didn't I already tell you that?"

"I know, kiddo, I know. But I want to make sure I've got all my ducks in a row here."

"I got a lot of frogs in a row, out in Vegas." When Mort looked at her as if she'd just grown another head, she said, "Okay, sorry, and yes, I've known both Tim and Jack since kindergarten."

Suzanna then spent the first two innings answering more questions, Mort taking a break only when Tim came up third in the bottom of the first. He grounded out to second, ending the inning.

When Mort finally ran down, and the game was between innings, Suzanna asked a question of her own. "Mort? Why would someone think Tim's been cursed?"

He looked at her strangely for a moment, then grinned. "Hey, I curse the boy every day."

"No," she said, shaking her head. "That's not it. Someone said something about a curse while we were in Pittsburgh, and I overheard a couple of reporters earlier tonight, talking in the hallway. One said Tim is going to be traded, or become a free agent at the end of the year, and the other one said maybe the curse will get him first."

"Oh, *that* curse," Mort said, taking out a large white handkerchief and wiping the back of his neck. "That's nothing. Private joke between a couple or so of the sportswriters. Only superstition."

Suzanna chewed on this for a moment and decided Mort was being way too casual for such an intense man. "Superstition? Tim's big into superstitions, you know, when it comes to baseball. He always wore the same socks when his team was winning. He always eats spaghetti before every game. He phoned a restaurant from the car on the way here to order some delivered to the clubhouse. He has to have three pieces of bubble gum stuck in his cheek. And then there's that thing he does at the plate. You know? With his bat? There's probably more."

Mort bent his head, scratched at his cheek. "He keeps a photograph of his mom and dad wrapped inside plastic, stuck in his right sock."

Suzanna felt a tug at her heart. Both Mr. and Mrs. Trehan were gone now, passing away about a year apart while she was still in California. It was just like Tim to do something like carrying their photograph onto the field with him. Neither one of them ever missed one of the twins' games, all through school.

"That . . . That's nice," she said, blinking quickly because her eyes had begun to sting. "So it's not some curse that guy was talking about? Just a superstition?"

"Right," Mort said quickly. Too quickly. "Nothing to worry about."

"Mort." Suzanna shifted on her seat, looked deeply into the agent's eyes. She'd read everything she could find on Tim and his career over the years, but never anything about a curse. A private thing between sportswriters? It didn't compute. "We can do this the easy way, or we can do it the hard way."

"What's the hard way?" Mort asked, obviously a man who always looked at all the angles.

Suzanna smiled. She could lie with the best of them when she put her mind to it. "The hard way, Mort, is me sitting behind a microphone at the press conference and stating, very firmly, that there is no curse. Then, when a reporter raises his hand, and tells me about the curse, and asks me why I don't think there is one, I can —"

"Okay, okay," Mort said, cutting her off just as she'd run out of lie. "I get the picture. What's the easy way?"

She looked up at him after recording the Cardinals' first out in the top of the third, a pop to short. "Need you ask? You tell me about the curse, Mort. Right here, right now."

Mort shook his head. "And you look so nice, too. That hair. It's cute, all sticking up like that. And you've got a great smile. Really terrific. Fooled me completely. You're as tough as Keely, aren't you? Maybe tougher?"

"I haven't met Keely yet, so I couldn't say," Suzanna told him. "Now, talk to me. I'll give you a peanut?"

Mort looked out onto the field, then pointed to Suzanna's program. "Myers struck out swinging," he said, so she could record it. Then he sat back, his bulk filling the chair. "Okay, the curse, the superstition, whatever you want to call it. It's about Jack."

"Jack? What about Jack?"

"He had to leave the game last year, before the season even started."

Suzanna nodded. "Yes, I know. Rotator cuff."

"So you know that. And, since you've known Tim since you all were kids, you also know that almost everything Jack did, Tim did at the same time, or right after. Broken bones, grades, the teams they played on, the colleges they were both accepted to — all that stuff."

"Go on," Suzanna urged, beginning to understand.

"What's to go on with? Jack got knocked out of the game, and Tim's worried he's next, that's all."

"But Tim's never been injured. Except near the end of last season, when he ripped a tendon in his finger."

Mort nodded. "And the two games he missed in spring training, after running into that wall chasing a foul pop-up. And the three-game series he missed three weeks ago because he hyperextended his knee trying to beat out a grounder at first. Jammed his leg on the bag. Damn near kept him out of the All-Star game."

The Cardinal left fielder made the third out, but Suzanna didn't record it. "And the other day? When Sanchez barreled into him at home? He was down for a while, Mort."

"I know. They're keeping count. The reporters, that is. Tim, the guy who never gets hurt, is getting hurt. Some jerk figured out that business about Tim doing almost everything Jack did, said something to Tim about it after a game, and everyone else picked up on it, like some sort of private joke. Drives Tim nuts."

"He believes it, doesn't he?" Suzanna asked, watching as Tim walked to the dugout, his mask off, his ball cap on backward, his uniform partly covered by his catching gear.

Long, tall, at ease in his own skin, he was the epitome of any boy's childhood dream, the perfect baseball player. He'd been born to play baseball; he lived for the game.

"Mort?" she repeated when the agent didn't answer her. "He believes it, doesn't he?"

"I don't know. Maybe. But he doesn't always do what Jack does. I mean, nobody saw any baby on his doorstep. And he's not — well, yeah, he is married, isn't he? How about that."

Then Mort stood up, started toward the back of the box as the door opened and Jack and Keely Trehan walked in. "Hey, you're late," he said, grabbing Keely in a hug.

Suzanna swiveled around in her seat to get her first look at Keely Trehan.

Beautiful. The woman was beautiful. Neither too tall nor too short. Huge brown eyes. Honey blond hair pulled into a casual knot of curls on top of her head — the sort of hairdo that took either forty minutes in order to look as if the person had just grabbed a rubber band and a few clips and tossed it up there, or the sort of hairdo that came so easily to those with naturally curly hair.

Suzanna would have placed a bet that Keely's hair curled naturally. This woman had too much life dancing in those brown eyes of hers to waste a moment of it with something as mundane as working hard for casual disarray.

Keely wore pencil-slim red slacks and a red-and-white-striped blouse that curved over her pregnancy-expanded belly. She looked like a candy cane, and the way her husband looked at her, it was clear he thought she was good enough to eat.

"Hiya, Jack, long time no see," Suzanna said, getting to her feet as Jack left his wife's side and headed toward her.

"Suze," Jack said, putting out his arms

so that she'd walk into them, let him hug her. "Just when I think my little brother's lost his last marble, he goes and does something brilliant." He kissed her temple. "Welcome to the family, sweetheart."

"Thanks, Jack," she said, hugging him back. "You don't mind?"

He put his hands on her shoulders, pushed her slightly away from him. "Mind? Why would I mind? This is perfect, just perfect. Tim needs a keeper."

Suzanna watched, bemused, as a hand with nicely rounded scarlet nails reached out, gave Jack a poke in the arm. "Introduce us, you dope, then go apply for that job as a smooth-talking diplomat. Right after you take your foot out of your mouth."

Jack grinned at Suzanna. "Suze? The lady with the good right arm is my wife, Keely. Keely, one of my oldest and best friends, and Tim's keep . . . er . . . wife, Suzanna."

Keely grinned at her. "Hi. Excuse the guy choking on his size twelves. He's a man, you know."

"I know. Sad, isn't it?" Suzanna said, returning Keely's smile. Her sister-in-law's smile. Wow, she had a sister-in-law. Well, Tim did. Surely she could think of Keely as her sister-in-law, too.

"Okay, okay," Jack said sheepishly. "I can tell when I'm not wanted. But be careful, Suze. Keely learned her interrogation skills with the FBI, I swear it."

"Go talk to Mort, he's looking ready to burst," Keely said, lifting her face for a quick kiss, and Jack obediently went away.

"Jack looks great," Suzanna said, watching Tim's twin go back up the few steps to where Mort waited. "And he looks at you like you're his whole world."

Suzanna watched as Keely, a very fair-skinned woman, blushed straight to the roots of her hair.

"He does, doesn't he," Keely said, then sighed. "We're so happy it scares me sometimes." Then she moved toward the seats, sitting down, patting the one beside her. "Now, come talk to me before I pull out two dozen snapshots of Candy and bore you into jumping over that railing."

The small Philadelphia apartment was quiet, the bedroom shrouded in darkness, with a spill of moonlight shining through the window and falling on the couple curled together on the king-size bed.

Suzanna, snuggled tight against Tim's chest, giggled.

"What?" he asked, stroking her bare arm. "I was laughable? I thought I was pretty damn good, personally."

"Oh, you were, you were," she told him, moving up so that she could kiss his chin. "I was just thinking about the press conference after the game, that's all. Mort's amazing. I swear, Tim, he knows more about me than I know about myself. How did he do that?"

"He probably pumped Jack all during the game. Which we won, by the way, so you can applaud again at any time. In which I hit a home run, not so by the way. To right center." He sighed theatrically. "I'm so good sometimes I even amaze myself."

Suzanna gave him a quick, playful punch in the gut. "Show-off," she said, then quickly removed herself from the bed before he could tickle her, covering her naked body with the thick white terry-cloth bathrobe he'd been given at some hotel he'd stayed in somewhere.

"Hey, where are you going?"

"Nowhere," she said, sitting down at the bottom of the bed. "I just think maybe it's safer down here."

He tried to look innocent. "But I don't even remember how ticklish you are, honest."

"Yeah, right, you forgot," she said, rolling her eyes. "No, Tim, I have a question for you."

She couldn't know it, but her spikey dark red hair was standing up all over her head. She looked like a firecracker, and he had to resist the urge to light her fuse one more time. Then again, why resist? They were married. They could make love all night if they wanted to. Except that Suzanna didn't look as though she wanted to make love.

So what did she want? She wanted to ask him a question? That couldn't be good.

"I take it we're going to talk now?" he guessed, suddenly feeling very tired. Not that he was getting old or anything, but crouching behind the plate for nine innings wasn't exactly a cakewalk.

"Only a little. I want to hear about the curse."

He opened his mouth to ask, "Who told you?" But then he closed it again, knowing that was the last thing he should say. So he shrugged, and said lazily, "Oh, that. Yeah, some sportswriters started that crap last year, when I ripped the tendon in my finger. It never even hit any of the columns. Just a private joke making the rounds among the guys. No big deal."

"No big deal? Jack has to leave the game

in the spring, and you get injured early in the fall, and it's no big deal to you? Now, why don't I believe you?"

Because you're too damn smart and you know me too damn well, Tim thought, then also wisely, did not say out loud.

"Maybe because I'm all grown up now?" he suggested.

"Really? Do you still chew three pieces of bubble gum during games?"

"I like gum. And nobody chews tobacco anymore." He did not like where this conversation was heading.

"Uh-huh. And you had spaghetti tonight, Tim."

"Carbs. Good to load carbs before a game."

He'd tell her. One day, he'd tell her. But not yet. Cripes, not yet.

"The line you draw on home plate?"

Tim was getting antsy, moving around in the bed. "Habit," he said, then went up on his knees, reaching for her. "Are we done yet? Because I'm starting a new habit. I begin right about here," he said, nibbling on her earlobe, "then sort of work my way down."

"Tim, we're talking here," Suzanna said, even as he pulled her onto her back on the bed, began working on the terry-cloth sash she'd tied at her waist.

"Wrong, we're not talking here," he said, pushing the robe out of the way before he lowered his mouth to her belly.

They were so damn compatible. In the past. Hopefully, in the future. As long as they didn't talk too much.

He kissed her flat stomach, then moved lower, trailing his lips down one thigh, back up the other.

"What . . . What are you doing?" she asked, her voice sounding nervous, and yet excited.

How he wanted her. Any way, every way. They were so good together, so very good. His good old Suze, just what the doctor ordered. He couldn't get enough of her. Gently, oh, so gently, he spread her thighs, lowered his head.

"Tim? Tim, I don't really know if I'd like — oh. Oh! Oh, *Tim*."

Six

I always hate to throw a guy out of a game, but sometimes it was necessary to keep order.

— Cal Hubbard, umpire

Suzanna turned on her laptop and went online to check for messages. There were three from the home office, and another two from Sean Blackthorne, owner of the company.

"What does he want?" she grumbled out loud in the Saint Louis hotel room, her finger hesitating after she'd moved the track ball to hit the OPEN icon.

Oh, hell, delaying things wouldn't help any. Sighing, she opened the first e-mail, scanned it quickly to see that Sean had decided to join her in Saint Louis later that afternoon.

"Oh, peachy," she said, deleting the e-mail and opening the second one. There was only one word in the message: *Dinner?*

"Dinner," she said out loud, hitting the Delete button once more. "Now, what does that mean?"

Suzanna quickly scanned the messages

from her office, saw nothing earth-shakingly important, and shut down the computer in favor of the Room Service breakfast that had arrived a few minutes earlier.

"Dinner," she repeated, knowing she was talking to herself, and also knowing that she'd been doing it for years and had ceased to worry that she might be going nuts. She'd been traveling alone for so long, living alone in so many different hotel rooms. She just liked the company.

"Could it hurt?" she asked herself, lifting the metal lid on her scrambled eggs, home fries, and ham. "We only dated a couple of times, and that was months ago, before I told him I didn't think dating the boss was a good idea. And the man knows I'm married now."

Tim. Her husband of almost two months. One month and a day short of three weeks, to be more precise about the thing.

Suzanna picked up the controller and turned on the television, flipping stations until she found ESPN. Tim and the Phillies were out on the coast, and even at home in Allentown the game wouldn't have come on TV until eleven o'clock. Not that Phillies games would be broadcast in

Saint Louis anyway.

She'd hit the sack here at nine last night, unreasonably tired after a day spent trying to undo the damage Forrester and Sons' resident computer guru had done to their newly purchased Blackthorne accounting system.

She looked at the scrambled eggs and decided they didn't smell all that appetizing and she didn't want them. Maybe just the wheat toast, that would be enough.

Munching the toast, she waited through recaps of a few other games before the announcers turned to the Phillies-Giants game.

As it had been lately, the recap of highlights of the latest Phillies' win looked pretty much like the Tim Trehan Show. Tim was on a tear, plain and simple. No home run last night, although he already had more four-baggers this season than any other catcher in either League. But last night it was a triple and two singles. Five RBIs. Three runs scored.

And one heck of a throw to second to cut down a base-stealing attempt to end an inning.

Suzanna turned up the volume when the tape switched to the clubhouse and she saw Tim sitting in front of his locker, a towel wrapped around his neck, fielding questions from reporters.

"It's been a good road trip," Tim was saying into a crowd of microphones shoved into his face. "Dusty's playing well, Rich Craig made one heck of a catch in the ninth to rob Gomez, and Jeff Kolecki started, what? Three double plays? We're just clicking, that's all. Everybody's giving one hundred and ten percent. A real team effort."

"And there he is, ladies and germs, Mr. Modest," Suzanna said, taking another bite of toast.

"Now we head home," Tim said, "and that's good. This has been a long road trip."

"Home to your bride, Tim?" one of the reporters asked, and Tim just grinned at him as the tape ended and the station went to commercial.

"Oh, be still my heart," Suzanna said, turning off the set, and then grinning herself, definitely pleased. What a smile that man had. Without effort, Tim could always have the whole world eating out of his hand.

Except that he was making noises about her quitting her job, going on the road with him when the team traveled, and she'd been resisting him.

She didn't know why.

Yes, she did.

One hundred million dollars.

They were married now, sure. But she didn't want to look like some sort of gold digger. Get married, quit her job the next day, wrap herself in Tim's money? No, just the thought made her nervous.

Besides, she'd worked long and hard to get where she was, and she liked her job. Loved her job.

Even if it had meant not going to the coast with Tim.

Maybe *because* it had meant not going to the coast with Tim.

Because there were flaws in her marriage, and she knew it.

One of them was that Tim had never told her he loved her, which meant that she sure as hell wasn't going to be the first one to say the words.

Besides, he had to know she loved him, had loved him for so long that she couldn't remember ever not loving him.

And he still called her "babe." She hated that he called her babe. It made her feel like one of a crowd of babes, maybe even interchangeable babes.

Except he'd given her a ring, and his

name. She'd moved her clothing into his house.

They were man and wife.

"So how come I don't *feel* like we're man and wife?" she asked out loud, heading for the bathroom, to take a shower, start yet another day.

It was Monday. By Wednesday night, Tim would be home, to begin a home stand against the Mets on Thursday. She'd be home herself on Wednesday, maybe even tomorrow if that damn computer geek at Forrester and Sons would just keep his sticky fingers off the keyboard until she could undo the damage he'd inflicted and get the company up and running again.

She loved Tim coming home to her, her coming home to him. They were like illicit lovers then, grabbing all the time together that they could manage . . . spending most of those hours in bed.

It still amazed Suzanna to realize the depths of her passion, the hungers Tim had discovered inside her.

All her dreams about Tim had been about his eyes, his smile, the house they would build with the white picket fence around it, the children they would have together. How she'd bake him cookies, and they would sit on the porch swing at night, holding hands. Mushy stuff. Romantic stuff.

The wild, hot sex had come as a bit of a surprise.

A nice surprise.

Suzanna stepped out of the shower, wrapped a hand towel around her wet head, began smoothing a lightly scented oil on her still-wet skin.

She was so aware of her body now. Tim had done that, too, awakened her to her own body, even her ability to reduce the man to a mass of heavy-breathing, sweating passion that left them both limp and shaking.

So much to be happy about, rejoice over.

Except they didn't talk.

Oh, they talked. They talked about the games. They talked about the past, a lot. They talked about their parents, how it felt to be an orphan, even at the advanced age of twenty-nine. Those were deep talks, holding a lot of truths, even a few tears. So they did talk.

They spoke to each other in general terms about the world, politics, even the cats. But whenever she wanted to get more serious about their relationship, talk about anything even vaguely resembling his feelings for her, hers for him, *why* he had decided, out of the blue, to marry her, he found a way to get her into bed, where she couldn't talk or think at all.

"This time," she said to her reflection as it was revealed in the mirror after she rubbed a towel over its steamed surface. "This time, we *talk*."

"It really smells great in here, Mrs. Butterworth," Tim said, strolling into the kitchen, his hair still damp from his shower. "Thanks a lot. I know Suzanna will be tired, flying in from Saint Louis and then taking the shuttle from Philly to here. She left her car parked at ABE when she flew out, or I'd go pick her up, take her out to a nice dinner. I wanted her to have more than some warmed-up pizza when she finally got home."

Mrs. Butterworth, who should have been short and soft and gray-haired, to match her treacle-sweet name, hitched up her denim overalls that threatened to slip off her slim shoulders and turned to look at Tim.

"Are you going to tell her about Margo tonight?" the woman asked, narrowing her eyes behind small, round wire-rim gold frames, the same frames she'd worn when Tim was in high school. Mrs. B. called it her John Lennon look. What was scary was that with her mop of brown hair, parted in the middle and swinging in at her chin, with the glasses, and with that beak of a nose the woman had, she sort of *looked* like John Lennon.

He was surprised that she hadn't said, "Hey, Jude, I'm going to bring you down."

Before she could say it, or anything close, he reminded her, "Now, Mrs. B., we can't be sure."

"The hell we can't," the woman said, turning back to the counter to spoon soft butter into the potatoes in the mixing bowl. "I may have taught history, Tim, but I minored in biology in college. One minute little Margo is dragging her belly all over the floor, howling like a banshee, and the next day she's curled up on the couch, no more pitiful howling, and looking like the cat that ate the canary. We won't even talk about the absolutely disgusting *smirk* on Lucky's face."

Tim pulled out one of the wooden kitchen chairs, turned it around, then straddled it. "But Margo's still a kitten, Mrs. B. Suzanna said so, said she wasn't quite a year old yet. Lucky's only about a year old himself."

"So Lucky robbed the cradle. Color me shocked."

"This isn't good, you know. Suzanna said she was thinking maybe she'd breed Margo. You know, with another pedigree Persian? Does it really take only one time?"

"With cats, with dogs, sometimes with people. Weren't you listening during Sex Ed?"

Tim dropped his head into his hands. "In my next life, I'm inventing condoms for cats," he grumbled under his breath.

"I heard that," Mrs. Butterworth said, then turned on the mixer. "Stop sitting there feeling sorry for yourself for lying to Suzanna, and fetch me the milk carton from the fridge."

"Yes, ma'am," Tim said, slowly unwrapping his long legs from the rungs of the chair and heading for the huge refrigerator that had been covered to match the cabinets — just one more of Keely's little tricks. First time he'd come into the kitchen, it had taken him a full minute to locate the damn thing.

"So, Mrs. B.," he asked, handing over the milk carton and watching as she opened it, poured some into the potatoes being smashed to smithereens by the electric mixer. "How long before . . . before Suzanna figures out I didn't have Lucky snipped?"

She looked over her shoulder at him. "Planning to build a bomb shelter out back to hide in?"

"I don't know. I mean, how mad can she get?"

"Suzanna? Oh, I don't know. Let's see. Do you remember the time Kurt Wheeler said something nasty about that sweet little Diane what's-her-name after the junior prom? Said he'd — well, you know, hit a home run with her? Poor Diane, the child wouldn't say boo to a goose, or whatever that saying is. But not Suzanna, when she found Diane crying in the girls' bathroom. Your sweet, dear Suzanna went looking for Kurt and then all but picked him up and slammed him into the lockers, told him to keep his dirty mouth shut or she'd shut it for him. She's got a righteous temper, Tim, and you know it."

"Yeah," Tim said, shoving his hands in the pockets of his jeans. "I know it. So, how long have I got before I get my head shoved into a locker?"

"Well, according to the care and feeding of cats book I picked up at the super-market last week, the first thing to notice is if Margo's nipples begin to turn pink and become erect."

"Oh, cripes," Tim said, half collapsing against the counter. "I don't want to hear all of this."

Mrs. Butterworth turned off the mixer and reached into the drawer in front of her for a spatula which she used to wipe the sides of the bowl before turning the mixer on again. "Well, tough toenails, Tim. You're hearing it. You'll also notice the fur around the nipples sort of becoming sparse, probably so the kittens will find it easier to nurse. At least that's the conclusion I came to. Not that I needed the book all that much, because Margo's little belly is growing."

"So there's no doubt?"

"None. From my calculations, and I used the night those two animals kept me up to all hours, running around my apartment and howling at each other until I could finally corral Margo and lock her in the bathroom — and knowing now that you can calculate gestation as one mating day plus sixty-three days — I'd say we'll have kittens in, oh, about another six weeks, give or take a few days."

"But Margo's already getting fat?"

"I'd say so, yes. She's so little beneath all

that fur, it wouldn't take much to give her a belly. The instructions in the book were very clear. Don't touch the cat's belly, especially long-haired cats, or you could injure the babies. So I haven't prodded at her or anything. Oh, and Margo should *not* have been mated during her first time in heat, not long-haired cats. I'm worried about that little girl."

She turned off the mixer once more, then glared at Tim overtop the rim of her glasses. "You men, you're all alike, thinking with your hormones."

"Hey," Tim said, stepping back and raising his hands, "how did I get dragged into this?"

"I'm not sure, other than your lie to Suzanna; but you're standing here, I'm worried about Margo, so you're getting whatever I want to hand out. Okay, that's about it. Roast is sliced and wrapped in foil in the oven. Gravy's simmering on the top of the stove, salad's in the fridge. Now, what time is Suzanna due home? I have a date."

Tim lifted one side of his mouth in a smile. "A hot one? Has he been snipped? You'd better be careful, Mrs. B."

"Ha-ha," she said, taking out a dinner plate to cover the metal mixing bowl, keep the potatoes warm. "Better you should ask that question about yourself. I swear, I'm surprised you ever let that poor girl out of bed when you're home."

And with that parting shot, Mrs. Butterworth — tall, slim, denim-overall-and-navy-knit-top-clad recent inductee to senior citizenship — sashayed out of the kitchen on her sneakered feet, on her way back to her garage apartment.

Leaving Tim to sink slowly back into his chair, desperately trying to recall Suzanna's answer to his question about birth control that he'd asked that first night.

"Cripes," he said, blinking. "Two out of three? Oh, Suze, get home. We have to talk. . . ."

Tim sat in his favorite chair in the den, glowering at his brother.

Suzanna hadn't been home long enough to do more than eat dinner, load the dishwasher, and change into soft pink sweats before the doorbell had rung and Jack and Keely had come barging in.

Oh, all right, so they hadn't *barged*. They had seen Suzanna's sedan as they were coming out of their own drive, on their way to the grocery store with Candy, and had waited another hour before packing up the kid and driving over, for a "visit."

When had the idea sounded so good — building his own house not a half mile away from his brother's?

So now here he was, sitting in the den with Jack, while Suzanna, Keely, and little Candy were in the kitchen, talking about whatever women talked about when there were no men around.

Him and Jack, probably.

And not that he wasn't glad that Keely and Suzanna had hit it off so well. They kept each other company when Jack was doing his TV and radio color commentaries for the Yankee games, and while Tim was on the road with the team. That was what baseball wives did when they didn't travel with their husbands.

Or when they weren't jetting all over hell and back, playing computer genius and leaving their husband at home to stew, or on the road looking at a redheaded roomie who most definitely was *not* Suzanna.

"Who's pitching for the Mets tomorrow night?" Jack asked, sipping the beer Tim had tossed to him earlier, when they had both been banished to the den.

Tim shrugged. "I don't know. Rimes? All they toss at me anymore are lefties."

"Yeah, like Sam's going to lift you for a right-handed batter. Good old ambidextrous Tim-bo just sashays to the other side of the plate. Your average is only twenty points lower from the right."

"And I'm batting .325 leftie," Tim reminded his brother, for there had always been a friendly competition when it came to their batting averages . . . considering that Jack's average had never risen to more than about .200. "Hey, we're identical twins. You could have tried the same thing. I learned how to catch and throw rightie, bat from both sides. Think what it would have been like if you could have said screw the bad left arm, now I'll pitch with my right."

"That would have gotten me into the record books all right," Jack said. "Get real. You started throwing rightie when you were seven or so, once you knew you wanted to catch. You don't start that stuff at twenty-eight. Besides, good average or not, you're not all that great from the left side every time. You looked pretty lame against Colon the other night. He had you swinging from your heels."

"He got lucky," Tim said, thinking about the left-handed Giant reliever who had struck him out swinging. "I wanted it low and inside so bad, and when it came in low and outside, I couldn't lay off it. I can't hit them all, you know, bro."

"No? I could have sworn you thought you could," Jack said, grinning at him. He lifted his beer can, gestured toward the kitchen. "You and Suze still doing okay? She doesn't mind the road trips?"

Tim looked into the opening of his beer can as if he could see straight to the bottom of the Black Hole of Calcutta, or something else just as depressing. "No, she doesn't care. I mean, she hasn't said . . . I haven't asked. And it isn't like she isn't always flying off somewhere, putting out fires for her company." He put down his beer. "Damn."

"Uh-oh," Jack said, sitting forward on his chair. "Want to talk about this?"

Tim eyed his brother coolly. "I don't think so. Besides, there's nothing to talk about. We're good. Hell, we're great."

"That's good. But you two did sort of rush into this marriage stuff, you know."

Tim sneered. "Here speaks the man who married his interior decorator, *after* he'd moved her in to take care of Candy. So we're not the sanest two guys out there. Are you saying you did it any better?"

"No, Tim, I'm not. And I think

Suzanna's the best thing that could ever happen to you. But there's something . . . I don't know. Call it twin telepathy, the way Mrs. B. does. But I get the feeling something's bothering you."

"Yeah," Tim said, standing up. "You're bothering me. I've been out of town for ten days, and now my wife's home, I'm home, and I'm knee-deep in relatives. Go the hell home, bro, okay?"

Jack raised his eyebrows. "Oh," he said, then grinned. "Interrupted your seduction scene, did we? Sorry about that, Tim. But Keely wanted to invite you guys over Sunday night, after the games, to celebrate Aunt Sadie's seventieth."

"Aunt Sadie's going to be seventy? You're kidding."

"Hard to believe, isn't it? She only retired five years ago and moved into my garage apartment and regressed to psychedelic teenager."

Tim shook his head. "Red convertible, all that weird junk she keeps bidding for on e-Bay. That baseball player figurine she made for me in her ceramics class — you know, the one with the bobbing head? I know she painted it to look like a Phillies uniform, and I know she put my name and number on the back, but when she told me

151

she thought she'd captured my face? If I looked like that, Jack, I'd have to wear a bag over my head. The damn thing has rouge or something painted on its cheeks, and lipstick, for crying out loud."

"Hey, don't tell me your troubles. Mine's wearing Yankee pinstripes — except they're going the wrong way."

Tim picked up his beer once more, laughing. "Sure, we'll be there for the party. We wouldn't miss it. My game's at one."

"So's mine. I do the post game wrap-up on radio, and I'm outta there. Keely's planning some kind of buffet dinner for around seven, just to be sure. Then we're on the road for almost two weeks. Do you think Suzanna will be working out of the Allentown office? I trust Aunt Sadie, when she's not trying to make me listen to her audition song for *South Pacific*, that is, but I'd be happier if Suzanna was around, to keep Keel company. She's almost seven months along, you know."

"I don't know where she'll be," Tim said, and his mood plummeted again, because he didn't know. He'd be home, the Phillies were starting an extended home stand, their last west coast swing over for the year, but Suzanna could be in Phoenix next week, or even Seattle.

This wasn't right. He was supposed to know where his wife would be. And she was supposed to be with *him*. Here, in this house, or in the Philadelphia apartment. Just with him.

He looked down, because a cat was rubbing against his legs. It was Lucky, the no-good, double-crossing Romeo.

That brought up another thought Tim really didn't want to have. Procreation. Margo's, most definitely, and the possibility that Suzanna might soon. . . .

"So," Tim said quickly, banishing that particular thought, "have you and Keel ever thought about getting Candy a kitten?"

Suzanna put away her toothbrush, still feeling what she believed to be a stupid thrill, seeing it sitting there, right beside Tim's, and headed back into the bedroom.

She loved this room.

Keely had told her that Tim, for all his bluster about just looking at pictures and then "picking stuff," had actively participated in every last detail of his house, both the building of it and the furnishings.

He'd picked this bed. A huge thing, with four solid posts and a wooden top that was all carved inside and had striped draperies tied to it, like something out of an English castle. It was so high that Suzanna used the small two-step affair that she'd always assumed was only used by modern furniture makers as a sort of affectation.

The room was done all in deep greens and golds and touches of navy. Oriental rugs were scattered on the hardwood floors, and the dresser and armoire were huge. Everything was huge, even the deep tray ceiling that had to be at least fifteen feet above her head.

And the window. How could she not love the triple-hung window with the stained-glass oriel top? Keely hadn't put any drapes there, because the architecture of the windows was more than enough, and the bedroom overlooked nothing more than the privacy of oak trees that had probably been growing on this rolling hill for about a century.

Coming home was like entering another century, actually. And that made sense, because English history and Mrs. Butterworth's classes had always been Tim's favorites. He was a thoroughly modern man, but he was also a traditionalist. And he might have said he liked the castle in that tapestry in the foyer, but she knew darn well he'd also be able to tell her when and where it had been made, how long it had taken to make it, and exactly what historical event the scene depicted.

Tim had made sure he had every modern convenience in his house, but, between them, he and Keely had managed to hide them all, so that there were no jarring surprises like air-conditioning wall vents visible next to a four-foot-high Chinese vase, or naked television screens marring the decor anywhere.

Even Tim's flat-screen wall TV in his den had been camouflaged by the painting of a hunt scene that rose toward the ceiling at the push of a button.

Amazing what money could buy.

And yet this was a home, not just a showplace. Keely had also made sure of that. Sure, Suzanna knew she'd add a few things, someday, rearrange some of the furniture if the spirit took her. But, by and large, this was Tim's home, and she was happy in it.

"Hi, there," she said, easing out of the filmy dressing gown that went with her new negligee — she loved negligees — and slipped into bed beside Tim, who was paging through a copy of *Sports Illustrated*. "You in there?"

He closed the magazine, tossed it onto the bedside table. "Not that week. It's the swimsuit issue. I forgot I had it."

Suzanna looked past him, noticing that he'd thrown the magazine so that the back cover faced up. "Swimsuit issue, huh? How lonely have you been?"

"Not that lonely," he said, reaching for her, and she decided that it was okay to talk later. Maybe even tomorrow. What was her rush?

Except that Tim stopped, just as he was about to kiss her. "Suze?"

"Hmmm," she said, reaching for the snap on his pajama bottoms. He didn't wear tops, but he had the sexiest collection of pajama bottoms.

"About . . . us."

He wanted to talk? Well, how about that.

"Us. Sure. What about us?"

"Well," he said, and she sat up to look at him, because his voice sounded sort of strained. Not at all like him.

"Yes?" she urged, getting nervous. "What about us?"

He sat up as well, pulled a pillow from behind him and laid it in his lap, rested his elbows on it. "Remember that first night, Suze?"

She smiled. "You just remembered who

seduced whom? If I give you a quarter, will you promise to forget again?"

"I think we can safely say it was pretty mutual, babe. But what I'm trying to remember is your answer to a question I had."

"You had a question?" Suzanna shook her head, not understanding.

"Yeah. Oh, hell," he said, throwing the pillow onto the floor. "Birth control, Suze. I asked you about birth control. I'm sure I did. And you said you were fine."

Suzanna felt her stomach coiling into one huge knot. "I don't . . . Oh, wait, yes, I do. You asked me if I was okay. That was it. *Okay.*"

"That's what I remember. And you said you were fine."

"I did?"

"Well, something like that. Maybe *never better?*"

"Never better? What's that supposed to mean?"

"You're asking *me?*" Tim stabbed his fingers through his hair. "I thought it meant you were on the pill, something like that."

"I see," Suzanna said, caught between anger and anguish. "You thought I had sex so often that I needed to be on the pill? Different city every week, different man every night? Is that it?"

"No! Oh, cripes, I hate this. I didn't think that, Suze. I guess I wasn't really thinking."

She looked down at her hands, saw that she'd laced her fingers together so tightly that her knuckles had turned white. "I thought you didn't care. I mean, I thought you never said anything. And then you never used anything, or asked me to use anything . . ."

Nothing. He didn't say a word. Silence clogged the room.

"Tim? Would it be so bad? I mean, if I were to get pregnant?"

"No," he said.

Squeaked, actually. The word had come out in a definite squeak.

"I see," she said, sliding out of the bed and picking up her dressing gown, which she'd laid over the bedside chair done up in stripes to match the hangings.

Then she took the dressing gown off again and climbed back into the bed. "No, I'm not leaving."

"Good. Ah, Suze," he said, reaching for her.

"*You* are," she said, pushing at his chest with both hands. "Get out, Tim. Out of this bed, out of this room. Now."

"You're kidding, right? What did I say that was so terrible?"

"It isn't what you said, Tim; it's how you said it. And how you looked when you said it. Like a deer trapped in headlights. You thought I was on the pill. You did, didn't you?"

He opened his mouth, then shut it again, probably so she couldn't listen to his tone and accuse him of anything else.

"And now that you know I'm not, you're trying to pretend it doesn't matter, that it would be just fine with you if I were to get pregnant. In a pig's eye, Tim. It's the *last* thing you want."

Now he did speak. "You're right, it is. Right now, Suze, just for right now. I mean, we just got married. Why can't we have some time to ourselves first? Jack's happy as a clam, having Candy, having Keely pregnant. I want kids. But I think I'd rather we waited a while, babe, that's all. You could maybe quit your job next year, travel with me when I go on the road? I mean, what's the rush?"

"Get . . . out," Suzanna said, pointing toward the door. "Go downstairs, Tim, sit in your favorite chair, and think about this, okay? Next wife, Tim, discuss birth control *before* you hop into bed with her every five seconds for seven weeks — almost two whole months."

He got out of the bed and actually headed toward the door, before stopping, coming over to her. "Are you saying that you're . . . you know?"

"No, Tim. I'm not . . . you know. Of course I'm not. So you can rest easy about that. You just can't do it in this bed. Not tonight. Now go away. Here, take this," she ended, flinging his pillow at him.

A second pillow hit the side of the door just as he was leaving. "And don't call me babe!"

It was only after he'd gone that Suzanna hopped out of bed and dug around in the desk in front of the window, hunting up a calendar, her hands trembling as she counted the days. . . .

Seven

Going back down to the minors is the toughest thing to handle in baseball.
— Gaylord Perry, pitcher

Tim shuffled toward the kitchen, rubbing at his stiff neck. He could have slept in the other furnished bedroom. He'd known that. But he'd been punished. Thrown out of his own bed. That pretty much meant he should sleep on the couch in his den, suffer on the couch in his den, so he could look pitiful and forgivable the next morning.

At least that was the way it worked in the movies.

"Are we speaking this morning?" he asked when he saw Suzanna, all dressed and brushed and looking well rested, sitting at the breakfast bar, sipping orange juice.

"I suppose," she said, not looking away from the morning news show playing on the small flat-screen television set usually hidden behind a wooden pull-down door Keely had called an "appliance garage."

"Good. What are we saying?"

"I don't know. Did you sleep well?"

"No. And I've got one hell of a stiff neck."

"Good."

"Yeah," he said, pouring his own orange juice. "I thought you'd like that."

He carried the glass over to the breakfast bar and sat down on the stool next to Suzanna.

She got up, carried her glass to the sink, ran tap water into it, and then began emptying the dishwasher.

"I'm going to go shower, okay?"

"I'm not stopping you," Suzanna said, and Tim flinched as she began flinging silverware into the drawer with more energy than he considered necessary.

His mom used to do that. Slam plates, bang cabinet doors. And his dad used to head for the hills until he could find a big box of candy with a red ribbon on it. Flowers, too, if Mom was mad enough.

Smart man, his dad.

What was that old saying? He that fights and runs away, lives to fight another day?

At least he lives.

"I'll . . . I'll just go take that shower now."

"Do that. But I'll probably be gone before you come back down. I have to get to the office."

Tim looked up at the clock. "But it's only six-thirty."

"Sean called a breakfast meeting."

Okay, so maybe him that fights and sticks around also has a point. "Sean Blackthorne? Your boss? The one who sent a contribution to some animal shelter in our name as a wedding present? That Sean?"

"It was a nice gesture," Suzanna said, beginning her assault on the clean dinner plates.

"What? As a kid, was he all impressed with Bob Barker on *The Price Is Right*? 'Don't forget, have your pet spayed or neutered'? Every show, every day, don't forget, have my — *your* pet spayed or neutered."

"And he's right. Except, of course, if you're going to breed your animal. An animal like Margo, for instance. I got her from Sean, you know. He breeds Persians."

Margo. With the pink and erect nipples. And another country heard from, Tim thought, and definitely hostile territory he didn't want to tread right now. "Margo, right. So, tell me, babe, are you still planning on breeding her?"

Suzanna shook her head. "No, I've decided against it. Sean was telling me the other night that Persians can be tricky.

Lots of possible complications. I love Margo. I don't want to take the chance. So I'm going to have her spayed."

There were three ways to go here, Tim knew. He could tell Margo what Mrs. B. thought. He could run like hell. Or he could get mad.

"The other night? What other night? You've been in Saint Louis for a whole damn week. Are you telling me this Sean Blackthorne guy was there with you? I thought he was the head honcho. What the hell was he doing there?"

She wouldn't look at him. Not that she'd been looking at him so far, but now she was *really* not looking at him.

"Suze? Are you going to answer me?"

"When you speak to me in that tone of voice? I don't think so."

He stabbed his fingers through his hair. "Again with the tone of voice? What's wrong with my tone of voice?"

She slammed the ceramic roasting pan onto the countertop. "I'll tell you what's wrong with your tone, what was wrong with it last night. I . . . I don't like it, that's what."

"Oh, well, that helped," Tim said, pretty sure he was using "that" tone again.

She left the roasting pan where it was —

which was probably a good thing — and walked over to him. "Last night you blamed me for not telling you I'm not on the pill. Like I'm trapping you into something, or something like that. Just in case you figured out that maybe marrying me was a crazy idea and I wanted to make sure you couldn't get out of it again so easily if things didn't work out."

"Cripes. When did I say that? I never said that."

"You didn't have to," she said, poking him in his bare chest. "I know what you meant."

"Then you're one up on me, babe, because I sure didn't know it."

"Don't . . . call . . . me . . . *babe*," she said, poking at him some more. "I am not one of your babes. I'm your wife."

"Fine," he said, getting angry. Really angry. "I'll call you ridiculous. It fits. What makes you think I want to make sure I'm keeping a door open out of this marriage?"

She stepped back a little. "Why else would you be asking me about Sean?"

"Blackthorne?" Tim shook his head. "Oh, wait a minute. Now you think I'm accusing you of having some sort of affair with your boss? I wasn't —"

"We dated, all right. Twice. Met at restaurants after work, drove home separately. He gave me Margo when he decided he couldn't keep her, that he had enough breeders. There was nothing else, Tim. *Nothing.*"

"You dated him?" Tim felt his temperature rising before remembering that he'd done his share of dating himself. "Okay, so you dated him. And now you're married. So why's he in Saint Louis with you? You told me this was a one-person job. That's what you said, Suze."

She rubbed her hands together. "I don't know. Maybe he was checking up on my performance. Maybe he was hoping to sell Forrester and Sons more software."

"And maybe he was hitting on you?"

"Don't be ridiculous," she said, but she still wouldn't meet his eyes.

"He tried to hit on you, didn't he?"

"Oh, all right, all right. He tried to hit on me. Just a little. I don't know why. We hadn't dated in at least six months. But I told him no, and he went away."

Then she lifted her head, glared at him. "And that's not the point. The point, Tim, is that you *thought* something was going on."

"It was. He was freaking hitting on you. You admitted it."

"I can't control what other people do. Not even you, when you're making an ass out of yourself. But I can expect you to trust me, Tim. The way I trust you when you're on the road."

"Big deal. I sleep in the same room with Dusty. What's not to trust?"

Suzanna held up her hands. "We're not having this conversation. We're just not. There's no time. I've got to go."

"Go see Sean," Tim said, damn sure now he was using "that" tone.

"Go to hell, Tim," she said as she picked up her purse and briefcase and stormed out of the house.

Tim sat down, tried to recapture their conversation.

Suzanna thought he was having second thoughts. That was clear.

What wasn't clear was — was *she* having second thoughts? Why else would she think he was?

He looked down to see Margo brushing at his leg.

"She's going to be very upset with you, you know," he told the cat, lifting her up, taking a quick, surreptitious look at the cat's belly. "But she's going to kill me."

But, he thought, she wouldn't toss Margo out on her rump. He wouldn't toss

Suzanna out if she were to get pregnant.

No, he didn't think the timing was right, not now. They got along really well — okay, so most of the time they got along well — but obviously not well enough, not yet. There were still some bugs to work out in this marriage.

So a baby wouldn't be a good idea. Not at all. Not right now.

Except, maybe it would be.

He'd have to think about that. Right after he just happened to drop in at Suzanna's office later today, to take her to lunch before heading to the ballpark . . . and size up Sean Blackthorne. Maybe flex his muscles a little.

Right after he stopped off somewhere to pick up a big box of candy with a red bow. And some roses. His dad had always brought home roses.

"Suzanna, can you stay a moment, please?"

Suzanna stopped, her back to the slowly emptying conference room, and turned around, returned to the table littered with Styrofoam coffee cups and boxes of dough-nuts. "Sure, Sean. What's up?"

"Nothing," he said, motioning for her to retake her chair.

He then sat down beside her.

Sean Blackthorne was a good-looking man. Tall, dark-haired, with a perpetual tan that came courtesy of a tanning salon, not from walking a sunny golf course or other outside activity. He should take up some sport. Sean was forty, she thought, and beginning to go a little soft. But he was still handsome, and he was sitting entirely too close to her.

"I want to apologize," he said, and she blinked, surprised.

"That . . . That's okay," she said, knowing she was lying, because it hadn't been okay. The guy had hit on her. Toasted her success with Forrester and Sons with diet soda over dinner, slipped his arm around her waist as they had walked through the hotel foyer to the elevators, and then asked if he could come up to her room for a nightcap, some talk.

Okay, so he hadn't attacked her in the elevator or anything, but she'd known what he was asking. And he'd known what he was asking.

Not so subtle was the kiss he'd forced on her just as the elevator doors opened on her floor. He'd aimed for her mouth, but she'd quickly turned her head, so that his kiss had landed on her cheek.

Still, he had kissed her.

"No, Suzanna, it's not all right. I know that you're married to that ballplayer. I guess . . . I guess I just didn't want to believe it. I was way out of line."

Suzanna nodded. There wasn't a lot a person could say to a statement like that one.

"And you're still here, you know? I thought you'd resign, after the wedding. It's not as if you have to work to support yourself anymore. I finally convinced myself that you'd begun to think you'd made a mistake, eloping to Vegas like that with an old high school sweetheart you hadn't seen in years, and maybe it was time for me to step in, let you know that I was . . . I was still interested."

"I'm . . . very happy in my marriage, Sean," Suzanna said, carefully banishing the argument of this morning to the far recesses of her mind. "So, although I'm flattered, I really think you should know that —"

"That it's hands-off. I understand. I just wanted you to know that I do understand, and that nothing like that will ever happen again. Don't leave, Suzanna. You're a real asset to the company."

"I have no intention of leaving, Sean," she said, getting to her feet once more.

"Tim understands that."

Sean stood with her. "So he doesn't mind that you travel a lot? I mean, you're not even married for two months, and you've been to Saint Louis, New Orleans, and back to Pittsburgh. That's a lot of traveling."

"And Tim's been to California and Arizona, Sean, some of that time while I was here, not on the road myself. It's not optimum, I agree, but we're handling it."

He gave a small shake of his head. "I couldn't handle it, not if you were my wife. I'd want you where I could see you."

"Oh, marvelous," Suzanna said, hefting her purse back on her shoulder. "You men, you're all alike."

He followed after her as she headed out of the conference room, toward her office. "Meaning? I thought you said your husband was okay with this traveling stuff? Look, Suzanna, if it's going to become a problem, I can make some changes. Send Gloria out more, keep you here in the office. I think she's ready to solo."

Suzanna stopped in her tracks. "We could do that?"

"Sure, why not? Gloria's single, and you're married now. It's not like I'm saying married employees can't travel — or like

I'm saying anything else that could get me in trouble with labor laws or anything — but if it's easier for you to stick closer to the home office, I'm willing to arrange it."

"Well, thank you, Sean. Tell you what. I'll get back to you on Monday, after I talk to Tim, all right? He's got a really important four-game series with the Mets starting tonight, so I don't know when we'll be able to sit down and talk."

"Sure. Anything you want. And I am sorry, Suzanna. I think I kicked myself all the way back here from Saint Louis."

She went up on tiptoe, kissed his cheek. "Don't be silly. I was sort of flattered."

"Let me take a wild guess here. You'd be Sean Blackthorne?"

Tim? Suzanna froze, her lips pressed to Sean's cheek as she sort of swiveled her eyes to the left.

Oh, yeah. Tim.

Suzanna jumped away from Sean as if she'd been scalded. "Tim. What are you doing here?"

"Nothing. Just thought I'd stop by, see where my *wife* works. I've got to leave for the stadium in an hour. Sam's called a lunch meeting."

Sure he has, Suzanna thought, trying not to grimace. Breakfast meeting, lunch meeting. If she could have one, he could have the other. Oh, Tim was a real scream, wasn't he? She should be laughing . . . if she wasn't contemplating homicide.

"I'm Sean Blackthorne," Sean said, as if Tim hadn't already mentioned it, sticking out his hand. "And you're Tim Trehan. Nice to meet you."

Put out your hand, Trehan, or prepare to have it hacked off, Suzanna shot at him mentally.

"Nice to meet you," Tim said, shaking Sean's hand.

Okay, she'd let him keep his hand. He might need it.

"I don't want to jump the gun here or anything," Sean went on, just as Suzanna was beginning to believe she just might make it through this meeting without having Tim punch her boss, "but I was just telling Suzanna that she doesn't have to travel anymore. I can make other arrangements, keep her here in the office."

"Really," Tim said, looking at Suzanna. "Keep her close, huh, Sean?"

"Exactly," Sean said, and Suzanna's estimation of the man's near genius dropped a couple of notches.

"Close to *you,* Tim," she said, walking over to stand beside him. "I was . . . I was just thanking Sean for the offer when you got here."

"You can really do that? That would be great, Suze. No more travel?"

"No more travel," Suzanna agreed, since she'd been cornered so neatly. "Sean? I guess I don't need until Monday to give you my answer. Thank you, and I accept. Now, if you'll excuse me, I'd like to walk Tim back out, say goodbye, since I'm not going to the game with him tonight. Come on, Tim," she said, grabbing his arm.

Once outside the low red-brick building, Tim took her hand as he led her over to his sports car parked in the lot. "I've got something for you. I would have brought it inside, but I always feel kind of dumb, doing stuff like this. Not that I do it, did it. I'm just doing it now."

Suzanna looked up at him. The man was nervous. Actually stumbling over his tongue.

"What don't you do that you're doing now, Tim?"

"Apologize," he said, quickly ducking his head into the passenger side of the car and coming back out holding a box of candy in one hand and a bunch of paper-wrapped yellow roses in the other. He sort of shoved them at her. "Here you go, Suze. I apologize."

She could skin him alive. He said the dumbest things, and she still didn't know if he'd meant any of them. And then he shows up at her job, calling her his *wife* in that same *tone,* and shakes Sean's hand with a grip that probably would bring most men to their knees.

Rough around the edges, for all the tutoring in manners he and Jack had gotten from their poor, beleaguered mother, Tim was still such a kid. Playing ball, chewing bubble gum.

But he was so cute. So absolutely adorable.

Look at him, standing here, jiggling from one foot to the other as if his underwear was suddenly too tight, his expression pretty close to hangdog.

"Oh, Tim, you're an idiot," she said, and stepped into his embrace. "We're both idiots."

Friday's game was a night game, and Suzanna had driven down with Tim to have an early spaghetti dinner at his favorite restaurant before heading to the stadium.

They were back to where they had begun. Friends again. Lovers again.

And as long as he could keep badgering

Mrs. B. into keeping Margo at her apartment, they would be doing all right.

As if picking up on his thoughts, Suzanna said on the drive to the stadium, "You know, I think Margo's deserted me for Mrs. B. She's always at the garage apartment. I think I'm jealous."

"You've always got Lucky. He's crazy about you," Tim said, inwardly wincing as he put in a good word for the feline Lothario. Once she knew the truth about Lucky, that damn randy cat would be "lucky" to get fed, let alone petted.

"You mean, like the cats got traded? Margo traded to Mrs. B., with me getting Lucky in return?"

"Along with two minor league cats to be named later, yeah," Tim said, pulling into his reserved parking spot.

Time to change the subject. "So, you're sure you'll be okay, alone in the box? I'm sorry Aunt Sadie bailed at the last minute, but she's practicing her audition song for *South Pacific* with the organist from the church."

" 'Bali Ha'i,' accompanied by pipe organ. I'm sorry I had to miss that."

"Yeah, well, Bali Hi-note is something you really might want to miss. Not that anybody but dogs can hear her when she goes for the top ones."

"I think it's sweet," Suzanna said, playfully bumping Tim's shoulder as they walked toward the elevator. "Although I have to admit that the grass skirt she showed me yesterday sort of scared me. Mrs. B. said Aunt Sadie will probably end up in the chorus, as usual."

"Not Mrs. B. Director Mrs. B. Do you remember the musical we put on for her our senior year?"

"*Oklahoma*, sure, I remember," Suzanna said, nodding. "O-k-l-a-h-o-m-a, except Tommy Crimmins always tried to sing it O-a-k. And he had the loudest voice in the chorus. I thought Mrs. B. was going to stuff a gag in his mouth."

Tim grinned at the memory. So many memories.

Could you build a life on memories?

Hey, it was working so far.

"Okay, here we are, specialized door-to-door delivery for the little lady. Now, how many home runs do you want me to hit for you tonight?"

"Oh, golly-gee, Mr. Trehan, you'd do that for me?" Suzanna said, teasing him.

"Can't impress you no-how, can I?" Tim asked, gathering her close in his arms.

"Yes, you can." She moved closer, sort of

ground her hips against him. "You can *impress* me anytime, big boy."

"You sure do pick your times," he all but growled, then swooped down to kiss her.

"Knock, knock."

Suzanna froze in his arms, then quickly stepped back as Dusty Johnson entered the super box, already wearing his uniform pants, topped by a sleeveless T-shirt with "Property of the Philadelphia Phillies" printed on it.

"Dusty? What are you doing up here?"

The first baseman scratched at his red head. "Well, nothin' much, Tim. I saw your car, and someone told me you might be up here. I just thought maybe I could meet the missus, that's all."

Tim frowned. "You and Suzanna haven't met yet?"

"Nope." He winked at Suzanna. "Keepin' you to himself, ain't he, ma'am?"

"No, that's my fault, Dusty," Suzanna said, shaking the boy's hand. "I haven't been able to come to many games. So nice to meet you. And, please, call me Suzanna. Ma'am makes me feel ancient."

"Yes, ma'am, I mean, okay, Suzanna." He turned to Tim. "Pretty as you said she was. Nice, too."

"Dusty's my roommate on the road,"

Tim explained to Suzanna.

"Yes, I know. You told me."

"Oh, wow, I forgot," Dusty said, slapping at his forehead. "When I told Sam I was comin' up here, he said for me to fetch you down. There's some reporter wants to talk to you."

"He can wait," Tim said, wishing Dusty out of the box, and himself alone with Suzanna and her apparent desire for some friendly fooling around.

"Nuh-uh," Dusty said. "Can't. She's already talked to everybody else, and Coach wants her outta the dressin' room before one of the guys gets frisky."

Tim snorted. "Sam said frisky?"

Dusty shot a quick look toward Suzanna. "Sure. Frisky. Well, he kinda said that."

"I'll just bet," Tim answered, knowing Sam Kizer's opinion of female reporters in the clubhouse. "Okay, before Kolecki decides to accidentally drop his towel, I'll go on down there. Suzanna? Are you sure you're going to be all right?"

"Tim, it's a box in a baseball stadium. What's not to go right?"

"Hey, I'll stay with her awhile, Tim, if that's okay with you. I can tell Suzanna all about how you talk about her all the time, and how much you miss her."

"I don't talk about her all the time," Tim said, but he was inwardly pleased. Why not let Dusty talk him up a bit? It couldn't hurt. He kissed Suzanna once more, quickly. "Just most of the time."

"Oh, go away," she said, playfully pushing at him. "If you're late again, Sam is going to make you stay in Philly during home stands and not let you come home."

"In his dreams," Tim said, and headed toward the clubhouse.

Listening to Dusty Johnson was a real treat. He was so young, so innocent, so sweet. Suzanna was surprised his mother let him out alone.

". . . and my mama told me I had to go to church every Sunday, just like at home in Tennessee, and I told Coach — Mr. Kizer — and he said then I could flap my wings and fly home from Chicago, because the plane was leavin' in an hour. It snowed all night, ya see, in April if you can believe that, so the Sunday game was already post-poned. We had a chance to get home early, and Coach took it."

Suzanna sucked on her straw one more time, then winced as it made an awful sound. She'd been so busy listening to Dusty's down-home stories that she hadn't

180

realized she'd finished the entire soda. "What did you do?" she asked, depositing the empty cup at her feet.

"Well, ma'am — Suzanna — I just said that if that's what I gotta do, then that's what I gotta do, because I promised my mama."

"So, Dusty, after they peeled Sam Kizer off the ceiling, what did *he* do?"

"Well, that's when Tim and me became roomies. Because Tim put his arm around me and said he'd stay with me, go to church with me. And then Jose said he'd go along with us, and then Dave Frey said he was staying, too. Next thing you knew, we were all goin' to church. Even Coach. Not a one of 'em was Baptist, neither. And we don't never fly on Sunday mornings ever since, no matter what."

Suzanna sat back in her seat and sighed. That was her Tim. No wonder she could never stay angry with him, even when he deserved it. "And now you and Tim room together on the road. That's nice."

Dusty rubbed at his shaggy red head. "It wasn't for a while, I can tell you. Those nightmares he was havin'?"

Suzanna perked up. Nightmares? He'd had one that first night. But not since then. At least not on the nights they had been together.

"They were bad, weren't they?" she said, figuring the best way to learn something was to pretend she already knew more than she knew.

"Oh, yeah. Real bad. The curse, you know?"

"Oh, the curse," Suzanna said, relaxing again. "Yes, I know about that. Some sportswriters saying maybe he'd get hurt, because Jack had gotten hurt."

Dusty nodded. "Yeah. And the rest of it."

Suzanna narrowed her eyes. "What rest of it?"

"You know. The baby, the weddin'."

Suzanna rested her elbow on the arm of the chair, dropped her chin into her hand. "The baby? The weddin' — I mean, the wedding?"

Dusty grinned. "What his brother did, he does. That's what Tim said. Man, and he'd *dream*. Sometimes it'd be dreams where he was injured. Sometimes, it would be about weddin' gowns. He'd see the pitcher when he was at the plate, and the pitcher would be wearin' a weddin' gown. Spooky, huh? But the worst? The worst was when the pitcher'd throw the ball to the plate, and it wouldn't be a ball, but a baby. Comin' straight for him. Old Tim'd sit up in bed, his hands out, yellin', *'No, no!'*"

She'd seen that. In Pittsburgh, during their first night together. Tim, sitting up in bed. She'd heard that. *"No, no!"*

Suzanna sat up straight herself, put her hands in her lap. Then she sort of clapped them together a time or two. She didn't know what to do with her hands. She didn't know what to do with her body. She just knew she felt as if she might just jump out of her skin.

"Bad . . . um . . . bad dreams."

"Oh, yeah. Then, the last time, he had all *three* things happen in the same dream. It just kept gettin' worse and worse for him. It was gettin' so as he couldn't play."

"The last time? When was that?"

"Let me think. Oh, okay. In Pittsburgh. Yeah, in Pittsburgh. Right before you two got hitched." He grinned at her. "I knew it would work."

"*You* knew it would work? You knew what would work, Dusty?"

He looked at her, suddenly nervous. "He didn't tell you?"

"Tell me what, Dusty?"

"Nothin'."

"Dusty . . . ?"

He sat forward, his elbows on his knees. "Okay. Tim does what Jack does. But not all the time. That's what he told me. Not all the time. Two out of five, I think he said. So I said, would that be one out of three? And Tim said sure, maybe. So I said, why don't you pick one and just do it, and then you won't have to worry about the other two. Next thing I know — bam! — you two go and get married. And we've been back on the road since, and no more nightmares. Isn't that cool?"

"Frigid," Suzanna said, summoning a weak smile.

"You knew, right?" Dusty looked frightened.

Suzanna nodded, forced herself to widen her smile. "Oh, certainly. Tim and I have no secrets. I'm . . . I'm just glad it worked."

"Good," Dusty said, bobbing his head as he stood up. "Well, I'd better get down there. Battin' practice starts in a coupla minutes. Anythin' you want me to say to Tim for you?"

"Nope," she told him brightly, blinking fast, to keep back the tears. "Not a thing."

. . . *why don't you pick one and just do it, and then you won't have to worry about the other two?*

Great advice.

And in walked good old Suze, right on cue, to help Tim out of a jam.

It was going to be a long game.

It was going to be an even longer ride home. . . .

Eight

I made a game effort to argue, but two things were against me: the umpires and the rules.

— Leo Durocher, manager

"Suze? Suze, wake up, babe, we're home."

Tim watched as Suzanna slowly opened her eyes and sat up. She'd wadded her sweater into a pillow and had been half leaning against the door all the way home — about as far away from him as she could get without crawling into the backseat — pretending to be asleep.

He knew she'd been pretending, because there had been a tension inside the car all the way home, a tension thick enough to chew on.

He also knew because when he'd met her outside the clubhouse door, she'd looked at him as if he'd just crawled out from beneath some rock, telling him she wanted to go home, not stay at the apartment, as they had planned.

So he'd kissed her.

And she'd stood there, like a statue.

"Want to stop for something to eat?" he'd asked.

"No, thank you."

"Tired, huh?"

"If you say so."

"Suze? What's wrong? Come on, smile. We won. We're tied with the Mets for first."

"Yippee-ky-o," she'd said without an ounce of emotion, and then headed for the car.

Two minutes after getting in the car, she'd rolled up the sweater and gone into her "don't bother me, I'm sleeping" routine.

He'd given serious thought to driving home via West Virginia, just to give himself more time to figure out what the hell had happened between their hot kisses in the super box and now.

The only thing he could come up with was Dusty Johnson, and that was ridiculous. Dusty was just a kid. A nice kid. Suzanna couldn't be angry that he'd left him there to talk to her for a while, keep her company.

Still, whatever had set her off had been stewing inside her for about five hours now, and he knew there was an explosion on his horizon, God help him.

Tim hit the lock release and walked around to Suzanna's side of the car, to help her out, be the gentleman, but she'd bolted from the seat the moment the locks popped and was already in the house.

She must have hidden the house key in her fist, to get inside so quickly.

"Nice night," he said, standing on the steps, looking up at the starry sky, then headed inside. "Wonder if I'll live to see the morning."

He could hear Suzanna in the kitchen, banging cabinet doors, clunking crockery on the counter.

Maybe he could go knock on Jack's door, beg him to put him up for the night.

"Suze?" he said, entering the kitchen. Well, standing at the entrance anyway, half in and half out, thinking about that wooden block of very sharp knives that sat on the counter next to the stove.

"I'm making herbal tea for myself," she said, holding the teapot spout under the faucet and jabbing at the single faucet handle.

None for him, obviously.

The water came out full force, missing the spout and splashing all over, spraying up at Suzanna's face.

"Maybe you should have taken off the

lid, filled it that way," Tim said, knowing he probably wasn't being helpful — to Suzanna, or to himself.

"Damn it! Damn it, damn it, *damn it!*"

Tim had always prided himself on his sharp reflexes. Not that he'd need them, because Suzanna would never throw a teapot at him or anything.

Except that when he looked at her as she headed for the drawer containing the dish towels, and she looked so silly — all wet and dribbling — he laughed.

Bad move. The next thing he knew, good old Suze had grabbed the sugar bowl, and it came winging toward him.

"Don't laugh at me!" she yelled at him as he ducked, and the ceramic bowl hit the wall beside him, taking a good-size chunk out of the plaster. Yeah, well, he was thinking maybe Keely had been right, and they should put wallpaper in here. Guess that was one decision now made for him.

"I'm not laughing at you, honest," Tim said, daring to bend down, pick up the bowl that had emptied, but not broken, and place it on the counter. "I'm still too busy trying to figure out who you are and what you did with my wife."

"Oh, really. Well, that's a good question, Tim. It really is," Suzanna said, grabbing enough paper towels to sop up a small flood, then going down on her hands and knees to wipe the wet floor in front of the sink. "And here I am, wondering *why* I'm your wife. Except I already know, don't I? Oh, yes. I *know*, Tim. All of it. You selfish, self-centered, opportunistic bastard."

Tim ignored the character attack and went down on his haunches. He grabbed the paper towels from her, finished the cleanup. "What in hell are you talking about? You're my wife because I asked you to marry me and you said yes."

She stood up, and he followed her toward the back stairs that led up to the bedrooms.

"But *why* did you ask me, Tim? Because you're crazy mad in love with me?"

She turned around as she passed the last step and stood in the hallway. "Let me help you answer that. No. You didn't marry me because you're crazy mad in love with me."

"I never said —"

"I know. Oh, God, do I know." She headed toward their bedroom.

He followed. "Look, Suze, I know I sort of rushed you into marrying me, but —"

"What rush? We don't see each other for ten years, and then we meet again, and less than a day later, we're flying to Vegas. And you didn't marry me because we went to bed together. Hell, Tim, if you married every woman you went to bed with since high school, you'd have more wives than some Saudi Arabian sheikh or something."

Tim summoned a small smile. "It did have something to do with it, Suze. We're great in bed."

"Yeah, sure. Great in bed. It's *out* of bed where we're not so great, right, Tim? Bastard."

There she went again: bastard. Was it becoming her favorite word? "What do you mean? I think we get along really well," he said, following her as she headed into her walk-in closet and began opening drawers, pulling out a ratty-looking set of green-and-blue-striped pajamas he'd never seen before. "Where did those come from?"

She looked at the pajamas. "They're my not feeling good pajamas. They're comfortable."

"They're ugly," Tim said, watching as Suzanna stripped out of her clothing right in front of him, pulling on the bottoms that had a hole in one knee.

"It doesn't matter if they're ugly. I'm sleeping alone."

"Yeah," Tim said, rubbing at the back of

191

his neck. "I sort of sensed that already."

She turned her back to him, unclipped her bra, and quickly pulled the top over her head, emerging from the neck hole with her hair all spiked and tousled. "Move it or lose it," she warned, and he stepped aside, let her pass.

But then he followed her. He wanted to know just what the hell was going on. But if she called him a bastard one more time, it was going to be no more mister nice-guy, damn it!

She took the decorative pillows off the bed, then turned down the spread. "You want to know why you married me, Tim?" she asked, tossing his pillow at him.

"I married you because I wanted to marry you. I *like* being married to you. And, until a couple of hours ago, I thought you wanted to be married to me."

"Well, you were wrong. I don't want to be married to you." She whirled about to look at him, and he could see tears shining on her cheeks. "You know what I do want? I'll tell you what I want, Tim Trehan. I want the curse to work. I want your career gone, I want you to have a wife who wants nothing but your money — and I hope someone leaves *triplets* on your doorstep!"

He sat down abruptly, on the striped

chair. It all made terrible sense now. "Dusty. That big-mouthed —"

"Oh, that's it, Tim. How like you. Blame Dusty. What did he do, Tim, other than tell me the truth? Now go away. I can't stand looking at you."

"No, damn it, I'm not going anywhere. We've got to talk. You've got to let me explain."

"Explain? Sure. Fine." She climbed into the bed, pulled the covers up over her stomach as she sat against the pillows. "This oughta be good. Go ahead, Tim. *Explain.*"

"Shit," Tim muttered under his breath as he stabbed both hands into his hair.

"Well, that was succinct," Suzanna said. "Tell you what. Let me help you. You've been having nightmares, Tim. For over a year now. Big, bad nightmares where you get hurt, have to leave the game. Just like Jack. Other nightmares, where you end up holding a baby, just the way Jack opened his door one day to find little Candy in a basket on his doorstep. Only yours comes via a curve ball."

Tim put out his hands, pressed them down as if trying to lower the level of intensity of this conversation. "It was a nightmare, that's all."

"Yes, a nightmare. Over and over again, a nightmare. The one with the pitcher dressed in a wedding gown must have been a real hoot. And then —"

"But —" Tim said, attempting to sit down beside her on the bed.

"*Don't* interrupt — and stay right where you are! You were having these nightmares, Tim. One at a time, even all three of them together, a real triple play. Waking in a cold sweat, your arms out, trying to catch the baby while all the time yelling, *'No, no.'* I was there for one of them, remember?"

"Vaguely," he said, feeling the pit widen beneath his feet. He should have told her. That night. At least before they had flown to Vegas. Anytime at all since then. Pick a day, any day. He should have told her.

"Vaguely? Cute, Tim. I know you, remember? The gum, the socks, the spaghetti. You're a hotbed of stupid superstitions, just like most ballplayers. The idea of having to leave the game because Jack did had to have been scaring you spitless, especially after you got hurt last year. This year it was even worse. Dusty told me how your game was off, how the dreams had started to screw up your performance on the field. Because you knew, you just *knew,* that at least one thing that had happened to Jack would happen to you. You're that *dumb*."

"Hey! You know me; you just said so. You know how Jack and I always follow each other. How I follow Jack."

"That, Tim, was coincidence. Kids break bones. Kids have crushes. Kids, especially twins, have most of the same interests, talents. Except I did most of your math homework, and Jack got A's all on his own. And two boys who've lived for baseball since they could walk could very easily both make the majors. It's you who made it all into some sort of woo-woo superstition. It's *you*, Tim, who let your mind give you nightmares."

"Woo-woo? That's cute."

"Drop dead."

"Ah, come on, lighten up just a little, okay? Let's talk this out. Maybe not all superstition, babe. You just admitted that twins often do the same things."

"As *kids*, Tim. If Jack jumped off a bridge tomorrow, would you jump off one next week? I don't think so."

Agreeing with her was probably a good idea. "Okay. So I'm stupid."

"*Oh!* You're *not* stupid! You're just a very smart man *acting* stupid. A curse? Get real, Tim."

"Okay," Tim said, willing to admit to anything short of fixing the last presidential election if it would make Suzanna happy. He knew where Judge Crater was buried, helped get rid of Jimmy Hoffa, could give her Elvis's current address. Anything. If she'd just let him talk, listen to reason.

One problem. One big problem. How was he going to make any of what he did sound even the least bit reasonable?

She swiped at new tears running down her cheeks. "How could you do this to me, Tim? *Use* me again, just like you've always used me. Good old Suze. She's crazy about me, always was. She'll help me out; she'll marry me. Dusty said so. Pick one, he said. And you did — and I never asked *why*. I'm so *stupid!*"

"You're not stupid, Suze," he began, figuring if she'd already said it, he could turn it around, say it back to her. "You're just —"

"Gullible. Pathetic. God! Jack knows, doesn't he? And Keely? Mort? Aunt Sadie? Oh, my God, Mrs. B.? They all know, don't they? Good old Suze, married because she was there, she was good old Suze, and she looked like the lesser of three evils."

She turned onto her stomach, burying her face in the pillows. "I want to die, Tim. I just want to *die*."

Tim put his hand on her shoulder, to comfort her, and she jackknifed up in the bed, to glare at him. "No. I don't want to die. Why should I? You know what I want, Tim?"

"You mean, besides wanting the curse to work?" He shook his head. If only she'd let him get a word in edgewise. He had a lot of convincing arguments, he must have them somewhere, but all he could think about right now was that he was lower than pond scum.

"Yes. I want you out of this room, now, and I'm taking me out of this house, first thing tomorrow morning. Me, Margo, and all my belongings. And then, Mr. Trehan, I want a divorce. You got that?"

"A divorce?" Tim felt the bottom falling out of his world. "You can't mean that, Suze. We're married; we're good together. I mean, I couldn't have a better friend than —"

He stopped, because her face was so white, her eyes so huge and sad. "We'll talk in the morning? Okay, Suze?"

"Will you get out of here if I say yes?"

"Sure. I'll leave. Just let me apologize, Suze. I know we got started on the wrong foot, as Aunt Sadie would say, but I think we've had a pretty good marriage so far. And now you won't be traveling, and we can be together more, and I like that, I really do. I can make this up to you. I know I should have told you, but once we were married, it didn't seem all that important to talk about why we got married. I think we're good together. I think —"

She sort of moaned, then turned on her side, her back to him, and he shut up. It was probably a good time to shut up. Because, he also knew, the only thing he could tell her was the truth, and the damning truth *was* that he had married her because of the curse, his damn stupid superstitions, those miserable nightmares.

And the unexpectedly great sex.

She already knew that. She knew he had tricked her, hadn't exactly played by the rules. And now she was tossing him out of the game.

A divorce. She wanted a divorce?

What would he do without her?

Tim picked up his pillow and headed for the den, and another stiff neck.

He figured he deserved it.

"So that's it, the whole story. Did you know?"

"No, Suzanna, we didn't know. Honest. Not for sure," Keely said as she poured tea for Suzanna, then sat down and picked up her glass of milk, made a face at it. "But, yes, Jack and I did wonder."

Suzanna nodded, poked her dark sunglasses back up on her nose. Her eyes were still red and puffy from a night of crying.

She wasn't sure why she was sitting in Keely's kitchen at seven o'clock in the morning. She only knew she couldn't stay in that house at the end of the lane another moment, and she desperately needed someone to talk to, someone who might have some sympathy somewhere to dish out to her.

"I love him, the bastard. The no-good rat bastard."

"Where is he now?"

"He left. I packed him a bag during the night and threw it at him this morning. He . . . He's staying in the Philly apartment until I can move out. He's being very co-operative, except when the big jerk says that he knows I can't stay mad at him just because he did one dumb thing and we'll be fine, just fine. Fine? What does that mean, Keely? Fine?"

"You're really moving out? Getting a divorce?"

Suzanna nodded. "But not the divorce. I can't. Not yet."

Keely took a drink of milk, then walked over to listen near the intercom, make sure Candy hadn't awakened yet. "Because it wouldn't look good? I don't know you that well yet, Suzanna, but I don't think you'd care about what anyone else might think it looked like, divorcing so soon."

Suzanna shook her head. "No, I don't care. It's because . . . because I think I might be pregnant. Strike two in Tim's nightmare. Serves him right," she said, putting a hand against her flat stomach. "Daddy rat bastard. Has a certain ring to it, doesn't it, Keely?"

Keely raced back over to the table, sat down, and grabbed Suzanna's hand. "Omigod! Pregnant? Have you taken a test? Seen a doctor? I've got this *great* doctor, Suzanna." She got up again, not all that swiftly thanks to her own pregnancy, and headed for the phone. "Let me call her. No, wait, it's too early for the office staff to be there. But that's okay; we'll call later, set up an appointment. Oh, would you listen to me? I'm babbling. We can't do that; it's Saturday. Okay, Monday. First thing Monday morning."

"No, I don't want to do that yet,"

Suzanna said, wincing. "I mean, I've skipped periods before. It isn't all that unusual for me."

"But you don't know. You should know as quickly as you can. Get vitamins, that sort of thing. How late are you?"

Suzanna sighed. Maybe coming here wasn't such a good idea. But she needed, desperately, to talk to somebody, and other than Mrs. B., Keely was pretty much it. There wasn't anyone else in her life, any of her old friends, she wanted to know about any of this.

"I haven't had a period since we were married. But," she added quickly when Keely gasped, "like I said, that isn't so unusual for me. I've never been regular. If I'm on the road, if I'm under a lot of stress? I can sometimes skip a month."

"But this is more than one month, Suzanna. You've been married for — what? Two months?"

"Nine weeks and four days, yes. So I guess I could have skipped two periods, now that I really think about it. I don't want to think about it."

"Did you . . . you know, use birth control?"

Suzanna felt her cheeks growing hot. "That's another reason I want him dead.

He says he thought I was on the pill."

"You weren't?"

"No. Why should I be on the pill?"

Keely shrugged. "I don't know. Some women use it to regulate their periods."

"I used to, years ago. But I decided I'd been on them long enough, and stopped them. I'm not real big on taking pills. My mom was on hormone replacement, and she swore that's how she developed some pretty scary problems after menopause. Who knows? But I stopped my pills when she told me."

"And Tim didn't use anything?"

Suzanna shook her head, trying not to blush. "Not even after we figured out what he thought. Me? I just thought he didn't care if we had a baby right away. You and Jack are, and you've already got Candy. I thought he thought it was okay."

Keely propped an elbow on the table and leaned her chin on her hand. "Don't talk much, you two, do you?"

Suzanna readjusted her dark glasses. "We . . . We've been busy. Either he's out of town, or I'm out of town, and when we're . . . together, well, we're just together."

"In bed. Yes, Mrs. B. was over one day visiting Aunt Sadie. She told us."

Suzanna reached into her pocket and pulled out a wad of tissues. "It was like one long honeymoon, Keely. More than a honeymoon. Like we were these secret lovers, who could meet only once in a while. We just wanted to be together. It was . . . It was romantic."

"And fruitful," Keely said, as Candy's chirping voice came through the intercom. "Come on, let's go get Little Miss Sunshine, and I'll see if I still have a pregnancy test left in the linen closet. I sent Jack out for one when I was late, and I swear he came back with half a dozen."

"I . . ." Suzanna said, getting up. "I'm not sure I want to know. Not yet."

Keely grinned at her. "I know, sweetheart. But there's one thing that's been true since the beginning of time. There's no such thing as being just a little bit pregnant. Sooner or later, everyone's going to know. Even Tim. Especially Tim."

"Oh, God," Suzanna said, following Keely up the stairs.

"But you don't start looking like you swallowed a basketball, the way I do, for a while. We can delay this a little bit, Suzanna, if you don't mind me butting in?"

"Butt away, Keely. I'm open to any suggestions."

"Good. I say you stay here tonight, in one of the guest rooms. Not that we won't tell Tim where you are, because I know he'll worry, and there is that party here for Aunt Sadie tomorrow night. You can see him then. But you can't be lying awake all night tonight, wondering if he's going to be coming home, bothering you. Or are you ready to see him?"

"I can't see him. Not yet. My mind's gone to mush. He lied to me. I could be pregnant. And when the pitcher throws the baby at him he yells, *'No, no!'* I'm not sure I can tell him, not ever."

Keely turned around, put her hands on Suzanna's shoulders. "I'll hide you out, keep Tim away until the party tomorrow, but I won't be a party to that one, Suzanna. He has to know. He has a right to know, even if I don't blame you for wanting to keep the news from him. What I'm saying is, you could delay it a little, until you know what *you* want."

"I . . . I want him to love me, Keely. That's all I've ever wanted. Even when I want to strangle the jerk, I want him to love me."

"And not just say so because you're carrying his baby? Is that what you're thinking? You think he'd say he loves you, even if he doesn't, because of the baby?"

Suzanna bit her lip, nodded.

"Okay. I understand, and believe me when I say I sympathize. Hear that little girl in there? There was a time I didn't know if Jack wanted me because he loved me, wanted to make a family with me, or if I was just a convenient body here to take care of Candy. You have to be sure."

"I do."

"And *I* had to be sure. I love Candy so much. How could I know if I loved Jack, or if I was just seeing some romantic notion of happy families?"

"How did you finally figure it out? That you two really loved each other?"

Keely smiled, a sort of dreamy smile. "Oh, when you know, you know. I can't explain it any better than that. But you'll know when you know. Trust me."

Then she grinned. "But, in the meantime, let's not put the cart before the horse, okay? We'll see if I still have one of those pregnancy tests somewhere around here, and then if you really are pregnant, we'll devise a few tortures for one Mr. Tim Trehan. Marry someone because he's superstitious? Does he really believe that's why he married you? What a jerk!"

★ ★ ★

It was midnight Saturday night. Tim sat sprawled in the big leather chair in the living room of his Philadelphia apartment, glaring at the telephone.

How could she do this to him?

He'd called a dozen times and gotten the machine every time.

He'd called Mrs. B., who had told him (sounding entirely too happy) that Suzanna had driven away early that morning, right after he'd gone as a matter of fact. No, she hadn't come back. No, she hadn't taken Margo with her. No, Mrs. B. hadn't seen any luggage. But, then, she'd been out shopping most of the day.

"Don't tell me you've misplaced your wife."

"She's mad at me, Mrs. B."

"That so?" The woman still sounded cheerful, which just proved what Tim had always suspected: Suzanna had been the teacher's pet.

"What stupid male thing did you do, Tim? Or did you tell her about Margo?"

"Not yet, no."

"No? Why not? You've got to tell her, Tim, before she figures it out on her own. Remember, there's no such thing as being a little bit pregnant," Mrs. B. had scolded with a positively evil laugh, and he'd invented an excuse to hang up.

Margo. Man, that cat had seemed like such a big problem only a few days ago. Now it didn't matter. Suzanna already hated him.

As a matter of fact, this might be a good time to tell her about the cat, about Lucky. Get it all over with at once.

Over? Was it over? Cripes, they had barely begun.

Tim lifted the can of beer to his mouth, then made a face when he realized the nearly full can had gone warm. What a mess he was. He couldn't even get drunk, drown his sorrows.

The Phillies had lost. Big time. Sixteen to two, a real laugher — for the Mets that is. And he'd gone hitless, striking out with the bases loaded in front of the home crowd. A few more poor showings like tonight's, and the infamous Philadelphia Boo-birds would be after him.

Hell, if he didn't figure out some way to get back in Suzanna's good graces, get his mind back in the game, he could end up like Phillies Hall of Famer Mike Schmidt, who had gone through such a bad slump one year that he'd actually run out onto the field one day with a wig and fake mustache on, pretending that the booing crowd wouldn't recognize him that way.

Wouldn't that be just great. Real great. . . .

It was Suzanna's fault. Oh, yeah, definitely Suzanna's fault. He hadn't slept more than a couple of minutes on that damn couch last night, he was going nuts, she didn't answer the phone, and he didn't know where she was, how she was, if she had moved out on him, left him.

How could she leave him?

"Divorce," he said, glaring at the television screen and ESPN's nightly baseball wrap-up. Just what he didn't need right now, a recap of the game that had dropped them a full game behind the once more first-place Mets. He picked up the remote, switched off the set.

"She didn't mean that," he said, trying to convince himself. "Suze has a temper. Mrs. B. said so, and I know so. And she has a right to be mad, definitely. Totally pissed. But I was going to tell her. One day. We were going to laugh about it. One day."

He knew what it was; it was Lucky's fault. He'd been so worried about telling Suzanna how that sex-crazed cat had knocked up her pedigree Persian, that he'd not thought enough about what could happen if Suzanna ever found out why he married her.

But damn it, it wasn't why he *stayed* married to her. He liked her. God, how he liked her, cared for her, enjoyed being with her. That wide smile of hers. The way she seemed to know him better than he knew himself, anticipated his every need. In bed and out of it.

And, oh, they were good together. They laughed at the same jokes, shared the same history. She knew his foibles and liked him anyway.

Loved him anyway.

"That's it," Tim said, getting up from the chair and heading for the kitchen and a can of soda. "That's the big one," he said, sighing. "She loves me."

He knew that. He'd always known that. Depended on it. Good old Suze.

Of course she married him when he'd asked. She loved him.

And he'd taken advantage of her.

But it got worse. When she found out, when Dusty told her what he should have told her himself, months ago, then Tim had said he liked her; she was his best friend.

He liked her.

Gee, that must have made it all better;

209

he *liked* her. And the sex was good.

Why couldn't he have told her he loved her? Why had the words stuck in his throat?

Because she wouldn't have believed him. Why should she? He didn't quite believe it himself.

He just knew that Suzanna was in his life, should never have been out of it, and he'd have no life at all if she left him again.

Was that love? It could be love.

It *was* love. Damn it, he loved his wife! He was in love with good old Suze.

"And if I tell her that, she'd have every right to tell me to go to hell. I can't tell her. I've got to *show* her."

He collapsed back in his chair and stared at the dark television screen. Okay, how was he going to show her? He didn't even know where she was.

But he'd find her. She couldn't hide; he'd find her. He'd find her and he'd tell her, and she'd take him back. Maybe not right away, but after a while, once he'd proved that he was sorry for what he'd done, how he'd deceived her in order to help himself.

He'd show her he loved her. Some way, somehow.

And, somewhere in there, he was pretty

sure he'd have to tell her about Margo, too.

"God. Someone ought to do a public service and just shoot me," he said, slipping low in his chair.

Nine

The more self-centered and egotistical a guy is, the better ballplayer he's going to be.
— Bill "Spaceman" Lee, pitcher

"So? What is it?"

Keely's questioning voice came to Suzanna through the bathroom door.

Suzanna sighed, called out an answer: "I didn't look yet."

"You didn't — oh, for crying out loud, Suzanna, let me in there."

"No! That is, just a sec, okay? I'm building up my courage."

The handle turned, and Keely walked into the bathroom. "You've been building up your courage since yesterday morning. It is now almost noon on Sunday. Rome was built quicker. Tim knows where you are now, thanks to my big-mouthed husband, and he knows you'll be here tonight for the party. So look. We've waited long enough."

"*We've* waited long enough?" Suzanna held tight to the pregnancy kit. "You're already pregnant. You have no surprises left.

You even know you're having a boy."

"The marvels of modern science. Now pull that thing open, twist it, bend it, say the magic words over it, whatever you have to do with it, and let's see the results."

"Jack told me you were pushy," Suzanna said, grimacing. "But he said he likes that."

"You'll learn to love it, trust me," Keely said with a laugh. "Now, let's see what you're supposed to see," she added, picking up the empty box. "Okay, it's a plus for pregnant, a minus sign for not pregnant. Not exactly rocket science. We can do this."

Suzanna sighed. This was silly. She either was or she wasn't. Waiting certainly wasn't going to change anything; fervent prayers to the fertility gods weren't going to change anything.

She turned the white stick over, looked at it, practically had to push Keely's blond head out of the way to look at it.

"And we have a winner!" Keely said, grabbing a numb Suzanna in a crushing hug. "Oh, how wonderful! Our babies can play together."

Suzanna put a hand to her stomach. "I think I'm going to be sick."

"No, you're not. You weren't feeling sick a minute ago, so you can't feel sick now.

That's psychological. Trust me, there will be days when it's not, but right now it is. Still, let's get out of this bathroom and sit in the kitchen. I'll make you some soup."

"I don't want soup," Suzanna said as they entered the kitchen, feeling mulish. "I want to go to Philadelphia and murder Tim."

Keely stepped away from the pantry, holding a can of chicken noodle soup. "Oh, I'm sorry, Suzanna. You're really upset? I guess I think babies are such wonderful news that I just went a little nutso. You don't want the baby?"

Suzanna sat down at the kitchen table. "Want the baby? Of course I want the baby. I want a dozen babies. It's the timing that's so terrible. I just don't want Tim to say he wants me because I'm having his baby, or say that he wants the baby because I just happen to be having his baby, or that he — no, I think that's it."

She leaned her elbows on the table and sighed. "I think that's enough, don't you?"

"Certainly enough for now," Keely said, opening the can and dumping the contents into a microwave-safe container. "Will you tell him tonight?"

Suzanna blinked back tears. "I don't think so. He's probably angry with me by now, you know."

"I know. Men get mad at us because they did something dumb and then we had the *nerve* to get mad at them for it."

"That, too," Suzanna said, summoning a weak smile. "But it's that they lost to the Mets last night. He went 0-for-5 last night, Keely, with two strikeouts. You do know, of course, that that's my fault? If they don't win today, and at least get a split with the Mets for the series, they end up down two games after being tied on Friday night. Well, I don't even want to think about it."

"Jack's the same way when the Yankees lose. I've learned to enjoy the game, and I know how much he loves it; but those two are so intense, aren't they? It is just a game."

"Keely, it was *never* just a game to Jack and Tim. Not ever."

"Also true. I met Jack right after he had to retire, and he was miserable. I thought he was just spoiled and self-centered, but I slowly came to realize that to Jack, his life was over; his world had ended. If Candy hadn't come along? I think he would have sulked forever. But the thing is, Suzanna, Jack learned that baseball isn't all there is to life. He still loves the game, but there's so much more now in his life. Candy, me, the baby. Aunt Sadie says the best thing that ever happened to Jack was tearing his rotator cuff. While I don't quite believe that one, I do think he's a happier man now than he ever was while he played. More . . . complete."

"Tim's always lived for the game. God, Keely, he married me because he was so afraid he might lose the game."

"So he says," Keely said, putting a bowl of microwaved chicken noodle soup in front of Suzanna. "So he says. But you know what, Suzanna? I think his subconscious is smarter than that. Somewhere, deep inside himself, that big dumb jock looked at you and outsmarted himself."

"What?"

"Oh, never mind. I'm pregnant. I get to say silly things once in a while. You'll see, it's in the expectant mothers' manual. Now, eat up."

Three out of four. They had dropped three games out of four to the Mets. What could turn out to be the most important series of the season, and they had blown it. Back out of the tie for first place they had grabbed on Friday, and now two full games out, with the Philly sportswriters already saying, "Choke city," and "Not enough good pitching," and, worst of all,

"What's up with Tim Trehan?"

Tim left Philadelphia behind him, gratefully, and headed up the turnpike to Whitehall.

By the time he hit the Quakertown exit, all thoughts of the game had fled, and he was wondering about his reception at Jack and Keely's when he arrived.

Suzanna would be there. Jack had said that Keely had said that Suzanna had said she'd be there.

What if she wasn't there?

And why there? Why with a house full of people, Aunt Sadie probably wearing one of those silly paper hats, a couple of leis, and a big button saying "Birthday girl" on it?

He didn't need a crowd. He needed to be with Suzanna.

God, how he needed to be with Suzanna.

She, obviously, didn't need to be with him. Because Jack had said that Keely had said that Suzanna had said she wanted him to come to the party, yes, but that she was still going to be staying in the guest room at his brother's, and that he was to pretend everything was just fine between them for Aunt Sadie's sake, for Mrs. B.'s sake, and not cause any trouble or she'd have to hurt him.

That was the message he'd gotten: she'd have to hurt him.

That was just a saying, an empty threat. He knew that.

So why was he already hurting?

And why did he feel as though they had all reverted to elementary school? *He told me to tell you that he said that she said — cripes!*

Tim pulled onto the narrow macadam road that led back to Jack's house and several other homes that were either brand new or under construction, and ended at the small bridge running across Coplay Creek to his own house.

His and Suzanna's house.

The one she wasn't in.

He was early — it didn't take long to lose two-zip. He could stop in at the house, hope that Suzanna might be there. Drop off his bag. Glare at Lucky.

Looking to his left as he neared his brother's house, Tim could see a huge black four-by-four parked in the circular drive. "Oh, great. Cousin Joey. The shorter the man, the bigger the vehicle."

He pulled into the drive, figuring he might as well check to see if Suzanna was there, before making an ass out of himself, running through an empty house, calling

218

her name like some pathetic loser.

Besides, it had been a couple of months since he'd seen his cousin, Joey Morretti. Used to be Joey called himself Two Eyes, back when he wanted to believe he was part of the Bayonne, New Jersey, Mafia. If there even was a Bayonne chapter of the wise guys.

Aunt Sadie had said Joey called himself Two Eyes so he could remember how many he had, a statement that pretty much summed up Joey Morretti.

Candy's biological mother was Joey's sister, Cecily, once known as the airhead of the family but now better known as the conniver, thankfully at a distance from Candy, both physically and legally. When Cecily had temporarily adopted the handle Moon Flower and gone off to Tibet to find herself — or so she'd said — she'd left Candy on Jack's doorstep.

Changing Jack's life forever.

Of course, along the way to his current happiness, Jack had found himself having to deal not only with Candy, and a fairly belligerent Keely, but also with Cousin Joey, who had tried to gain custody of the baby.

Which, Tim thought now, would have been about the same thing as handing the kid over to be raised by penguins or something.

Still, in the past year or so, Joey had changed. For the better.

"Like he could have gotten worse?" Tim muttered to himself as he got out of his car and looked at Joey's license plate that read, STUDLEY1. "Cripes. Studley One? Studley five million and six, I would have believed."

As he approached the door to his brother's house, it opened, and Studley One came skipping out. "Hey, Tim-bo! Just coming out to check on my wheels. Can't be too careful with this baby, ya know. I don't want it boosted."

Tim looked at his cousin. Still short, of course, but with his dark blond hair no longer dyed black to make him look more like the Italian side of his heritage. No longer dressed head-to-toe in black, either. Although plaid Bermuda shorts and black Banlon socks were never going to take the fashion world by storm.

"I think your wheels are safe here, Joey," Tim said, adding to himself, *at least the ones that haven't already fallen off your trolley.*

"Yeah, guess so. Hey, nice wife, Tim-bo. I brought a wedding gift with me, ya know, since I wasn't invited to the wedding."

"Nobody was invited to the wedding, Joey. We eloped to Vegas."

"Uh-huh, heard that. So, wanna know what it is?"

"What what is?" Tim asked, stepping left, then right, trying to get past his cousin. Suzanna was in there. If he had to pick his cousin up and toss him on top of his "wheels," he'd do it.

"The present. Don't you want to know what I got you guys? It's one of those things that shoots salad all over the place. The deluxe model. Nothin' but the best for my cuz, ya know. Besides, if you're looking for Suzanna, she's not here. She and Jack went to the store for more liverwurst for Aunt Sadie. Bruno already ate it all."

"Bruno? Who's Bruno?" If Suzanna wasn't inside, he might as well stay outside. Because if he was in for lectures from Aunt Sadie and Mrs. B., he could wait to hear them.

Joey rolled his eyes, then hitched up his plaid Bermuda shorts. "Ya know. *Bruno.* Bruno Armano, my fighter. Well, used to be my fighter, until he went to cooking school. Now he's assistant to the pastry chef in this really hotshot place in Bayonne."

"There's really hotshot places in Bayonne? Just kidding. So, your fighter, huh? Oh, yeah, I remember now. The mountain you tried to pass off as the muscle that was going to hurt Jack if he didn't hand over Candy to you. I thought he was called Sweetness."

"Yeah, well, not anymore. Seems someone asked him his name one night when we were hanging at a local bar — because we're still friends, ya understand? I'm loyal that way, ya know. Anyway, Bruno says his name is Sweetness, and this guy, he takes exception."

Tim was barely listening. He was too busy listening for a car to pull into the driveway, with his wife in it. "How so?"

Joey made a face. "People are strange, Tim-bo, ya know that?"

Tim looked at his cousin, noticing that he was wearing about half a dozen gold chains around his neck, one holding a large round charm that looked like it contained a tiny photograph of the cast of *The Sopranos*. "Yeah, Joey, I've heard that. I even believe it."

"Well, this guy, this really *strange* guy, he takes exception to Bruno calling himself Sweetness, which was just his boxing name, ya know? Sweetness, the Beast of

Bayonne. He says to Bruno, he says, 'Hey, there's only one Sweetness and you ain't him.' "

Tim nodded. "Walter Payton, right. Chicago Bears. Hell of a player, and a real class act as a man. I can't really blame the guy if he was a fan."

"Yeah, that's what the guy says. Football player. Damn phenom, Payton was, ya know. The best, just the best there ever was, right? We all know that. But Bruno, he don't follow football; he don't know nothin', ya know? He picked the name Sweetness because he likes sweet stuff. So he looks at this guy, blinks his big dumb baby browns, and he says — 'Who?' And the guy yells out, *'Heresy!'* — and then decks him. Pow! You remember Bruno's jaw?"

"Glass, right?"

Joey shook his head sadly. "Crystal. Down he goes, splat. When he got up, he said that's it, from now on he's Bruno again. So, he's Bruno again. Don't call him Sweetness, Tim-bo, not unless you want to see a six-foot, six-inch guy ducking behind Candy — for cover, ya know. According to Bruno, you never know when there's another fan out there somewhere what could take exception."

Tim smiled. Good old Joey, always good

for a diversion. "I'll remember," he promised, then stepped past his cousin, who finally seemed willing to let him go, as he was already moving off to check his wheels. "Is the birthday girl inside?"

"No, the birthday girl is standing right here on the porch, waiting for her kiss. Terrible game, Timothy. I've seen better swings on a rusty gate."

"Thanks, Aunt Sadie, I can always count on you for a pep talk," Tim said, climbing the steps to drop a kiss on the woman's papery cheek. Sure enough, there was the paper hat, the leis, the birthday button, the whole nine yards. "You look great. Not a day over ninety."

She aimed a slap at his behind as he entered the house, then followed after him. "No need to be facetious, Timothy. And if you're looking for your wife, she's not here. And, if you're planning to be sulky or nasty or anything else we don't like, I'm warning you now that Keely, Margaret, and I, solely or once formed into a very small but very nasty mob, will throw you out of here on your ear."

Tim turned to look at his aunt. "Jack said that Keely said that Suzanna said that I was to act like nothing was wrong. But you know?"

Sadie Trehan sniffed. "Poor, poor Timothy. We're women. Of course we know. We know *all* of it, every last little detail. And I'm horribly ashamed of you, Timothy. I always thought you were the smart one."

"No, you didn't. You always thought Jack was the smart one."

She leaned close to whisper, "I just tell him that to make him feel better."

"But I'm supposed to be the handsome one. I kind of liked that."

Aunt Sadie gave an exaggerated sigh. "You do know you and Jack are identical twins, correct?"

He gave her another kiss on the cheek. "What I know, old woman, is that I'll never get anything past you, will I? Now, where's Mrs. B.? I want to know what she's told Suzanna about Margo."

"The unwed mother, you mean? Margaret hasn't told her anything. We've decided to leave that up to you. Ah, such a sad frown, Timothy. Were you hoping we'd do it for you?"

"Until this moment, no, I hadn't thought about it. But if you guys want to, hey, that's okay with me."

"I'll just bet it is. Don't be a wimp. Ah, there's Suzanna now; they must have parked out back and come in through the kitchen. I recognize her laugh. Make her cry, Timothy, and I'll have to punish you."

"You'd have to get in line, Aunt Sadie. Suzanna's got first dibs. Now, if you'll excuse me . . . ?"

Tim headed down the hallway toward the kitchen, pursuing the sound of voices, of laughter.

"Sure," he muttered under his breath. "Happy, happy. Let's all be happy."

He nearly jumped out of his skin when Mrs. Butterworth piped up from behind him, "Poor boy. And just think, only yesterday, all Tim's troubles seemed so far away."

He turned, slowly, and glared daggers at his old teacher. "I'll bet you've been waiting *days* to say that one to me."

"Hmmm, maybe years. It's always the ones who ride the highest that have the farthest to fall. That's not the Beatles. That's the old pride cometh before the, etc. Oh, and you look terrible."

"Only because I crawled here from Philly on my hands and knees. Is Suzanna in the kitchen? I thought I just heard her laugh."

"Yes. She laughs, she talks, she is proving that other than her ridiculous notion that you're one of the good guys, she is a sensible human being. You married her because she seemed the lesser of three evils, Tim? What were you thinking?"

He rubbed at the back of his neck. "Thinking? I wasn't thinking, Mrs. B. I was . . . I was temporarily insane. No sleep except for nightmares, my game was going to —"

Mrs. Butterworth made a face.

"— heck, going to heck. Reporters with their secret joke about the Trehan curse, and that was going to hit the papers any day if I didn't start hitting again. And then there was Suzanna, smack in front of me like manna from heaven, and we had such a great time, and the next thing I knew . . ." He put up his hands as if to end, "And that was that."

"What a sorry excuse for an excuse that was, Tim," Mrs. Butterworth said, shaking her head. "An excuse, by the way, that mentions nothing about why you haven't told Suzanna about your stupidity, and how lucky you are that everything worked out so well, that you now know that you love her. You know, Tim, all that mushy stuff?"

"I was working my way up to it?" he offered hopefully.

"Nope. Not good enough. You've had

227

nearly three months to work your way up to it."

"But I was getting close, honest. It was probably the Margo and Lucky thing that got in the way," he said, trying again. "I didn't want to confuse things."

"And that's just pitiful," Mrs. Butterworth said, rolling her eyes. "Really, really pitiful, Tim. If those are your arguments, your excuses, then Sadie's right. Unless you're up to a siege, Tim, Suzanna is going to run, not walk, toward the nearest exit."

Okay, this was good. Mrs. B. was going to give him some hints. She knew Suzanna; she was a woman. She'd tell him how to fix this.

"Siege?"

"You do remember your history, don't you? Attacking forces surround the castle until those inside surrender?"

"Gee," Tim said, his hopes not so high after that statement. "And here I left my catapult in my other slacks. What in he— heck are you talking about, Mrs. B.?"

"Think, Tim. You need to lay siege to Suzanna. Not toss rocks from a catapult or starve her out, for goodness sake. Use your imagination. You have to lay siege to her *heart*."

He leaned one shoulder against the wall

in the hallway and looked at Mrs. B. thoughtfully. "To her heart. Siege. So, what you're saying is, I don't go into the kitchen, grab Suze, take her outside, and tell her that I'm the world's biggest jackass, but I love her?"

"That's what you were planning?"

"Yeah, well . . . sort of. I mean, I'm not so sure it would work, and it probably won't, but I've got to start somewhere, right? I decided on the drive from Philly that I can't go too slow. It would drive me nuts."

Mrs. Butterworth stuck her slipping glasses higher on her nose. "How did your gender ever think it could rule the world? Answer me that one, Tim. No, don't bother. I taught history. I know how badly you men have been doing it. So, *no*, Tim. Caveman tactics . . . Well, they went out with the cavemen."

"I thought sweeping a woman off her feet was romantic," he said, laughter coming to him from the kitchen again while he stood there, feeling as if he'd stepped in quicksand.

"In some cases, yes. But you're not one of those cases. You tricked the woman, Tim. You lied to her, if only by omission, and now you're hanging on by a thread, boy. One wrong step, and it's all over."

He walked three quick paces toward the kitchen, turned around, walked back to Mrs. Butterworth. "I can't believe I'm having this conversation. Okay, okay. What do you and Aunt Sadie think I have to do?"

"And Keely," Mrs. Butterworth reminded him. "It's all three of us."

"Three of you? Like the witches in *MacBeth*?"

"Don't you sass me, Timothy Trehan," Mrs. Butterworth said, wagging a finger under his nose.

"I'm not, I swear. I want your help. I *need* your help. But, first, are you also *helping* Suzanna? Because you can't be pitching for two teams, Mrs. B."

"I'm old. I can be anywhere I want to be," she said rather smugly. "Now, here's the plan."

Tim leaned closer.

"You are going to *court* your wife."

He backed up. "Oh, come on. That's really your plan? This siege thing?"

"You have a better one?"

He shoved his hands into his pockets. "No. But I'd already thought of that one. Make nice, don't push her, prove to her that our marriage was — is — a good idea.

But you know Suzanna. She can be so damn . . . darn stubborn. It could take *months*. I'd hoped you'd have a better plan. A faster one?"

"Faster? Oh, I get it." Mrs. Butterworth looked at him from overtop her glasses. "I suggest cold showers, Tim," she said, and then she turned, sort of swirled an invisible cape, and headed back toward the foyer. He could almost swear he heard a witchy chuckle as she went.

Suzanna had seen Tim's car parked in the circular drive and was grateful when Jack had driven around to the garages, giving her another moment or two before she had to face the inevitable.

The inevitable was that she was pretty sure she was going to melt like warm butter when she saw Tim, the jerk. And if she did that, not only would Aunt Sadie, Mrs. B. and Keely never forgive her, but she'd never forgive herself.

A one-sided love was doomed from the beginning. She'd figured that out during her senior year in high school, and then applied only to west coast universities, knowing that Jack and Tim were staying on the east coast.

Yes, a one-sided love was doomed from

the beginning. She'd forgotten that some-where during one crazy night in Pitts-burgh, of all places. But she remembered it now.

Tim knew she loved him, as she kept re-minding herself. He'd have to be com-pletely unconscious not to know that. He'd always known.

And she'd always been his good old Suze.

He was going to come waltzing in here with his hangdog look, his eyes all puppy sad, looking so damn adorable, and push all her buttons, hoping she'd still react the same way she'd always done:

I fell asleep after practice, Suze. Could I copy your English homework in first period study hall? Come on, Suze, save my life.

Hey, Suze, you're not going to believe this, but I've got a flat and my spare's no good. I've got this date tonight? Jack's already called dibs on Dad's Chevy. Do you think you could swing it so that I could borrow your mom's car? Help me, Suze, save my life.

All the way back to elementary school: *Suze? Was today the day we were supposed to bring in popsicle sticks to make an African hut? Because, you know, I just plain forgot — hey, you brought extras. Good old Suze, you saved my life.*

Every time, the hangdog look, the puppy eyes.

Every time, she'd give in, help out, "save his life," come to the rescue. Break her own heart.

Now, there was a history to be proud of — if she were a masochist.

And here they were again.

He had to be expecting her to give in, having made him suffer for a couple of days. He had to believe she was too good-hearted, and too stupidly in love with him, to do anything else.

And he was pretty close to right.

Except, she'd learned a few things over the years. She'd learned that she could live, function, even succeed, without Tim in her life. That had been an important lesson.

If she had to, she could learn it again.

Because, no matter what, she was *not* going to hang on to him because there was a child involved now, not hang on in a marriage begun in deception, be the one giving love, always giving love, and getting Tim's sincere thanks in return.

She'd "sincere" him, the bastard.

Oh, how she hated him! Oh, how she loved him!

Oh, where in hell *was* the man? Was he

planning on hiding out in the living room or something, hoping she'd come to him?

Fat damn chance, bucko!

And then, suddenly, there he was. Walking through the kitchen and into the den, heading toward her, no sign of a birthday present for his aunt in his hands — undoubtedly figuring that she'd "saved his life" and signed his name to her own present. And he was right, of course.

She clutched Candy to her protectively, tight enough to make the child begin to struggle to be free. Clearly Candy wasn't old enough to join the Association to Shun Tim Trehan, because the little girl was holding out her arms, squealing for her uncle to take her.

"There she is," Tim said, grabbing Candy and kissing her. "There's my girl."

No, Stupid, I'm *your girl.*

Maybe shunning him isn't enough. Maybe some rope, some honey, and a convenient anthill?

Suzanna turned away, realizing she'd gone just a little hysterical. Now she was jealous of a sweet baby like Candy? What kind of sick, twisted, pathetic mind would even give out signals like that, let alone believe them, even for an instant?

Had to be being pregnant. Keely had

sworn there would be changes in her moods and thinking processes that would sometimes startle her, surprise her, even embarrass her.

Being jealous of a baby because Tim had called her "my girl" had to be one of those hormone-induced aberrations.

Either that, or she was going nuts.

"Hello, Tim," she said, lifting her chin, praying her tone was light, her smile at least halfway believable. After all, there were at least twenty-five guests milling around in the kitchen and den, all of them knowing that she and Tim were still relative newlyweds. She had no choice but to put a brave face on things, hope Tim did the same.

"Hi, babe," he said, then winced. "Sorry. I mean, hi, Suze." Then he bent down, still holding Candy, and kissed her hello. Smack on the mouth.

Suzanna felt her stomach flip, and psychological or not, she went racing out of the den, heading for the powder room, where she promptly brought all of the orange soda she'd drunk on the way home from the store back for an encore.

Ten

The sun don't shine on the same dog's ass all the time.
   — Catfish Hunter, pitcher

"What the — ?"

"Just shut up and come with me, bro," Jack said, as Tim had started after Suzanna. "Come on. You don't want to go chasing her right now."

Tim looked back over his shoulder as Jack led him out the kitchen doorway and darn near dragged him all the way down to the pool, where a couple of kids Tim had never seen before were playing Climb the Bruno in the shallow end.

"Did you see her?" Tim said once Jack had let go of his arm. "She turned green when I kissed her. *Green,* Jack. Does she hate me that much?"

"She doesn't hate you, Tim. Look, it's . . . complicated, okay?"

Tim narrowed his eyes. "Now, there's a news bulletin I already got. Just tell me one thing, Jack. Whose team are you playing for?"

Jack grinned, then stretched out his length in one of the chaise lounges. "You mean, am I pitching for Tim's Trials and Tribulations, or Suzanna's Sinister Sisters?"

Tim grabbed a mesh folding chair and pulled it over next to the chaise lounge, sat down. "Exactly. Suzanna's already got Aunt Sadie, Mrs. B. — your wife. Who have I got? Joey? Cripes, I might as well just forfeit the game now."

"It's not the guys against the gals, Tim. It's nothing like that." Then Jack grinned. "We're all pretty solidly on Suzanna's side."

"Gee, thanks."

"Candy still seems to like you."

"Candy's not all that discriminating. You'd better watch that when she gets to be a teenager. She might end up falling for some guy like me."

"Oh, come on, you're not so bad. As a matter of fact, I was you, not so long ago. It's just time to grow up, bro."

"Tell me about it. And then tell me *how.*"

Jack shrugged. "Do you love her?"

Tim avoided his brother's eyes. There were just some conversations Tim stayed away from, even with Jack. This was one of them. "I've always loved Suzanna."

"Sure. Suzanna the pal. The buddy. The great kid. The *convenience*. There were times, Tim, when even I could have decked you for the crappy way you treated her, knowing she was crazy about you."

Tim tried to get angry, but it was hard to get mad when you knew yourself to be wrong, dead wrong, and guilty as sin. "I was a kid. We were all kids."

Jack stood up, motioned for Tim to follow him as they walked away from the pool area when a splash came too close. The kids were sitting with a couple of women now, and Bruno was entertaining them, doing cannonballs into the deep end. Diving whales displaced less water.

"We were all kids, Tim, you're right. And Suzanna had so much going against her. The braces, the extra pounds, the fact that she was smart as a whip. Remember how Mom and Dad had to convince us that we could have brains and still be popular? But being good at sports helped us. Suzanna didn't have that luxury. She was just good old Suze, to you, to me, to everybody. Did she even go to the proms?"

"She was on the committees," Tim said, wondering if there was anything lower than a snake's belly, because if there was, he was it.

Jack led Tim to the garage, where he picked up two gloves and a baseball, handing one glove to Tim, then headed out onto the lawn.

"Bet it was a heck of a shock, seeing Suzanna again, and with her looking so great."

Tim, backing up on the lawn, caught the ball Jack threw, and threw it back to him. "You know, it actually took me a minute to recognize her at all. That smile? She hardly ever smiled in high school, probably because of all that hardware in her mouth. She should have smiled more. God, I'm crazy about that smile."

"The rest isn't so bad, either," Jack said, throwing the ball a little harder this time.

Tim snagged the ball out of the air, palmed it a few times, then sent it winging back at his brother. "You're going to think I'm nuts, but it wasn't that she'd gotten so pretty, and with that great body, and all. It was the smile, Jack, and how we could just sit down and talk after all those years, just like we'd never been apart."

He grabbed the ball low, spinning in a circle, pretending Jack's velocity had forced him into that spin, and threw it back with equal force. "Not that I'm complaining about the rest of it, you understand."

Jack caught the ball, kept it in the glove, and walked toward his brother. "So. You're crazy about Suzanna's smile. You like talking about the good old days. God, Tim, would you listen to me? Are we really old enough to even *have* good old days? I guess so."

"We're getting to current events now, right? To my nightmares? The Trehan curse?"

"Nope. Those are water under the bridge, as Aunt Sadie would say. Now you have to figure out what you're going to do next. And *why* you're going to do it. That's most important, bro, the *why* of it. Answer carefully, Tim, because otherwise, I'm not going to help you."

They put the gloves and ball back on the shelf in the garage and headed up the hill once more, toward the house.

"I was wrong," Tim said, collecting his thoughts. "Wrong not to tell her, wrong to take advantage of her, wrong to be so stupid as to believe in something as dumb as a curse, or superstition, or whatever the hell I was thinking."

"That's a good start. Keep going."

"We're great together. I mean, you can't spend your life talking about high school. I'm not dumb enough to believe that one.

But we always got along; we were always friends. Who would have believed what happened when I kissed her? I mean, I just about fell apart. There was this spark . . . no, this *blaze*. I mean, I couldn't get enough of her."

"Talk slowly, bro. Keely is going to want the details."

"Hey, this is brother to brother. Keep the women out of it, okay? Aren't I already suffering enough?"

"All right, but only if you say the right thing. Because then I'll be in just as deep as you, and Keely would murder me if I told her that I told you what I might tell you."

Tim stopped, looked at Jack. "You know, we're twins. We have twin-speak, always have. We can talk in shorthand to each other, understand each other better than most people. But I'll be damned if I can figure out what you just said."

"Just answer one question, Tim. Don't avoid it, don't twist it, just answer it, because it's important. Do you love her?"

Tim rubbed at his forehead. "Yeah. I love her."

"Okay, same question, part two. Are you *in* love with her?"

Tim nodded. "Yeah. That, too. I'm

about as sloppy about Suze as a person can get, and I'm not ashamed of it."

His brother slapped him on the back, sending Tim stumbling forward a few feet. "Well, okay then. I hereby declare myself a free agent, and I'm ready to sign with your team, Tim, if the price is right."

"Should we call Mort out here?" Tim asked, shaking his head. "He does handle all our contracts. I'm sure I saw him in the kitchen, scarfing up potato chips."

"We don't need him for this one. Mostly, I'm only going to tell you what you already know. You can't expect Suzanna to forgive you right away. Hell, you're just lucky she's agreed to go home, not stay in the guest room."

"She did?" Hope flared in Tim's chest.

"Don't get too happy, bro. I heard her telling Keely that she's already moved all of your stuff into another bedroom. She likes the tester bed, or whatever it is, and figures you don't deserve it."

"So I've been tossed out?"

"Not all the way out, Tim. You're still in the house. Be grateful for small favors. Keel would have thrown my stuff on the lawn, then set fire to it and invited the neighbors over for a marshmallow roast. Now, to continue?"

Tim made a motion with his hand. "Be my guest."

"You did a lousy thing, Tim. A selfish thing. And, being you, you pretty much landed on your feet for a while there. Without knowing it, you married exactly the right woman, for exactly the wrong reasons. In other words, every dog has its day, and you've had plenty of them — but not today, bro, because this time you royally screwed up. And now you're going to have to earn your way back into her trust."

"Lay siege to the castle of her heart. Heard it already. That message has been delivered."

"I figured it was. So, my last question. This is the big one, Tim, for all the marbles. Are you going to do what everyone feels you should do? Court Suzanna? Convince her that you love her? Eat some crow, do some groveling, pay for your mistake? Take it slow, take it easy, give her what you stole from her, flying her off to Vegas like that? If it takes weeks? Even if it takes *months?*"

Tim nodded. "I already know that telling her I love her is only going to get her mad. She wouldn't believe me, and I can't blame her." Then he frowned. "Months?"

"But you'll stick it out? Even if it does

take months? Hell, you're lucky it probably won't take years, even luckier that she even seems willing to give you a chance."

"Cold showers, right. Candy and flowers, got it. Courting?" He made a face. "How am I going to do that one?"

"I have no idea, Tim. And now, because you answered my questions the way I hoped, and because you're looking so pitiful, here's a little present. Something the girls don't want you to know, something you can't let *anyone* know you know. But you're my brother, and I can't go along with that one. You're two-for-three for the game, Tim, and at two-for-three, I don't think you have to worry about being injured anymore. Two-for-three is more than you've ever done in our follow-the-twin game."

"Two-for-three? Are you telling me — ?"

"Yup. Suzanna's pregnant. That's why she ran off, to toss her cookies. Morning sickness, Tim, and as I've found out, that doesn't just hit women in the morning. And it sure doesn't make women always feel all warm and cozy about the man who gets none of the problems, but just gets to hand out cigars. You're going to be a daddy, bro. Welcome to my world."

"Pregnant? *Pregnant?* And that . . .

You're saying that's why she . . . ?

"You got it, Ace. Just remember, you've got to play dumb here. Well, dumber than usual, bro. You can't let her know you know."

Jack chuckled softly, patted his brother on the shoulder, and walked away, heading into the house, leaving Tim to stand there, unconsciously rubbing at his own stomach.

Suzanna watched Tim as he pulled a can of beer from the refrigerator, grabbed a piece of cold, rare roast beef, and rolled it in one slice of rye bread, then headed into the den.

Most of the guests were outside now, as Aunt Sadie had asked them all to come see her birthday present to herself, a brand-new, compact four-by-four in bright blue. With racing stripes and a bright yellow Tweetie Bird painted on the hood, a Sylvester the Cat painted splatted against the tailgate.

Aunt Sadie knew how to enjoy life.

It was too late to go with them, so Suzanna just sat there, waiting for Tim to join her.

"You should eat more than that," she told him as he sat down beside her on the couch. "Keely made enough food to feed a small army."

He chewed on his half sandwich, swallowed, then said, "This is just an appetizer. I'm having filet of crow for my main course. How are you, Suze? Contact a hit man yet? Maybe Joey could help you out there."

She gratefully grabbed on to the subject of Joey Morretti. "*Joe* is taking courses at his local community college. Criminology."

She beat on Tim's back as he choked on the last bite of sandwich.

"Joey is taking classes in crim— criminology? He wants to be a cop? Now, there's a switch. If you can't join 'em, beat 'em, is that it?"

"I think it's very good for him. Keely told me all about how Joe had a few problems, how his sister got all their parents' attention, so that Joe sort of drifted into some . . . some small fantasy about joining the Mafia. He just wanted attention, that's all. Someone to notice him."

"Suze, Joey's been a weirdo from day one. He threw my new mitt in the toilet when I was about ten. I almost made him dive in after it, but my dad stopped me."

Suzanna nodded. "Obviously he tried to get your attention, too."

"Oh, really? Let me take a wild guess here. You took some psych courses in California? Bet those La-La-Land wackos put a hell of a spin on that stuff."

"For your information, I found the courses very . . . enlightening. Especially those on being an enabler. Oh, and in case your east coast university didn't cover that, that means I should have let you either get in trouble or do your own damn English homework."

He took a sip of beer, then looked at her closely. "Is it easier to fight about stuff that happened long ago than to talk about what happened to us since we met up again?"

"I don't know," she said, blinking back tears. "I may have to start with kinder-garten, and the day you talked me into eating paste, and work up from there. Un-less you think it would be easier for us to just get a divorce."

"No divorce, Suze. I'm going to make it up to you, for all of it. I promise."

"All right," she said, inwardly rejoicing, even as she wondered if, even with Tim's best intentions, they would ever be able to get past what he'd done. "Just as long as you know you'll be making it up to me from the guest room."

She could feel his eyes on her as she stood up, walked away. She even heard him as he muttered, "Kindergarten? Cripes. It's gonna be one hell of a long siege."

And she smiled. He was so adorable.

She still wanted to kill him. He didn't even ask if she felt better. Did he think only of himself? Or was he trying to save her embarrassment?

Maybe she didn't know Tim as well as she'd always thought she did.

"So I reminded him about the paste in kindergarten. How he tricked me into eating some."

Jack nodded, then forked more of Keely's great chocolate cake into his mouth. "I remember that one."

"But what you probably don't remember, and I'm sure Tim doesn't remember, is that I liked the taste of it. I ate paste through at least the second grade."

Jack laughed. "So, Suzanna, is this the plan? To drag up every stupid, selfish thing Tim ever did and make him apologize for it, pay for it?"

Suzanna shook her head. "No. It isn't as if he was holding a gun to my head. I wanted to be near him, and I'd have done just about anything to accomplish that."

"That's another thing," Jack said, waggling the fork at her. "Why Tim? Why not me?"

"What do you mean, why not you?"

"Well, hey, we look alike. Remember those old reruns of that TV show Patty Duke was in? The look-alike cousins? How did it go?"

"Oh, I remember. There was this theme song . . . ?"

"Yeah. Dressed alike, and what else? They walked alike, at times they even talked alike? That was Tim and me, until we could finally talk Mom out of dressing us the same. But, back then, we were pretty interchangeable. Just two dumb kids. Was it because of the alphabet? First in the row, Jack Trehan. Second, Tim Trehan. Followed by one Suzanna Trent. I guess what I'm asking is, if I'd been named Walter, or something, would that have changed anything?"

Suzanna took a bite of her own slice of cake. She'd gone from feeling sick to wanting to eat everything in the kitchen. How long had it been since she'd tasted homemade, baked from scratch chocolate cake? Years and years.

"No, Jack, that wouldn't have changed anything. I've always liked you, but it was always Tim who caught my attention. With his silliness, his mad dash through life, the scrapes he'd get himself into all the time, then get back out of again without a scratch. His confidence in himself, even his arrogance. Always Tim."

"Interesting. Keely says she likes Tim, thinks he's a riot and a nice guy, but if she had to live with him, she'd probably have to put a large dose of rat poison in his cereal within a month."

"So you're not as alike as you think you are," Suzanna said, smiling. "Keely and I are your proof."

"I guess so. Everybody always points out our similarities. You and Keely see the differences. Interesting."

"I told Tim that you're the angel, and he's the devil."

"The angel? That sounds boring."

"Not to Keely," Suzanna reminded him.

His grin was sheepish as he watched Keely walk by, Candy on her hip, or what pregnancy had left her of her hip. "Yeah. She's crazy about me."

Suzanna rolled her eyes. "And there's one of the similarities. You're both so damn cocksure of yourselves, although it was always Tim who, I could tell, would never even *conceive* of the idea of ever failing at anything he tried to do. I always envied that."

Jack looked at her for a long moment.

"You do know that you're beautiful, don't you? That you're smart, you're talented, have a great heart — all that good stuff?"

Suzanna shrugged, feeling the flush of embarrassment rising in her cheeks. "Let's just say I'm one of those people who looks in the mirror and still sees teeth braces, baby fat, and a bunch of silly romantic dreams that had a snowball's chance in hell of ever coming true."

"You still feel that way?"

"I hadn't been, not for a lot of years, ever since college, I guess. And when Tim looked at me, seemed to *want* me, I was so . . . so . . . And then I found out *why*, and I just . . ."

She sighed. "Well, I'm back to that hopeless romantic in the mirror, I guess. And now I'm going to get fat again. All I need is to dig out my old retainer, and I'll just be good old Suze."

"In another age, we could have hired someone to horsewhip him."

Suzanna smiled. "He's sorry, Jack. He really is."

"I know. He's the sorriest guy I know right now. Let me count the ways."

"Oh, Jack, thank you, but you don't have to be so hard on him. He's your brother, and you love him. I don't mind. I'm not totally innocent in all of this, remember. There were about two dozen questions I should have asked, any sane woman would have asked, and I asked none of them. I just hung on, and went along for the ride."

"I think he loves you."

Suzanna shook her head, blinked at the sudden stinging in her eyes. "I think he thinks he *should*. And, if I tell him about the baby, that's the first thing he'll say to me. 'I love you, Suze.' "

She looked at Jack, feeling one tear escape, roll down her face. "If he does that, Jack, I'll never be able to believe another word he says."

Tim sat on the floor in the den, his legs tucked up in as close to a Yoga position as a ballplayer with aching knees could get, wearing the paper hat his Aunt Sadie had forced on him earlier. She'd called it a "cone," but he was pretty sure it was a dunce cap.

The sun was going down on one of the longest days in his life, after one of the longest weekends in his life, and he was alone in the rapidly darkening room.

He looked at the toy he held in his hand, one of the toys he'd been picking up, tossing into the toy box in the corner of the room.

Soon he'd be doing this same job in his own house, for his own child.

Damn. There it went again. His stomach, doing that rotten flip it had been doing on and off all afternoon. He'd eaten a little of everything, because Keely liked it when people showed that they liked her cooking, and now all of it was sitting like a rock in his gut, topped off by a huge wedge of chocolate birthday cake.

He wasn't really sick to his stomach. He couldn't be. He had a cast-iron stomach; everybody said so. He'd never been able to dredge up any desire to drink anyone else under the table, even in college, but he could eat most anybody under the table. A full restaurant meal, followed by a stop later for tacos, some hot salsa dip to cleanse his palate, a few of those round green peppers that made most people start to perspire under their eyes, and maybe a couple of hot dogs picked up on the way home, with chili sauce, mustard, and onions, just to top everything off.

And he'd sleep like a baby.

Baby.

There went his stomach again. Cripes. He clenched his teeth together hard, tried to ignore the bitter taste at the back of his throat.

He wasn't going to make it. No way. No way in hell.

But he was going to have a baby.

Okay, Suzanna was going to have a baby.

His baby.

He swallowed a sick burp.

But, hey, he'd been cool. He'd talked to her, lots of times. Mostly, she'd been with the other women, the lot of them probably plotting against him, with Aunt Sadie, Mrs. B. and Keely as the ringleaders.

If he could just go home, lie down, he'd feel better.

What time was it? He looked toward the clock on the mantel. Damn near ten. A lot of people, those with kids who were in Candy's play group, had already left, as well as some of Aunt Sadie's friends from ceramics class and the theater group.

There were still a few neighbors hanging around, and Joey of course, along with Bruno.

Good kid, Bruno. He'd kept the children occupied all afternoon, as pool float, jungle gym, even as a sort of maypole for a while.

Would he be as good around his kid, Tim asked himself.

His kid.

Cripes! He was going to have to make a run for the bathroom, just the way Suzanna had done.

His kid. Okay. But his pregnancy?

That was pushing things.

He pulled a handkerchief out of his back pocket and wiped at the perspiration gathering on his forehead. Man, it was hot in here. Too many people, even for a state-of-the-art air-conditioning system.

Really hot.

And his gut was giving him fits.

Where was Suzanna? He wanted to go home. Why didn't she come take him home?

"Oh, thanks, Tim," Keely said, walking into the den, flipping on the wall switch that turned on the recessed ceiling lighting.

Tim blinked at the sudden brightness. "No problem. I wasn't doing anything else," he said, tossing yet another toy into the box.

Keely bent with a small groan, to pick up a few colored blocks, and looked straight into his eyes. "You feel all right? You don't look well."

Tim shoved the handkerchief back in his pocket and stood up. "I'm fine, really. It's been a hell of weekend, one way or another. And who was that bozo in the green-and-white-striped shirt?"

"John Donnelley? He's one of our neighbors. And he's not a bozo; he's an orthodontist. Why?"

"Nothing. Just that he cornered me for about ten minutes, telling me he thinks I'm holding my left shoulder too high at the plate. Everybody's an expert. Hey, Keel? I . . . I want to thank you for taking care of Suzanna for me. I know she was upset."

"Upset? I've never thought of you as a master of understatement, Tim. She was pissed."

Tim grinned weakly. "Okay, she was pissed. She's still pissed."

Keely took his arm and led him over to the couch, and he held on to her as she lowered her bulky figure into the soft cushions. "This couch is a man-eater, but Jack insisted," she said, patting the seat beside her. "Sit down, Tim. I think we should talk."

Tim looked toward the kitchen, hoping to see Suzanna there, come to rescue him. "I . . . I was thinking about going home, Keel. Like I said — been a long day."

"Tim — sit."

He sat.

"You did a terrible thing, Tim," Keely

told him; this sweet, blond, wonderfully chubby, *blooming* woman said to him, "When Suzanna came here Friday morning, she was devastated."

"I know. I've had all the lectures."

"You didn't have mine, Tim," Keely said, rubbing at her stomach. "Oh, he kicked me! He can be quiet for hours, and the moment I want to be quiet, he thinks it's party time."

Tim pressed a hand against his mouth, because his stomach was doing flips again.

"Want to feel him kick?" Keely asked, then took Tim's hand before he could say no, or run away, or move to Antarctica and change his name, or any of the other things he could think of in half a second.

"There! Feel it? That's his foot, the little bugger."

Tim smiled weakly as he felt the baby's foot push against his hand, as he watched Keely's swollen belly almost stand up, circle, and settle back down. "Wow," he said, swallowing hard. "Doesn't that hurt?"

"Not a bit. Oh, okay, so it can be uncomfortable sometimes, when he tries to get that foot out through my mouth, I swear. But it's also wonderful. Life, Tim, growing inside me. Part mine, part Jack's, all ours. I didn't get to have that feeling with Candy, so this little guy is making up for it, reminding me that heartburn and fat clothes are okay; but they aren't what really makes you parents. Candy is the child of our hearts, you know? Jack and I are so blessed."

Tim leaned over and kissed Keely's cheek. "Jack's a lucky man, Keel."

"Thank you, but you're still going to get the lecture. Oh, never mind. I've been watching you, Tim, and you look like you're already suffering. In fact," she said, pushing herself up slightly and looking toward the kitchen, "I think you've suffered enough that maybe I should help you out a little here."

Oh, no. Not more help. Any more help, and Tim was pretty sure he couldn't *help* but screw things up even more than they were now.

"Keel, that's okay. I already know I have to take it slow, get Suzanna to trust me again, get her to understand that I want this marriage. I really want it."

"That's very commendable, Tim. However, intelligent as Suzanna is, levelheaded as she is, I don't think appealing to her intellect is going to get you too far."

"Oh, great! Finally, one person agrees that I should toss her over my shoulder and carry her off to my cave."

She hit him on the chest. Not hard, but she had a pretty good backhand swing. "Idiot! You can't do that. And, even though I know you love her, even if *you* don't know that yet, you can't tell her that, either. Not in her condition."

Tim suppressed yet another bitter burp. Maybe he had a virus.

"Being pissed, you mean?" he asked, hoping Keely would just shut up.

"No, Tim, that's not what I mean. Look, Suzanna would kill me if she knew I was telling you this, and Jack, too, because we've all agreed to keep Suzanna's secret. But I really believe you should know that Suzanna is . . . well, she's . . . Let's just say she might be having some mood swings right now. Stuff that she'd usually not do, or say, but that she might do or say right now. So you can't get angry with her if she doesn't react the way you might expect, okay?"

How dumb did he have to play this, so that Keely wouldn't murder Jack?

"Okay," he said. "I upset her. I understand that."

Now Keely kissed his cheek. "You know, Tim, a woman would have understood what I just said. But I can see I have to draw you a map. As long as you promise you won't tell Jack or anybody. And for God's sake, don't let Suzanna know you know. That would be a disaster."

"No disasters on my horizon, Keel, other than the one we all know about," he lied with hopeful sincerity, "because I have absolutely *no* clue as to what you just said."

And then she said it. The darn woman just went ahead and said it: "Suzanna's pregnant, Tim."

The path Suzanna had taken to the powder room had included a deft step around the huge ottoman. Tim hurdled straight over it. . . .

Eleven

There's a soft liner, which is caught by the second baseman. And the ball game is over! For this inning.
— Jerry Coleman,
San Diego Padres announcer

Suzanna watched as Tim walked through the hallway, automatically touching the head of one of the wolfhounds incorporated into the tapestry. He did it every time, and probably didn't even know he did it.

Another superstition? Or just habit?

She put down her purse and followed after him, as both were carrying what Keely laughingly called "leftovers" from the party. There were enough of them to have another party.

"Why didn't you tell me you were sick?" she asked as Tim stood back, holding open the refrigerator for her, so she could stash the silver foil covered tins beside the ones he'd carried in from the car.

"I don't know. It was Aunt Sadie's party. I didn't want to be a wet blanket."

She put a hand on his forehead, pretending she wasn't using the excuse to touch him. "You don't feel hot. Keely said you threw up."

"Yeah. Well, don't worry about it, okay? I'm fine now."

Suzanna followed after him as he went into the den, picked up the TV remote. "But you could be sick."

"You threw up," he said, punching in the numbers for ESPN. "And you're fine now, too, right?"

"Right," Suzanna said warily. So that was it? He saw that she'd felt better, and then decided either not to mention that she'd been sick, or hadn't cared enough to ask. No, he cared enough. He was a good man. She was angry with him, disappointed in him, but she couldn't go blaming him for every vice in the world.

"See? You're all right; I'm all right."

"Yes, but —"

"Did you see today's game?"

She shook her head. "No, there wasn't time. I'm sorry. Candy decided that today would be a good day to want to hang on Keely's leg, so I took her out for a walk, then helped Keely once the baby was down for her nap. What did I miss?"

"Another loss," he said, just as the recap of the Phillies game came on the screen.

"So you didn't see it?"

"No, I said I didn't," she said, stepping closer to the large-screen set.

"Good." He turned it off. "Nothing much to see. One of the . . . um . . . Brandenberg tried to take me out at the plate. Barreled into me, into my gut, but I held on to the ball." He rubbed at his stomach. "I guess I took a bigger hit than I thought."

He was lying. The man was standing there, looking straight at her, and lying through his teeth.

Why? She decided to push him.

"Really. You know, Tim, maybe there's internal bruising. Even internal bleeding. Let's go."

"Go? Go where?"

"To the Emergency Room, Tim. You got hit; you've thrown up. Maybe it isn't your gut. Maybe you have a concussion. What did the trainer say when he checked you out?"

"He said I'm fine, that's what he said," Tim told her, his voice tight as he threw the controller onto the couch. "Let's go to bed; I'm wiped out."

"Don't you want to talk?"

He rolled his eyes at her. The man was picking a fight!

"I mean it, Tim. We . . . We really should talk."

"About what? I screwed up, you caught me at it, and now you're punishing me. Oh, yeah, I heard all about it, Suze. About my clothes being moved to another bedroom. Everybody's having a lot of fun at my expense, laughing at me."

Tim Trehan, Suzanna knew, didn't give a rat's ass about what the world thought of him — unless he thought badly about himself.

"You were embarrassed," she said, nodding her head. "I'm sorry. I shouldn't have gone to Keely."

"No," he said quickly, rubbing at the back of his neck. "That's not what I meant. What I mean is . . . Oh, hell, Suze, I don't know what I mean. Look, let's just go to bed. Where did you put me?"

"In the back bedroom. It's the only other one that has furniture, remember? You don't mind?"

"Of course I mind," he said, and she was pretty sure it was the first really *honest* thing he'd said to her all evening.

He stepped closer to her, put his hands on her upper arms. "I missed you, Suze. I missed you so much."

Give in, her body cried out, even as her

brain delivered a mental kick to her backside.

"We've been apart longer than this, Tim. Ten days for one of your road trips, another week when I had to go to Seattle. Ten years, when we went off to college."

He rubbed his hands up and down her arms. "This was different. I didn't know if you'd be here when I got back. I . . . I need you, Suze."

She had to say it. She had to say something, because if she didn't, she'd fall into his arms, give in, give up, and they would spend the rest of their lives reliving the old patterns. That old pattern where Tim asked, and she gave.

"Because of the curse? Because, otherwise, you could get hurt? Have to leave the game?"

"Screw the curse, Suze. It was stupid. I was stupid."

"Yes, you were. And so was I. This isn't just about the curse, or your superstitions, or some crazy belief that you'd end up doing at least one of the three major things Jack did this past year. There's more to it than that, Tim. A lot more."

He dropped his hands from her arms, and she sighed in relief . . . and in loss.

"Kindergarten. Paste. La-La-Land psychology. We're back to that?"

"You don't see the pattern, Tim?"

He made a face. "No, I don't see the damn pattern. We were kids."

"We weren't kids in that hotel room, Tim. And yet you reverted straight back to the old days. You had a problem, and good old Suze could help you out. You seduced me, Tim."

"Yeah, that took all of ten seconds," he grumbled, just like a man, and she was suddenly *so* glad she hadn't forgiven him.

"Go to bed, Tim," she said, turning her back on him.

"Ah, Suze, I'm sorry. That just came out. I didn't mean it."

She turned back to him. "A part of you did. Tim," she continued, sighing, "either we divorce now, admit we made a mistake, or we work on this. But you can't expect a lifetime of Tim asks and Suzanna jumps to be resolved with one quick 'I'm sorry.' Do you understand that? You have to decide just what it is you want from me, what you think you need from me, and I have to decide if what I feel for you is what a wife should feel, or if I've finally thought I've won one, and the victory was more important than whether or not I still *wanted* it."

If she had hit him with a lamp, he

couldn't have looked more shocked. It had never occurred to the man. Never. She might not want *him?*

He'd seen some glimpse of light, realized that he'd made a mistake. Had even suffered, a little. But, deep in his heart, he was so damn sure she'd forgive him.

Rocked your world, didn't I, Tim-bo?

He changed the subject. "We have a free day tomorrow, just a practice, so I can come home again in time for dinner. Then the Cardinals are in Tuesday and Wednesday, we're off Thursday, and the Cubs will be here for a three-game weekend. Then we hit the road, for two with the Marlins and two more with the Braves, and then to Shea Stadium to finish the season with three against the Mets."

"And?" she said, trying to get his point.

"I just thought I'd tell you, that's all. That's what husbands do, right?" he said. "So you can plan? We could go out for dinner tomorrow night? You could come stay at the apartment Tuesday and Wednesday? Didn't you say you still had some vacation time coming to you?"

"We'll see," she said, feeling rather powerful. It was a new feeling where Tim was concerned. Not that he was exactly *pleading* with her, but he was close. "Now, go to bed, Tim. You got knocked down, remember?"

"I'm still on the floor," he said, grimacing.

"In the *game*, Tim, in the game. You go upstairs."

"Aren't you coming? Oh, I know, I know, separate bedrooms. But it's late, Suze. You need your rest, too, right?"

She looked at him suspiciously for a moment, then decided he was just trying to get her upstairs, where he'd make his next move. Well, good luck to him, because she had found the key to the master bedroom door.

"I'll be up soon," she said. "I brought the cats home today, before they forgot who we are. I just want to make sure they have some dry food and fresh water. Otherwise, Margo will be standing on my chest, nose to nose with me, at five in the morning, yowling."

Tim just about knocked her down as he headed over to the plastic pad on the floor in front of the pot-and-pan closet and picked up the dishes. "I'll do that."

She pulled out the foil bag of cat treats and shook it. "Thank you. But you forgot Margo's nightly treats. I'm surprised she wasn't waiting for us when — ah, here she comes. She heard me shake the bag."

Suzanna went down on her knees and poured a few treats into her hand. "Come here, sweetheart. Look what I've got for you."

Margo was a great cat, but like many Persians, she also was very much her own cat. She was the queen, and she made very sure everyone knew it. Big, bad Lucky never approached the feeding dishes until Margo was done eating. She allowed affection, gave much in return, but even Suzanna couldn't turn her into a cuddly lap cat. Still, she kept trying.

As Margo finished the last of the treats, Suzanna picked her up, hoping for a little purring, and maybe a lick on the nose, which was either Margo's way of saying, "I love you," or "Okay, I've been good, I've let you hold me for three complete seconds, so now let me down."

"Oh, look, Tim, she's letting me cuddle her," she said, smiling up at him as she stroked Margo's long, lush coat. Margo was all fur, and looked twice as big as she actually was. At her last appointment at the vet, she'd weighed in at only six and one-half pounds.

Funny. She felt heavier tonight.

"Okay, they've got fresh food and water,"

Tim said, sort of nudging Lucky with the toe of his sneaker, as if pushing him out of the kitchen and into the hallway.

Suzanna bent her head so that Margo could lick her nose, still running her hands over the cat's body.

"Tim?"

"Hmmm? I was just heading upstairs. You coming?"

"Not yet. Tim, I think Margo may have worms or something. Do you think she could have worms? Her belly's sort of tight, and fuller than it's ever been. You know how she can stretch out on the couch? She looks like she's three feet long, and pencil slim. Lucky goes outside, so God knows what he gets into and could bring home to Margo. When did you last have him at the vet?"

"It's . . . It's been a while," he said, nudging Lucky again with his foot. "But he didn't have worms then. Dogs get worms. I don't think cats get worms. Probably not. So, no, Lucky didn't . . . didn't give her anything. Maybe she's just eating a lot. Aunt Sadie may have been overfeeding her."

Margo was still cuddling, her purr loud and rumbling.

"Her nose is cold and wet, and I think

270

that's good. But this isn't at all like Margo, Tim. It's probably all my fault. I know Mrs. B. takes very good care of her, but she's more used to Mrs. Josephson, I guess. And I've been away from home so much lately. Do you think she senses tension in me, and is trying to comfort me?"

"If she knows I've been benched, yeah, I guess so. Come on, it's late. Let's go upstairs."

Man, he was antsy. What was his problem? He looked . . . Yes, he looked *guilty*.

Suzanna's internal radar, which had been trained on Tim for most of her life, turned itself on, scanned the room, and landed on Lucky.

Did Lucky look guilty, too? Could cats look guilty?

Was Margo sick, or just being unusually sweet? Or did she think that she and Suzanna were kindred spirits?

"Tim," she said, dragging out his name. "Lucky is fixed, right? That is what you told me."

He scratched at a spot just above his left ear, a sure sign he was about to say something she wouldn't like.

"Tim?"

"About Lucky getting snipped . . ." he

271

said, grimacing as if every word was painful.

"Timothy Patrick Trehan," Suzanna said, still holding Margo as she got to her feet. The cat objected, cried out, and Suzanna let her down before walking straight up to Tim and pointing a finger at him. "You didn't have him fixed, did you?" She poked her finger into his chest. "*Did* you?"

He let out a long breath. "You wouldn't understand. It's . . . It's a *man* thing, Suze. How could I look Lucky in the face if I did that to him? Snipped? Cripes. I just couldn't do it. He's only about a year old, Suze; he hasn't even *lived* yet. How does a guy do that to another guy? But . . . But I was working my way up to it, honest I was. I'd made up my mind to have a little man-to-man talk with him, explain things, and then get him an appointment. But then Mrs. B. told me —"

"Mrs. B. *told* you, Tim?" Suzanna's eyes narrowed. "She told you what, Tim? She told you that Margo was *pregnant?*"

He gestured awkwardly with his hands. "She bought this . . . this book about it. Said something about nipples getting pink and big, and no hair, and, well, I tried really hard not to listen."

Suzanna glared at him for a few moments, then went looking for Margo, who was sitting on the kitchen table, daintily licking her paws. She picked up the cat, her hands gripping the animal behind her front legs, and went face-to-belly with Margo's stomach.

"Oh . . . my . . . *God*," Suzanna said as Margo struggled to be free. She put down the cat and whirled around, to face Tim once more. If her eyes could turn to lasers, he'd be just so much dust on the floor.

"You said she was pretty much still a kitten," Tim said quickly. "Lucky's not a kitten, but he's not that old, either. I thought I had time. You know, to break it to Lucky gently?"

"I could kill you. I could just *kill* you," Suzanna said. "How can I believe *anything* you say to me?" she asked him, and then she stomped up the back stairs.

The Cardinals came and went. So did the Cubs.

The Mets were on a tear, winning three of five on the road.

And the "Phightin' Phils" were now three games out of first. The rest of the team had been great, but Tim's play could pretty much be summarized as stink, stank, stunk.

He had taken to putting music disks in his car radio and avoiding the call-in all-sports talk stations.

Two errors in five games. A solid Golden Glover, and he'd made two stupid errors in five games. And his batting average had dropped seven points so far in September. That was a big drop, this late in the season.

Not that Suzanna cared.

She hadn't come down to a single home game, because she'd gone out of town, to San Diego. She'd told him she'd have to travel with Gloria for a while, show her the ropes, but Tim wasn't buying it.

She had gone out of town because she wanted to be out of town while he was at home, and now she was home again, and he was on the road.

That was what he got, telling her his schedule.

She'd planned her absences around it.

"You have to put it all out of your head and concentrate on the game, bro," Jack told him, long distance.

Tim sat down on the edge of the Atlanta hotel bed, the cell phone pressed to his ear. "How am I supposed to do that? She's avoiding me. I call home, and I get the answering machine, have to listen to my own stupid voice. I call Mrs. B., and she tells me Suzanna's home; she can see her car in the driveway. She's using the Caller ID and just not answering. Next thing, Jack, she'll be moving out. Lay siege to the castle of her heart? Sounds good, if soppy, on paper, bro, but we're never in the same place."

"You will be if you keep dropping games while the Mets keep winning. In fact, the way I figure it, unless you sweep the Braves and take two out of three games from the Mets, win this thing outright, you'll be lucky to get a wild card and play in October at all. All while hoping the Mets drop at least two of their three to Cincinnati before you head to Shea. Statistically, you're not out of it, but you've got to win, Tim. You've got to win."

"Don't remind me," Tim said, unconsciously rubbing his belly. He'd just been sick again. Hell, he'd been sick every morning, waking up with his stomach roiling, so that the moment he picked his head up off the pillow it had been a mad dash for the bathroom.

He felt like shit.

"So, she went to the doctor? You did say she had an appointment, right?" Tim asked, not able to concentrate on baseball, not able to think about anything but Suzanna.

"Yeah, bro, she did."

"And she is?"

"Oh, yeah. Even had a sonogram, because she wasn't sure when you two got lucky."

"Don't say Lucky. I'm still thinking about strangling that cat."

"I'm not talking about that Lucky. Want the due date?"

"Margo's?" Tim rubbed at his clammy forehead. "I don't think so."

"Not the cat's, Tim, for crying out loud, although I do know it. Aunt Sadie figures it'll be next week, around October fifth. If you guys get into the divisional series, you'll probably be out of town, playing."

Tim sighed. "I can live with that."

Jack laughed. "I'll bet you can. I've been teasing Keely that I'm going to be out of town the last two weeks of October. She isn't amused."

"Keely's due already?"

"Nine months isn't that long a time, bro. She's due October twenty-eighth. Do you want to know when Suzanna's due? Seems like you were a busy boy in Pittsburgh."

"In Pittsburgh? How would anyone know that?"

"The sonogram, Tim. Pay attention. Now, do you want to know the doctor's estimate on the due date, or not?"

"Go ahead," Tim said, lowering his head almost between his knees, because the nausea was coming back.

"April fourteenth. I checked the schedule for next year. Lucky for you, that's three days into a ten-day home stand."

"April," Tim repeated. He'd been throwing up for two weeks, every damn morning for two weeks, ever since he found out about the baby. April? He wouldn't live until April. "Is she . . . Is she okay? Or is she still having that morning sickness stuff?"

Maybe, just maybe, if Suzanna stopped, he'd stop. Which was about the damndest, dumbest thing he'd ever thought of, because that was just not possible. He was sick, damn it! Sick!

"I really don't know, Tim. I do know that she and Keely made hot fudge sundaes last night after dinner. When I was stupid enough to say that maybe Keel shouldn't have whipped cream, she shot some at me, straight out of the can. So, mostly, I'm staying away right now."

Tim bit down hard, clenched his teeth for a few moments. "How can she eat that crap?" he asked, his mental picture of ice cream, fudge, whipped cream, all making him want to head for the porcelain bowl again.

"That's the way it goes, Tim. First they're sick, and then they're eating all the time. Although Keely's getting heartburn at night, a lot. She did that in the beginning, but it had gone away. Last night, she slept sitting up in the recliner in the den. I'll be glad when this is over, although probably not as glad as Keel will be."

Heartburn? Tim relaxed his shoulders. He didn't get heartburn. Not ever.

"What else?" he asked, pulling the notepad and pen from the bedside table. "We've got morning sickness, heartburn . . . and what else?"

"You're worried? Don't worry, Tim. Suzanna's going to be fine."

"I know that," Tim said quickly. "Just humor me, okay?"

"Okay. Let's see. Keely had morning sickness for, oh, about three months, to tell you the truth. And some heartburn. Then she was pretty good for a while, until her ankles started swelling. That's when she had to cut out salt, salty foods. And she did start to gain a little too much weight, so we had to watch her diet. Still do, except she keeps slipping those sundaes by me. Now heartburn again. Some aches and pains she says are nothing. Oh, and the mood swings. How could I forget the mood swings?"

"I have to buy a book, or something," Tim muttered, pretty much to himself.

"Don't bother, bro. We've got plenty. I'll sneak them to you when you get back home. Because, you know, it's not just the woman anymore. Everything is directed at both mother and father. *We* are pregnant, not just Keely."

"Uh-huh," Tim said, reaching for his can of soda. Ginger ale. It settled his stomach sometimes. So did soda crackers. They came free when he ordered soup. He'd started collecting little packets of soda crackers.

Jack was talking again. "And then there's the classes. That breathing stuff for natural childbirth? Keely says she's pretty sure she'll want drugs, lots of them, but she felt she should at least take the classes. You can do those over the winter, Tim, be Suzanna's coach."

Tim's head was swimming. He was getting way too much information. "Hey, gotta go. Sam wants me at the stadium early, for some extra batting practice. Good luck to your Yankees tonight, Jack. Shame we're going to beat them in the Series."

"In your dreams you'll beat them, Tim," Jack shot back. "But let's not jinx it. We still all have to get through the playoffs, take the pennants."

Tim hit the button, ending the call, and slowly got to his feet. He felt so old. Too damn old.

He stepped into a pair of jeans, then frowned as he noticed that the waistband seemed big. How much weight had he lost? He rummaged in his bag, pulled out a belt, and slipped it on, pulled it two notches past the worn bit of leather that indicated where he usually wore it.

"No good," he said to his reflection in the mirror over the low bureau. "I guess it's time to see Jerry."

The bathroom door opened, disgorging Dusty Johnson and a lot of steam. "Jerry?" Dusty repeated, rubbing at his wet head with a hand towel. "Who needs to see Jerry? You? You sick again?"

"Not really," Tim said, turning away. "I just thought I'd check with him, see if he could give me something to settle down my stomach."

Dusty nodded. "Sounds like a good idea. He ain't a doctor, but he's close."

Tim picked up his jacket and headed for the door. "I'll meet you over there, okay?"

"Sure thing," Dusty said, hanging on to the towel wrapped around his waist. What a kid. He undressed in the dark, carried his underwear with him to the shower room after a game. Mr. Modest. His mama probably told him never to get naked with anybody he wasn't already married to — if even then.

Tim grabbed a cab to the ballpark and hunted down Jerry in the training room making use of the whirlpool.

"What did you do, Jer," Tim asked, pulling up a chair next to the whirlpool, "throw out your shoulder wrapping Rick's ankle? Or maybe you're just checking the temperature, to be sure none of us burns in there?"

"Put a sock in it, Trehan," the trainer said, sinking lower in the tub. "What can I do for you?"

Tim picked up a ten-pound weight someone had left on the floor and absently began doing curls. "Nothing much. I've just got . . . a small problem."

Jerry sat up, displacing a good bit of water. "Tim, there are no small problems. Not when we're three games out of first, with five to go, two of them against the Mets. Now give — what's the problem?"

"It's my stomach," Tim said, standing up, beginning to pace the room. "I keep . . . I keep throwing up. In the mornings mostly."

Jerry was out of the whirlpool, wrapping a towel around his ample middle. "Any pain? Like, on the right side, or around your navel?" He put a hand on Tim's forehead. "No fevers?"

"No, why?" Tim asked as Jerry dripped all over his imported loafers.

"Could be chronic appendicitis, that's why. How long has this been going on?"

Tim mentally counted backward, ending at Aunt Sadie's birthday party. "Today's eleven days."

"And you're sick every day?"

"Yeah," Tim said nervously. "Chronic appendicitis, huh? How do we know for sure?"

"We don't. Usually, it's pain, elevated white blood count, fever. That's acute. But chronic? That one's harder. We can start with blood tests, but it really doesn't sound like appendicitis, Tim. You said you're only sick in the mornings?"

"Once or twice at night," he said, trying to steer Jerry back to that appendicitis thing.

"But mostly in the morning?"

"Okay, yes, mostly in the morning."

"And no pain, no fever?"

"Cripes, Jerry. You want I should put it in writing? No pain, no fever."

Jerry shrugged. "Then, that's it. You're pregnant."

"*What!*"

"I said, that's it, you're —"

"I heard what you said," Tim shot back, glaring at him.

"Hey, I'm kidding, Tim, I'm kidding. Men don't get pregnant."

"Gee, and we all wondered why you didn't go all the way, become a doctor. You're such a freaking genius."

"Oh, yeah? Well, I'll have you know, buddy, that even if men can't get pregnant, they can *feel* pregnant. My cousin, Fred? You remember him? The guy with the six kids, all girls? Fifth one, he got pregnant along with Maryanne. She threw up, he threw up. Her breasts got sore, his . . . chest got sore. She burped, he did the encore. She waddled like a duck, he — well, you had to be there, Tim. We were sure

283

he'd go into labor with her, but it didn't get that bad."

Jerry chuckled. "Of course, that's only because Fred passed out when Maryanne's water broke, bam, smack in the middle of our Fourth of July picnic. Hit his head on a croquet mallet, got a concussion, and was admitted to the floor above Maternity. We've got it all on video."

Tim was shaking, but he hopefully hid his reaction from the trainer. "Jerry, that's a great story. What the hell does it mean?"

"It means, Tim, that sometimes the man gets symptoms, right along with the woman. It's all mental, of course. We think that with Fred it was because he wanted a boy so bad that he talked Maryanne into another pregnancy. Once they had the tests, learned it was another girl? He started getting sick. But it didn't happen again, with the sixth girl. Fred just said that with six you get eggroll, something like that. And it was Maryanne who wanted the sixth one. Probably to see if Fred would start barfing again."

Tim chewed on this for a few moments. "So, Fred was feeling . . . guilty?"

"Guilty? Yeah, I suppose that was it. Guilty. But it doesn't matter, right? Your wife's not pregnant. Or is she?"

Tim shook his head. As long as Suzanna wanted the pregnancy kept a secret, he wasn't going to say a word to Jerry the Mouth. "Nope. So we're back to that appendicitis stuff?" he added hopefully.

"All right, I guess we have to follow up on this. I'll arrange for blood work at the local hospital, some time this afternoon. And, now, if you'll excuse me, I've got some ankles and knees to wrap."

"Sure, thanks, Jer," Tim said, collapsing back into the chair once the trainer left the room.

Guilt? He could be throwing up because of guilt? And who could he ask about it, anyway? Suzanna? No. Because he wasn't supposed to know she was pregnant, and because she'd taken those psych courses in La-La-Land.

And no shrinks! No way was he going to a shrink. Sam went to a shrink, and look where that got him, for crying out loud. The man had started humming some sort of mantra when he got his shorts in a knot. And eating sunflower seeds. Now he was making noises about group meditations before games.

So no shrink. No Suzanna. And no Jack, because he liked his brother, and if the guy laughed, he'd have to kill him.

Which left . . . What? Who? Who could he talk to who wouldn't go running to Suzanna? Who could he talk to who wouldn't start rolling on the floor, laughing at his expense?

Who else cared that his game had gone to hell, his life was going to hell? That he was two quick seconds away from calling a cab, heading for the airport, and saying screw it to the rest of the season?

He headed back outdoors, pulling out his cell phone. He pressed the second button on the speed dial, waited.

"Mort? You got a minute . . . ?"

Twelve

They usually show movies on a flight like that.

— Announcer Ken Coleman,
calling a long home run

"Well, here we are," Keely said, settling into her seat in the private super box Mort had wrangled for them at Shea Stadium. It was Friday night, and the first of the last weekend of games in the regular season. The Phillies were two full games behind the Mets, with three games to go.

"Yes," Suzanna answered nervously, "here we are. Thanks for coming with me."

"You're welcome, although Jack can't quite understand why I didn't go to Yankee Stadium with him. Big deal, they clinched their division weeks ago. Although I can't believe I'm going to be rooting against my very own Mets."

Suzanna looked at her new friend, her dear friend. "Jack says you can't name a single player on the Mets team."

"Can so," Keely answered, lifting her

chin. "I just won't give him the satisfaction, that's all."

Suzanna laughed, shaking her head. "You're a nut; you do know that, right?"

"Oh, absolutely. Jack's still a little torked that I didn't recognize him as the great Jack Trehan when we met. And then, when I did find out, I told him I'm a big Mets fan. Mets fans are *never* Yankee fans, Suzanna. It drove Jack nuts. You have to keep them in line a little, Suzanna, keep them guessing. Although I now can name every player on the Yankees, and if Tim's Phillies end up playing them in the Series, I'll be rooting for the Yanks. I hope you don't mind."

"With Jack as a former Yankee, and now their color commentator? How could you do anything else?"

"Oh, look, Suzanna, some little kids are going to sing the Anthem. Aren't they cute? Isn't that sweet?"

Suzanna stood and watched as Tim joined his team at the edge of the dugout for the playing of the National Anthem, then took his place on the bench.

"He doesn't look sick," Keely said, turning a pair of binoculars on her brother-in-law. "Maybe Mort just said that, so you'd show up."

Mort's voice came from behind them. "What? Me — lie? I never lie."

Keely gave Suzanna a quick poke in the ribs. "Did you hear that? More and More Moore, super agent, never lies. Duck, Suzanna, I think there might be a lightning bolt heading in this direction."

"Very funny," Mort said, making his way down the steps inside the super box, planting kisses on their cheeks. "Suzanna, you can't tell Tim that I talked to you about anything other than offering you this super box for the weekend. I think he thinks I'm like a priest in the confessional, or something like that. What we talk about is sort of sacrosanct."

"Okay, that's it, definitely a lightning strike," Keely said, pushing herself to her feet. "And I've got to go visit the little girl's room again. Remind me not to drink too much, Suzanna, or the limo will be making pit stops every ten minutes on our way home."

Suzanna watched Keely go and wondered, not for the first time, if she would be as laid back about her own pregnancy when she got to the elephant stage. She doubted it.

"Sit down, Mort, and tell me how he is tonight."

"He's good, good. I saw him this morning. I gave him the books he asked me to buy for him, told him he's not being all that peculiar. Did it with a straight face, too, just the way I didn't act surprised when he told me you're pregnant, seeing as how Sadie told me all about it the day of the birthday party. I didn't let on that I knew, or that he isn't supposed to know — none of that. I'd say I'm up for sainthood, but then that lightning Keely talked about would be sure to strike."

"I still wish he didn't know," Suzanna said, feeling tears gathering behind her eyes. They kept doing that. Gathering, waiting, ready to spill over. She was turning into a damn sprinkling can. "I didn't want him to know."

"Yeah, Sadie explained all of that. But since he doesn't know that you know he knows, it's okay, right? Although I have to tell you, sweetheart, I think you're both nuts."

"I can't explain it, Mort, but I have to do what I'm doing. If I give in now, the way I've always given in, we'll never be happy." She pulled a tissue from her pocket and dabbed at her eyes. "Except now he knows I'm pregnant, so how am I ever going to know if he really loves me?"

"He's throwing up every morning; that should give you some clue," Mort said, pulling out a cigar, then looking at Suzanna, replacing it in his shirt pocket. "And he can't play for sh— Sorry. He isn't playing well; that's what I meant to say."

"But he knows I'm here tonight?"

Mort nodded. "That should make a difference, don't you think? Even if I told him you're going home with Jack and Keely, and that you don't want to see him."

"I'm coming back tomorrow night, too," Suzanna said, twisting the tissue in her hands. "Aunt Sadie's coming with me. And then it's Mrs. B.'s turn, on Sunday."

"Last regular game of the season. Two out of three aren't enough. We have to sweep and win it all outright. I hate going down to the wire like this. Ages me, I swear it."

"Poor Mort," Suzanna said, smiling, but she was also nervous. "He'll be fine. He's been better lately, and had good games against Atlanta."

"He's a professional. He has to be able to push everything else away and concentrate on the game. I had a pretty hefty Come to Jesus moment with him about that the day he called me, and he's sucking it up, concentrating on the team. Tim was always a real team player."

"I know, and I shouldn't be making it hard on him, not right now. My timing has never been really good."

"Are you kidding? Your timing was great, showing up in Pittsburgh like that in July. He was going down, Suzanna, straight down. Look at the August he had — fantastic. All we need now is to clinch the division, and I defy management to tell me they won't meet our price."

Suzanna sat back in her seat and looked at the agent. "That isn't why Tim plays, Mort. You do know that, don't you? He'd play for free, just so he could play."

"Oh, boy, do I know that. Tim and Jack both. Why do you think they need me?"

"Aunt Sadie says you've been great. Especially after Mr. and Mrs. Trehan died. Like a loving uncle, or something."

"They were good people, Suzanna, and they raised good sons. Okay," he said, leaning forward, his elbows on his knees. "Here we go. I brought you a program, in case you want to keep score again. Kolecki just singled."

"Thank you, Mort," Suzanna said, feeling those darn tears threatening again. "Just remember, Mort. This is just between the two of us. Jack and Keely and everybody know Tim wasn't feeling well, but they don't know why. I couldn't do that to Tim."

"You love him a lot, don't you, sweetheart?"

"Yes, I do. That's why this is so hard."

It would be easy, so very easy, to just give in, let what would happen just happen.

But then she'd never know, would she? Did Tim love her? Or did he need the "luck" she brought him? Did he think babies were neat in general, or that a baby they had together would be special?

Aunt Sadie and Mrs. B. said Tim was coming along, but he still had some growing up to do.

Maybe, Suzanna thought, pressing a hand against her belly, she did, too. . .

She was here, in the stadium. Mort wouldn't tell him where, or what he'd said to get her here; but she was here, and Mort had relented enough to tell him that Jack would be picking her up outside the players' entrance after the game.

It wasn't all he wanted, but it was a start.

She knew what the game meant to him, what it had always meant to him. She'd been with him from the start. Playing on the same team in rubber ball when the coaches had to remind them where first base was, then keeping the stats on every other team he'd ever played on. Good old Suze.

He didn't want good old Suze. He wanted Suzanna. His Suzanna.

But, for now, he'd take what he could get.

He stepped to the plate, smiled, because the Mets thought so little of his hitting anymore that they didn't care if he batted leftie.

Didn't they know that was the best way to get his juices up? Suzanna knew.

He looked up at the stands, toward the luxury boxes, and waved, then pointed to right center field. Shared a moment, shared their private joke on the Mets.

Lowering the bat, he drew an imaginary line across the plate. He took two quick swings, then coiled the bat, stared at the pitcher, sure his nod to the catcher meant he'd just agreed to a low fast one, outside.

You think I can't hit that one? Come on, wise guy, try it. Just try it.

He waved at the super boxes again as he rounded the bases and headed home behind Jeff Kolecki, his tape measure home run making it two to nothing in the top of the first.

He got to the dugout, where he shared high fives with his teammates, then raced into the clubhouse and threw up a whopping helping of ziti in marinara sauce.

Suzanna had planned, hoped, to be gone before Tim could track her down; but Jack's game had run late, and they were still waiting for the limousine to pick them up when Tim came outside and spotted them.

"Good game, Tim," she told him with an overly bright smile, then turned her head so that his kiss landed on her cheek. "One down, and two to go."

"They're already selling playoff tickets at home," Mort told him, clapping him on the back. "And, best of all, I've got a meeting in Philly next Wednesday with the money man."

"Uh-huh," Tim said, obviously not paying attention to Mort, as he kept staring at Suzanna. "How are you feeling?"

"Fine," she said, then frowned, hopefully a perplexed frown. "Why do you ask?"

"No reason. Hey, I'm just glad you're here. You, too, Keel."

"I wondered when you'd see me. I didn't think I was invisible," Keely said, putting both hands on her huge belly. "But you never know."

Suzanna tried not to look directly at Tim. He looked so good, if a little thin. *Sure. I get fat and he gets thin. Women are cursed.*

"Suze?"

"Hmmm?"

"I was thinking. Maybe, instead of driving all the way back to Whitehall, you could, you know, stay here with me?"

She shook her head. "I can't, Tim."

"You mean you don't want to," he said, his voice becoming slightly sharp.

"No, I mean I can't. Didn't you know that Sam sent out telegrams to all the wives? No cohabitation until this series is over. He said that cohabitation would sap your strength. Except he said it a little differently. It was probably all the *stop*s in the telegram that made it seem a little, well, tacky."

"Cripes!" Tim shoved a hand through his hair, which still bore the indentation from his cap. "What does the man think? That we're all going to have orgies, or something?"

Suzanna felt her cheeks growing hot. "Tim," she warned quietly, wishing Keely would stop giggling.

"No," he said, avoiding the hand she tried to place on his arm. "No, it's dumb, stupid. We're grown men, for crying out loud. Curfews on the road, the team bus, the damn meditation crap he pulled with us tonight. And now *this?* Stay here, I'll be right back."

Suzanna watched as Tim, looking so damn sexy in his black pullover and khakis, slammed back through the door, leaving the three of them standing there.

"Mood swing," Mort whispered quietly, so that Keely wouldn't hear. "I read a few chapters before I handed over the books. Typical mood swing."

"Oh, here we go," Keely said, pointing to the long black limousine that had pulled into the restricted parking area. "And here's my hero. How did it go, darling?" she asked as Jack stepped out of the limo and took Keely in his arms.

"We lost," he said. "I don't think the guys can get themselves up for the games, knowing we've already clinched. But that's not good. Streaks are streaks, winning or losing. They'll be better tomorrow. But you're not coming in, right, Keel? I think you're done with trips to New York until after the baby's born."

"Yes, master," Keely said, rolling her eyes at Suzanna. "See? They get all bossy when they think they can. Jack already knows this is my last trip to New York, because I told him so. He's just trying to look like macho-daddy."

"I think he's sweet," Suzanna said, those ready tears stinging her eyes once more.

"And I think I'm out of here," Mort said, kissing both women. "Sadie said when I couldn't remember who knows what and who I lied to last, it was time to get back behind my desk. See you tomorrow night, Suzanna?"

"Sure, Mort," she told him. "I'll be here, promise."

"What was all that about?" Keely asked, watching Mort walk away. "There's only one lie, that we don't know you're pregnant. And that's not even a lie, not really. I mean, if Tim *asked,* and we said no, then that would be a lie. This is just a secret, right?"

"Right," Suzanna said sincerely. One secret. Plus the one that Mort had told her about Tim. That Tim knew she was pregnant, and that he was throwing up every morning. Keely and Jack, and all the rest of them, couldn't know that. Of course, since Mort knew, it was always possible that Aunt Sadie also knew, although she probably wouldn't tell anyone else. Except maybe Mrs. B. But not Jack and Keely.

And *she* wasn't going to confide in Keely, not this time.

It was getting difficult to remember who knew what or, as Tim might say it, how to tell the players without a scorecard.

Suzanna smiled, thankful to see Tim heading toward them once more. "Look at that face. I don't think he won this one," she said to Jack.

"I have to go back to the hotel on the team bus," Tim said, his eyes still sparking blue fire. "But that doesn't mean you can't sneak into the hotel, get a room. Dusty wouldn't tell on me."

"Dusty?" Suzanna shook her head. "Would that be the same Dusty who told me about the one-in-three odds? That Dusty?"

"Never mind," Tim said, then muttered something under his breath. "Okay, okay. So I've got to stay with the team this weekend. But after we take this series —"

"Ah, there's the Tim we all know and love. Not a doubt in his mind."

"Shut up, Jack. Like I was saying, after we win this series, we'll have a free day before the divisional playoffs begin, but we'll need that for travel. That means another trip out of town for a five-game series we'll win in three. Your turn, bro."

"Me? I'm not going to say a word, Tim. You think you can win six in a row — with Phillies pitching? Hey, go for it."

"Thank you. Now, after we take the division, we go best of seven for the pennant. That's another week, more if we get rained out. Then four more to beat your Yanks, Jack — maybe six, if you're lucky — and then, by damn, I'm coming home."

Suzanna mentally added up the days, for games, for travel, possible rain outs. "But . . . But that means it could be well into the middle of October before you're home."

Tim put his hands on her upper arms. "I'll call every day, Suze, promise. And you still can come to the games, stay with the other wives who travel with the team. I really wish you'd do that, Suze."

"But . . . But Margo's going to have her kittens. I mean, Aunt Sadie isn't sure of the day, but we're pretty sure it will be within the next week or two. I can't leave her."

Tim backed up two steps. "You're kidding, right? I'm going to be playing for a chance at the World Series, and you're going to stay home and watch a cat?"

Suzanna tipped up her chin. "Yes, Tim, I'm going to stay home and watch a cat. You have a problem with that?"

He did, obviously. Oh, boy, did he ever.

But, instead of exploding, he surprised her by taking a deep breath, letting it out slowly, then saying, "Okay. Okay, Suze. Just come back tomorrow, and Sunday. After that, we'll play it by ear."

"And you're not angry?"

"Me? No, I'm not angry. It's all my fault anyway; everybody knows that. I should have had Lucky . . . snipped."

"Sam's waving at you from the bus, Tim," Jack said, with an inclination of his head. "I think you have to go. So do we. Time I got little mother here tucked up in bed."

"Ah, so thoughtful. And my feet hurt, Jack. Maybe you could carry me over to the limo?"

"How about I go find a wheelbarrow, sweetheart," Jack shot back at her, and Keely laughed as she took his hand, dragged him to the limousine.

"That's another thing, Tim," Suzanna said once Jack and Keely were in the backseat of the limo. "Keely's due October twenty-eighth. But Dr. Phillips . . . I mean, but her obstetrician told her she's showing signs that she may be earlier than that. If the Yankees make the Series, Jack has to be there for the radio broadcasts, so someone will have to stay with Keely."

"Aunt Sadie will be there, and Mrs. B."

"Mrs. B. is going to Tampa, to visit her sister. She leaves Tuesday and won't be back for at least two weeks, remember? Then, when she gets back, there's rehearsals every night."

"I forgot," Tim said, edging closer to her again, looking like he might want to kiss her. "Still, there's Aunt Sadie, right?"

"Tim," Suzanna said, sighing. "How do you want Keely to get to the hospital? In Aunt Sadie's little red sports car, or after trying to climb into that four-by-four with the Tweety Bird on the hood? And, before you answer, remember that I've driven with the woman. She's got a lead foot and thinks Stop signs really only mean *pause*."

Tim was silent for a few moments, a silence broken only by Sam Kizer's bellow of "Get your ass on board, Trehan!"

Then he said, "This is a conspiracy, isn't it? I've got this whole pack of women conspiring against me. Cripes, Suzanna, when will you think I've suffered enough?"

"This isn't about suffering, Tim. I'm not a vindictive woman. This is about learning what you want, and why you want it."

"I know why I want you, Suze," he said sincerely.

"Yeah. You won tonight. I know. And I'll be here tomorrow night, and again on Sunday. I promised Mort, who said I owed it to the team, even if I didn't owe it to you. But after that, Tim, you're on your own. I'm not expecting you to give up the pasta, or the bubble gum, or any of the rest of it. I just want you to decide if you want me because I seem to have stopped the curse from getting you, or because you want *me*."

"I just *said* that I —"

"Tim, your bus is waiting. Jack and Keely are waiting, and if she has to wait much longer, she'll want to go back inside and visit the ladies' room again, and we'll never get out of here, and I'm exhausted. So go. Please go."

He went.

She glared after him. He'd just shut his mouth, and he'd gone, without looking back.

Suzanna glared daggers after him. Since when had he become so damn amenable?

Tim sat in the last row of the chartered plane, scribbling on a notepad.

Jack knew Suzanna was pregnant, because Keely had told him, and Jack had told his brother.

Keely knew Suzanna was pregnant, because Suzanna had told her, and then Keely had told him.

Aunt Sadie and Mrs. B. knew Suzanna was pregnant, because either someone told them or they read it in the vegetables swirling around in their witches' cauldron, along with the bat wings and eye of newt.

Mort knew that Tim had been told by both Jack and Keely that Suzanna was pregnant.

The only one who knew nothing more than the fact that she was pregnant was Suzanna.

Interesting. The major player in all of this was the only one who seemed to be out of the loop.

But only Mort knew about the morning sickness and all the rest of it. And, unless the man wanted to see all of his toupees strung together, weighted down with rocks, and tossed into the nearest river, he'd keep his mouth shut.

Which meant, realistically, bottom line, that only Aunt Sadie and Mort knew about the morning sickness.

Mrs. B. was out of the picture, at least for two weeks, visiting her sister in Tampa.

Margo was nesting, or so Aunt Sadie called it, constantly having to be dragged out of closets and boxes and back to the padded bed Suzanna had bought for the birthing.

Lucky had come back from the vet yesterday morning, okayed for surgery, and was hiding out at Aunt Sadie's. According to his aunt, the cat would not be allowed back in the main house until the kittens were at least six weeks old, because otherwise he might hurt them.

Banished. Just like his master. Tim decided he was lucky he wasn't Lucky, or he'd be "snipped," too.

It was October eleventh, and the Phillies had won the playoffs, three to two in five games, and were now on their way to the next series, and the pennant. No time to go home, only time for meetings and more practice and Sam's latest innovation, Yoga.

Except that the manager had canceled the Yoga sessions after Romero's right leg had gone into such a cramp in the Lotus position that Jerry had had to get out of the whirlpool to help unbend him.

He still phoned Suzanna every day, and she still said she was fine when he asked her, and he still said he was fine when she asked him. Then they talked for a few minutes about the games, about Margo, about how much he hated his hotel rooms, and they hung up again.

Tim looked at his watch, then at the phone stuck into the back of the seat in front of his. It would be too late to call when they landed.

He grabbed the phone, read the directions, and dialed.

"Trehan residence," a male voice said after five rings, just as Tim was wondering if the machine would pick up and he'd end up talking to his own voice again.

Tim took another quick look at his watch. It was after nine. "Who the hell are you?" he asked, sitting forward, so that his seat belt grabbed at his hips.

"Oh, is that you, Tim? This is Sean. Sean Blackthorne. I'm afraid Suzanna can't come to the phone right now."

"Wanna bet?" Tim said, breathing heavily through his nose. "Get her . . . now."

"No, really, Tim, she can't. You see, Margo has gone into labor."

Tim closed his eyes, tight. "She's having the kittens?"

"Yes, she's gone into labor. Since I breed Persians — Margo's from one of my litters, you know — Suzanna asked if I'd come over when the big event was imminent."

"To answer the phone for her?"

"Oh, oh no, no, of course not. It's just

that Margo seems to have decided to have her kittens under your bed, Tim."

"My bed?" Cripes! Why didn't she rent a billboard? Tell everyone they slept in separate bedrooms.

"A lovely piece, Tim," Sean was saying. Tim barely heard him through the red haze that was building behind his eyes, inside his ears, everywhere. "Tester. Early Tudor. A very good reproduction."

The haze cleared a little. Blackthorne was talking about *his* bed. His and Suzanna's bed. Okay, okay, he could deal with that.

"So why can't Suzanna come to the phone?"

"Why? Because, Tim, she's under the bed, with Margo. Thankfully, it's a very high bed, but we still have to get her out from under there. Really, Tim, I hate to be rude, but I really do have to go help Suzanna."

"Uh-huh, okay. Sure," Tim said, stabbing his fingers into his hair. "Look, Suzanna already knows where the team is staying tonight, but she'd have to call before midnight, because Sam makes sure the switchboard won't put calls through to the rooms after that. So have her call me just as soon as Margo . . . just as soon as you know anything. Leave a message at the desk if she has to, okay?"

"Fine," Sean said, then added, "You're doing very well, Suzanna tells me. Congratulations."

"Don't watch, huh?" Tim asked, sure Suzanna could never be attracted to a man who didn't like baseball.

"I play the occasional game of handball at my gym," Sean said rather proudly, "but I'm afraid I don't really follow sports, per se."

Wuss. No wonder she'd dropped him after a couple of dates.

"That's great, Sean," Tim said, trying to relax. "Look, Margo's okay, right? I mean, Suzanna's crazy about that cat."

"She'll be fine. Unless, of course, she isn't. Breech births, things like that. She really is too young to be having a litter. She's already ruined for showing, mating with a common domestic shorthair, and who on earth would want nonpedigree kittens? I told Suzanna to have her aborted, but she wouldn't hear of it."

Tim hadn't known about that. But if he had heard about the option of aborting the kittens, he could have told Sean that Suzanna wouldn't go for it. Not unless a vet had told her it was the only way to save

Margo, which obviously he hadn't, because Suzanna had taken the cat straight to the vet.

"Again, I really have to — oh, good, Suzanna, you've got her. Wonderful. Tim? I have to hang up now."

"You'll tell Suzanna to call me — cripes!" he ended, talking to a dead phone.

Thirteen

There's no crying in baseball.
— Tom Hanks,
in *A League of Their Own*

Suzanna stood in front of one of the large windows in the living room, watching the rain, watching for headlights coming up the drive.

She'd been standing here, in this same spot, for over an hour, ever since Mort had phoned to say that finally Tim was on his way home from the stadium.

To lose, that was bad. To lose in front of the hometown crowd, that was awful. Terrible. The pits.

They had lost the first game of the league playoff, the one that would give them the National League Pennant. Then it had rained, for four straight days. And not just rain, but a minimonsoon.

How many hours had Tim spent on the phone with her from his hotel room? She'd played cheerleader, shoulder to cry on, devil's advocate and, all too often, weather person, telling him she was sure the storm would blow out soon, and they would be able to play again.

But when the rains stopped, the losing went on. They had come home down two games.

She'd wanted to go to the stadium, wanted to see him. Wanted. Just plain wanted.

But Dr. Phillips had put Keely to bed because she'd spotted a little, and Candy was just too much for Aunt Sadie to handle all day long. So she'd had to say no, I'm sorry, I just can't. "But I'll be watching every game, and cheering so loud you'll probably be able to hear me."

How hard it had been to sit in front of the television set and watch those games in Philadelphia. The Phillies had won one, and Tim had hit a home run; but they had dropped the next game when their ace reliever had walked the bases loaded in the tenth, then walked in the go-ahead run as Tim had argued vehemently that the last pitch had been a strike.

"Umpires always hate Philly," he'd told her later that same night, on the phone from his hotel. "We not only have to play better than the other team; we've got to work twice as hard to get past the bad calls."

"I know, Tim," Suzanna had said, glad he couldn't see her face.

"It's true, damn it. Oh, okay, most of them are pretty good, pretty fair. But there's a couple who really do hate us. It just figured that one of them would be behind the plate tonight."

"It was a ball, Tim. I saw the instant replay, five times. And, if that one had been a strike, the next one would have been a ball. He had you diving all over the place to save him from wild pitches. Sam should have taken him out when he walked the leadoff batter."

"And put in who? We've been working the bullpen hard, Suze. And Dave is our closer. He's had forty-eight saves this year."

"I know, Tim, I know, really I do. But I wish you could have taken him out. He was just plain wild tonight. He didn't have it."

"Whose side are you on?" he'd shot back, and she'd just sighed, then waited for him to calm down. He had a temper, but it always blew hot, then cooled quickly. She just had to wait him out.

"Okay, enough of that," he said in a few moments. "Can you come down tomorrow night?"

"Maybe, since Jack might be home before the Yanks go on the road. But I think it's going to rain."

And she'd been right.

Down three games to one, the rains had made it across country, to Philadelphia. Two more days of postponements followed before they finally took the field in a fine drizzle that soon turned into a near downpour.

But they played. The Yankees had already won the American League Pennant, although Jack couldn't get home, with all the pre-Series telecasts to do, and October was rapidly approaching November.

They had to play.

"Poor baby," Suzanna said, wiping away a tear. They had tried so hard, but trying to come back from a four-to-two deficit when the rain just got worse and worse as the innings went on was darn near impossible.

Suzanna closed her eyes, able to see how the national television cameras had zeroed in on Tim as he sat in the dugout and watched, through a veil of rain, as the new National League Champs celebrated on *his* field.

She would have expected him to stand in the dugout with his teammates for a few

313

moments, and then take off for the club-house, to throw a few things, to kick something. That she could have understood.

It had been so eerie, watching him.

He'd just sat there, holding his bat, because he'd been due up next if only Craig could have gotten on base. Two out, two on, down two runs, and Craig had popped up to the pitcher in the bottom of the ninth, leaving Tim to stand on deck, his bat in his hands. His useless bat in his hands.

Five minutes, maybe more, Tim had been shown sitting in that dugout. All by himself. Holding that bat.

Finally, as Suzanna sobbed, he'd picked up his catching gear, angled his mask over the top of his head, and walked away.

Half-drowned puppies dragged out of a sack tossed into a river didn't look so pitiful.

"Did they have to keep the camera on him so much?" Suzanna said now, wiping away new tears.

It was her fault, of course. She should have been there. Not because of any stupid curse, or superstition, or anything like that. But because she was Tim's wife, and he'd wanted her there. She had failed him, plain and simple.

Mort had kept her up to date on Tim's symptoms. The poor guy still got sick in the mornings. She wished she could tell him that she didn't, but how could she do that, when he believed that she didn't know he knew about the pregnancy?

Tim wasn't shy. He'd never been the reticent sort. If he wanted her to know that he knew about the baby, he would have come right out and told her. He hadn't, and he must have a reason.

Just as she had a reason for not telling him.

The same reason: their marriage had to be a real marriage first, based on real love and real commitment, and then and only then could either of them see this baby as anything else but a reason to stay married.

Not that he wouldn't have to give up the pretense of not knowing soon, even if she didn't tell him the news. Lord, but she was blossoming, much faster than Keely had, to hear her friend tell it. Her slacks were way too tight, so that she'd bought new ones, with elastic waists, and even those were getting snug. She'd have to buy more, in a larger size.

She could do that when she bought some new bras, also in a larger size.

Still, she felt good. Remarkably good, as

a matter of fact, while Tim was getting worse.

He'd had to leave one game, Mort had reported to her, with stomach cramps. He'd had two nosebleeds, which didn't make a bit of sense to Suzanna, but a check on the Internet — *everything* was on the Internet — told her that, yes, nosebleeds were also common with men experiencing "male pregnancy symptoms."

The article she'd read had termed the phenomenon "sympathy pregnancy," also noting that psychiatrists called it *couvades* syndrome, which was from the French word for "hatching."

And Tim, poor Tim, was textbook.

Maybe if she told him she knew.

But what good would that do? She'd never know, not really, if he was having the symptoms because he felt guilty, or if he was just doing what the article said that twenty-two to seventy-nine percent of all American dads-to-be did, at least to some degree.

The reasons given had not included guilt, but had only mentioned that the symptoms could come from sympathy for the mother, temporary, unexplained hormonal changes in the father, or feelings of displacement, which meant that the father felt the wife was getting all the attention and wanted some for himself.

That didn't sound like Tim, but when she'd read the words "make people know that he is a *major player* in the pregnancy," well, that one had definitely worried her.

But it didn't matter. None of it mattered, not tonight. Tonight, her big bad warrior was coming home, a loser. There would be no World Series against the Yankees. No trophy, no ring. No "Hey, Tim Trehan, now that you've been named MVP of the World Series, what are you going to do next?"

"Who wants to go to Disney World anyway? Seen one mouse, you've seen 'em all," Suzanna muttered, then blinked as she thought she saw headlights approaching through the tree branches that still held so many leaves this late in the fall.

She ran to the front door, waited until she heard the beep of Tim's car's alarm system engaging, and then opened the door, praying she'd know the right thing to say, now that he was here.

He had his head down as he approached the steps, then stopped, looked up at her, the rain rapidly turning him into a drowned rat.

"Hi, Suze. I'm late, I know, but I had to

stop for gas. You want to hear something? Something Dizzy Dean once said? You remember Dizzy Dean, don't you?"

"I remember, Tim. A famous pitcher, and a very quotable man. You and Jack were always testing me with famous baseball quotes. Come inside, and you can tell me what he said that you thought about tonight."

Inwardly, she was hoping it wasn't one she remembered: "The good Lord was good to me. He gave me a strong body, a good right arm, and a weak mind."

"No, that's okay, Suze. I kind of like being in the rain. I've been in it so much lately, I think I'm growing fins. Anyway, I stopped to get gas, and I thought about Dizzy Dean. You remember now?"

"No," Suzanna said, blinking back tears. He was being so brave. Her heart was breaking for him. "You'll have to tell me, Tim."

"Okay. He said, and I think I've got this one exactly: 'It puzzles me how they know what corners are good for filling stations. Just how did they know gas and oil was under there?' Isn't that a riot?"

"It's very funny, yes," Suzanna agreed, twisting her hands together, fighting the impulse to run down the steps, into his arms. "Tim . . . ?"

"We lost, babe," he said after a moment,

lowering his head. "We lost."

"I know," she half whispered, not caring that he'd called her babe. "I'm so, so sorry."

He looked up at her, and his smile flashed white in the light from the lamps on either side of the door. "Hey, no big deal. Somebody has to lose. Besides, I've just saved Jack ten bucks. He bet me we'd lose to his Yanks in the Series."

Suzanna tried to wipe at her wet cheeks as if the rain had hit her. "Ten bucks, huh? Well, it's nice to know Candy and the baby won't have to go without new shoes. Tim? Please, come inside."

"I won't be good company," he told her.

"I wasn't planning on asking you to entertain. But you're getting very wet, and you're going to drip on the foyer floor. Now come on, come inside, get a hot shower, and then I'll make you some soup or something."

Finally, he walked up the steps and into the foyer. "I'm not hungry."

"I am," she said. "I'm thinking chicken noodle, and then I can show you the kittens. You're going to just love them, Tim. The biggest one? He's already starting to open one eye."

"Uh-huh," he said, heading for the stairs.

"Maybe in the morning, all right? I'm beat."

She looked after him, watching as he held on to the banister, seemed to have to half pull himself up the stairs.

"Are you sure?" she asked him, feeling as if she'd just been rejected, deserted, proven useless to help him. "Because I could make something else. Ham and bean soup? Chili?"

"Night, Suze," he said, rounding the second-floor landing, heading for the back bedroom.

"Night, Tim," she said quietly, then walked into the kitchen, because the box of tissues was in the kitchen and she was pretty sure she was going to have herself a good cry.

Suzanna picked up the newspaper Tim had left on the kitchen table, and read the headline on the sports section one more time: CHAMPS AGAIN; YANKS IN FIVE.

Jack had to be so happy. With Keely due in only another six days, the last thing he'd wanted was for the Series to stretch to the full seven games.

Tim had sat with her to watch the away games, and he had driven to the Bronx to sit in the booth with Jack for the home games. How he had done it, Suzanna would never know, but Tim had been great, helping with the commentary on radio, complimenting the National League Champs, all that good stuff.

He smiled for the cameras, talked to all the reporters, answered all their asinine questions.

And then he came home and went straight back into his mummy act.

How long was the mourning period for losing a ball game? Suzanna was darned if she knew, but she was getting pretty tired of tiptoeing around Tim as if his best friend had just left him and his dog had died.

He slept, all the time, and when he wasn't sleeping, he was playing tapes of the playoffs. Watching himself catch, watching himself hit, watching himself strike out.

Keely had told her that Jack had been pretty much of a basket case when she'd met him, having just had to retire from the game because of a career-ending injury. She'd said he'd sulked, been snippy — yes, she'd said snippy — a general pain in her hindquarters.

Hey, why not. They were identical twins.

But enough was enough. Tim's career wasn't over, far from it. Mort had called

Tim to Philly only five days ago, to ink a new contract with so many zeroes in it that Suzanna got dizzy trying to count them.

He still had next year. He had lots of next years before he retired.

So, hey, get over it!

Suzanna stepped outside for some fresh air, saw the mailman turning around at the dead end, and headed down the drive. She walked back up the hill after collecting the Saturday mail, sorting through it as she walked.

Three of the envelopes intrigued her. One had a local postmark and was handwritten, obviously by a child, and the other two were from the two Philadelphia children's hospitals, CHOP and Saint Christopher's.

"Tim?" she said, dropping the rest of the mail on the kitchen table and heading into the den, where he was just sitting, the television set off, staring at nothing. "What are these?"

"Hmmm?" he said, as if just waking up and trying to rouse his mind.

"I said, what are these?" she repeated, waving the envelopes in front of him.

He reached for them, and she kept the handwritten envelope, handed him the other two.

"Oh, they're nothing," he said, tossing them on the coffee table.

"Requests for donations?" she asked, sitting down beside him.

"No, not donations. Aunt Sadie handles that end. These are different requests. Now that we have the schedule for next year, everyone wants to get their dibs in. I'll look at them later."

"No, I'll look at them now. Dibs? What sort of dibs?"

Tim sat back, sighed. "For my private box, Suze. I keep that Tiger's Den in right field for the kids groups, PAL, stuff like that, but the sick kids, well, sometimes they need to be somewhere more private. That's all."

Suzanna opened the first envelope and unfolded the letter, quickly scanning it. "You mean you loan out the box to sick kids? I knew about the Tiger's Den, and I think that's wonderful; but I didn't know you did this, too. That's really sweet of you, Tim."

"Yeah, well, it was Aunt Sadie's idea. We went to one of the hospitals one year, to see the kids, sign some autographs, and I came home pretty jazzed. I mean, those kids were so sick, and yet we could make them smile. I wanted to do more, more than just go there once in a while, or just send a check for new toys for the playroom or something. This is what Aunt Sadie came up with."

"You're a good person, Tim," Suzanna said, folding the letter that had been effusive with thanks even while requesting certain dates for the use of the box next season. "Sometimes, when I want to slap you silly for moping around here, I forget that."

He turned to her, grinning, and put his arm around her shoulders, surprising her straight down to her toes. It was the first time he'd touched her since before that awful night of their final loss. "As long as you're feeling so warm and fuzzy about me, what do you say we go upstairs?"

"How romantic," she said, pulling away from him before she could give in. Sex was the one absolute no-no. They were living together, coexisting, but not because they had great sex. They had to get to know each other again, know each other better, as grown-ups. Love each other. Then, and only then, was there going to be any sex.

He knew. She knew it.

"What's in this one, I wonder," Suzanna said, trying to make it look as if she was only reaching for the envelope and not trying to avoid him. "May I open it?"

"Sure," Tim grumbled, slouching against the back of the couch once more. "Knock yourself out."

The letter was filled with horrible misspellings, so that Suzanna knew no parent had seen it. "I wonder how he got your home address? Oh, here, he explains it. He's our paperboy. And he wants to know if you'll sponsor his baseball team next year."

She kept reading. "Oh, dear. It seems that Hardcastle Plumbing has decided not to be a sponsor anymore, and Scott — that's our paperboy — thought you'd like to do it, since it's your old team."

"You're kidding," Tim said, grabbing the letter from her. "Jack's and my old team? Yeah, here it is, he says so — they play on that old field behind the Fire Hall, just like we did. Man, when that alarm went off, we had to stop the game until the noise died down. My dad started that league. Hey, this is great. I'll bet they need new uniforms. We always needed new uniforms. You remember, Suze, right?"

"I remember the year you all got head lice because nobody ever washed out the batting helmets," she said, grinning at him, knowing he was only half listening to her.

"Yeah, that, too. And we had to share our gloves, and there were never enough bats or balls. Look, he put his phone number at the bottom," he said, standing up. "I'm going to go call him, okay?"

"Sure," Suzanna said as he headed for the phone in the kitchen and the scratch pad and pencil she kept there. "I think that's a great idea."

One step forward, she thought, resting her head against the couch cushions. Bless Scott. And bless baseball. Because baseball may taketh away once in a while, but then it always giveth again.

Tim eased himself into the seat between Jack and Suzanna, shaking his head. "It's a madhouse back there," he said, having just returned from backstage in the Whitehall High School auditorium. "A palm tree fell down, the female lead has a frog in her throat — I heard her talk, and I mean that literally; I think she swallowed one — and Mrs. B. is having one of her dictator on a rampage moments. Remember those?"

"You mean, when she starts warning everybody that if they don't shut up and shape up, she's walking straight out the door, and they can all just fall on their fannies by themselves?" Jack asked. "That kind of moment?"

"Oh, yeah," Tim said, grinning at Suzanna. "I remember you trying to calm her down before *Oklahoma*. I've always privately wondered if you have some sort of death wish."

"She'll be fine," Suzanna said, rolling her program into a log, then gripping it with both hands. "She just gets a little . . . emotional."

"Teenage boys catching a glimpse of Jennifer Lopez get a little emotional. Mrs. B. goes ballistic."

"Cute, Tim," Suzanna said, then picked up her head when a hand landed on her shoulder. "Oh, hi there, Joe. Aunt Sadie said you were going to be here. Hello, Bruno, so glad you could make it."

"Yes, ma'am," Bruno said, looking at the seat behind him as if wondering how anyone could truly believe the seats were one size fits all. "We wouldn't miss it, would we, Joe?"

Joey Morretti leaned down next to Tim. "I've got a minitapee stuck in my pants. Powerful little sucker, ya know. We'll be able to get it all on tape."

"Gee, that's . . . great, Joey. You planning to copy them, sell bootleg tapes to the cast?"

"Just at cost, just at cost," Joey explained quickly. "And, ya know, and a small . . . service fee."

"Of course," Tim said, shaking his head. "One thing about you, Joey, you know how to work all the angles."

"Hey, it's business. It's family, sure, but it's business," Joey said, sitting down in a huff just as Aunt Sadie came rushing up the aisle in her grass skirt.

Tim tried to sink lower in his seat, pretending not to know her.

"Bruno!" Aunt Sadie called out in a voice that was made to be heard in auditoriums, if the auditorium doubled as the floor of the New York Stock Exchange in the middle of a bull market. "Thank God you're here. We need you backstage."

"Me?" Bruno said, standing up. Bruno, standing up, was sort of like finding yourself in the shade of an elephant. "What'dya need, Aunt Sadie?"

The woman took several quick breaths, fanning herself with one of the leis around her pudgy neck. "It's Willard Osslid. He's not coming. I don't know," she said, fanning faster. "Something about emergency open-heart surgery, as if any of us believes that. The man's always bragging about his great lipids. Anyway," she went on, waving that off, "now we need a new islander. This is, after all, *South Pacific.*"

Tim raised his hand, as if he wanted to be called on in class. "Wait a minute. Willard Osslid? The janitor in the middle school? How's Bruno going to fit into his costume? The guy's about five-foot-three."

"It's not that small a costume," Aunt Sadie said, rolling her eyes. "Besides, the palm tree keeps tipping, and Bruno can just stay on stage and hold it up while he's being an islander."

"I don't know, Aunt Sadie," Bruno said, raising his shoulders as he seemed to be trying to sink his head between his shoulder blades. "I'm not real good at singing, and I don't know the words or nothin'."

"No, no, you won't have to sing, sweetheart," Aunt Sadie said, standing on tiptoe, to pat Bruno's cheek. "You just have to stand there. That's all." She lowered her head, adding quietly, "And keep everybody's mind off the fact that Marilee Wescott's voice sounds like metal scraping across the bottom of a very deep barrel."

Tim stood up, motioned for Aunt Sadie to back out of the row, so he could talk to her privately. "How small is this costume you want to put on Bruno?" he asked.

She shrugged. "He's an islander. They didn't wear fur coats, Timothy."

"Okay. And, since I just saw Willard Osslid peeking his head out from between the curtains, whose idea was it to use Bruno?"

"It . . . It was sort of a joint decision, Timothy. Margaret and I just thought . . ."

"You are a shameless, wicked woman, Sadie Trehan," Tim said, trying to be stern.

"Thank you, Timothy. Now, if you'll excuse us? Curtain is in five minutes, the overture any moment now, and we still have to adjust the loincloth."

Once Bruno and Aunt Sadie were gone, Tim sat down again, laughing quietly.

"What?" Suzanna asked. "What's so funny?"

"You'll see," he said, and took her hand in his. "I don't know why I thought this was going to be boring."

The orchestra hit the first notes just as Jack's cell phone went off, and he quickly pulled it from his pocket, put it to his ear.

"What? I can't really hear — you *what?* Three minutes? Did you say three minutes?"

"What's up, bro?" Tim asked, because his brother was looking pretty pale.

"Okay, okay. You just stay there, honey. What do you mean, where else would you go? I know you, Keel, you'll take a cab if I'm not there in ten minutes. So you just stay there. Did you call the doctor?"

Suzanna leaned across Tim, put her hand on Jack's knee. "Jack? Is it Keely? Is she all right?"

Tim didn't say anything. He was suddenly too busy trying to keep down the steak and French fries he'd had for dinner. Now he was having pregnancy symptoms for Keely? What in hell was the matter with him?

Jack flipped his cell phone closed and grabbed his coat from the empty seat back in front of him. "Gotta go, Keely's in labor. Damn woman's been in labor all day, she says now, but she didn't want to spoil Aunt Sadie's big night. Someday I'm going to kill that woman, I swear I am."

Suzanna was already on her feet, shoving her arms into her own coat. "I'm going with you, Jack. Someone has to stay with Candy."

"Me, too," Tim said, starting to rise, but Suzanna pushed him back down. "No, you stay here. Aunt Sadie has to have someone from the family in the audience."

"So, like now I'm chopped liver?" Joey

groused from the next row. "You guys never did want me around."

"Not now, Joey," Tim said, then turned and looked at his cousin. "Hey, wait a minute. You're Candy's uncle, you go. Suzanna and I can stay here, then drive Aunt Sadie and Mrs. B. over to the hospital. How's that, Suze?"

"Reasonable, I suppose," she said, also looking at Joey. "Candy's already in bed for the night anyway. Joe? Is that all right with you?"

"I dunno. Can I leave my minitapee with you?"

"Sure," Tim said, wincing as Joey reached into the front of his pants and pulled out a small black rectangle that was warm when he took it in his hand. "Maybe you could sterilize this thing first?"

"Picky, picky," Joey said, making his way to the aisle.

"Okay, gotta go," Jack said as Suzanna grabbed him, gave him a quick kiss. "I'll . . . I'll — see you later."

Tim nodded, then put his hand on his brother's arm for a moment before Jack sighed once more, then turned and ran up the aisle just as the overture ended and the curtains opened.

"Hey, down in front," someone called

out from behind them. Tim helped Suzanna off with her coat, and they both sat down once more.

"How long is this show?" he asked her.

"I don't know. Two hours? Oh, Tim, look! Look at Bruno."

Tim looked at the stage, and the mountain of a man standing at the extreme stage right, one shoulder propping up a papier-mâché palm tree, both hands crossed in front of him in the hope, the very vain hope, that nobody would notice that he was almost entirely naked.

"We're going to get raided and have to bail Aunt Sadie and Mrs. B. out of the pokey," Tim said, and Suzanna pressed her face against his shoulder, laughing.

Fourteen

Predictions are difficult, especially about the future.

— Yogi Berra

Suzanna and Tim arrived at the hospital, Aunt Sadie and Mrs. B. in tow, within an hour after *South Pacific* ended to a standing ovation, and some raucous cheering when Bruno took his individual bow.

"Excuse me," Tim said, approaching a nurse on the Maternity floor. "I'm looking for Jack Trehan?"

The young nurse looked at him quizzically. "Aren't *you* Jack Trehan? Where's your greens? I gave you greens. You can't go back in there, you know, until you're in your greens."

"Greens? What the hell are — oh, no. Wait. I'm not Jack Trehan. I'm his twin brother. Where is he?"

"Tim? Hey, bro, I thought that was you," Jack said, walking down the hallway. "How was our star? Where's your roses? We bought you roses," he asked, kissing Aunt Sadie's cheek.

"Never you mind about me, and the roses are in the car," Aunt Sadie said. "How is Keely?"

"You mean, other than driving everyone in here nuts?" Jack asked, grinning.

Suzanna stood to one side, the newest member of this family, and let them all talk. Besides, she had seen the nursery as they had passed, and was longing to go back, take a good hard look at all the babies.

"What's she doing?" Tim asked as Jack led the way to the waiting room.

"Oh, nothing much. Just telling everybody she thinks her labor stopped, so she wants to go home."

"Her labor stopped?" Tim looked at Suzanna. "Can it do that?"

Suzanna shrugged. "I have no idea."

"It can," Jack said, holding up a pair of green wrinkled cotton pants with a drawstring waist. "Man, these are weird. Anyway, the doctor's here, and she says Keely should please shut up and let the experts decide. In this case, the expert is a big monitor they've got strapped around her belly, and it's recording contractions. It's terrific. We can hear the baby's heartbeat, everything."

"So she stays put?"

"Oh, yeah. Even if the labor stops, she stays put. They already broke her water."

Tim sat down, and Suzanna thought he looked a little green himself. "Broke her *what?*"

Jack stripped off his shirt and pulled the green scrubs top over his head. "It's the damndest thing, Tim. I read about this stuff, and we talked about it in parents class, but to see the doctor walking in there with this big . . . this big *hook?* Let me tell you, I was pretty happy when the nurse said I had to leave, to get these scrubs on."

Suzanna sat down next to Tim. "Are you all right?"

He rubbed a hand across his mouth. "Sure, I'm fine. So you're going back in, Jack? They're going to let you stay?"

"Because I took the classes, yeah. I'm her coach."

"Do you know what he's talking about?" Tim asked Suzanna.

"Jack and Keely took classes, Tim. On how to breathe, when to push, that sort of thing. Jack helps Keely time her breathing, cheers her up, wipes her forehead, every-thing. Right, Jack?"

"That's it. Head cheerleader. And she concentrates on her focal point. For Keely, it's Candy's rubber duck," he said, then slipped into the bathroom to put on his scrubs pants.

"Keely is hoping to try natural childbirth," Suzanna explained to Tim, longing to touch a hand to his forehead, because he looked as if he might have a fever. "She's also investigated all the different drugs, and may use some, if it gets too difficult."

Tim nodded, took two deep breaths. "Okay. So how long? She's already been here for at least three hours, right?"

Aunt Sadie sat down on Tim's left, and told him, "Oh, honey, this is a first baby. We could be here until morning, even longer."

"Isn't that a long time?"

"No, Tim," Mrs. B. said from her chair across the small room. "Keely has to dilate, and that takes time. There are three stages to labor. The cervix has to —"

"That's okay, Mrs. B. I'll just wait," Tim interrupted quickly.

Suzanna found all of this fascinating, a sort of rehearsal for the day she'd have her own baby. Tim, on the other hand, looked as if he was rehearsing his trip to the guillotine, poor thing.

Jack came back into the room, looking rather adorable in his greens, and Suzanna thought about how Tim would look when his time came. Probably as green as the scrubs, if he didn't stop having all these male pregnancy symptoms.

"Why don't you guys go get some coffee or something?" Jack said. "I'm going to go stay with Keely."

Tim was the first on his feet. "Good idea," he said, taking Suzanna's hand. "Come on, my treat."

They all followed Jack to the door, then stopped behind him as he put his hands on either side of the doorjamb. "Wasn't that — Keely? What the hell? *Keely!*"

"Mr. Trehan?" the nurse who had been behind the rapidly moving litter asked, looking at Jack, then Tim, then at Jack again.

"Me," Jack said, poking himself in the chest. "I'm Mr. Trehan. See? Scrubs? What's going on? I thought Keely would give birth in the room she's — she was already in?"

"There's been a complication, Mr. Trehan," the nurse said; then Tim grabbed Jack with both arms as his brother moved to run down the hallway after his wife. "Don't worry, Dr. Phillips is very good."

Mrs. B. stepped past the twins and confronted the nurse. "Susan? Remember me?"

"Mrs. Butterworth? Hello!"

"Yes, dear, hello. Nice to see you again, even if you never got more than a C in my class. I suppose your talents lay elsewhere. Now, what's going on?"

The nurse looked from Mrs. B. to Jack, who was still struggling to get out of Tim's grip. "Ah . . . the placenta, Mrs. B. It started separating all of a sudden, and the baby's heart rate dropped."

"What does that mean?" Jack asked, his voice tight as Tim finally let him go.

"It's called placenta previa. It means, sir, that Mrs. Trehan has started to hemorrhage, and we have to take the baby now. Dr. Phillips may have to do a C-section, but she's hoping not, because the cervix dilates all the way when the placenta separates. We just have to get that baby out now, and the doctor wanted your wife in the operating room. I'm sorry, but you can't go in there."

"Oh, God," Jack said, slipping down in a crouch, his back against the wall, putting his head back and looking up at the ceiling. "Oh, my God . . . Keely."

Suzanna pressed both hands to her mouth as she looked at Jack, who was rapidly falling apart.

And that was when Tim stepped up to

the plate. "Have you seen this before, Susan?" he asked, his voice calm. "How serious is this? To Keely? To the baby?"

The nurse looked to Mrs. B.

"Tell him, Susan," she said in her teacher voice. "We're all adults here." She bent down, put a hand on Jack's shoulder. "This man has a right to know everything."

"Yes, ma'am. It's not without its risks, sir, to both mother and child," Susan answered, "but I've seen more good results than bad. Please, let me go check and see how things are progressing. Whatever happens, happens very quickly."

"Sweet Jesus," Jack said, burying his head in his hands as Tim half lifted his brother to his feet and clumsily gathered him into his arms. "We were going to have a baby, Timmy. That's all. People have babies every damn day. This isn't supposed to happen. . . ."

Suzanna brushed back tears as she walked down the hallway, toward the operating room. Jack needed a private moment, with family, and she had this overwhelming need to be closer to Keely, as if she might be able to *will* everything to be all right.

The nursery was ready back at the house. She and Keely had put it together while Jack and Tim were gone. Knowing the baby would be a boy, Keely had done it up in blue and green, with a wallpaper border of baseballs, mitts, and bats.

The diaper holder was stacked and ready. All the little shirts and kimonos were neatly in their assigned drawers.

There was a huge teddy bear sitting in the crib.

Just no baby. All they needed now was the baby, and the baby's mother.

Suzanna approached the double doors and tried to look through the glass, but she couldn't see anything but people in greens, so many people, all with their backs to her.

She pressed her hands against the glass, closed her eyes, willed Keely to be strong.

"You're a fighter, Keel," she whispered. "A real fighter. You won't let anything bad happen, I know it."

How long she stood there she didn't know. Hours, minutes. The longest minutes of her life.

And then she heard it. She heard the cry. A baby's cry. The most beautiful sound in the world.

"Jack!" she called out, running back down the hall and into the waiting room.

Jack got to his feet, brushing away his brother's hands. "What? What is it?"

Before Suzanna could say anything, Susan was there, and she was smiling. "Mr. Trehan? You can come with me now. It may look a little messy in there, but everybody's just fine. Your wife, your son."

Jack just stood there, his shoulders heaving, so Tim gave him a small push. "Go on, Daddy. Go see your wife and baby."

Jack nodded, just nodded, then slowly walked toward the door. He stopped, looked back. "It's all right," he said, tears streaming down his face, the look of joy still edged by fear on his face difficult to witness. "Keely's all right."

And then he was gone, and Suzanna walked into Tim's outstretched arms, to cry against his shoulder.

Three days later, Keely and John Joseph Trehan, Jr., were home in Whitehall, with Keely holding court from the den couch as the baby napped in his bassinet beside her.

"Me, me," Candy said, holding out her arms to her mother, and Keely helped the child climb up onto the couch to get a better look at her little brother.

"Are you sure you can hold her?" Suzanna asked. "She's all elbows and knees, Keel, and you're still pretty sore."

"I'm okay, Suzanna," Keely told her, kissing her daughter's curly blond head. "Candy has to know that she hasn't been replaced. Don't you, sweetheart?" she asked, nuzzling the child's neck.

"Me, me," Candy said, which was pretty much her answer to most anything, her question for most everything. In fact, Aunt Sadie had been rechristened Me-Me by the child, and seemed to revel in the name.

"Can I get you anything? Tea? Some of those sugar cookies I baked the other day?"

Keely looked at Suzanna quizzically. "And here I thought you liked me," she said, then grinned.

"Oh, come on, they're not so bad; you said so yourself. Although they're certainly not my mother's, even if I used her recipe."

"Not unless your mother was into baking sugar-coated hockey pucks, and I'm pretty sure she wasn't. We'll get back to your lessons in the next week or two, I promise. In the meantime, though, Suzanna, I think you're going to have to do some studying. You know, like learning that a capital T means tablespoonful, and a lower case t means teaspoonful. Just the basics."

"Got ya," Suzanna said, walking over to

the bassinet as little Johnny began to stir. "Do you think he's hungry?" she asked, wishing she didn't feel so nervous around the baby. But he was so small, and his entrance into this world had been so traumatic.

"No, I don't think so. He ate only an hour ago. Maybe he'll settle down again."

As if his mother's suggestion was an order from on high, Johnny closed his eyes and went back to sleep.

"Oh, he's so adorable," Suzanna said, blinking back tears. It was silly, but she'd been crying on and off for three days now, and her emotions showed no signs of calming down. "He's the most beautiful baby I ever saw."

"Sure. That's because he came flying out in such a rush when Dr. Phillips grabbed him. He didn't have time for his little head to go all cone-shaped or anything. But he is cute. I think he has Jack's mouth."

Suzanna grinned. "When he's sleeping, or when he's crying?"

"Both," Keely answered, rubbing Candy's back, as the child had now stretched herself belly to belly with her mother and was noisily sucking her thumb. "And I think he's going to have that same blond streak Jack and Tim have. Not that he has much hair right now, but I think I can see the different shade near his temple."

"I wonder if our . . ." Suzanna began, still leaning over the bassinet, then quickly stopped when Jack and Tim walked into the den. "Hi, guys," she said, standing up straight once more. "Did you find the right kind?"

Jack lifted a small plastic bag. "Do you people have any idea how many different kinds of pacifiers are out there? I know what you said, Keely, but when we got there, and saw them all, my mind sort of went blank."

"So he bought one of each," Tim said, giving his brother's shoulder a playful punch. "Johnny's going to have his pick. Suze? Ready to go home? Aunt Sadie's on duty in ten minutes, but maybe we could give Keely and Jack some time alone?"

"How considerate," Keely said. "Thank you, Tim. God bless Aunt Sadie, and Mrs. B., and everyone, but I was never alone in the hospital, and now I'm never alone here, at home. Not that I'm not happy for all the help."

Suzanna looked at Tim. "Well, I don't know about you, but I can take a hint. Come on, Tim, let's go."

That had sounded good, she thought as she and Tim exited the front door for their walk back to their own house. She'd sounded light, and upbeat, and all that good stuff. She didn't think anyone would even come close to guessing that the last thing *she* wanted was to be alone with *her* husband.

"Keely looks good," Tim said as they cut across the grass rather than walk down the curving drive to the road. "And Johnny's a lot better."

"He still has to take sun baths," Keely said, talking about the child's elevated bilirubin that had kept mother and baby in the hospital an extra day so that Johnny could be put under special lights in the nursery. "But his little nose isn't so orange anymore, is it?"

"I don't know; I didn't look," Tim said, guiding Suzanna so that she walked at the edge of the road, where macadam met lawns, and he took the outside position. Very mannerly and correct, just as his mother probably taught him, even if there were seldom any cars on this private road that led nowhere but to the houses built there.

"No, you haven't, have you?" Suzanna said, frowning. "Why is that?"

"I don't know. I look at Johnny, and all I can think about is holding Jack, feeling him tremble and shake, listening to him cry. My brother, crying? I don't think I've heard that since we were kids. Not even when Mom and Dad died — or if he did, he did it in private. He just fell apart in that waiting room, Suze, like his whole world was ending. Is it worth it? He could have lost Keely."

"But he didn't. Keely's fine, Johnny's fine, and they're all happy as pigs in mud. Tim, you can't stop living just because sometimes things don't work out the way you think they're supposed to. Why, if everyone thought like that, nobody'd have babies. Or get married, for that matter."

"You're right, you're right," Tim said, then sighed. "I just . . . I just didn't realize how *complicated* it all could get, I guess."

She wanted to tell him, longed to tell him. I'll be all right, Tim, please don't worry. *Please.*

"At least Margo had an uncomplicated birth, and the kittens are so adorable. I shouldn't like the one that looks just like Lucky, but I have to admit that he's my favorite."

"Candy gets one, right?" Tim asked, taking her hand in his. "And Sadie wants one, but I'd like to keep the other two, if you don't mind. One mini-Margo, one mini-Lucky."

"Four cats? You want us to own four cats?"

"Hey, why not?" he said, grinning.

They turned into their own property, crossing the bridge that ran above the Coplay Creek, and she stopped there, walked over to the railing.

"It's so pretty here," she said, looking at the tall, nearly bare trees, the red and gold leaves swirling in the water as it tumbled over smooth rocks. "So quiet, so peaceful. Oh, look, Tim — geese."

Tim rested his arms beside hers on the railing. "They'll be heading south soon, for the winter. Then the seagulls will be here."

"Seagulls?" she repeated, turning away from the railing and heading up the long, curved drive. "In Pennsylvania? You're kidding, right?"

"Nope. It started a few years ago, I don't know why. Used to be you only saw seagulls at the shore, when we'd go Jersey to the beach house Jack has there. But, a couple of years ago, we started seeing them in the wintertime, in the parking lots of the local malls. Now we even get them up here. Aunt Sadie feeds them, which could be one reason. Then, in the spring, they're gone again. I guess they decided all birds should have a winter home."

"They probably come here for the food, once all the tourists leave the shore," Suzanna said as she waited for Tim to open the door, turn off the alarm in the kitchen hallway. "I mean, think of all the restaurant dumpsters around here."

"Possible," Tim said, looking through the mail Suzanna had placed on the kitchen table before heading over to Keely's. "So, Suzanna — when are you going to tell me you're pregnant?"

"Wha— what?"

He put down the mail and turned, looked straight at her. "I said, when are you going to tell me you're —"

"I heard you," she said, pulling out a chair and sitting down before she fell down.

"Heard, but haven't answered," he pointed out, walking over to the counter and lifting the lid on the cookie jar. "I like these," he said, holding up one of her hockey puck sugar cookies. "If we're ever attacked by marauding seagulls, we can use them as weapons."

Suzanna heard him. She saw him. She just didn't understand him.

"Tim, I —"

"Do you want to know how long I've known?" he asked, his tone still light, although his eyes seemed to have gone cold. "Do you, Suze? I've known since Aunt Sadie's birthday party. Nearly two months, Suze. I've known for almost two months. I even know your due date, April fourteenth. It's November, Suze. So I'll ask you again, when were you going to tell me?"

This wasn't going right. When Suzanna thought about this moment, she thought about him coming to her, telling her he loved her desperately, with or without a baby, with or without the Trehan curse, with or without anything but the fact that he loved her. *Her.*

Didn't he understand that? First he would tell her he loved her, and *then* she would tell him about the baby.

But he hadn't said a word. He still slept in the back bedroom. He rarely even tried to kiss her. She still went to work each day, and he still spent most of his free time with Jack, the rest of it overseeing his bowling alley and the irrigation project at his golf course. They were living together, but they were living separate lives.

"I . . . I was working my way up to it," she said at last, knowing he was waiting for her answer, knowing that answer sounded lame, so very lame.

"Uh-huh. Why?"

"Why?" She looked at him, her eyes wide. "What do you mean, why?"

"I mean, why were you working your way up to it? You're pregnant. I'm the father. I *am* the father, right?"

Suzanna felt the blood drain out of her cheeks. "You . . . you *bastard!*"

"That's what I thought. Relax. I know I'm the father, Suze. I always knew that. But you'd be surprised at the insane thoughts that can dig into your mind when you know your wife's pregnant and she won't tell you."

"I . . . I never thought of that . . ." she said quietly.

"No, I know you didn't. I'll bet you also didn't think about what it was like to call here from the road and wonder if you were still here, or if you'd decided to leave, have our baby somewhere, send me divorce papers."

"I wouldn't have — oh, Tim. I . . . I never looked at any of this from *your* side, did I?"

"No, babe, you didn't. I'm in a pennant race, and I'm going nuts every moment, wondering where my wife is, why she's hiding things from me. If she'll even be there when I get home. Not a lot of fun, Suze."

She nodded, embarrassed, and sorry, and — wait a minute. He was pushing all the old buttons, and she was still responding in all the old ways.

"Excuse me, Tim, but when did this all become about *you?*" she asked, getting up from her chair. "What about me?"

"Come again?"

"Me, Tim. Your wife. You know, the woman you married because she was the lesser of three evils?"

"I explained that," he said, putting down his half-eaten cookie.

"Sure, you explained that. Right after Dusty spilled the beans, you explained that. Was that supposed to make it all better? Tell me, Tim, what would have happened if you'd gotten hurt? Couldn't play anymore? Had to retire, like Jack? Would that have meant that good old Suze had failed to come through for you this time? Would I have been expendable then? You don't want this baby. We never even talked about babies, except when you got all weird about birth control."

He made a face. "That's nuts. We're married, and we're going to stay married. And I want this baby."

"Oh, really? And I'm supposed to believe this?"

"Yes, damn it, you're supposed to believe this."

"Why? Because you *say so?* Let's replay this, from *my* side. I'm pregnant because my husband doesn't even speak to me enough about the *real* things in life to tell me he doesn't *want* a baby right now, and I'm going nuts every moment, wondering why my husband married me, what else he's not telling me. Because he lies to me. Lies about why he married me, lies about a damn cat. Lies, or hides, or just plain ignores. You knew I was pregnant? Well, Tim, *I* knew you knew I was pregnant. I even know you're feeling so damn guilty you're having male pregnancy symptoms. But did you say anything? Ever? No, you didn't. Because we don't *talk,* and when we do, you *lie* to me. Like you said, Tim. *Not* a lot of fun."

"Damn it," Tim said, leaning against the counter. "What happened, Suze? We used to be able to talk to each other. Why has getting married ruined such a great friendship?"

"I . . . I don't know, Tim," Suzanna said, heading toward the back stairs to the bedrooms. "Maybe it wasn't such a great friendship in the first place. Maybe it was all me, giving, and all you, taking. Did you ever think about that?"

He didn't follow her when she climbed the stairs, and a few seconds later she heard the back door slam.

Tim cut around the house to the front and headed for the bridge, and maybe Jack's house. Because Coplay Creek was just that, a creek, and not deep enough to drown himself in.

He walked along, his hands dug deep into his pockets, replaying his and Suzanna's fight in his head.

She was right. Damn it, she was right.

Good old Suze.

God, how he hated that. How he hated himself for ever thinking that, ever saying that.

Suzanna was right. He was a bastard. Selfish. No good. Immature.

Nauseous.

But he loved her. He did, damn it.

At the hospital, when everything started going south with Keely and little Johnny, he'd held his brother, but all he could think about was Suzanna. What would he do if something ever happened to Suzanna?

He couldn't live without her. He didn't

want to live without her.

And yet today, after three days of near agony, when he'd decided it was time, way past time, for him to let her know he knew she was carrying his child, everything had gone from bad to worse.

He needed to talk to somebody. He needed to talk to Jack.

No, not Jack. Jack was busy being a happy father, he and Keely playing happy family. He couldn't rain on that parade.

So who was left? Not Mort, not this time, because he had to be the one who had told Suzanna about his pregnancy symptoms. Not even Jack knew about those.

Not Aunt Sadie, because she was at Jack's house, and not Mrs. B., because she was substitute teaching all this week.

There was nobody. Nobody. He was all alone.

"Hey, Tim–bo!"

"Oh, shit," Tim muttered under his breath. "Is the whole world out to get me?" he asked as Joey pulled up beside him in his humongous four-by-four.

"Hey, thought that was you. I was just going to see the kid; but when I saw you, I let Bruno out, and I kept coming. We came to see the baby, ya know, but that can wait.

What ya doin', walking around out here?"

"Trying to be alone?" he answered, knowing there was little hope that suggestion wouldn't just go zinging right over his cousin's head.

"You look pretty bad, Tim, like you just lost your last friend," Joey called out as Tim kept on walking. "Just let me park this thing, and I'll walk with you, okay?"

"Why not," Tim grumbled. "God's punishing me, and I deserve it." More loudly he said, "Sure, Joey, and then you can help me with my troubles, right?"

Joey hopped down out of his vehicle, hit a button on his key chain that activated the security system, and jogged over to Tim. "Me? Help you? There's a switch. Okay, let's try it. How can I help you?"

Tim looked around, and his gaze landed on some boulders the builders had bulldozed into a pile on the lot where a three-story Georgian colonial was almost under roof. He'd have new neighbors soon after Christmas. "Let's sit down," he said, motioning toward the boulders.

"Hey, sure," Joey said, bounding toward the boulders and hopping up on one of them, like a kid just offered a treat. "Man, this is cool. We never talked, ya know that? Never."

"Yeah," Tim said, selecting another boulder for himself. "There's a lot of my not talking going around."

"Huh?" Joey asked, shaking his head. "You been, ya know, tippling?" He lifted an imaginary bottle to his lips.

"No, but it was going to be my next choice," Tim said. "Joey? Do you know that Suzanna's pregnant?"

"Me? Naw, I don't know — oh, okay, sure. I knew. Everybody knows. Why?"

For the next twenty minutes, maybe longer, Tim talked, and Joey listened. He told his cousin everything: about the curse, about meeting up with Suzanna in Pittsburgh, about the birth control — or lack of it — even about Lucky and Margo. And when Joey just sat there, looking almost pontifical, he went for broke and told him about the male pregnancy symptoms, and the fight he and Suzanna had just had.

"You screwed up, Tim-bo," Joey said at last, nodding sagely. "Big time."

Tim slapped his hands on his knees and stood up. "Leave it to you, Joey, to tell me the obvious. Hey, never mind. Thanks for listening. I think I needed to say it all out loud, you know?"

He started walking away, but Joey clambered down from his boulder and followed him. "Hey, wait. You want help? I'll help you."

"You?" Tim shook his head. "Thanks, but —"

"No, really. I'll help you. I'm taking this psych course at the community college, and — what? Why're you rolling your eyes like that?"

"No reason. Go on, Joey. Let me have it. Tell me how I've got to court her and take things slow, and prove that I love her. I don't know how to do any of that, now that she hates me this much, but you can tell me anyway."

"I'm not telling you anything like that, Tim-bo. She's just as in the wrong as you are."

Jack stopped, tipped his head to one side. "*She's* in the wrong?"

"Heck, yeah. You're tossing your cookies. Your nose is bleeding — you might want to dab at it there with something, Tim-bo. You've got headaches, and cramps, and you're telling me you have a toothache? You're telling me you read about all these symptoms, and you're having all of them? Sounds to me like you're already suffering plenty, ya know? So what's she doing? Except maybe busting your chops."

Tim chewed on this for a few moments,

after getting over the idea that he was actually listening to his cousin. "So, what you're saying is, we're both at fault? Not just me?"

"Hey, mostly you, definitely. But she's not being any walk in the park, now, is she?"

"No, she's not," Tim said, thinking about his lonely bedroom.

"You wanna know what's lacking here, Tim-bo? I'll tell you what's lacking here. Trust. T-r-u-s-t-t, trust. You can't have anything else if you don't have trust. I know that, because we're studying it."

"Only two *T*s, Joey," Tim said absently, as the gears in his head had begun to spin. His wacky cousin had a point, a real point. Hadn't he and Suzanna just been yelling at each other about how he couldn't trust her to be there when he came home, and she couldn't trust him to stay with her for any reason except that she was pregnant? Trust. Yeah. That was it. There was no damn *trust*.

"You're nodding your head, Tim-bo. That means you think I'm right, right?"

"Right, Joey," Tim said, putting his arm around his cousin's shoulder. "Now, what do we do about it?"

"Well," Joey said, hitching up his pants,

then swiping a finger under his nose. "First, you prove to her how much you want this baby, but you want her even more, right? She needs to know that, right?"

Tim nodded, wiping at his own nose, his handkerchief coming away with a few spots of blood on it. "Right."

"And no pressure, okay? None of this chasing her around the table, stuff like that. Women don't want sex so much as they want holding hands, and intimate dinners, shit like that."

"You learned this in psych class?"

"Naw, my mom told me, years ago, back in high school. Right after she found the condom pack in my wallet on prom night. So, you gonna listen to me? It's going to take time, because you two really screwed up, but I think you can do it. Trust her. Give her time to trust you."

"Okay. I'll try it," Tim said, looking over his shoulder, in the direction of his house. His and Suzanna's house. "What have I got to lose?"

"What have you got to lose? You're asking me? Okay. Everything, Tim-bo. You've got everything to lose," Joey said with a shrug, and Tim looked at his cousin with new respect.

Fifteen

You can lead a horse to water, but you can't stick his head in it.
— Paul Owen, player

Since Tim knew anyway, Suzanna finally broke down and headed to the maternity shop in the mall, Aunt Sadie going along with her.

"Fat clothes," Suzanna said, holding up a pair of jeans with a huge elastic front panel in them. "I don't want to wear fat clothes."

"This from the woman who just downed two hamburgers and fries? How much have you gained, dear?"

Suzanna hung her head. "Fifteen pounds, seven of them this month," she said, a sudden memory of her mother, years ago, gently steering her away from potatoes and toward the broccoli invading her head. "Dr. Phillips told me that the month I really begin to show is the month I'll gain the most weight. At least that's been her experience with her patients. I've got a thirty-five-pound limit, so I'm still doing okay."

Aunt Sadie began ticking off on her fingers. "December, January, February, March, most of April. Five months, divided by twenty, leaves four pounds a month. Can you keep to that?"

Suzanna held up a knit, turtleneck top, cut on the bias, and large enough to use as a couch cover. "I have to do this, Aunt Sadie. I used to be fat, and I don't ever want to be fat again. It's all Tim's fault, you know."

"Oh, good, let's blame Timothy. He deserves it."

"No, seriously, Aunt Sadie. He used to feed me. Constantly. His mom was such a great cook, and he always shared with me so I'd share the great lunches my mom packed for me. Except he got the home-cooked roast beef sandwiches, and I got the lemon sponge cake. He'd eat two sandwiches, I'd eat two desserts. And, believe me, the last thing I needed every day was two desserts. But it didn't stop there."

Aunt Sadie pulled a nursing bra off the rack, looked at it, quickly put it back. "No? Where else did it go?"

Suzanna sighed. "I started eating to feel good. There's really no other explanation, although nobody had that one back then. It's only in the last few years that science has started talking about eating as a comfort in teenagers. Tim went to a dance; I stayed home and ate a half gallon of chocolate marshmallow ice cream. Tim gave Mindy his class ring, and I ate a whole bowl of raw chocolate-chip batter. God, I was sick for three days after that one. Not that I only started in high school. I was already pretty hefty in grade school, thanks to my mother's own great cooking." She looked at the other woman. "Do you suppose that's why I don't cook? Because, if I did, I'd eat it all?"

"Could be, I suppose. But it was baby fat, Suzanna, and gone now."

"Only because I finally wised up, realized what I was doing, and changed my diet. And moved away from Tim. Now I'm back and what do I get — baby fat."

"And a baby," Aunt Sadie reminded her. "This is entirely different."

"Yeah? Explain that to my stomach, would you? All I want to do is eat. Eat, eat, *eat*. When I'm upset, it's all I do. Eat."

"Keely ate everything that wasn't nailed down for several months, as I recall, once the morning sickness stopped. You know you're trying to make a perfectly rational reaction to being pregnant just another thing that's wrong in your life, don't you, dear?" Aunt Sadie said, moving on to the rack of maternity underwear. "Now, these don't look so bad."

"Am I, Aunt Sadie?" Suzanna asked, taking a pair of underpants off the rack. "Darn, and I wanted to blame Tim."

"Hello, ladies. Which one of you is expecting a great event?"

"Cute," Aunt Sadie said, "but nothing but a discount is going to get me to open my purse any wider than I've already planned."

"Oh, Aunt Sadie, that's not why I brought you with —"

"I know, dear, but I've planned your wardrobe as my Christmas present to you. Your wedding present, too, since we never got to throw you and Tim a party."

The clerk looked from Suzanna to Aunt Sadie, measuring both of them, an avaricious glint in her eyes. "You want to start with undergarments? That's a good place to start. When are you due, dear? You're definitely blooming. How about we go into the dressing room, dear, and I'll measure you?"

"Oh, God," Suzanna said, wincing. "I'm going to hate this."

And she did. She hated that maternity bras, while not really terrible, weren't exactly great, either. She hated that maternity underwear, as explained by Martha, the salesperson, was to be worn with the waistband inches higher than her rapidly disappearing waist.

Standing in front of the mirrors — why on earth anyone would put three-panel mirrors in a maternity shop dressing room was *totally* beyond Suzanna — dressed in nothing but maternity bra and the above-the-waist underpants, she decided that the next time Tim saw her naked would be in his *dreams!*

Because there was no way in hell he was going to see her looking like this.

Aunt Sadie came into the room without knocking, carrying an armload of slacks, sweaters, blouses, and a few dresses. "Ready to start?"

"Ready to go hide," Suzanna said, grabbing a pair of the slacks and quickly stepping into them. Oh, this was great. These fit around her expanded waist . . . and now the underwear stuck out above them. "Quick, hand me one of those tops."

A very long ninety minutes later, Suzanna and Aunt Sadie sat in the pizza parlor across from the maternity store with several bags on the floor beside them, Aunt Sadie sipping a soda, Suzanna working on her second slice of pepperoni pizza. She'd skipped the garlic bread, and figured she was at least making a start on eating more sensibly.

"Martha told me she thinks you look just a little too advanced to be only four months along. She wanted to know if you've had a sonogram."

"Had one," Suzanna said around a mouthful of pizza. "On my first visit. I don't get another one for a couple of months, as long as I'm doing well. Why? What does Martha think?"

"Other than that, if she's on commission, she's made one great sale today? Well, dear, she mentioned twins. So I told her that Tim was a twin, and —"

"Grrrummmmff!" Suzanna quickly picked up her napkin and coughed her half-chewed pizza into it before she choked. Then she grabbed another napkin and wiped at her eyes. *"That* is not amusing, Aunt Sadie."

"Funny. I thought it was," Aunt Sadie said with a grin. "When do you go to the doctor again?"

"Next week, and Tim insists on going with me."

"He's concerned."

"He's *nuts,* that's what he is," Suzanna

grumbled. "Like I want him there when I step on the scale? I don't think so."

"But he's going?"

"Yes, he's going. I warned him that I'm going to tell Dr. Phillips about his male pregnancy symptoms, and he doesn't care. He says they're not so bad now. But I saw him downing some antacids last night, so he's lying to me. I'm telling you, Aunt Sadie, the man is driving me crazy."

"How?"

Suzanna looked at the rest of her pizza and knew she wasn't hungry anymore. "How? It's school lunch all over again. He takes me out to dinner, that's one. He rents movies and insists I watch them with him, then pops popcorn — with butter — and all but hand feeds it to me. And he *reads*. He has more books on pregnancy and delivery than Dr. Phillips, I swear it. He's *obsessed* with my labor and delivery."

Aunt Sadie nodded sagely. "Because of Keely. He's worried, Suzanna. He's really worried."

"Well, he should be," Suzanna said, knowing she was being entirely irrational. "He is the one who got me this way, remember."

"You know, dear, some would call you heartless."

Suzanna bit her lips together.

"I mean, he's being so good, trying so hard. We told him to court you, and he's —"

"Wait. Back up a moment. You *told* him to court me? Who's *you?* Keely? Mrs. B.? Or did you just send out postcards all over Whitehall, asking for a vote?"

Aunt Sadie nodded, not realizing that suddenly, Suzanna had designs on the woman's neck, and her hands squeezing it. "He's been so lost. We know he made a mistake, Suzanna; but he really meant well, and we told him he'd just have to take his time, prove to you that he —"

Suzanna held up her hands, really angry now. "You can stop there. I think I get it. Does anyone in this family have any idea what the concept of *private lives* is all about? Since when did Tim and I become some darn committee project?"

Aunt Sadie didn't even blink. "Since the two of you began making total asses of yourselves, I suppose."

Suzanna's mouth opened, then shut again, and she sagged in her seat. "Oh," she said in a small voice. "Okay."

"He loves you, Suzanna," Aunt Sadie said, reaching across the small table to take one of Suzanna's hands in hers. "He didn't know it when he married you, but he knows it now."

Now the tears were threatening. "He doesn't say anything."

"Doesn't he? He's reading all the books. He wants to go to the doctor with you. He's popping you popcorn."

"With double butter," Suzanna said, trying to maintain her anger, but it wasn't working.

"It's you now, isn't it, dear?" Aunt Sadie asked, giving Suzanna's hand a final squeeze, then sitting back in her chair. "You're the one who isn't sure."

Suzanna lowered her head, feeling the heat rush into her cheeks. "I love him . . . but . . ."

"But you think maybe it's leftover puppy love, like the puppy fat you got rid of years ago?"

Suzanna looked at Aunt Sadie, blinking back tears. "How can I know? How can Tim know? We got married for all the wrong reasons."

"Tim, to save himself from a worse fate, and you, because you figured it was time you finally won one?"

Suzanna made a face. "That's it, in a nutshell." She put a hand on her belly. "This baby deserves better than that, Aunt Sadie."

"Yes, dear, he does. Or she does. Or" —

Aunt Sadie paused, smiled — "*they* do."

"Oh, God . . ." Suzanna said, sinking in her chair once more.

"Don't look. You promised not to look."

Tim dutifully turned his back as Suzanna stepped on the scale, then turned around as the nurse, obviously not part of Suzanna's secrecy plot, brightly called out, "One hundred forty-three. Hmmm, that's another eight pounds, Mrs. Trehan. Dr. Phillips is not going to be happy."

Suzanna mumbled something under her breath as she stepped off the scale, then glared at Tim. "Not one word. Not a single damn word, you got that?"

He held up his hands. "Who? Me? I wouldn't even think about it."

Then he grinned, once Suzanna was walking ahead of him, into one of the examination rooms. What was she worried about? She looked cute, damn cute. Her cheeks were fuller, her breasts were — no, he couldn't think about her breasts, not if he wanted to sleep nights. And her backside? Hey, there was a handful. He had a flash of a Lone Star song in his head, one of his favorite groups. Something about hating to watch a lover leave, but sure loving watching her go.

"Are you coming, or what?" Suzanna asked from the doorway, and Tim quickly caught up with her, then wished he hadn't.

Small room. Big table. Those stirrup things for Suzanna's feet — somebody would have to hunt him down and tackle him to get him in that position.

And artwork. A huge poster showing the nine months of fetal development, in color. Another showing the stages of labor — the one showing the baby's head half out of the mother was particularly vivid.

And a sort of plaster of paris wall hanging with arrows drawn on it and words like cervix, and uterus, and vulva and . . . Well, he really didn't want to look.

After helping Suzanna onto the end of the table, where she sat, glaring at him, he found a pamphlet and decided the safest thing he could do was take a chair and read it.

He put it back down when he saw it was a breast feeding instruction pamphlet, with photographs. Not line drawings. Photographs.

What was he doing here? He felt about as out of water as a fish on top of the Alps.

"You could go back to the waiting room," Suzanna said as he stared at his feet. At least they were his feet. He could trust his own feet.

"No, that's okay," he said, rubbing at his gut. The burrito he'd had for lunch was lying there, like Gibraltar. "I have some questions for the doctor."

"You're kidding."

He looked up at her. She looked so cute in that long sweater and those slim jeans. Didn't she know how cute she looked? "No, really. I want to know about those parents classes."

"Birthing classes? Tim, I don't think you want to do that."

"Why not?"

"Because, then you'd have to be in the delivery room, remember? Like Jack?"

"Jack never made it to the delivery room," Tim said, feeling the muscles clenching in his jaw.

"You know what I mean."

"Yeah, I know what you mean. You don't want me there. You don't want me to be your cheerleader."

"Oh, Tim —" Suzanna said, sighing. Then the door opened, and Dr. Phillips and a nurse stepped into the room.

Tim ran a hand under the collar of his shirt, suddenly claustrophobic. What was he doing here with all these women and all these pictures of . . . women stuff? His had been a male household, except for his mom, who definitely had been outnumbered.

He had a sudden flashback of the day he'd been looking for another bar of soap and found his mom's sanitary products under the bathroom sink. He'd asked what the box was for, and got his one and only sex education lesson from his mother.

After that, he did his best to stay away from "women stuff."

Now he was surrounded by it.

"Mr. Trehan, how nice to meet you," Dr. Phillips said, extending a hand to him as he stood up, remembering his manners. "You look very much like your brother."

"Yeah. Identical twins."

"Interesting. One sperm, one ovum, and a split. Fraternal twins are more common. Well, Suzanna," she said, turning to her, "I take it any morning sickness is definitely all gone?"

Suzanna blushed to the roots of her hair. "I gained eight pounds. I know."

"You're still under the limit, and even limits have extensions; but I would like to measure your belly if that's all right with you?"

Suzanna nodded, then lay back on the table, the nurse draping a paper sheet over her.

"I . . . I mean, maybe I should . . . ?"

"No, no, Daddy," Dr. Phillips said. "You're a part of this."

Yes, he was, wasn't he? Tim stepped closer to the table.

"What's that?" he asked as the nurse squeezed something from a tube onto Suzanna's now bare belly, and then Dr. Phillips began moving a small plastic rectangle across Suzanna's skin.

"I'm looking for the baby's heartbeat," the doctor told him, and Tim had this sudden urge to sit down again. But he stood there, waiting. And waiting. And waiting.

"Ah, here we are. Hiding, weren't you?" Dr. Phillips said as a quick *thump-thum-thump* echoed in the room. The nurse held up her arm, watched her wristwatch. "So?"

"One-forty-four, Doctor."

"Thank you. All right, now let's measure."

Expecting something else high-tech, Tim was surprised to see the nurse hand the doctor a regular cloth tape measure. He looked away as she pulled Suzanna's slacks lower, then measured from there to Suzanna's navel.

She glanced over at Suzanna's opened chart, then looked at the tape measure again.

"Hmmm, let's do that one again, shall we?"

"Why? What?" Tim asked, instantly panicking.

Dr. Phillips ignored him. "No, that's right. Suzanna, when was your last sonogram?"

"Why? What?" Tim asked, reaching the second level of panic. After this, it was either the doctor talked to him, or he grabbed her by the shoulders and shook her until she did.

"Nothing's wrong, Mr. Trehan," Dr. Phillips said, going over to the sink and washing her hands as the nurse helped Suzanna pull up her slacks and sit up once more. "It's just that your wife's uterus is growing faster than I expected. Unless we've got the due date wrong, of course. Suzanna? Are you sure of the date?"

"No, I told you I wasn't. The earliest I can figure is near the end of July," Suzanna said, looking at Tim.

He flinched, remembering the day he'd tossed that "if I am the father" line at her in the heat of anger.

"Yes, I remember now," Dr. Phillips said, paging through Suzanna's chart. "Irregular periods. All right, this is what we do. We get another sonogram. Iris? Set it up, please."

"So that's it?" Suzanna asked. "You think I'm farther along than we thought? But I can't be."

"Then maybe we've got multiples."

"Multiples?" Tim asked, the sound of the ocean somehow rushing in his ears.

"Twins, Mr. Trehan. I only got one heartbeat, but twins can be tricky. One could be hiding behind the other one."

Tim didn't remember hitting the floor. . . .

It was the longest ten days in Suzanna's life, waiting for the appointment at the hospital, and the sonogram that would tell them if, just maybe, she was carrying twins.

"Are you okay?"

She looked across the car at Tim as he cut the engine in the hospital parking lot. "I'm fine. Please stop looking at me as if I'm going to *explode* at any moment. You're driving me crazy."

"Sorry," he said, pulling the key from the ignition. "It's just that . . . I mean . . . *twins?*"

"Or I'm just fat," she said, opening the door and stepping out into the late November cold. She pulled her jacket around her, but it didn't quite reach, so she couldn't zipper it. She needed a new coat.

Maybe a horse blanket, if she hoped to wear it for the entire winter.

There had been a light, early snow two days after Thanksgiving, and the cold temperatures had kept it from melting, so she was glad when Tim took her arm as they walked through the parking lot.

"You feel okay?"

"Tim, please, just stop asking that. If it's twins, it's twins. There's not a whole lot we can do about it now."

"I know, but I feel . . . responsible."

She rolled her eyes, trying not to laugh. "That's because you are, dummo. You and your little swimmers."

She loved doing that to him. Anything faintly related to conception made him go all confused and flustered.

Except this time, he didn't get flustered. "I wonder, do you think they were doing the backstroke? Or did they do a fifty-yard dash while your egg stood on the street corner, her skirt hitched up, and a come-hither look in her eyes?"

"Tim!" Suzanna exclaimed, blushing. "Control yourself."

"Hey, if we can't joke around at a time like this, when can we, Suze? Or aren't you as nervous as I am?"

"Oh, I'm nervous," she said as they approached the desk in the Ultrasound Department. "Suzanna Trehan, here for a sonogram?"

"And Mr. Trehan," Tim piped up immediately.

"Okay," the desk clerk said, smiling at both of them. "Dr. Phillips is in the hospital and asked that we page her when you showed up. If you'll just sit down over there? We'll be with you as soon as possible."

Suzanna looked at Tim, then took his hand. "She's here? She just got the report the first time. I don't like this, Tim."

They sat quietly, still holding hands, until a technician called their names, and they followed him into a darkened room filled with several large pieces of medical equipment.

Suzanna got up on the table, and there she was again, bare belly sticking out with Tim standing right there to see it all. How glamorous.

"Good morning, everybody," Dr. Phillips chirped happily as she came into the room in scrubs and a white lab coat. "Just delivered Miss Elizabeth Anne, seven pounds, three ounces. It's a lovely day."

Suzanna squeezed Tim's hand, trying to relax. After all, Dr. Phillips was smiling.

"That's nice, Doctor," she said. "Isn't that nice, Tim? Elizabeth Anne. What a pretty name."

"You two have any names yet?" Dr. Phillips asked, washing her hands at the sink, then taking the piece of equipment the technician handed her.

"No."

"Yes."

Suzanna looked at Tim. "You've looked at names?"

"Just a couple," he told her, grinning. "Hermione, Archibald. You know, the usual stuff."

"Idiot," she said, wanting to hug him. He was being so sweet, and she was being such a bear.

But she was so scared.

Let it be one baby; let it be twins. Quintuplets, she didn't care. Just let them be healthy. And bless Tim for understanding that this baby was all-consuming to her right now, that even he had to at last take a backseat in her life.

As long as he came along for the ride.

"So, how did it go?" Jack asked, walking into the pro shop at the golf course.

Tim was there, taking some inventory. The course was closed, but the pro shop was still busy with Christmas shoppers, although they would close soon after the holiday, reopening when the course did.

"Okay," he said, his back still turned to his brother as he counted golf gloves. "The baby's fine."

"Just one baby? Keely told me —"

"Nope. Just one. Dr. Phillips spent a lot of time, sure there were two, but she never found another one, or another heartbeat. She says that happens sometimes. We get another sonogram next month."

"Bummer. So you still don't know for sure?"

"Nope," Tim bit out, putting down the stack of gloves. He'd lost count anyway. "Want a soda?"

"Sure," Jack said, following him into the snack bar, then sitting down on one of the stools as Tim went behind the bar and pulled out two cans. "Hey, your head looks all healed. That must have been something, fainting like that?"

Tim rubbed at the spot where a large scab had finally dried up and fallen off. He'd not only fainted like a jerk, but he'd hit his head on one of the damn stirrups on the way down. "It was embarrassing; that's what it was. Damn nurse, leaning over me, shoving that smelly thing under my nose."

"You had a shock," Jack said, trying to hide a smile, and not succeeding.

"I made a jackass out of myself, bro. Just say it."

"I don't have to; you just did. How's Suzanna?"

"Fine, I guess. Relieved. Dr. Phillips says the baby looks extremely healthy to her."

"Good," Jack said, turning the soda can in his hands. "Hey, bro, would you do me a favor?"

Tim looked at his brother, wondering at his serious tone. "Sure. An arm, a leg, a kidney. Name it."

"Nothing that serious, thank you anyway," Jack said, grinning. "Keely and I want you and Suzanna to stand as godparents to Johnny. Would you mind?"

"Mind?" Tim thought his grin might split his face. "God, that's great. What do we have to do?"

"Take godparent classes, for one thing. First one is next Friday."

"Friday, huh? That's okay. We start parents class on Thursday."

Jack held out his hand to high five his brother. "Way to go! She's agreed to let you be her coach?"

"As long as I promise not to faint, yeah. Dr. Phillips says I have to master that one, or nobody will let me in the delivery room. Well, she'd let me in, but she warned me that if I keel over, they're just going to let me lie there and step over me."

Jack shook his head. "Big, bad Tim the Tiger Trehan. Hitting the floor. I still don't believe it."

"It wasn't my most shining hour," Tim admitted, downing the last of his soda. "Hey, did I tell you? Suzanna's resigning, effective the end of the year. She's staying home."

"Fantastic. And you don't leave for spring training for a couple of months after that. Well, almost a couple of months. This is good. You need time together. Maybe you can take a trip, have that honeymoon."

"Honeymoon? You mean Suzanna, me, and her belly? I don't think so. I'm still sleeping in the back bedroom. The cats don't even sleep with me."

"Well, there is that," Jack said, scratching at the side of his cheek. "No progress, huh?"

"Some. She talks to me. She cooks for me."

"That's progress? Keely says Suzanna's got a long way to go before she should solo in the kitchen."

"No, really, she's getting pretty good. You know Suzanna. When she puts her mind to something, it usually gets done, and gets done right. Although I have re-membered that she was kept off high honors twice in our senior year because she got C's in home economics. Now I know why."

They were both silent for a few minutes, thinking their own thoughts, before Tim said, "Do you think she'd do it?"

"Do what? I was just taking a moment to catch up on my sleep. Johnny thinks we run an all-night diner."

"Go away with me. After the first of the year, I mean, once she isn't working any-more?"

Jack shrugged. "I guess you'd have to ask her, bro. Keely and I, and everyone else, have resigned from the Help Tim Club, you know. Suzanna got pretty peeved when she finally figured out that we all told you she was pregnant."

"Joey's still giving me advice," Tim said as they walked back to the pro shop.

"You're kidding."

"No, really. He sent me some psych books, and a couple of letters. I don't think they teach spelling in Bayonne. Anyway, he's coming up for Christmas, with Bruno. Suzanna invited them. I think he thinks he's Dear Abby or something."

"He sure has changed, hasn't he, now that dear sister Cecily's out of the picture."

"And good riddance," Tim said. "The last thing Candy needs in her life is a visit from Cecily."

"That won't happen. Candy's all legally ours now, and Cecily hasn't so much as sent a card since the day she left. Joey told me he'd heard that she's in South America, doing God only knows what. She just sends home for money."

"Señorita Cecily. Has a certain ring to it, I suppose. Wonder if she's starting a revolution — she could do that, you know," Tim said, locking up the pro shop and heading to the parking lot, where only his and Jack's cars waited. "Well, time to go home to Little Mother. Wonder who she's going to be tonight."

"Meaning?"

"Meaning, bro, that either I come home to a house smelling of supper cooking, or I come home to a woman waiting for me, coat over her arm, so we can go to Tony's for dinner. Good mommy day, dinner at home, where we actually talk to each other a little, some television, early bed. Bad day? Well, the early to bed stays the same."

"Tony's, huh? That's not so bad. I like

their desserts. Banana cream pie? Could do worse, right?"

"Right. Except that Suzanna always makes sure she sits with her back to the dessert case, and then gives in and orders something anyway. Then she glares at me, like it's all my fault."

"Ah, pregnancy. Those were the days, Tim. I'm not looking forward to the next time."

"Next time? After what you and Keely went through? Are you nuts?"

"No, Tim," Jack said, as his tone went quite serious. "We want more children, definitely. Dr. Phillips says the odds are very high that this will never happen again. Life is life, Tim, and we have to live it. For Keely, and for me, that includes more children. If they come along, great; if they don't, then we'll live with that. But we will live."

Tim put his arm around his brother's shoulders, gave him a squeeze. "You've always been my hero, Jack, do you know that?"

"And you're mine, except when you swoon like some Victorian lady. Now, let's go home to our wives."

Twenty minutes later, Tim walked into the kitchen to see Suzanna frowning over something in a frying pan on the stove.

"Problem?" he asked, leaving the door open before the smoke alarm could go off, then making his way through the haze, to the stove.

"Oh, Tim, I burnt the pork chops," Suzanna wailed, turning to him. "One minute they were fine, and the next —"

He held his arms out to her, and she allowed him to hold her, comfort her.

"It's okay, babe, it's okay. I wanted some banana cream pie anyway, honest." Then he kissed her hair, snuggled her closer. He could swear he felt his heart growing larger, warmer, inside his chest.

It was a start.

Sixteen

He slud into third.

— Dizzy Dean

"Excuse me, Father. We have to *what?*"

Tim quickly took Suzanna's hand in his, gave it a squeeze. "Shhh, babe. Let's just listen. This is for Keely and Jack, remember?"

So they listened. And then they both nodded their heads, and then they stood up, left the rectory, and drove home. In silence.

"Married," Suzanna said at last, once they were both standing in the kitchen. "We *are* married."

"But not in the eyes of the Church," Tim said. It had been a long ride home, and you would think he'd gotten every last secret grin out of his system. Sadly, he had one left, and he grinned it now.

"Don't you smile, Timothy Patrick Trehan," Suzanna said, glaring at him.

"Ah, yes, that's me, all right. I, Timothy Patrick Trehan, do take thee, Suzanna —"

"Oh, stuff it," she said, filling the teapot.

"I'm almost six months pregnant, Tim. What's it going to look like? Me? At the altar? Getting *married?*"

"Oh, I don't know. It's not like you'd be the first one to put the cart before the horse." Damn, but he was enjoying himself.

She turned and glared at him. "Shut . . . up."

"Oh, come on, Suze. We can do this. Father O'Mara said he'd cut all the red tape, just marry us real quick. Nobody has to know."

Her expression had been mulish. Now it turned sad. "I . . . I wouldn't mind if Keely and Jack were there. And . . . and maybe Aunt Sadie and Mrs. B.?"

"And Joey, and Bruno, and Candy, and Johnny," Tim added, putting his arm around her.

She laid her head on his shoulder. "I can't wear white."

"Because you're not a virgin?"

"No, because I'd look like the iceberg that took down the *Titanic,*" Suzanna said, wiping away a tear. "Oh, I can't believe we're doing this. Las Vegas was one thing. But this . . . This is so *final.*"

"What God has joined together . . ." Tim said, pressing a kiss against her hair.

She stepped away from him. "We're doing this so we can stand up for Johnny, Tim."

"Right. Sure. Definitely. We're handing each other a life sentence, right? For the kid — and for our own kid. Hey, count me in. Although I have to say that living-in-sin stuff did have its benefits, at least for a while."

"I can hate you sometimes," she said, narrowing her eyes.

"No, you don't. We're getting somewhere, Suze, and this is just another step in the right direction."

He watched as she walked into the den and stood in front of the Christmas tree they had put up together a few days earlier.

They had had fun doing it, too. They had shopped together for the lights, the ornaments. They had picked out a tree at a local tree farm, and Tim had cut it down himself with the saw the owner provided.

Suzanna's cheeks had been bright red from the cold, and her eyes had sparkled as he tried to load the tree into the back of his four-by-four, without much success.

They had driven all the way home with half a tree sticking out the back, Suzanna's bright wool scarf tied to it to warn other motorists.

And then she'd made hot chocolate, and

they had struggled with the tree stand, and Suzanna made him move the whole thing twice, to either side of the living room, and finally to the den.

"What's the sense of having it if we can't enjoy it. We're never in the living room." That was what she'd said, and he'd agreed. He'd have agreed to almost anything if it meant he didn't have to drag tree and tree stand another inch.

"It looks great, doesn't it?" he said now, walking up to stand beside Suzanna, who was carefully repositioning a crystal bell. They both ignored the fact that Margo and the kittens had taken up residence under the tree. How much harm could they do?

"I remember when I was a kid," Suzanna said, not looking at him. "Dad would put the lights on, and then Mom would put the ornaments on, and then I'd ruin the whole thing by throwing handfuls of tinsel all over it. This is so much prettier, but maybe it's too perfect."

"Just wait. One day our kids will be throwing tinsel, and you'll be wishing it was perfect again."

He felt her stiffen slightly as he dared to slip an arm around her waist.

"Suzanna?"

"Tim?"

"You go first," he said, as they had both spoken at the same time.

"No, that's okay. You first."

"I've been first long enough, Suze, don't you think? Come on, what's on your mind? Are you having second thoughts about saying yes to Father O'Mara?"

"No," she said, sighing. "I want everything right for this baby, and that means getting married again, I suppose. This is something else. I . . . I was just wondering if — oh, this is silly."

"What?" he asked, gently grabbing her arm as she turned away from him.

"The kettle's whistling, Tim. I have to turn off the stove," she said, continuing on into the kitchen.

He was close behind her.

"So?" he asked after she poured herself a cup of decaffeinated tea, then added three heaping spoonfuls of sugar. She was doing a little better, but she still had that sweet tooth biting on all cylinders.

"Well," she said, turning to face him. "It's just that," she began, then stopped, shook her head. "Oh, this is just too silly. Tim, there are five bedrooms upstairs. I'm in one, you're in another, and the other three are still vacant except for the carpets you picked out for each one, right?"

"Right. There was no reason to rush, not with the rest of the house to furnish. Keely said one guest bedroom would work for now."

"And she was right, to a point. I mean, we'll be turning the front bedroom into a nursery," Suzanna said, then hastened to add, "but not yet, Tim. I . . . I don't want anything done until the baby's born. We can plan, we can maybe buy a few things, but I don't want to do much until the baby's born."

He nodded, remembering how she'd sobbed into his chest that night at the hospital, going on about empty nurseries and broken dreams and jinxing things.

He wasn't the only superstitious member of this branch of the Trehan family.

"Okay, no nursery until the baby comes. Plan it, know what we want, and then send me shopping, right?"

"Thank you, Tim. Keely promised to help. She says she'll have everything organized and make her assault — she called it an assault — on the stores the moment the baby arrives. I'm just going to pick two different color schemes."

"We could have learned the baby's sex during the sonogram, Suze. Dr. Phillips said she was ninety-nine percent sure. Why didn't you want to do that?"

"I don't know." She shrugged. "I like surprises?"

"No, you don't. Otherwise, we'd be sleeping in the same bed by now."

She dipped her head slightly, then looked at him. "That's . . . That's what I wanted to talk to you about. It's the bed."

"Which bed? I'm being invited to bed? Man, we should have gone to see Father O'Mara a long time ago. I didn't know getting married again would work so well."

"Down, boy," Suzanna said, holding out her arms, so that he stayed where he was, when he wanted to be where she was. "I'm just trying to tell you that I can't climb into that high bed anymore." She sort of wrapped her hands around her belly. "Actually, it's climbing out again that's such a pain. I go to the bathroom at least twice every night, and I'm afraid I'll take a wrong step, miss the stool, and . . ."

"I'll saw off the legs," Tim said, and he meant it. "I can saw a tree; I can saw bed legs."

"No, no. I just want us to change beds, that's all. You can have your bedroom back, and I'll take yours."

He thought about it a moment. That was all it took, one moment. "No."

"Thank you — what did you say?"

"I said, no. I have a better idea. I move back into *our* bedroom, and I help you in and out of bed. You just wake me up, and I'll help, honest. And Jack told me Keely was always a lot more comfortable if he helped her arrange pillows, between her legs, under her belly. And then he'd lie back to back with her, to help support her. I can do that for you, Suzanna. I *want* to do that."

She pressed a hand to her mouth as she blinked rapidly, her eyes shining with unshed tears. "Oh, Tim," she said, walking toward him. "We can't have sex. I'm not ready for that. I know you're trying, and I'm trying, but please, don't push it. Not now. Not yet. I'm so sorry . . ."

He took two steps back. "Who the hell is talking about sex?" he asked, stunned to realize he was actually angry. "You're my wife, you're pregnant, and I'm just trying to help. Don't make it sound like I'm only trying to get into your pants, for crying out loud. Give me a little credit."

Her face paled. "You don't want to have sex with me?" she asked, her voice small, her whole body going small — and at the rate she was growing, that wasn't an easy trick. "It's because I'm so fat again, isn't it?"

"No! You're not fat, Suze, you're pregnant. And you're beautiful. You're blooming, you . . . you *glow*. And I like your hair."

He winced. He thought he might be getting somewhere for a moment there, but then he went and mentioned her hair.

Instantly, she put both hands to her head. "You can't like my hair."

"I liked it when we were twelve; why shouldn't I like it now?"

"Because I can't color it while I'm pregnant, and because it's all growing out and it's all *orange* again. That's what I am. I'm just one big, fat orange. I'm surprised someone hasn't stuck a Sunkist sticker on me."

"And the mood pendulum swings to the other side," Tim muttered under his breath, going toward her, quickly gathering her into his arms. "I wouldn't be pregnant for all the tea in China, babe. How do you do it?" he asked, cuddling her close to his chest.

"I don't know," she said, sniffling. "How do *you* do it?"

He laughed softly. "I get to take antacids. You don't," he said, kissing her short, spiky hair. Her, yes, sort of orange hair. "But I'd be lying if I didn't tell you I can't wait until this baby is born. I'm getting pretty sick of being sick to my stomach."

"That's because I do the cooking," Suzanna said, and he could tell that she was going to start crying again.

"Come on," he said bracingly, taking her hand and leading her toward the stairs. "I'm moving back in, babe, and I'm going to behave, promise. But we've got to make this a team effort. Isn't that what they called it in parenting class? A team effort?"

" 'Ray, team," Suzanna grumbled, sniffling. But she followed him.

He was rounding first, heading to second. . . .

Suzanna held Johnny high on her shoulder, patting his little back so he could bring up a really big burp. The kid had no shame when it came to burping, that was for sure.

"I can't believe how much better I'm sleeping now that Tim's in bed with me."

"Maybe you want to rephrase that?" Keely said as she sat on the couch, a mountain of clean baby clothes beside her as she folded each piece precisely. "I mean, it isn't much of a compliment to the guy, is it?"

Suzanna made a face. "You know what I mean. Sometimes my back just *aches* by the end of the day, but when I get into bed, Tim lies down right behind me, supports my back. And the warmth isn't so bad either, considering how cold it is outside. That, and all the cats sleep with us."

"So he hasn't tried anything? Bummer."

Suzanna wiped Johnny's little mouth after his burp, then laid him back in the bassinet. "I think he's being wonderful. Considerate."

"Yeah. You get married tomorrow, Suzanna. Don't tell lies the day before you get married."

"All right, so maybe I think he could try to do more than kiss me good night."

"Ah, honesty. Now, there's something that's been sadly lacking around here, between the two of you. Oh, that Joey, he's *so* smart about these things."

"Joey? *Our* Joe?"

"Uh-hmm, our Joey. He's been tutoring Tim. Didn't you know that? Not that Tim needs any more help. God knows we gave him enough to screw everything up royally. This is helping Joey, and I think Tim's wonderful to pretend to listen to him."

"I don't understand," Suzanna said, picking up a small shirt and folding it neatly, adding it to the pile. "What's Joey saying to him?"

Keely looked at her for a moment, as if deciding what to say. "Nothing much, Suzanna, and certainly nothing Tim didn't already know. He's just telling him that you have to learn to trust each other."

"And how are we to do that?"

"I'd say, by doing just what you're doing. Taking it slow and easy, step by step, day by day. And I think it's great that the two of you are going away for a few days. You need to be alone together."

"I'm sort of scared about that," Suzanna admitted, picking up another shirt. "Dr. Phillips said no flying, so we're just driving to Atlantic City, but Tim acts as if we're packing for an expedition to the North Pole. I looked into his suitcase, and he's got two childbirth books, a list of emergency phone numbers, and an extra prescription for my prenatal vitamins. He even bought a new charger for the cell phone, as if Atlantic City doesn't have phones. Oh, and my focal point thingamajig. You know, the baseball trophy Tim won in fourth grade and gave to me?"

"How organized. And this is the same man who, just last year, handed me his design for his bedroom, totally forgetting to put *windows* in it? Amazing."

"He told me he picked the house plans from a book Aunt Sadie sent him."

"Oh, he did, he did. But then he changed everything. The builder and I had to beat him down a couple of times, but his ideas are, by and large, pretty terrific. He and Jack aren't just jocks, Suzanna. They're two very smart guys."

"I know," Suzanna said, rather shamelessly swelling with pride. *Opposed to just swelling,* she thought, *which I'm also doing.* "But, if he's so smart, why doesn't he know I want him to sleep with his arm around me instead of back to back?"

"Maybe he needs you to tell him."

"I suppose. But we're taking it slow."

"He won't think you're fat, Suzanna. Trust me."

"I know. It's my hang-up, not his, and I'm fighting it. Childhood trauma and all of that junk. Maybe I was frightened by a chocolate cake sometime in my past. Maybe next week . . ."

"You'll be having another sonogram then, won't you?"

Suzanna nodded. "Unless Tim and his X-ray eyes can tell us more. He keeps *staring* at me."

"You know what I hated?"

"Those stupid stretch panels in your slacks?"

"No, silly. I hated that everyone thought it was fine to touch my stomach. I mean, total strangers, or close to it. They just come up and put their hands on your belly. And Jack would just stand there, beaming. If anyone tried that when I wasn't pregnant, he would have clocked them. But, hey, get pregnant, and you're free territory. It's weird."

"Tim hasn't asked to touch my belly yet. He knows the baby's moving, but he hasn't asked."

"Probably because he's afraid he'll throw up."

"There is that. Poor Tim," Suzanna said, and they both laughed.

Suzanna looked down at the rings she'd taken off last night, then had Tim slip back on her finger earlier today, in front of God and several witnesses.

For the first time, the very first time, she felt married. Not playing at married. Married.

She walked through the casino hotel suite, admiring the brass fixtures on the sinks. Boy, were there sinks! Two in one bathroom, one in the other, and yet another in a serving bar tucked into the short hallway between the living room and the bedrooms. There were as many sinks as there were television sets. In each bedroom, in the living room, even one sort of suspended from the ceiling in the bathroom, over the whirlpool tub that was large enough to float a small battleship.

"We don't need all this room," she told Tim as she entered the living room.

Tim stretched out on one of the cushy leather couches. "Hey, can I help it if the desk clerk is a fan?" He finished stretching, then stood up. "You ready to go downstairs? I'm feeling lucky."

"Speaking of Lucky," Suzanna said, and watched Tim's smile fade. "You already cancelled twice, you know. You are keeping his appointment next week, aren't you?"

"Nope."

"Tim —"

"*Lucky*'s keeping that appointment. I'm just the traitorous bastard who's taking him on his last ride as a man."

"Oh, okay," Suzanna said, smiling. "That's what I meant."

"I know you did. But it still makes me cringe. And what about Margo?"

"She goes next week, too. I probably

should just change vets, go to yours."

"Why?"

"Why what?" she asked as he held open the door for her and they stepped into the hallway.

"Why change vets? And, if someone does, why shouldn't it be me? You don't always have to do what I do, Suze."

She pushed the DOWN button on the wall. "Tim, believe it or not, and I know this is hard, considering how moody I've been, but it just would be easier to go to your vet. Mine's way across town."

"Oh," he said, stepping into the elevator behind her. "But do I get good marks for being cooperative?"

She reached up and kissed his cheek. "Definitely. Now, let's find me one of those machines with the frogs. I'm also feeling lucky."

Tim looked at the plate Suzanna put on the table before the attentive waiter helped her into her seat once more. She'd been a good girl at the salad bar, until she'd hit the cheese section, and the dressings. A couple of calories for the greens, definitely a few more for the black olives and the shredded cheese, and then a mountain of them for the bleu cheese dressing.

"What?" she asked, looking at her plate. "What's wrong now?"

"Nothing. Not a darn thing. Hey, did I ever tell you the story about Joey and red meat?"

She lifted a forkful of salad, then let it hang there as she said, "No. And maybe I don't want to hear it. I like Joe. I think he's sweet, and definitely smarter than you all give him credit for being."

Tim rested his elbows on the table. "Five bucks says you won't think so after I tell you the red meat story. You on? Your luck's been running pretty good all day."

She took a bite of salad, then motioned with her fork for him to tell her the story.

"Okay, here we go," Tim said, trying not to laugh. Every time he thought of this story, he laughed. "We're out to dinner. For Keely's birthday, I think, not that it matters. We've all ordered steaks, New York strips. You with me so far?"

"Hanging, breathless, on your every word," Suzanna said, rolling her eyes.

"Good. So we're eating, and we're talking, and we're eating, and then Joey says, 'That's it for me, this meat is too red.' "

"Too *rare*," Suzanna said, correcting him.

"You wish. But that's what we thought

403

he meant, too. He'd eaten most of it, leaving the center. That's when he said it was too red. Too rare, that's what we all thought. He then explained to us that he *likes* it red, but he's learning how to eat it *not* so red. Do you want to know why, Suze?"

"You're dying to tell me. Go ahead."

Tim grinned. "He said, and I swear we didn't laugh at him at the table — although Keely had to quick excuse herself to go to the rest room — he said, in all seriousness, 'The doctor says I shouldn't eat so much red meat.' "

Suzanna just stared at him.

He sat back in his chair, folded his arms across his chest. "That's okay, I'll wait. This is one of those slow-building things."

"He . . . He was eating steak."

"Uh-huh. Keep going."

"But steak is red meat."

"To you and me and the rest of the world, sure. But not if it's well done, according to Joey. I think his doctor should have realized that with Joey, sometimes it's better to explain using words of no more than two syllables."

Suzanna raised her napkin to her mouth and looked at Tim, her eyes sparkling. She coughed politely, lowered the napkin, and said, "That's funny. I mean, that's really —"

And then she laughed. And Tim laughed.

All through dinner, Suzanna would smile, exchange glances with him.

She giggled a time or two as she sat next to him at the roulette table, saying, "You know, the longer you think about that, the funnier it gets."

On the way back up the elevator to their suite, she suddenly said, "The doctor says I shouldn't eat so much red meat," and giggled again. "How can I ever look at Joe again? I'll just burst out laughing."

"I've got a million more Joey stories, but they'll keep. I can just drag out one every time you need a good laugh."

"Is that so often?" she asked as he slipped the key card into the door of their suite.

"No, babe, it's not. Hey, this is our honeymoon. Should I carry you over the threshold? Maybe I should have done it earlier."

"Yeah, about six months earlier," Suzanna said, giving him a quick punch in the arm. "Sam would kill me if you threw out your back two months before spring training."

"Now, there's a dare if I ever heard one," he said, and he quickly swooped down, grabbed her under her knees and around her back, lifting her high into his arms. "Where to, madam?" he asked, walking into the living room of the suite.

"The bathroom, unfortunately. I shouldn't have had that bottled water while we were downstairs."

"Your wish is my command," he said, and walked down the hallway to the main bathroom, the one that would have been just one huge playground, if Suzanna wasn't pregnant. And if she would have let him near her, which she hadn't done in a very, very long time.

"Thank you, kind sir, you can go somewhere and groan now," she said as he put her down just outside the bathroom. "I'll be right back."

Tim continued on to the bedroom, pulled down the bedspread, and then opened the large suitcase holding the special pillows he'd brought from home.

His wedding night. His second wedding night. The first had been more exciting.

But this one meant more, so much more.

Suzanna rejoined him about ten minutes later, dressed in one of his Phillies T-shirts and a pair of his sweatpants, pulled high above her waist, her face clean and sort of shiny.

She was the most beautiful woman in the world. His heart swelled with love.

"I'm really tired," she said, rubbing at the small of her back. "Its been a long day."

Tim took a quick look at the bedside clock. It was five minutes after eleven, definitely past Suzanna's bedtime. "I should have cashed in earlier."

"No, don't be silly," she said, lowering herself onto the bed, then allowing him to swing her legs up onto the mattress so that he could position one of the pillows between her thighs. "Oh," she said on a satisfied moan, "that's better."

He remembered when she'd moaned for him for quite another reason. But he batted down that thought and helped her carefully wedge a much smaller pillow just beneath her belly. "Comfortable?"

"Hmmm," she said, smiling up at him.

That's one of us, he thought, turning off the lights and then walking around to his side of the bed, wishing his libido had gone wherever Suzanna's had, considering that they were both having these damn pregnancy symptoms.

He crawled into bed and moved across

the mattress, putting his back against hers. "Better?"

"No," she said, her voice small. "I . . . I think I'd like you to turn around. You know, like spoons?"

"Spoons," he repeated, not understanding.

"You know, Tim, like spoons in a drawer? You lie with your front to my back, and — oh, just turn over, okay?"

He didn't need any more urging. Lifting the covers slightly, he turned onto his left side, then shifted so that he was curled close to Suzanna's body. His belly against her back, his knees bent so that their legs also touched.

And, unless she was already asleep, she knew that he was aroused.

Problem was, he didn't know what she'd do if he tried to get . . . closer.

And then there was his right arm. There was nowhere to put it.

"Oh, what the hell," he muttered, and slipped his arm around her, so that his hand fell somewhere on her belly. Any higher, and he'd probably get tossed from the bed entirely.

"That's so nice," she said, her voice sleepy.

"I think so, too," he said, beginning to

run coaching signs through his head, to take his mind off how he was feeling, south of the border. But her hair smelled so good, and she was so soft, and he wanted her so damn much he'd — what was that?

He said it: "What was that?"

Suzanna sighed. "Oh, he does that every night now. I try to rest, and he thinks it's time to party. Did you feel it?"

Tim swallowed hard as he pressed his palm flat against her belly, and was rewarded soon after by the feel of a healthy kick.

His stomach did a small flip, and he wished he'd skipped the chocolate mousse for dessert. His brow broke out in perspiration. But he couldn't move his hand. "Will he do it again?"

"Keep your hand there," Suzanna told him. "I think he sort of . . . gravitates to the warmth."

Tim closed his eyes, waited for the next kick. And there it was. His nausea subsided as he smiled in the darkness. "He's real, babe. He's really real."

"I know, Tim," she said, putting her hand on top of his.

They were still lying that way the next morning, after both of them spent a very restful, uninterrupted night's sleep.

Tim used the smaller bathroom, leaving the large one to Suzanna, and he sang as he showered, feeling good about life, feeling good about Suzanna, feeling good about himself.

He'd passed second and had just slid into third.

Home plate was looking closer and closer. . . .

Seventeen

Q: *Do you want french fries?*
Yogi Berra: *Okay, but no potatoes. I'm on a diet.*

Suzanna turned pages in the magazine, not seeing a single word.

Why couldn't Tim be here with her? He'd wanted to, she knew that, but both he and Jack had to fly to California the previous day, to appear in the commercial Mort had set up for them months ago, and Tim had totally forgotten about, or he would have canceled it.

He must have told her that a dozen times: "I would have canceled the damn thing."

But how was he to know that Dr. Phillips would break her ankle, skiing, over the holidays, and postpone the sonogram?

So here she was, all by herself. Keely couldn't come, because Candy was down with a cold, and so was Aunt Sadie. Mrs. B. was substitute teaching again, and Joey was in Bayonne.

Until she believed she could look at him

411

with a straight face, she hoped Joey would *stay* in Bayonne.

"Mrs. Trehan?"

Suzanna looked up, to see the same male technician motioning for her to follow him.

She pushed both hands against the arms of the chair and got to her feet. She had a scale at home now, thanks to a Christmas present from Tim, whom she could have cheerfully murdered as he stepped on the thing, showing her that it printed out digitally — in half pounds.

So she knew she'd gained another eight pounds this month, and nothing she did seemed to mean anything when she looked at food. It all still cried out, "Eat me, eat me!" Why couldn't she be nauseous, like Tim? Not that she actually could envy him that one. . . .

"There you are, Suzanna," Dr. Phillips said as she entered the room, hobbling a little on her purple, knee-high cast. "I'm sorry for the delay, but since you saw my associate in the office, I know you're still doing just fine. Still blossoming, I see?"

The technician helped Suzanna up onto the examining table. "Flowers blossom, Doctor," she said. "I'm a mountain being pushed up by some shift in the seismic plates."

"And now we're going to find out, once and for all, I hope, just why you're gaining so quickly. I'm still thinking multiples, you know, even if my associate couldn't find a second heartbeat. Babies can hide really well."

"I think the Twinkies have something to do with my weight gain. Tim watches me like a hawk, but I still found a way to hide them in the laundry room, a place he never goes. I'm shameless, and I know it. I complain about my weight, and then I eat."

Dr. Phillips chuckled, then took charge of the sonogram, moving the sensor over Suzanna's bare stomach.

"Where is your husband, Suzanna? I was sure he'd be here."

"In California," Suzanna said, sighing, and also trying to look at the screen on the machine. It looked like a piece of pie. Everything looked like a piece of pie to her. "He's filming a commercial, then has to stop in Saint Louis on his way home, for some autograph show. What do you see?"

"Well, I'm still just checking, but I can tell you without hesitation that you did not swallow a watermelon seed. You're definitely pregnant. Ah, nice full bladder, good."

"I always have a full bladder," Suzanna

groused, wishing Tim were here, holding her hand. She was so nervous.

"Uh-oh."

Suzanna lifted her head as far as possible while lying on her back. "Uh-oh? What uh-oh? Is . . . Is something wrong."

"It would be, if I seriously believed your baby has three arms. As it is, I'd say we're looking at twins." The doctor did something with the dials that caused a white square to appear on the screen, then pushed a button that made it sound as if she'd snapped a picture. "Got you, you little dickens. Did you really think you could keep avoiding me?"

Suzanna heard the doctor as if from a distance. *Twins.* Not one life growing under her heart, but two. Double the reasons to make this marriage work. Not only work, but thrive.

"Tim's going to faint," she said at last, when she could speak again.

"Yes," Dr. Phillips said, taking more pictures. "How is he, anyway? Still struggling with his *couvades* syndrome?"

"Yes. He had another nosebleed last week, which is silly, because I don't have nosebleeds. I'm waiting for his ankles to start swelling."

"The nosebleeds are part of it, probably

something hormonal. There are several conflicting opinions. Do you know that many physicians believe that male pregnancy symptoms are a good thing? They believe it brings father, mother, and baby closer. And they'll disappear as soon as the baby — the babies — are born. Now, just a few more pictures for my trophy wall, okay?"

"Okay," Suzanna said quietly.

"I can give you the sex of one of them, but that second little bugger is still being pretty modest, hiding behind the other one. Woman to woman, Suzanna, no wonder you're having backaches. So, do you want me to tell you?"

"No, please don't. Tim and I — well, me, actually — I decided I didn't want to know."

Once the examination was over, Dr. Phillips told her that from now on she wanted to see her weekly, because although she was due in mid April, she might be as much as a full month early, which was not all that uncommon with twins.

"Isn't that too soon?" Suzanna asked as the technician helped her off the examination table.

"Not for twins, no. And, since we're still

not sure of your due date, and considering your size, and the size of those babies — you're feeding them well, Suzanna — I wouldn't be at all surprised if you were early. Don't worry."

"March? Oh, no. Tim will be in Florida in March, for spring training. He leaves the third week in February. If I tell him this, he won't go."

"I don't want to butt in here, but he's your husband, Suzanna. You have to tell him."

"Maybe," Suzanna said, sighing. "Are you sure I could be early?"

"They're babies, Suzanna. Nobody can be sure of anything."

"Maybe I shouldn't tell him we're having twins," Suzanna said, mostly to herself. "But if I tell him I might be early, then he'd ask why, because he knows I couldn't have gotten pregnant any sooner than last July."

Dr. Phillips motioned for the technician to leave the room, then said, "Suzanna, I don't want to pry, but I'm not just treating you and the babies; I'm treating all of you, your family. When I last saw Keely, she told me you and Tim are still, well, still getting used to the marriage?"

"We're . . . We're doing okay. Even better than okay, lately."

"Good, that's very good. But I don't recommend keeping this a secret from him, even if you think it's for his own good. He needs to know, then make his own decisions."

Suzanna sniffled, then wiped at her eyes. "I know. Thank you, Doctor. I'll . . . I'll think about it. But, in the meantime, can I please ask you to keep my secret."

"Against my better judgment, yes."

"Who speaks for this child?"

"We do," Tim and Suzanna said together.

They stood in the large vestibule of the church the first week of February, where the baptismal font was located, Suzanna holding Johnny, Tim standing beside her.

Jack and Keely stood on either side of the priest, beaming at them, Candy held high against Jack's shoulder.

Aunt Sadie sniffled into a white handkerchief with yellow ducks printed on it, and Mrs. B. stood with her chin lifted, as if to make sure the priest wouldn't drown Johnny when the time came to drip water on his little head.

Joey was recording the entire thing with a palm-sized video recorder while Bruno held up portable lights, high above his head — which was pretty high.

Mort was outside, for the second time, talking into his cell phone.

Tim was grateful Father O'Mara had rehearsed them so well, because he was feeling decidedly queasy, again. The closer Suzanna came to her due date, the more his symptoms snuck up on him at the damndest moments. He could tell Suzanna was worried about him — because most nights she suggested they eat out, rather than experiment with her home cooking.

"We do renounce him," he and Suzanna said, then continued through more responses, Suzanna's voice more steady, clearer than his. Ten minutes later the christening was over, and Keely had grabbed a definitely unhappy Johnny back into her arms, quickly stuffing the pacifier into his mouth.

"Poor baby," she crooned as Suzanna helped her rebutton Johnny's long white gown. "They strip you down, they get you all wet, they put salt on your tongue. You've had better days, haven't you?"

"That's not it. He's crying because he's wearing a dress," Jack said, earning himself a nasty look from his wife.

Tim walked outside to join Mort, grateful for the cold, crisp air. "What's up,

Mort. You missed the whole thing."

"Nothing," Mort said, flipping his phone closed and sticking it back in the pocket of his topcoat — the cashmere one with the fur collar. "Oh, all right, if you're going to drag it out of me. It's Sam. He's had a heart attack."

Tim blinked, unable to take in Mort's words. They had come flying toward him from so far out in left field that he couldn't believe them. "Sam? Our Sam? Sam Kizer?"

"Yeah, that Sam. Hell, Tim, he was a walking time bomb, and we all knew it. Anger management class? That was like trying to put out a forest fire with a thimbleful of water. Not to mention the cheese steaks he ate every day. But he's okay. He's had the surgery."

"Open-heart?"

"I suppose so. At home, in North Carolina. I was just on the phone with his wife. He wants to see you."

Tim pressed both hands to his chest. "Me? Why? I mean, sure, I want to fly down and see him, but why now? He's still in the hospital, right?"

Mort took Tim's arm and led him down the walkway to the street. "Tim, who's been on this team the longest?"

"Me," he said, still not understanding. "I've never been anywhere else. You know that."

"Right. And who's captain of the team? You again, right?"

"So? I'm a player, not a manager. And Sam's coming back, isn't he?"

"His wife says so, once the doctors give the okay. Remember Dan Reeves? Football coach?"

"Yeah. He had open-heart. And he's still coaching."

"So why should it be any different for Sam, right? Maybe I can get him one of those cholesterol-lowering commercials. Ask him about that, okay? Hey, Jack, come over here."

Jack, carrying Candy, walked over, looked from Mort to Tim. "What's up? I can feel Mort's radar quivering. Mort?"

"Sam Kizer had open-heart surgery eight days ago. They've kept it from the press, all hush-hush, but they'll be going public later this afternoon. He wants Tim there with him tomorrow, when he's released from the hospital, to do a quick press conference. I couldn't talk his wife out of it."

"Why?" Jack asked, echoing his brother.

"Well, here's the thing. The pitchers report early to Florida, and for some reason, Sam wants Tim there then, too, before the rest of the team."

"What the hell for? The minor league catchers will be there."

"That's what all the phone calls were about. Sam's got it in his head that Tim's the stability on the team. That he'll keep everyone calm, keep the program going."

"He's got a full staff of coaches, Mort," Tim pointed out, trying to be reasonable. Of course, using "reason" and "Sam Kizer" in the same thought was pretty ridiculous no matter what the situation.

"But he wants you. You're good with the press. Face it, Tim, most of his coaches talk in grunts. And Larry Watkins stutters when he's upset. He never talks to the press. I can't help it if you're the silver-tongued devil, Tim."

Jack shook his head. "Doesn't Sam know Suzanna's pregnant?"

Mort shrugged. "Bigger question, Tim. Does he care? And tell me, how do you turn down a guy with a zipper in his chest? You've got Jack and Keely here, Tim. Sadie, right? What could go wrong?"

Tim looked back toward the church, watching Joey as he kept his hand on Suzanna's elbow, so that she didn't slip on any remaining patches of ice left over from last week's fifteen-inch snowfall. Joey was being a real brick, driving up from Bayonne, helping Suzanna whenever he could. But leaving Suzanna with Joey? "Cripes," he said. "It's bad enough I was going to be leaving in a month. How am I going to tell her this one?"

Suzanna sat on the bedside chair and watched as Tim packed his suitcases. "Are you sure I can't help you?"

"No, that's okay. You just rest. We stayed longer at Johnny's party than we should have. I've got to catch the last flight out of here tonight. Are you sure you're going to be all right?"

She pinned a bright smile on her face, even as she looked down at her swollen ankles as she rested her feet on the footstool Tim had dragged over to her. No more salt. That was it, no more salt! But Keely baked such a wonderful ham, she hadn't been able to resist. "I'm going to be fine. I'm surrounded by people who will take care of me, you know that. And I've got the cats to keep me warm at night."

"And you see Dr. Phillips again tomorrow? I wish I could go to the appointments, but I've been so busy since that damn snowstorm took out half the roof at the bowling alley."

"I know. But Mrs. B. has been a brick. And she even stops at Stop signs. Besides, it usually takes two hours of sitting in the waiting room to see Dr. Phillips for five seconds. You went to all of the classes. Thank goodness we got them out of the way early, because of your spring training."

He shoved several long-sleeved knit shirts into a duffel bag, and Suzanna winced, trying not to think what they would look like when he took them back out again.

"You're doing a lot better with your weight," Tim said, reaching into his sock drawer.

"I know. Only five pounds this month. I still weigh less than you do. When you stepped on that scale, and I realized that I was actually only thirty pounds lighter than you? It was a real wake-up call, I can tell you."

"You were skinny when we met up again. You could have used a couple of extra pounds."

She rolled her eyes. "*Now* he tells me. Although I'm sure you didn't mean this many extra pounds."

He stopped packing and walked over to

her, going down on his knees beside her. "Are you going to be all right at night? I mean, without me there to . . ."

"I've already decided to sleep in the back bedroom, and I'll just stuff some extra pillows behind me. And remember the cats — although they won't replace you. I'll be fine, Tim, just fine. And you'll be home as often as you can."

"Every weekend, I swear it. Damn it," he said, getting to his feet again. "Two steps forward and one back. That's what my mom always used to say. We're doing so well, Suze. I don't want to leave."

Suzanna looked up at him, blinking back tears. "And I don't want you to go."

He was beside her again in an instant. "You don't? Why, Suze?"

She reached out to cup his cheek in her hand. "You know why, Tim Trehan, but I'm not going to say it first."

He grinned. "If I say it, will you say it second?"

"Probably," she said with a watery smile. "Try me."

"Okay — wait. Will you believe me when I say it? Have I proven myself yet? Do you . . . Do you trust me now?"

"Oh, Tim, I trust you. I really do. Everything you've done these past months?

Putting up with me when I've been so . . . so silly? How can I not trust you? I love you."

His grin went nearly ear to ear. "Made you say it first," he crowed, then took her hands, pulled her to her feet, and took her into his arms. "Ah, babe, I love you, too. I love you so damn much it hurts."

"Promise?" she whispered against his chest as he stroked her back, holding her, but gently, as if she might break.

"Promise," he said, kissing her hair. "You're my life, Suze. It just took almost losing you to realize that. I'm a slow learner."

"I make you look like the class genius," she said, pushing her head back so that she could look up into his face. What she saw there made her knees go weak.

He was crying. Her Tim. Crying.

"Oh, Tim," she said, slipping her arms up and over his shoulders. "If I could only get closer."

"Yeah," he said, blinking. "Someone's come between us, huh?"

She began playing with the hair at his nape. "Do you think there's an early flight tomorrow? Do you have to go tonight?"

He put his hands on her shoulders. "Oh, babe, you do pick your times. There's nothing I want more than to hold you, to love you, but the books I read —"

"The books are just books. Dr. Phillips says it's all right until it's not comfortable anymore. I think I could be . . . very comfortable."

He sneaked a look at the bed. "Really?"

"Really," Suzanna said, not caring that her belly button had, just in this last week, decided to become an "outie" rather than an "innie." Not caring that she was far from the slim-waisted woman who had fallen into bed with Tim last July. Not caring one single bit.

Because he loved her; he'd proven that in so many, many ways. Because he looked at her as if she were the most beautiful creature in the world.

Because she loved him. So much. Not the way she'd thought she'd loved him, when she was young, and idealistic, and stupid. She loved him for the man he was, not the boy she'd put on a pedestal, worshipped from afar.

They had both grown; they had both changed. And now here they were.

At last, at long last, here they were. And it had all been worth the trip.

"Tim? You're not afraid of me, are you?"

He looked down at her, smiled with just

one side of his mouth, but with both eyes. "Only when you cook, babe," he said, and then he led her toward the bed.

She felt like a princess as he guided her up onto the two-step affair that had first intrigued her, then troubled her, and now would help lift her on the way to a new paradise.

While she stood balanced on the top step, Tim put out his arm and, in one quick motion, swept stacks of his clothing to the floor.

"Tim! I ironed some of those things."

"I'll send them out to be pressed," he said, pulling down the bedspread.

She half turned, to sit on the bed, and he helped her raise her legs onto the mattress. She was half sitting, propped against some of the many pillows that had become part of her bedroom ensemble.

He was stripping off his slacks as he rounded the bed to climb in the other side. He knelt on the mattress, pulled his shirt and crew neck sweater off in one quick motion, then grinned at her. "I don't believe this."

She looked down at her Phillies shirt and sweatpants. "It's not quite how I pictured this moment either," she admitted, putting both hands on her swollen belly.

Tim reached down and pulled up the sheet and one blanket, covering both of them to the waist, then leaned on one bent arm and grinned at her. "How are we going to do this?"

"I have no idea," Suzanna said, feeling herself blush. But then he touched her breast, her swollen breast, and she closed her eyes, sighed. He lowered his hand, slipped beneath the T-shirt, then claimed her again, rubbed a thumb across her super-sensitive nipple. "Oh, that's good. That's so good."

"If this is baby fat, Suze, I'm all for it," he said, pushing up the T-shirt, then lowering his face to her breast, taking her nipple in his mouth.

She held him, one hand on his back, the other cupping his cheek, as he kissed her, whispered to her, went on a gentle investigation of her changed body. As he roused her, as he made her feel beautiful, and cherished, and oh, so very loved. . . .

Keely put her elbows on the kitchen table and dropped her chin into her hands as she looked at Suzanna. One of those people who seemed to do two things effortlessly at the same time, she was also jiggling Johnny's infant seat with her foot, keeping the baby happy. "I don't get it. Tim's gone, and you've been looking better, happier, than you have in months. I mean it. These past three or four weeks you've been positively *glowing*. Have I been wrong all this time, and you don't love him?"

"Oh, I love him," Suzanna said, knowing her smile bordered on the dreamy side of lunacy. "He calls me five times a day, I swear it, sometimes to moan and groan about being away, having to deal with the press, the owners, but mostly to tell me he loves me. He loves me, Keel. He really does. And I love him. It's real. For him, for me."

"I told you you'd know when it was real, didn't I? So, when was your moment?"

Suzanna lowered her head as she sipped tea, sure Keely would be able to read her expression. She'd kept this secret to herself and didn't plan to be more than vague now. "Oh, I don't know. The day of the christening?"

"Really. That long ago? We were all pretty busy that day, and then Tim was gone the next morning. What did I miss?"

"Nothing you're going to learn from me," Suzanna said, toasting Keely with her teacup. "Now, do you want to hear my other news? I've been keeping it secret for a while now, thank goodness, or Tim wouldn't have been able to help Sam, but I have to tell someone or I'm going to burst. Well, I'm definitely going to burst; that much is pretty obvious, isn't it?"

"I know I didn't get that big, but you told me Dr. Phillips said you're going to have a big baby."

"Or two small ones," Suzanna said, then giggled as Keely's mouth dropped open. "Okay, definitely two small ones."

Keely jumped up so quickly that Johnny began to cry, but she ignored him as she raced around the table to hug Suzanna. "Twins! I don't believe it! And you've been keeping it a secret? From us, right. Not from Tim."

Suzanna waited until Keely had picked up her son before she spoke again. "I haven't told Tim."

"You haven't — well, we know his cell phone number. Let's call him. This news is too good to — wait a minute. *How* long have you known this?"

"Over a month," Suzanna said, playing with her teaspoon so she could avoid Keely's eyes. "I swore Dr. Phillips to secrecy."

"Why? I don't get it. You're telling me

you and Tim are in love — not that everyone didn't know that. You're telling me everything's hunky-dory between the two of you. So why didn't you tell him?"

"I . . . I didn't want to worry him," Suzanna said, then winced. "Oh, okay, so that's only partially true. Keely, he's got all these pregnancy symptoms. He even gets backaches now."

"He'd get them anyway," Keely pointed out reasonably.

Suzanna sighed. That was the problem with talking to people. They were always so reasonable.

"And Dr. Phillips says twins are often early. Even a month early, although for some reason they're very developed, their lungs and everything, so they're just fine. I've been reading about it."

"Nope," Keely said, sitting back in her chair, Johnny snuggled into her shoulder. "I still don't get it."

"Keely, think. The baby's due the second week in April. Tim will be on a ten-day home stand then, so that's all right. He's only an hour away from home and has already planned to drive back here every night. But if I go into labor in March? He'll still be in Florida."

"The hell he would," Keely said, making

a face. "He'd be right here, waiting for you to pop, and nobody'd stop him. Oh, I get it. He'd go AWOL, right?"

"Exactly. It was bad enough thinking about that before Sam's heart surgery. But now? Sam is rejoining the club next week, the first of March, but he's still relying on Tim. He talks to the press, he's been keeping Sam up to date on everything, evaluating the pitching staff — who better to do that than the catcher, who's going to tell the whole truth, when the pitching coach just might not? To put it bluntly, Sam isn't a very trusting soul. Besides, spring training gets under way tomorrow for everyone."

"So you *were* going to tell him?"

"Yes," Suzanna said, nodding. "Yes, I was. I had to get used to the idea first, but I was going to tell him. The day of the christening, as a matter of fact. It seemed like a good day for it."

"The same day you both knew for sure that you're in love with each other. The same day he learned about Sam. Busy day, Suze."

"Exactly. Still, I wanted to tell him. I was going to tell him. But then we got . . . distracted." Suzanna quickly took another sip of her now tepid tea.

"Okay. I understand. No, damn it, I don't understand. He has to know, Suzanna. He deserves to know."

"And I agree. I almost told him last weekend, when he got home, but he was so exhausted he slept most of the weekend. I'll tell him this weekend."

"Wrong," Keely said, going over to pick up the cordless phone. "You'll tell him now. You were at the doctor's today. He's expecting a report. Tell him today. Don't let him know you've known yourself until today. I mean it, Suzanna. I know you're pregnant, I know you're scared, and I know you and Tim love each other. But we've already been around this park, and I know you don't want to go there again. Don't screw this up."

Suzanna looked at the telephone, then took it. "Man, you're bossy."

"It's what I do. My Aunt Mary always tells me that a person should go with her strengths," Keely said, hefting Johnny higher in her arms. "Now, *dial.*"

Dusty Johnson sat down on the bench outside the open lockers in the clubhouse and looked at Tim. "Hey, you feelin' all right?"

Tim looked at him, blinked, tried to remember his name. He knew him. He had carroty hair, just like Suzanna. "Oh. Dusty. Hi."

"Yeah, hi. What's wrong? Too much Florida sunshine today?"

"No, no, that's not it. I'm fine." Tim slipped his cell phone back into his pocket, stood up, looked around as if trying to orient himself to exactly where he was. "I've . . . Look, I've got to go."

"Go? Go where? We still have one more practice today. And then we're all gettin' together to plan Sam's welcome back party, remember? We elected you to be in charge."

Tim sat back down again. "Oh, yeah, I forgot." He swallowed hard, then stabbed his fingers through his hair. "Look, if you don't mind, I'd sort of like to be alone for a few minutes."

"Sure, no problem," Dusty said, standing up. "We can talk later, if you want to."

"Yeah, thanks," Tim said, already forgetting that he'd even spoken to his teammate.

Twins. He was going to have twins. He and Suzanna were going to have twins.

He reached back and absently rubbed at the backache that had been nagging him on and off for weeks, then closed his eyes, tried to picture what it would be like having twins.

His mom and dad had survived it, survived him and Jack and those wild years when his mom had called them Double Trouble. Jack was Double, and he was Trouble.

Always had been.

"Twins," he said, trying the word out loud.

Two cribs, two high chairs, two car seats, two of everything.

Double the love.

His stomach did a small flip, and he knew he'd be heading for the bathroom any time now to toss his cookies. That hadn't happened in a while, but it didn't surprise him.

The other night, on the phone, Suzanna had teased him that he'd probably go into labor with her. He'd laughed, but it wasn't funny.

He couldn't fall apart. He was her coach. And now she'd need him twice as much. He couldn't fail her.

Taking a deep breath, he willed his stomach to stop roiling, then headed back out onto the field. It was a good thing he was building up all these good deeds with Sam, because the moment he thought Suzanna needed him, he was outta here.

Eighteen

"Watch that baby . . . Outta here!"
— Phillies announcer Harry Kalas, calling a home run.

One thing about winter in Pennsylvania, it was never predictable. Tim could remember years he'd played golf on New Year's Day; it was that warm. Then there were occasional winters like this one, where eastern Pennsylvania had more snow than Buffalo, and colder temperatures than Nome.

Years like this one, you could almost count on a late March snowfall. A big one.

He hadn't been able to come home in two weeks, because of all that snow. It would have taken him longer to wait out airport closings and rerouted flights than it was worth, and he might not get back to Florida on time, and Sam would have another heart attack. Besides, Suzanna worried about him, and he didn't want her worried about him.

But Joey was there. He'd taken the semester off from community college, just so he could be there.

He owed Joey, big time. And Bruno, too, who drove up on weekends and cooked, then filled the freezer for Suzanna with meals for every night until he came back again, whisk and measuring cup in hand.

Tim had tracked down Dr. Phillips long distance, and when the doctor had returned his call, he'd bombarded her with questions about Suzanna, about the babies.

So he knew. He knew that the April date was just a target now, but might be nowhere near the bull's-eye.

He phoned Suzanna every chance he got, sometimes five or six times a day. Then he'd chew a couple more antacids and get back to work.

One good thing, the weather in Pennsylvania had finally turned warm. The snow, mountains of it, was melting at a good clip. Suzanna also thought it was a good thing, because she was pretty sure that one of these days, Joey was going to kill himself with the snowplow as he zipped up and down the long drive. He'd already taken out part of the railing on the little bridge over the Coplay Creek.

So March had come and gone, and then Tim was gone, off to Saint Louis, to open the season. March went, and the April rains came, so that the home opener was rained out. Shades of the lousy way the last season had ended. It was a good thing Tim had decided not to be superstitious anymore . . . although he did carry a copy of the latest sonogram with him wherever he went.

Tim stood at the window overlooking the drive, shaking his head. Rain, rain, rain. Sure, it was melting the snow; even little Coplay Creek was high and rushing fast, trying to pretend it was a river. When would it stop raining?

It was dusk, not that the day could get much grayer, and he watched as Joey's headlights flashed as he turned into the drive. He'd just driven Aunt Sadie home, and both he and Bruno would be here for the rest of the weekend, even if the rain did stop and they could get in at least one of their games against the Mets. Nothing like playing in Philadelphia in April. Rain, damp, usually cold. Did the words "retractable roof" mean nothing to people?

Tim remained at the window, cursing the never-ending downpour, then noticed that Joey's huge four-by-four was still at the bottom of the drive, the headlights pointing in a pretty strange direction.

Next thing he knew, Joey was running up

the drive, holding both hands over his head — as if that might keep him dry.

He met his cousin at the front door. "What's going on?"

"It's . . . It's the freaking bridge. It freaking *broke*. I got one wheel stuck straight through it, and I can't get it out. I guess I need to rock it, ya know? Come help me."

"I'll get my coat," Tim said, heading for the hall closet.

And then he saw her. She was standing in the doorway leading to the kitchen, and she had the strangest look on her face.

"Suze? What's the matter?"

"My . . . I think my water just broke."

Tim pressed a hand over his mouth, to keep down the five-alarm chili Bruno had fed him for lunch, and looked at the floor. "I . . . I don't see anything," he said, then winced. Stupid! What a *stupid* thing to say.

"It's . . . It's not *rushing* out, Tim. I'm . . . I think I'm *leaking*. It's the strangest feeling . . ."

"Oh, babe," Tim said, rushing to her, taking her in his arms. "Let's get you sitting down, okay?"

"And get some towels for me to sit on, please," she told Bruno, who was draining boiled potatoes in the sink. He dropped the pot. "I don't want to make a mess. Joey? Dr. Phillips is number four on the speed dial. Will you call her, please?"

Tim knelt down on the floor in front of Suzanna, taking her hands in his. "Are you having contractions? Do you need to breathe?"

"Tim, I *always* need to breathe," she told him, touching his cheek. "But, yes, I guess these are contractions. I just thought my backache was getting worse."

"How long?" he asked, squeezing her fingers. "How long have you had this backache?"

She looked up at the clock. He looked, too. It was almost six-thirty. "I woke up with it."

"And you didn't tell me!" He closed his eyes, swallowed. "Okay, okay. No big deal. Remember what Mrs. B. said? First babies take a long time. We're good, we're good. We just get your bag and get you to the hospital. Joey? Did you get Dr. Phillips yet?"

Joey remained silent.

"Joey?"

"Um . . . I got her service. She's, um, she's outta town. Her associate is somewhere; they just have to find him."

"Find him? How the hell did they lose him?"

"The service said he's in Easton, some-where like that."

"Easton? That's a half hour away — more, in this damn rain!"

"Tim, you're shouting."

"Sorry, Suze," Tim said, getting to his feet. He looked at Joey; dripping wet Joey. "Oh, cripes. Joey, we have to get that damn monster truck of yours off the bridge. It's our only way out of here."

"Naw," Joey said with a wave of his hand. "My vehicle goes anywhere. We can go over the lawn, over the snow, through the trees. You name it. Of course, you got a lot a trees, Tim, and a lot of creek. But we can do it."

"But you said you were stuck on the bridge," Tim said, rubbing at his aching back.

"Oh, yeah," Joey said, raising his eye-brows. "Wow."

"Tim?" Suzanna said, tugging at his arm. "What's going on?"

"Nothing, babe, nothing. Are you all right here with Bruno? Joey and I have to go do something with his truck. No, wait. Bruno, you come. Joey, stay. Sit. Wait for the phone call. Oh, and call Jack. Wait, don't call Jack, he's not home, he's in Bal-timore. Damn!"

"We could call Keely," Suzanna suggested, looking at the three men.

"No!" they all said in unison.

"Oh, okay, right. She'd want to know why Joey's truck is stuck on the bridge. Men," she said, rolling her eyes. "You never want to look bad, do you? Ohhh . . ." she ended, slowly sitting up very straight, "there's another one. They hurt now, Tim. And I can feel more water coming out every time I move even a little bit. Could you please move Joey's truck?

"Bruno — now!"

"This isn't happening; this isn't happening," Tim repeated as a sort of mantra, as he and Bruno ran down the hill, toward the truck. The headlights were still visible, but they seemed to be a little yellow now. "Shit! Joey turned off the engine and left the damn lights on. His battery's going," he called to Bruno as they ran. "We've got to get that piece of junk the hell out of there."

Which was, once Tim shined the flashlight on the driver's side rear wheel, or what could be seen of it, going to be a neat trick if he could do it.

It had been all that snow, and then all this rain. And Joey banging the snowplow into the bridge, probably more than the

442

single time Suzanna saw him do it.

"This thing isn't going anywhere," Tim called through the sound of the rain slamming onto the bridge, the four-by-four. The bridge, narrow anyway, was totally blocked. He reached into the driver's side and turned off the headlights, throwing the whole area into full dark. "Come on, we have to call a tow truck."

"Are we going to have to do it?" Bruno asked, trotting up the hill beside Tim, toward the lights of the house.

"Call the tow truck? Sure."

"No, I mean, deliver the babies."

Tim stopped, bent over, and lost the chili.

Suzanna looked at the baseball trophy Tim had given her so long ago. Just a little thing, and the bat had long ago broken off the plastic batter poised on top of the small block of wood. But she loved it. The trophy had traveled with her to college, and she'd kept it on her bedside table all these years. Like some dumb groupie.

But that was okay, because it was a great focal point.

"Anything else?" Joey asked, sort of bouncing on the balls of his feet as he stood in front of her, rubbing his hands together. "I've got your suitcase, your pillows, that focus thing. Come on, Suzanna. Help me here. Anything else?"

"You can call Dr. Phillips's service again," Suzanna said, doing her best to remember not to hold her breath when the pain gripped her again.

She wasn't having cramps, at least not the way she'd read about contractions in the books. She felt very little pain in her belly, except very, very low. It was her back. Her back was killing her. She felt as if she were being bent like an archery bow being pulled on, could bend backward until her head touched the kitchen table. "I . . . I think I'd like to lie down."

She stood up, which may have been a mistake, because suddenly it was Niagara Falls, right there in her kitchen. Lucky, who had been lying on the floor beside her, yelped, and ran for the den.

"Good for you," Suzanna groused as she watched the cat. "See? Do bad things, and God always gets you back, sooner or later."

"Damn," Joey said, also jumping back. "This isn't good, is it?"

She motioned for him to let her alone as she sat back down again. "Just call, Joey."

"Give me the cell phone, then get me the phone book," Tim called out, running into the kitchen, skidding to a stop. "Suze? What's the name of that place down the road? You remember? Don Hunsinger's dad owns it?"

"Hunsinger's Towing?" she offered, worrying because Tim's face looked so pale, and he'd asked such a silly question.

"Okay, that's it," Tim said, paging through the thick book. "Got it."

"What's he doing, Bruno?"

"Calling a tow truck, Suzanna. Joey's truck is really stuck on the bridge."

"Oh," Suzanna said, but then didn't say anything else, because another contraction had her locked in its grip. She managed to look up at the wall clock. Less than three minutes since the last one, and they seemed to be holding on for about forty-five seconds. "Tim? I think you should call the police instead. And, and an ambulance? And Keely? Oh, Tim, this hurts."

Joey took out his own cell phone and punched in 9-1-1 even as Bruno hit Keely's number on the kitchen phone's speed dial.

"Wasn't Alexander Graham Bell a wonderful man?" Suzanna said, sighing.

"Nobody answers at Don's dad's. Bruno, Joey, get that damn monster of Joey's off that damn bridge! I can make it past the hole with my car," Tim yelled, racing to Suzanna's side.

"Hey, that thing cost a bundle, Tim," Joey protested. "He'll rip the under-carriage or something."

"I'll buy you a new one. Come on, babe, my car's right out front. We'll get you in the backseat, and Bruno will get the truck free." He grabbed the trophy, stuck it in the pocket of his rain slicker, and helped her down the hallway.

"I . . . I need a raincoat. Or an um-brella?"

"Right, right," he said, leaving her for a moment as he stripped off his slicker. "Here you go. Wait. I want the cell phone."

He raced back into the kitchen, slid on the mess she'd left there, and cannoned into the side of the table.

"Damn!"

Suzanna giggled. She knew she shouldn't, knew it was pretty much a giggle bordering on hysteria. Still, she couldn't help herself. She felt as if they were in an episode of *I Love Lucy*.

"Comfortable?"

Suzanna raised her head from the slightly soggy pillows Bruno had shoved beneath her head as she lay in the backseat, and glared at her husband. "Don't ask dumb questions. Can we go now?"

"Little problem," Joey said from behind Tim. "The rest of the bridge? It, ya know, sorta *broke?* We were rocking the truck, and it was doing pretty good, and then —"

Tim dropped his head into his hands. "All right, all right, I get the picture. What about the police, Joey? The ambulance?"

"How they gonna get up here, Tim?" Joey asked. "My truck's in the middle of the bridge, there's about five feet of it missing now in one spot, behind the truck, and the creek is pretty deep. Nice creek, running all around your property, ya know. But right now it's one of them knight things."

Tim shook his head, and Suzanna said, from inside the car, "A moat, Tim. Joey means a moat. Ooh! Here I go again."

Brakes squealed down at the bottom of the hill, and a car door slammed, quickly followed by Keely, running up the hill, waving a huge flashlight.

"Where is she? I got Aunt Sadie to watch the kids, and — oh, brother," she said, shining the light into the backseat of the car. "What's she doing out here? You can't go anywhere." She pushed Tim away and leaned into the car. "Suzanna? How often are the pains?"

"All . . . all the time. I think I want to push."

"No!" Tim slammed Keely out of the way and all but jumped into the car. "No pushing, Suze. No damn pushing."

"Let's get her inside," Keely said, but now it was Suzanna's turn to say *no.* She wasn't moving. She couldn't. Really, she couldn't. She just wanted to push.

"Can't she, ya know, cross her legs?" Joey asked, and Keely gave him a punch in the arm. "Hey, don't hit me. I could help, ya know, except we didn't get to the delivering a baby part of my course. Cops do it all the time. Except we're not there yet. Now, if she were, ya know, choking? Then I could —"

"Shut up, Joey," Tim and Keely said at the same time.

"Honey?" Tim asked, looking at Suzanna. "You really need to push?"

"Uh-huh," she said, and reached for him. A new pain gripped her, and she grabbed at Tim's shirt, nearly ripping it off him as she twisted the material in her fist. Man, she was strong. . . .

Keely opened the front door and climbed into the bucket seat. "Let go, honey, let go. Where's your focal point, Suzanna?"

Tim reached into the pocket of the slicker that was on the floor of the car now and pulled out the trophy. Keely grabbed it and held it balanced on the back of the front seat. "Okay, Tim, now help her get her slacks off. No, wait. Bruno? Run inside and get the afghan from the couch in the den. Tim, I'm assuming you've called for an ambulance? And why don't we drive down to the bridge. That way we're closer, when help comes."

Tim agreed, just waiting for Bruno to return with the afghan. He arranged it over Suzanna's hips, then helped her remove her sopping wet slacks and underwear. "Wait. I read about this. I mean, I read it all, cover to cover. We need a shoelace."

Suzanna groaned.

"No, really, we do. To tie off the cord. And newspapers, to wrap the babies in. Oh, God, I can't do this."

"How about string?" Keely asked. "I'm sure there's some in the kitchen."

"Tim-bo?" Joey said as Bruno went running back into the house once more. "Phone's for you."

Tim looked at the cell phone. "Are you nuts?"

"No, I mean it. Phone's for you. Dispatcher. They traced my call."

Bruno slammed out the front door with a plastic bag holding newspapers and ball of twine and ran to the driver's side door, climbing in as Joey landed half on Keely's lap. "Ready?" The boxer turned chef turned chauffeur asked, and then gunned the engine, moving the car all the way down to the bridge.

In the meantime, Tim, half falling on Suzanna, was yelling into the cell phone. "Hello? Hello? Who is this? Where's the ambulance? And we need a tow truck."

"Hey, Tim, that you?"

Tim looked at the cell phone for a moment, then pressed it to his ear once more. "Who is this?"

"It's Don. Don Hunsinger. I'm working Dispatch tonight. I understand you've got a little emergency? Something about a baby?"

"Two babies, Don, two. And where's the tow truck?"

"Dad's on his way, don't worry. So's an ambulance, and a couple of cops who won the bet and got the job. So, how's the little mother?"

Tim looked at Suzanna, who was staring fixedly at the baseball trophy visible in the interior lights Bruno had turned on. She was also panting. Panting real, real fast.

"About to give birth. How soon can you be here?"

"Soon as we can, Tim. Hell of a crackup at MacArthur and 329, what with the rain and all. That's where Dad is now. We're sending for another ambulance. In the meantime, how about we play ball?"

Tim's head was going to explode. He just knew it. He was nauseous, his back ached, and Suzanna needed him. "Play ball? What the hell are you talking about?"

"Here," Joey interrupted, holding out a headpiece attached to a plastic-coated wire. "Headphone, just for cell phones. So you don't get all that radio stuff from the battery. I love stuff like this."

"Radiation," Keely said, grabbing the wire. "Good going, Joey. Here, Tim, give me the phone for a second."

Within seconds, Tim had the headphone snapped over his head, the cell phone clipped to the belt on his slacks. "Don? You still there?"

"Still here, Timmy," his high school friend said, his tone unbelievably calming, which was nuts, because Donnie was the same guy who had, for a joke, glued his own finger to his nose in fifth period study hall. "Ready to play catcher? Are you behind the plate? Ready to go?"

Tim took a deep breath, willed himself to be strong. "I'm not a catcher here, Don. Just a utility player."

"No, you're going to be the catcher. That's what we call the OB guys. Mama does the work, and you just catch."

"Okay, okay," Tim said, looking at Suzanna, who was still staring at the trophy. "You okay, babe?"

"Don't . . . call . . . me . . . babe," she said, and then she grinned. "Oh, Tim . . ."

"Tim? Tim, where are you? Let's start with that, okay?"

"In the car, Don, near the bridge on the drive up to my house. There's a truck —"

"Four-by-four. Jeez," Joey yelled in Tim's direction, earning himself a cuffed ear from Keely, who had already complained that Joey could at least try to keep his elbows out of her back as she knelt on the front seat.

"It's stuck on the bridge, and the bridge is pretty much out. The creek's high, and I don't know how you're going to get in here, Don."

"Oh, we'll get in there. Do you hear sirens yet? They just left the accident on 329."

"Nope. Nothing yet. Why the *hell* do I live in the country?"

Suzanna reached up and grabbed his hand, squeezed it until he figured his circulation might be cut off, permanently. "Do you want to push, Suze?"

"Pushing . . ." she said between breaths. "Pushing . . ."

"She's pushing!" Tim yelled into the phone as he lifted the afghan and ducked his head underneath it, between Suzanna's already raised and bent legs. A moment later, Keely's huge flashlight was under there with him. "Oh, cripes. I think I see a head," Tim said, sure he was going to faint.

"Okay, Tim, don't panic. We've got a real barn burner here, huh? Gut check time, Tim. It's not a head, Tim; it's a can of corn. Isn't that what we call it? An easy catch, can of corn. All you have to do is wait for her to push and get ready to catch."

"Would you please stop pretending this is a damn baseball game?" Tim complained, then took in a deep breath as Suzanna lifted her hips off the seat. "Uh-oh, here we go."

Tim thought he heard sirens, but he couldn't be sure, because Keely was yelling

453

for Suzanna to breathe, and Joey was yelling that Keely was kneeling on his hand, and Suzanna was just plain yelling.

And pushing.

"Did she push? Talk to me, Timmy."

"Tow truck's here," Bruno yelled, opening the car door. "I'll go help them."

"Me, too," Joey said, also getting out of the car.

"Tim? Come on, you have to talk to me," Don said, still in that calm, measured voice. "Is she pushing?"

"She did, she did. But now she stopped. I can see more of the head, but not all of it. It's . . . Cripes, it's stuck."

"No, you're fine. Ambulance driver says they're at the bridge now, throwing a rope across so the EMS can get to you. Now listen, Tim, next push might just do it. A real bang-bang play, at the hot corner, okay? You ready?"

"I never freaking played third. You played third," Tim gritted out, blinking back the perspiration that was running down his forehead.

"Tim?"

"Suzanna!" Tim said, pulling his head free of the afghan.

"I'm sorry, Tim. Nothing seems to work . . . work the way we planned."

He didn't know how he did it, but he grinned at her and said, "I wouldn't have it any other way, babe. You all right?"

She nodded, and then her eyes grew wide as another pain hit her.

"Where are they?" Tim yelled into the headpiece as he dived under the afghan once more.

"Another pain, huh? Okay, Tim, maybe it's time for a Hail Mary pass."

"Football? Make up your damn mind. I thought we were playing baseball!"

"I don't know what you're playing, but I'm Mary. How about you let me take over?"

Tim felt the hand on his back and sat up, pushed the afghan away, and looked at the second most beautiful woman in the world. She was about forty, her hair was dripping wet, her uniform was too tight on her pudgy body, and she was holding a medical bag.

"You're Mary?"

"I am, and you're in the way. I've been listening in on Dispatch, so I know we're close. Why don't you go around to the other side of the car and hold your wife's hand? Better, help her sit up a little for these final few pushes."

"Gotta go now, Tim," Don said into his ear. "Good luck."

"Yeah. Yeah, Don, thanks. I owe you."

"Just invite us all to the christening."

"You got it!" Then he ripped off the headpiece and grabbed Mary's shoulder. "There's . . . There's two of them in there," Tim said, scrambling out of the car. "Do you know there's two of them?"

"Ah, double the pleasure, double the fun. Don't worry, I've already spoken to Dr. Bracken. He's on his way back from Easton and will meet us at the hospital. Hi there, Mrs. Trehan. Come here often?"

"Suz . . . Suzanna," Suzanna gasped, her smile more of a grimace.

"Okay, Suzanna. Pretty name. I'm just plain Mary," she said, pulling on latex gloves, then climbing into the backseat. "Pretty exciting night, isn't it? What do you say we have some babies."

"O-okay," Suzanna said as Tim opened the door and slipped into the car. "Tim!" She reached back, grabbed his hand. "Don't leave me."

"Not a lot of places I could go, babe," he said, kissing her forehead. "I love you, Suze."

"Oh, Tim, I love you, too — *oh!*"

"All right, here we go. One hand on her back, one helping her hold up her head, and then sit her up a little," Mary instructed tersely.

"Hey, what's going on in — whoa!" Joey said, quickly drawing his head back out of the car. "Okay, I'm gone. They got my four-by-four moved, Tim-bo, and they're laying planks."

"Did you guys sell tickets?" Mary asked, then disappeared under the afghan once more.

"Here it . . . Here it comes . . ." Suzanna gasped, and Tim held her, telling her she was great, she was the best, she was magnificent, and he loved her. He loved her so much.

"Ohhhhh," Suzanna sighed at last, collapsing against him, and the next thing Tim heard was a baby crying.

After that, everything was sort of a blur.

The car was surrounded by cops in yellow slickers, EMS personnel, even the tow truck driver, Donnie's dad. Rain still came down in sheets, and there was even a little lightning, but somehow the baby was kept dry and transferred to the ambulance that had crossed the makeshift bridge on the newly laid planks.

The second baby was born as the ambulance, sirens blaring, pulled under the canopy at the hospital.

Girls. Two girls. They looked like two peas from the same pod. Identical.

Mama and babies were taken upstairs and settled into dry beds, while Tim and everyone else — half the world, it seemed — lingered in the lobby of the Emergency Room.

"Two girls. That's so sweet," Keely said. "Do you have names yet, Tim?"

"I think so. Allison and Elinor, for both our grandmothers," he said, rubbing at his back, which — miraculously — didn't hurt anymore, although it was still sore. "Suzanna was great, wasn't she?"

"You weren't so bad yourself, Tim-bo," Joey said, clapping him on the back.

"You were great, too, Joey," Tim said, holding out his hand to his cousin. "Thank you. Thank you for everything. You, too, Bruno."

"Well, okay, guess we'll head back to the house, huh?" Joey said, scuffing his foot against the tile floor.

"Sounds good. Aunt Sadie will want to hear all the news, and I've still got to call Jack," Keely said, going up on tiptoe to kiss Tim's cheek. "Congratulations, Daddy. Here's the keys to my car; I'll ride home with Joey and Bruno. Go kiss Suzanna for us, then go home yourself, get dry."

"Thanks," Tim said, his voice choked, because his throat was tight. *Daddy.*

Second best word in the English language, next to *husband.*

He headed for the elevator, still wiping his face with the towel Mary had given him. He was directed to Suzanna's room, but stopped at the nursery first. "Trehan twins?" he asked a passing nurse. "I'm . . . I'm the father."

"Oh, they're not here, Mr. Trehan. Since they were born outside the hospital, they can't be in the nursery with the rest of the babies. Sanitary regulations. They're in the room down the hall, with your wife. And they're fine. The pediatrician just finished checking them out. Oh, Mr. Trehan?" she asked as he headed down the hall. "Maybe you'd like a set of greens? You're pretty wet."

"Okay," he said, because he was cold, he definitely was wet, and he wanted to hug his wife. "Thanks."

Suzanna was asleep when he finally got to the room, and the room was dark except for a small light near the floor.

He tiptoed over to the two clear plastic bassinets to see two small pink bundles wearing pink knitted caps. They were sound asleep. "Had a busy night, didn't you?" he whispered, carefully kissing both of his daughters' foreheads.

And then he walked over to the bed. There was Suzanna, still fast asleep. His love, his life. Her orangy hair stood up in damp spikes, and the pale blue hospital gown had drooped halfway off one shoulder. She was lying on her side, one hand tucked under her cheek.

Tim stood there for a long time, just watching her, then finally lifted the sheet and blanket and climbed into the bed, to lie down, spoon fashion, behind her, one arm draped across her belly. . . .

Epilogue

"Talk to me, Suze," Tim said falling into the chair next to her on the grassy sweep behind his brother's house.

Suzanna swiveled her head toward him. "Ma-ma, Da-da, Me-me. That's it, that's all I can muster at the moment. Sorry. Get back to me, okay?"

Tim reached over and kissed his wife's cheek. "Ally said *Margo* this morning. At least I think that's what she was saying. Mostly, I was trying to get the poor cat's tail out of the kid's mouth."

"Margo's been a brick, hasn't she?" Suzanna said, reaching for her glass of iced tea — in which all the ice cubes had melted long ago, when she'd first tried putting the sixteen-month-old twins down for a nap on a blanket safely located outside the fenced-in pool area.

"Yeah, well, they're asleep now, and we can maybe have some grown-up talk."

"About what?" Suzanna said, putting down her glass after taking a sip of watery, lukewarm tea. It seemed like the only hot tea she drank was cold, and the only iced

461

tea she drank was always warm. She didn't even want to think about the temperature of her mashed potatoes last night when she'd finally gotten to sit down at the dinner table.

Tim took a deep breath, then took the plunge. "Jack and Keely have offered to take the twins after the season's over, so that you and I can go away. Have a real honeymoon, like maybe a whole week's worth."

Suzanna was silent for so long that Tim leaned over once more, gave her a little nudge. "Did you hear me?"

"Shhh," she said, her eyes closed. "I'm trying to imagine it. You, me, and nobody else? You're kidding, right? And where would we go? I mean, not that it matters. I can be embarrassingly overjoyed to go food shopping on my own."

"I know I'm not home enough, babe, but the season will be over in two months."

Suzanna stood up, and he took her hand, walked with her toward the pool area. "Unless — until — you make the playoffs. Realistically, if we put in time enough for the World Series, we couldn't get away until the third week of October."

He slipped his arm around her, nuzzled the side of her neck. "Paris has to be terrific in October."

"Paris?" Suzanna's face went white beneath her tan. "Oh, no, I couldn't — we couldn't do that. That's too far away from the babies."

"Hey, I thought you said you'd like a vacation from them. As a matter of fact, I distinctly remember you saying those exact words after Ellie climbed out of her crib the other night, and we found her in the kitchen."

"I know, I know," Suzanna said, then bit her bottom lip. "Couldn't we be away . . . but closer?"

Tim pulled her toward Jack and Keely, who were preparing hamburgers and hot dogs on the gas grill located inside the pool fencing — a safety precaution Keely had insisted on to protect curious little hands.

"Hey, get this. You guys offer to take the Terrible Twosome so I can whisk my wife off to Paris, and she says that's too far away."

Keely placed another hamburger pattie on the grill, and smiled at Jack. "Told you. That's five bucks you owe me, buster."

"What?" Tim asked, looking at his sister-in-law. "But you're the one who suggested Paris. Oh, wait a minute. You set me up, didn't you, Keely. Jack and me both."

Jack made a face. "It's embarrassing. The woman will do anything for a sure five bucks. I think she's going to be a very bad influence on our children. Hey, Candy — not so hard!"

Candy giggled as she walked along the outside of the fence, half-leading, half-pulling her fuzzy black cat, Brownie, by his leash and halter.

"Remind me to give Brownie some extra catnip tonight," Keely said, lining up rolls on the top shelf of the grill. "I guess we should just be grateful she isn't trying to drag Johnny."

"My son doesn't have a halter," Jack said huffily.

"Just wait. I find him trying to climb up on the kitchen counter one more time, and he will."

Suzanna slipped her arm through Tim's. "That's it, Keely. You're so busy with your own two. How could you even think to offer to take our girls on, just so that we can go away?"

"Oh boy here we go," Jack said. "Never tell this woman she can't do something."

"Smart-aleck," Keely said, stepping closer to Jack, so that he put his arm around her. "Seriously, Suzanna, I've got it all figured out. Mrs. B. and Aunt Sadie will be here, and you know Uncle Joey and Uncle Bruno would have to be beaten away with sticks, to keep them from helping. My biggest problem will be keeping Joey from saying 'youse kids' so much that the children pick up on it. Don't worry about a thing. Really."

"Okay?" Tim said, leading Suzanna back toward the blanket spread under a large oak tree, and to the two sleeping toddlers.

"Look at them, Tim," Suzanna said. Ally was on her belly, her knees tucked up under her, her rump in the air. Ellie lay sprawled on her back, her head resting on the stuffed rabbit that went everywhere she went. "Aren't they beautiful?"

"I do like them with their eyes closed," Tim said, earning himself a half-hearted poke in the stomach.

He looked down at his daughters, his girls, his babies, as Suzanna unfolded a light, lacy blanket and spread it over them.

Three redheads. The love of his life, and a pair of angels, both the picture of their mother, who had given him even more of Suzanna to love.

Suzanna stood up once more, and wrapped her arms around Tim. "I love you all, so much. So very much."

"And I love you, babe," Tim said,

turning her fully into his arms. "What do you say we go home for an hour, and let Keely and Jack practice being baby-sitters a little?"

"Do we dare? The girls will be up soon, and tearing all over again. We don't want to give Keely and Jack a reason to beg off, do we?"

"Good point," Tim said, "but I think we can risk it. Think about it, Suzanna. A whole hour. Alone. You and me. Me and you. A whole hour. Do you remember what I can do in an hour?"

Suzanna looked at her babies, and then at her husband. She had the whole world here . . . but, once in a while, she wanted her whole world to be Tim, only Tim.

"Not Paris, Tim. But how about New York City? I could go to Manhattan, and not worry."

"New York City it is. But what about now?"

Suzanna's smile was positively evil . . . He loved it when she was evil.

"Race you to the car," she said, and he ran after her, knowing she'd let him catch her.

The employees of Thorndike Press hope you have enjoyed this Large Print book. All our Thorndike and Wheeler Large Print titles are designed for easy reading, and all our books are made to last. Other Thorndike Press Large Print books are available at your library, through selected bookstores, or directly from us.

For information about titles, please call:

(800) 223-1244

or visit our Web site at:

www.gale.com/thorndike
www.gale.com/wheeler

To share your comments, please write:

Publisher
Thorndike Press
295 Kennedy Memorial Drive
Waterville, ME   04901